P9-DKD-395

0 00 30

7-00

CROSS DRESSING

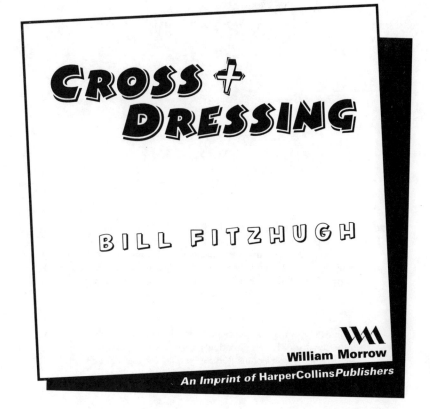

CROSS + DRESSING

BILL FITZHUGH

William Morrow

An Imprint of HarperCollinsPublishers

HarperCollins books may be purchased for educational, business, or sales promotional use. For information please write: Special Markets Department, HarperCollins Publishers Inc., 10 East 53rd Street, New York, NY 10022.

FIRST EDITION

Designed by Kellan Peck

Printed on acid-free paper

Library of Congress Cataloging-in-Publication Data
Fitzhugh, Bill.
Cross dressing / Bill Fitzhugh.—1st ed.
p. cm.
ISBN 0-380-97756-7
I. Title.
PS3556.I8552 C76 2000
813'.54—dc21   99-058658

00 01 02 03 04 RRD 10 9 8 7 6 5 4 3 2 1

For my siblings,
John, Ann, Mike and Liz,
who also survived Catholic school
and who give me great support.
And, as always and forever, for Kendall.

ACKNOWLEDGMENTS

I rely on a great number of people to help me get things right. Where things are wrong, it's my fault, not theirs. My thanks to the following:

Karen Vaughey Marble for telling me the story, way back in 1992, that turned into this one.

Matthew Scott Hansen for cowriting the original story whence this one came. Also for notes on this.

Sister Nicki Thomas of St. Mary's School in Los Gatos, California, the best "nun consultant" a lasped Catholic writer ever had.

The Very Reverend Jerry McBride of St. James Episcopal Church in Jackson, Mississippi, a busy man, doing good work.

Andrea Sinert and Elliot White for advertising insights and tidbits.

Dr. Bobby Robbins, Dr. Mary Mallette, and her sidekick, Dr. Bob Mallette, for various medical expertise. Dr. Judith Mitrani for helping with Ruth's medication.

Geoff Young for coming up with the title in five minutes after someone stole my first one.

Tom Dupree, my editor, for making the whole thing work when I was unable to do so. And his able assistant, Kelly Notaras, for assisting so ably.

Jimmy "Ninth Life" Vines for getting me hooked up. Howie "I'll send a messenger" Sanders and Richard "I believed in it from the beginning" Green for the big deal and for hanging in for so long. Avanti deMille for her patience.

Tom Shadyac, Jim Brubaker, Heather Leyton, Winston Stromberg, and everyone at Shady Acres. Holly Bario, Tony Grana, and Marcia Dripchak at Universal. And Tina Fortenberry too.

Michael Maren for permission to use facts from his *Newsweek* article, "The Faces of Famine." He is the author of *The Road to Hell: The Ravaging Effects of Foreign Aid and International Charity* (Free Press, 1997).

William Finnegan for permission to use facts from his *New Yorker* article, "The Invisible War." He is the author of *Cold New World: Growing Up in Harder Country* (Random House/Modern Library); *A Complicated War: The Harrowing of Mozambique* (University of California Press), and other books.

Tracy Weber for permission to use facts from her *Los Angeles Times* article, "Caretakers Routinely Drug Foster Children."

Colin Nickerson for permission to use facts from his *Boston Globe* article, "Worldwide Relief Efforts Booming."

Jennifer Miller, Leonard Gershe, and David Victor Hawkins for their input.

Finally, thanks to the dedicated professionals at the world-renowned Glenlivet Distillery. It's been a pleasure to agree to feature their fine products at several strategic points in the following tale.

Going to church doesn't make you a Christian any more than going to a garage makes you a car.

—LAURENCE J. PETER

Crouching behind a truck that was built Ford tough, Dan Steele had but one simple question. "How the hell did she end up with a gun?"

The man in the white jacket crouching next to Dan shrugged. "It's L.A. How do I know?"

Dan tugged habitually on his goatee as he considered how to deal with the armed woman who had taken the hostage from the nursing home and who was now hiding behind the driving excitement that was a Pontiac. Since Dan's job required him to deal with crises on a daily basis, he was usually calm, cool, and collected when this sort of thing hit the fan, but this was a different sort of thing. Dan seemed to be taking this personally.

It was just past ten o'clock and already it was ninety-two degrees. It was going to be another miserable day in the San Fernando Valley, with hot yellow-brown air triggering another Stage Three Lung Alert. Dan carefully raised himself until he could see his reflection in the truck's side mirror. Given the circumstances, Dan thought it only appropriate that he looked like a sweaty cop in a good suit when in reality he was the creative director at an advertising agency.

Dan looked like the sort of guy you would see in a television beer commercial, playing football in the background with other guys who weren't quite good-looking enough to be featured in the spot. He had been a swimmer in college and had put on a little weight but had not gone completely to seed. The upwardly arching lines in his forehead looked like ripples coming off his eyebrows, resulting in a cheerful appearance unmatched by his present disposition. His thick, dark hair was styled into a fashionable helmet. With his adequate physique, respectable looks, and not-too-shabby income, Dan seemed to have it all. But Dan, being in the advertising business, knew better than anyone that things aren't always what they appear to be.

He pushed his Armani frames up the slippery bridge of his nose, then looked quickly over the hood of the truck. The woman and her hostage were ten yards away. Dan ducked back into hiding position and turned to the man in the white coat. "Okay, here's the deal," Dan said as though he were in charge. "I'll create a diversion. You go for it."

The man looked at Dan and snorted. "*You* go for it."

Dan did little to hide his contempt. *Who does this six-dollar-an-hour yahoo think he is?* Out of force of habit, Dan assessed and categorized the man in marketing lifestyle-segmentation terms: unmarried, high-school-grad, apartment-dwelling, domestic-beer-drinking, TV-sports-watching, lower-middle-class nonvoter. He was a perfect sample from the psychographic cluster those in the advertising business called "Single City Stiffs." And wasn't this present scenario a perfect example of why we had demographic distinctions in the first place? People like Dan Steele didn't rush out from behind cars attempting to subdue armed crazy people. That was a job for rent-a-cops and other ambitious minimum-wagers. Unfortunately, the man in the white coat didn't share Dan's feelings on social Darwinism, so Dan was screwed.

Dan cupped his hands around his mouth and yelled. "All right, I've had enough of this crap! On three, we're coming in! This is your last chance!" He waited for a moment to see if that would end matters, but the hostage taker didn't respond. Dan pulled some cash from his pocket and turned to Single City Stiff. "All right. You go that way," Dan said, pointing east. "I'll go that way." He pointed west before handing the man a couple of twenties. The man nodded agreement. A second later Dan started. "One! Two!"

FWUMP! FWUMP! Dan cringed at the fat sound of two rounds slamming into the other side of his hiding place. "Three!" Dan turned to the man in white. "Go!"

In one swift motion the man stuffed the forty bucks into his pocket and made his move. He was just four feet from the truck when the woman opened fire. The blood red exploded across the man's white coat. He staggered backwards and fell at Dan's side. "Jesus!" Dan hadn't been prepared for this, not outright murder.

The man's eyes and mouth were open wide. He'd been hit three times. His breathing was frantic as his hand groped about his bloody chest. "Oh my God! Oh my God!"

"I don't believe it!" Dan said. "She . . . she shot you!"

The man's expression relaxed a bit. He suddenly didn't look like someone who had just taken three in the torso. "Wait a minute . . ." The man probed his wounds, then put his bloody fingers to his mouth and tasted the red. He spit.

Dan knew something was hinky. He reached down and felt the wounds himself. "The hell is this?" He rubbed the blood between his fingers, then sniffed. "She's got a *paint* gun?"

The man in the white coat sat up, confused as much as anything else. "She said she was armed. She didn't say with what." The man suddenly grabbed Dan by his shirt and pulled him close. "Hey, asshole," he said. "You didn't go." He was angry. "You said we'd go on three and you didn't go for shit."

"I did," Dan insisted, "but I, uh, twisted my ankle." He rubbed the joint and winced. "Ow! I think I sprained it pretty bad." He touched it tenderly. "Might be broken, I'm not sure."

"Uh huh." Single City Stiff wasn't buying it. "So now what?"

Dan was trying to think of a no-muss, no-fuss solution when his cell phone rang. Dan wiped his red fingers on the man's white coat, then drew the phone like a gun. "Steele."

"Which one do you want first?" It was Rose, Dan's assistant at the ad agency. Her favorite game was "good news, bad news."

"I'll take the bad," Dan said. He listened for a moment, then looked skyward. "What?" He banged his head against the side of the truck. "You have got to be kidding."

"No," she said. "I am *not* kidding. I don't have time to kid around with all the work my idiot boss gives me, especially in light of the fact that *his* idiot boss just called an emergency meeting of all department heads. You're due here in thirty minutes."

Dan peered over the truck toward the hostage situation. "Look, I'm handling a small problem right now," he said. "I'll be there as soon as I can."

"Hey, you'll be dealing with a problem called unemployment if you don't get your sorry butt into the office for this meeting."

Dan wondered what he had done to deserve all this. "Rose, darling, do me a favor and delay it. Call in a bomb threat, start a small fire. Be creative."

"On my salary? Forget it. Now, the good news. Beverly What's-her-name called. She's in town and wants to get together, nudge-nudge, wink-wink. You now have twenty-nine minutes. Gotta go." Click.

Suddenly smiling, Dan slid his cell phone back into its soft, warm holster, thinking of other things. This was indeed good news. Beverly was the woman of his wettest dreams. She was a commercial director in a porn queen's body. Over dinner, after directing one of Dan's television commercials a couple of months ago, Beverly confessed to having an exotic sexual appetite that had never been fully satisfied. A day hadn't passed since then that Dan hadn't thought of her confession and the implied possibilities. Beverly promised she'd call Dan the next time she was in town, and lo and behold, his day had come.

All he had to do now was solve this hostage situation and get to the meeting on time. But even if he left this instant, Dan knew it was nearly impossible to get from Northridge to Century City in under thirty minutes. Dan yelled over the car again. "I don't have time for any more of this crap! What's it gonna be?"

The woman yelled back. "You don't take me alive, coppers!" She coughed up a nutty little cackle.

"Great," Dan said. "Now she's Jimmy Cagney." Dan had wasted entirely too much time on this. He had other things to do, vastly more important things, and this was just serving to piss him off. Dan wasn't sure if he was more aggravated by the fact that he was having to deal with this crazy woman or the fact that he was paying someone else to do it. *I work my ass off for the money I get*, he thought. *Why do I get so little in return? Where's the complaint department?* Dan cupped his hands and yelled again. "All right, I'm going to stand up and come over there and we'll talk! And no shooting!" Dan waited for a response, but none came. "I'm not armed!"

The man in the white coat looked at Dan. "You gotta be crazy. She'll ruin that suit."

"Sometimes you feel like a nut," Dan said. "Sometimes you don't." He shook off his coat, hanging it on the truck's side mirror. He then braced himself and stood. A second later, a round of dark red paint exploded on his clean starched white shirt. He took a deep breath. "Dammit," he screamed. "Put down the gun, Mom. The show's over."

Five minutes later Dan was standing at the front desk of the nursing home looking like an angry performance art piece. His suit was ruined, his mood foul. He pulled out his checkbook and looked at the nurse behind the desk. Dan pegged her demographically as a "Midcity Service." She was a canned-hash-eating, *People*-magazine-reading, associate-degree-carrying renter, with bad credit card debt. "Can't you increase her Thorazine or something?" Dan asked.

"Your mother isn't on Thorazine," the nurse said. "She's on divalproex sodium."

And for good reason. After decades of increasingly wider mood swings, Dan's mom had been diagnosed as suffering from bipolar disorder. As a manic-depressive she was the poster girl for what mental health professionals called biphasic mood dysfunction. In her manic phases she was a marvel to behold. The mania manifested itself in what were usually harmless escapades, like using a paint gun to take hostages at the nursing home where she lived. On the downside, her depression could be paralyzing. Overwhelming despair and a sense of emptiness diminished her interest in all activity. Her appetite would disappear and, if the depression went untreated, she could quickly lose fifteen pounds on a frame that couldn't really afford the loss. She sometimes found herself obsessed with death. The words "recurrent suicidal ideation" had found their way into her permanent record.

Her name was Ruth. As children, Dan and his twin

brother, Michael, had seen her more than once on the floor of her room curled into the fetal position, crying for no apparent reason. Having nothing to compare it to, they assumed everyone's mom was that way. That many years ago Ruth was just one of the millions suffering, undiagnosed, from dysfunctional mood swings. Unaware of alternatives, she had simply tried to cope with it, never knowing why she felt the way she did—assuming it was her fault—and trying to deal with being the mother of two boys whose father had disappeared, leaving them in near poverty.

The poverty is what Dan hated the most, or at least that's what he thought. Being poor forced them to accept charity. Nothing was more humiliating. In fact, humiliation and wanting were the primary emotions of Dan's childhood. Raised by television as much as by his troubled mother, Dan was constantly taunted by commercials. By the time he graduated from high school, Dan, like all American teenagers, had been exposed to around three hundred and sixty thousand advertisements for all the desirable, sexy products available to the American consumer—all the things Dan couldn't have. As a child, Dan wanted nothing more than to grow up and be a consumer. To have all that stuff. If he had that stuff, he thought, then he'd be happy. And he wouldn't be humiliated anymore.

When they got older, Dan and Michael came to understand that their mother's behavior wasn't normal and they got her to a doctor for diagnosis. Actually, they went to several doctors, each of whom diagnosed Ruth differently. The first doctor said she was a bipolar III. The second doctor said she was bipolar I. The third said bipolar II. This wasn't an exact science, they said. And although the diagnoses were technically different, they were close enough to help Ruth deal with her problem.

She was on lithium for a while, but since it was less effective on patients who were "rapid cycling"—as Ruth had been recently—the doctor had switched her to divalproex, which worked fine, as long as she took it.

"Well, then increase her divalproex," Dan said to the nurse. He looked nervously at the balance of his checking account. *Damn good thing I've got two jobs.* He needed the double income to afford his excessive lifestyle and to keep his mom at the nursing home and on psychotropics. *It always comes down to money.*

"She doesn't need a dosage increase," the nurse said. "She just needs to take what we give her. She doesn't always do that." The nurse's tone was meant to imply that if Dan didn't like the way they were taking care of his mom, then Dan could just take her home with him and see for himself how difficult she could be.

Single City Stiff stood a few feet away in his stained jacket. He had a firm grip on Ruth's arm. She was wiggling like a big piece of gray-haired bait. Ruth was in her mid-sixties, though she looked older. Her minxy looks, once a warning to fainthearted men, were now losing the battle with age. She had silvery blue eyes, wiry and mischievous as her slim build. "I don't see what all the fuss is about," Ruth said. "I was just having some fun. Why can't I stay with you?"

Dan kept writing the check. "Mom, you know I love you," he said. "But I'm not a baby-sitter. And if you'll recall, I missed an important presentation that time the cops found you jogging up Sunset Boulevard."

Ruth was defiant. "I was getting my exercise. Doctor's orders."

"You were buck naked," Dan said.

"Yes, I was, wasn't I?" Ruth smiled blissfully, then turned on the guilt. "Michael would take care of me."

Dan stopped writing and looked directly at his mother. "Yes, but he's not here, is he?" Dan didn't bother to hide his bitterness. His identical twin had skipped the country,

sticking Dan with their mom, both financially and emotionally. Dan ripped the check from the register and handed it
to the nurse.

Single City Stiff turned to take Ruth away. "Better put
some ice on that bad ankle," he said over his shoulder.

The nurse looked at Dan's check. "I'm sorry, Mr.
Steele, it's four thousand a month now."

The woman sitting across from the loan officer had a habit.
In fact, she had two or three habits, which isn't unusual
for a nun; they get dirty, after all, and they need to be
cleaned now and again—the habits, that is, not the nuns.
While most nuns had stopped wearing the traditional habit
of their order, opting instead for the "dress of the day"
protocol, Sister Peg still wore hers, especially when she was
dealing with the bank. She hoped it would give her an edge,
playing on the romantic notions most people had about
nuns.

In the old days, a nun's habit was such a distinct uniform that a knowledgeable bishop could tell from a hundred yards whether a sister was with the Congregation of
the Sisters of the Third Order of St. Francis of Perpetual
Adoration or was one of the Sisters of Notre Dame de
Namur. You wouldn't confuse one for the other any more
than you might confuse a baseball uniform with a hockey
outfit.

Sister Peg's habit was unique. It had a little Sister of
Mercy in the pleats, some Carmelite in the yoke and gathering, and the floating sleeves of the White Sisters of Cardinal
Lavigeri. The outfit conveyed piety, devotion, and resolve.
While one might be unable to determine the exact order
to which Sister Peg belonged, it was obvious she was a nun,
or more precisely, a sister, since, strictly speaking, nuns took
solemn vows and were usually cloistered while sisters were
free to wear blue jeans and go to Starbucks.

Sister Peg's face, peeking out from the headdress which was one part Little Sisters of the Poor and two parts Reformed Cistercians of La Trappe, was sweet and soft. She was in her late twenties or early thirties. It was hard to tell for certain, given that her habit revealed only her hands and face, but Sister Peg might have been quite pretty underneath the whole thing.

But none of that mattered to Mr. Larry Sturholm. He had business to take care of, and the business at hand was the delinquent mortgage with Sister Peg's name on it. Larry was sitting behind his flimsy little associate's desk on the floor of his branch bank in a dull pocket of the San Fernando Valley. He was thin, befitting his modest income, and his shirt collar was loose around his chicken neck. His dark eyes seemed a size too large for their sockets. They looked as if they might pop out at any moment.

Sister Peg sat across from Larry worrying her rosary as he flipped through her loan file. Finally he looked up from the documents. "I'm sorry, Sister, what was your question again?" He seemed quite good-natured.

"Well," Sister Peg began, "the last person I spoke with here, a Mrs. Barclay, said that since I'd shown good faith by paying what I could, she wouldn't put us in default on the mortgage. But then we got this foreclosure notice, so here I am." She smiled meekly and continued her silent prayers.

"Us?" Mr. Sturholm said, his brow knitting in confusion. He scanned the documents again. "I don't understand who you mean by 'us.' Yours is the only name I see." He turned the file around so Sister Peg could see it.

"Well, yes, technically, I would be the one in default," Sister Peg said. "By 'us' I simply meant the people at the Care Center. The people I take care of."

"Oh, of course," he chuckled. "*That* kind of 'us.' I thought you meant 'us' like there might be someone else who could make the payments." He looked at something on one of the documents, then looked up at Sister Peg. "Sister, what exactly is your affiliation with the Catholic Church?"

Sister Peg looked startled. "What do you mean? I'm a nun." She said it as though that was all anyone needed to know.

"I was just wondering if I should talk to someone at the diocese about these payments. Are you like an employee?" He flipped through several documents looking for something, then smiled and looked up. "You know, I went to Catholic school through tenth grade, the good old Sisters of Mercy, right?"

Sister Peg smiled anxiously and nodded without making eye contact.

Larry gestured at her. "I can see you're not one of them, right? I mean I can tell by your habit, unless they've changed. It's been a while since tenth grade." He rolled his eyes, then looked back at the file folder. "What order are you?"

Sister Peg dropped her hands into her lap and tried not to look exasperated. She wondered why this sort of thing was so important to people. "Mr. Sturholm. It's not important what order of nun I am. What's important is keeping the Care Center afloat."

Larry shrugged. She certainly acted like a nun, he thought. He flipped through a few more pages of the contract, studied a few clauses, then pointed at one of them. "Ahhhh, here we go," he said. "Now I see what the problem is." He shook his head ruefully, as though it were a common mistake.

Sister Peg was relieved. "Wonderful," she said. "I knew it was just some sort of mix-up. I know how those things can happen." She moved to the next bead on her rosary.

"The problem was Mrs. Barclay," Larry said. "She was

terminated two months ago and I inherited her loan portfolio." He gestured at a tall stack of loan files on one corner
of his desk.

"They fired her?" Sister Peg asked. "But she was so
helpful."

"Well, yes," Larry said, sadly. "I understand she was
quite friendly." He folded his hands on his desk. "Believe
me, Sister, I wish we could just give our money away. But,
well, I'm sure you understand." Larry smiled at Sister Peg.
"I wish there was something I could do, Sister, honestly.
But my job is to bring all delinquent loans current." Mr.
Sturholm held his hands up as if to say there was nothing
he could do. "I know it won't be easy, but I'm sure you'll
think of something." He smiled again. "What's the old saying, the Lord works in mysterious ways?" He closed the
file and put it in the "delinquent" box.

This wasn't the reply for which Sister Peg had been
praying so hard. If she didn't get an extension or if she
couldn't get Mr. Sturholm to lose the paperwork for a little
while, she was going to lose the Care Center. And if that
happened, a lot of helpless people would be tossed onto
the street. The problem with that was that Sister Peg had
made it her life's work to take care of these people. Every
time she took someone in, Sister Peg made a personal
vow—a promise that no matter what happened, she would
take care of them. It was a promise she took very seriously.

The Care Center was a large old house in a poor neighborhood in Sylmar, a few miles northeast of the old San
Fernando Mission. Sister Peg had been running the place
for years. She and a few volunteers did what they could to
take care of all those who slipped between the cracks of
what few government programs were left to help the poor.
The Care Center was licensed by the County Department
of Health Services as an in-home congregate care facility.
They took in abandoned and abused children, drug addicts,

abused elderly, prostitutes and gang members trying to get out of the life, and anyone else they could help.

In regard to the delinquent mortgage, the main problem was that Larry Sturholm was right. No matter how hard she tried, Sister Peg had been unable to keep up the payments. Over the past eight years, Sister Peg and others like her had seen their caseloads quadruple. Upon learning there was little profit margin in helping the poor, the private sector had failed to respond the way Republicans had suggested it would. And, in part because of declining attendance, the Church was going through some belt tightening of its own and wasn't providing as much financial help as it once had. Regardless of the reasons, Sister Peg was now three months behind on the mortgage, and she and the rest of the Care Center residents were looking at being thrown out of their home in just over thirty days.

Mr. Sturholm stood to indicate that the meeting was over. "Well, good luck, Sister," he said. "I tell you what, I'll keep my eyes open for a cheap rental property for you."

Sister Peg turned to leave. She was disheartened, certainly, but not defeated. She took a few tentative steps toward the door.

"Oh, just a second, Sister." She paused, hoping that Mr. Sturholm had suddenly thought of a solution. When she turned around, she saw that Mr. Sturholm was holding his hand out toward her. "Here," he said. "Have a free calendar."

Scott Emmons was sitting across the desk from the head of Human Resources suffering his annual job performance evaluation. There was so much acid in Scott's stomach that he couldn't spell relief with all the letters in the alphabet. Scott was a forty-three-year-old second-string copywriter who had never been able to rely on his looks to get anywhere in life. He was slight and pasty, the result of an aversion to exercise and too many years under fluorescent lights. Making matters worse, Scott had gone with the ill-conceived hairstyle strategy that was the home-perm kit. With his thinning brown tuft agonized into feeble curls, Scott looked like a malnourished, middle-aged Jody from *Family Affair*.

Leslie Zimmer was the head of Human Resources. She was young and perky and had all the confidence that came with a brand-new M.B.A. "Scott, it comes down to this," she said. "You've been with The Prescott Agency for how long?"

"About ten years."

"And how many Clios have you won?"

Scott shrugged a zero.

"Effies?"

Scott shook his head.

"Addys?"

"I got short-listed for a nomination for my flea-collar campaign."

Leslie looked at Scott's file. "That was . . . when?"

"Eight years ago."

"Uh huh." Leslie made a note of that.

Scott had been in advertising all of his professional life and he had a great deal of nothing to show for it. Other than the flea-collar campaign, Scott's only claim to fame was a tag line he wrote that became a catchphrase in a small Midwest market for a couple of weeks. All he got in return was twenty-nine thousand a year and a crummy benefit package, neither of which went very far in L.A. Understandably, Scott had been hoping for a raise after this evaluation, but Leslie didn't seem to be heading in that direction.

"What are you working on now?"

Scott perked up. "A regional radio ad for a new panty liner," he said. "It's pretty good."

Leslie seemed unimpressed. "Scott, here's the deal. You need to come up with something. Bring in a new client, come up with a new campaign for an existing client, anything. Otherwise I'm afraid we'll have to give you notice. Do you get what I'm saying?"

Scott couldn't believe it. They were going to fire him? His breathing became shallow. If he stopped getting a regular paycheck, he'd be eaten alive by the "minimum amount due" payments on his credit cards. Scott knew he'd never get hired by another agency, not with his meager track record. If he got reduced to unemployment checks, Scott would have to move back in with his father, a fate worse than death. At least when you're dead, your father can't harp on what a loser you are. Scott wanted to ask Leslie how the hell he was supposed to win awards when he never got to work with anything better than flea collars and panty liners, but he lacked the courage to ask such a question.

Leslie looked across the desk. She felt sorry for Scott, and not just because of his hair. "I tell you what," she said. "Mr. Prescott has called a meeting about a new client. I'll see that you can be there, but you've got to come up with something," Leslie said. "Or else."

Dan didn't believe in God any more than he believed in the Tooth Fairy, but after making it from the bowels of the San Fernando Valley to his parking spot in Century City in less than thirty minutes without killing anyone, he was tempted to start. Still, since he would be attending Mr. Prescott's emergency meeting in a paint-splotched suit, Dan believed that if there was a theological being at work in his life, it was most likely Satan.

All things considered, Dan had every reason to be pleased with the way his life was working out. He had clawed his way up through the ranks of the advertising business to become creative director at The Prescott

Agency, a well-regarded midsize shop in Los Angeles. Dan was famous for the series of humorous spots he had created for California Air. The campaign was so successful that California Air became the region's number one airline after sucking hind tit for a decade. The campaign went on to win every major advertising award and it put Dan on the map.

What happened next was the sort of thing that happens only in Hollywood, and then usually just in the movies. Dan got a call from a development executive at Cinema On Demand, the nation's hottest new premium cable channel. COD, as it was called, was in the process of creating a weekly satirical-sketch comedy show that would be unfettered by the censorship imposed by network Standards and Practices departments. Among other things, the show would feature commercial spoofs, and they wanted Dan to write and produce them. The money was great and there was no telling what a TV screen credit and a few Cable Ace awards might lead to in a town so desperate for material that they rewarded the likes of Pauly Shore.

Typically, creative people in the advertising business weren't allowed to sell their services on the side like that. But Dan's boss, Oren Prescott, was enthusiastic about it. The way Oren saw it, having Dan work on the show would put him in proximity to some major-league celebrities, and that might be useful on some future ad campaigns.

In keeping with the COD theme, the sketch comedy show was being called *Comedy On Demand*. Dan was the producer for the "Commercials On Demand" which ran on each week's show. Dan's job was to conceive, write, and produce one commercial spoof every two weeks. Combined with his work at the Prescott Agency, this meant Dan worked eighty-hour weeks now and then, but the glamour appealed to him—as did the extra dough.

Riding the elevator up to the thirtieth floor of his Century City office building, Dan thought about this week's spoof. He wanted to do something on law firms, but he didn't have an angle. As was his habit when he was brainstorming, Dan began snapping his fingers like frantic castanets while his torso twitched left and right. Snapsnapsnapsnapsnap. He looked like a flamenco dancer paralyzed from the waist down. Sometimes the ideas just arrived; other times Dan had to work for them. As he passed the twenty-fifth floor it appeared that this week's COD would require some work.

The elevator doors opened to the entryway of The Prescott Agency. As always, the reception area was tense with earnest young people looking for their big break. It was all portfolios, résumés, and hair with attitude. Dan stepped off the elevator and waded through the Ogilvy wanna-bes. The receptionist looked up. "Nice shirt," she said. "Hand-painted?"

"Bite me." Dan figured he was going to get a load of shit about the shirt if he didn't come up with something better than the truth. By the time he reached the conference room, he had it. He laid a hand on the stain, put on a pained expression, and rushed into the meeting.

Everyone gasped. "Jesus, Dan," someone said. "What the hell happened?"

Dan grimaced just so and waved his free hand. "Don't worry, it looks worse than it is."

"It looks like you got shot!"

Dan took his place at the table. "No, some punk pulled a knife on a woman in the parking garage. I think she was pregnant. Anyway, I tried to get him to drop the knife, he lunged and got me here. Paramedic said it was pretty close to my heart. Then the cops showed up and, anyway, that's why I'm late, sorry."

A focus-group survey on Dan's story would have shown the room was split into four groups. The first group skewed young demographically. Lacking much business experience, they swallowed Dan's whopper like a Big Mac. The second group was thinking, *Bullshit*. Those in the third group, all of whom knew the story was bullshit, were thinking, *Good story!* The last group, which included Dan's boss, was thinking, *What heart?*

Oren Prescott was at the head of the huge slate conference table. He was a slick-looking huckster in his sixties—silver-haired but still firm. Tanned, but not in that leathery George Hamilton way, he looked as smart and conniving as he was. Demographically speaking, Oren was a graduate-degree-holding, three-alimony-paying, expense-account-abusing, mutual fund shareholder. His lifestyle segmentation category was "Power Circle Fringe."

The other seats around the table were filled with the butts of various department heads. Sitting in the chairs against the wall were two media buyers, a woman from the production studio, and Scott Emmons. Oren nodded at Dan as he spoke. "I'll keep this short so you can go get some stitches or whatever," he said. Mr. Prescott was concerned because he needed Dan to live long enough to work on the project he was about to announce. Oren placed both of his hands on the table, then stood slowly before addressing the room. "This morning I got word that Fujioka Electronics is looking for a new shop."

A buzz swept the room. The Fujioka account was worth a hundred million dollars in annual billings. For the past ten years they had been with Hawkins & Nelson, one of the world's oldest and largest ad agencies. The problem with such a big agency was that you ended up with a committee writing copy, compounded by a bureaucracy that slowed down an inherently retarded creative process. Fujioka now wanted some newer, younger blood to rattle the stick in the swill bucket—a brilliant group of young people who could tell all the old lies in exciting new ways. At least that's what Oren Prescott heard. The truth was more complicated than that, however. The truth was that Fujio-

ka's marketing director had heard rumors about an un-
planned career change for himself, so he immediately
instituted a full agency review in the hope of buying himself
six months to a year before being tossed into the garbage
like a crappy piece of direct mail.

"Christ, Oren, are you serious?" Dan's mind began to
race. This was a breakout opportunity. If he could bring
Fujioka into the fold, Oren would have to make him a
partner, lest Dan walk with the client and start his own
shop.

Scott knew it too. This wasn't flea collars or panty liners. This was exactly what Scott needed. He pulled out his
notepad and wrote *Fujioka!* across the top in bold letters.

"They want more . . . pizazz," Oren said, betraying his
old-school mentality.

Scott wrote it down. *More pizazz.*

"They're launching a new line of electronics that are
bigger and more powerful than anything ever made," Oren
said. "And they want a campaign that dazzles."

Scott scribbled *more powerful than anything.*

Oren slapped his palms onto the conference table.
"We're talking more sizzle than a steak-sauce ad!"

More sizzle, Scott wrote. He underlined the word *more*
and looked at it. Oren continued to talk, but his voice faded
in Scott's mind. He began to circle all the *mores* on his
notepad, then he drew lines connecting them to one another, and a moment later it dawned on him. The whole
thing. The slogan, the visuals, the strategy. Scott was on
his way.

"People," Oren said. "Landing Fujioka would *double*
our billings." He slowed his speech and continued in a
lower voice. "If we somehow fail to get this account . . ."
There was no need to finish the sentence. Oren simply let
the threat hang for a moment. "Dan, get started on this
right now. I want something on my desk by end of business

tomorrow. I'm talking full brand review—the works, and don't worry about strategy, we can always fake one later to fit a good idea."

With his left hand applying pressure to his ersatz wound, Dan's right hand began snapping its castanet. His eyes all but rolled back in his head. "Already on it, sir." Snapsnapsnapsnap.

Scott was paralyzed. He just sat there trying to talk himself into saying, "Mr. Prescott, I have an idea." It was an idea Scott believed was brilliant. Of course, it wasn't brilliant in a cure-for-cancer sort of way; rather, it was brilliant in that Scott believed it tapped into whatever caused the American public to become enthralled by phrases like "Where's the beef?" It was, in short, the best idea Scott Emmons would ever have. Unfortunately, before Scott could muster the courage to say anything, Oren said, "That's it, people. Fear for your future and get back to work."

Scott despised himself for remaining mute. He could still hear his father's voice reminding him of what a loser he was. "You wouldn't even know a diamond if you held it in your hand," was one of his favorite put-downs. Scott's father thought that was the best way to build character in his weak son. But somehow the method had failed to work, and now Scott was—at least in his own mind—exactly what his dad had predicted, a loser.

Mr. Prescott stopped Dan on his way out of the conference room. "How's it going with COD, Mr. Hollywood? Did you meet Jacqueline St. Georges last week?"

"Yeah, we had a nice chat. I told her she'd be perfect for Au Naturel Cosmetics."

"What'd she say?"

"Having won a Golden Globe award for her last film role, she denounced commercial work as vulgar until I told her what a certain former sitcom star made on those Clairol spots," Dan said. "At which point she saw the artistic merit of my argument."

Scott stood a few feet away, unable to assert himself. He wanted to speak, but he simply couldn't, and it wasn't for lack of trying. For the past six months, Scott had been listening to the "Grab All You Can!" series of motivational tapes in the hope of becoming more aggressive at work. He wondered why the results were so long in coming. The ads had promised results in two weeks. Scott decided to return to his cubicle and listen to another one of his tapes. He was determined that this time would be different. He would tell someone his idea.

Oren gave Dan a fraternal punch in the shoulder. "On my desk tomorrow afternoon," he said. "And remember, I want sssssssssizzle."

"Consider it done." Dan clapped his hands together. "In fact, I've got a great idea already." As Dan watched Mr. Prescott disappear down the hall, he stood there thinking, *What idea? I got shit for ideas.*

Back in his office, Dan changed shirts and began mentally rearranging his schedule. He'd have to put COD on the back burner for a day. The Fujioka campaign was too big an opportunity to screw up. Now all he needed was inspiration. Dan raised his hands to fill his peripheral vision and he began his trademark snapping ritual. He hoped the staccato valving of energy would focus the creative genius within. Snapsnapsnapsnapsnap. A hack at heart, Dan always started by looking for a tag line. "Fujioka . . . Fujioka . . . It's better than a poke in the eye with a sharp stick. A dull stick. A stick of gum. Uh, Fujioka . . . not just another Japanese corporation that makes shit better than Americans . . ." This went on for an hour.

Dan tried closing his eyes, standing on his head, and holding his breath. He laid himself across his desk like a sacrificial lamb. He sat cross-legged on the floor. He stood and paced. Snapsnapsnapsnapsnap. But nothing came. He was spinning around in circles in his chair when his inter-com buzzed. "Scott Emmons to see you," Rose said.

"Blow him off," Dan replied, still spinning.

"Says it's very important."

"I bet." Dan stopped his chair. "All right, send him."

Scott opened the door and poked his head in. "Mr. Steele?"

"It's Dan."

"Dan, right, I'm sorry." Two words and he had already screwed up. In the advertising business there was an unwritten rule about not using the titles *Mr.* and *Ms.* The practice of allowing all employees to call the president by his first name was designed to give them the sense that everyone was on equal footing. The idea was to prevent formality from interfering with creativity. That way junior employees felt free to share good ideas with superiors, who could then pass the idea up the chain of command until someone near the top claimed the idea as their own. Like much of advertising, it was a transparent yet surprisingly effective ploy.

"I've got an idea I want to throw at you," Scott said. "It's about Fujioka."

Dan glanced at his watch. "Two minutes." He wasn't trying to be rude so much as he was trying to be left alone.

Scott immediately began to doubt both himself and his idea. What had gotten into him? Was he nuts? Scott decided that as soon as Dan told him his idea wasn't worth shit, he was going to throw out those motivational tapes. There was no good reason to put himself through this kind of torture just because some latter-day Norman Vincent Peale was peddling positive thinking.

Dan put Scott in the "Backsliding Climber" lifestyle segment. He was a Paul McCartney–listening, dating-service-dependent, United Way–supporting, one-bedroom-apartment-renting model hobbyist. "Time's wasting," Dan said.

"Oh, right," Scott replied. He was clutching several sheets of paper, still warm from his printer. He cleared his throat. "I think I've got the answer to the Fujioka question." He waved the papers feebly.

"So you said." Dan looked at his recent phone messages, savoring the one from Beverly. "Minute fifty, I'm waiting."

Scott spread all but one of the papers onto Dan's desk. They were comps—rudimentary ad layouts, a little artwork, and sample copy that Scott had thrown together on his computer in the last few hours. It was crude, admittedly, but at the same time, there was something inspired about it. Dan saw that right away.

"It's a reverse Zen thing, okay?" Scott pointed at one of the pages. "Here's our spokesman. An old, wise-looking Japanese guy, like . . . like Master Po on *Kung Fu*."

"He was Chinese," Dan said, glancing at his watch again. "Minute thirty."

Scott's stomach tightened as he continued, wanting just to get this over with. "Okay, Chinese. Anyway, he's in a lotus position, right? Sitting by a pool reflecting the Fujioka logo."

Dan glanced at the documents. "Yeah, yeah, yeah." He yawned.

Scott was dying, but there was no turning back. "Okay, you know how Fujioka wants to position themselves with the whole bigger-louder-brighter angle, right? So here's the tag . . ." Scott pulled the last piece of paper from behind his back with a tepid flourish. He held it up for Dan to see and read it aloud. "More Is More," Scott said. He paused briefly to let it sink in. "Get it? It's a twist on the Zen thing, less is more, but it's More Is More. See, it—"

"I get it already. A chimp would get it, okay?" Dan

knew instantly that Scott had created the perfect campaign for Fujioka. It was elegant, it appealed perfectly to the target demographic and its bloated desire for conspicuous consumption, and best of all, it had legs. Given this, there was only one thing Dan could say. "This is crap. Why are you wasting my time with this?"

Dan might as well have disemboweled Scott with a staple remover. "Crap?" Scott asked.

Dan was suddenly conflicted. A lot of guys in Dan's position would have attached themselves to the idea and shared in the certain glory. But with the price of his mom's care going up, Dan couldn't afford to do that. He needed this one all to himself. "Scott," he said, "I know you mean well and I know you'd like that associate creative director position, but I just don't think this is it. Good try, though."

Scott wanted to die. Why had he done this? "Is it really that bad?" he asked.

"Let me try to put this in sort of a 'less is more' way . . . yes. And I'm not trying to be mean, but Fujioka would never go for it. They'd be over at Ogilvy's by lunch if we pitched this." Dan stacked the papers and held them up. "Who else has seen this?"

"Nobody," Scott said. "Why?"

Dan dropped the papers into the trash. "Keep it that way. Oren doesn't take kindly to employees working outside the team concept. *Capisce?*"

Scott could hear his father's voice chiding him. The little ego he had left quickly withered. He looked sadly at the trash can. "Could I have that?" His voice was timid. "It's the master copy."

Dan waved him off. "Scott, it's a waste of time, shake it off. You're better off forgetting it. Now, shoo, I've got work to do." Dan picked up the phone and dialed. Emmons slouched out of the room, defeated, yet oddly reassured that he had nothing to offer. When the door closed, Dan hung up the phone and shook his head in wonder. He reached into the trash can and retrieved the documents. "More Is More." His eyes twinkled. "Why the hell didn't I think of that?"

2

It was nearly midnight and Sister Peg was creeping down Sepulveda Boulevard looking for a hooker. She drove slowly for a couple of reasons. First, she wanted to get a good look at the girls who were working that night. Second, she didn't trust the brakes on Bertha, the twenty-six-year-old Chevy Suburban that was the Care Center's sole mode of transportation. Every time she touched the brakes, Bertha made a nasty grinding noise that sounded like money going down the drain—money she didn't have.

Sister Peg eased through the intersection at Nordoff and continued down the boulevard, her eyes scanning the corners and the sidewalks. Several of the working girls recognized the old beater and waved to the nun behind the wheel. Hers was a familiar face, since she had cruised the boulevard for years. Sometimes she stopped for these girls, but not tonight. Sister Peg was looking for one particular girl, but so far she was nowhere in sight.

As Sister Peg approached Parthenia Street, she caught a glimpse of herself in the rearview mirror. She'd been up since five-thirty that morning. She made breakfast, did several loads of laundry, cleaned some bedpans, then spent an hour on hold waiting for a federal bureaucrat who eventually told her the Care Center didn't qualify for the program they administered. Then she made lunch, served it, cleaned the kitchen, and started the entire process over again, finally turning out the last light around eleven. It was her usual routine, and for the past several years she had managed to maintain the schedule without taking on the appearance of the walking dead. But after her meeting with Mr. Sturholm earlier in the week, the pressure showed. She touched the lines by her eyes and wondered how long they'd been there. *I used to be prettier than this*, she thought. She kept cruising.

Finally, just past Roscoe Boulevard, Sister Peg saw who she was looking for. Josie was tall, thin, and had long straight lemon blond hair. She wore a shiny black and purple Lycra getup that was cut low in the front to reveal the ample, yet firm, goodies. Josie was perched high atop a pair of glittering four-inch platforms. The soles flared at the bottom and provided extra stability when she did a job standing. The clingy outfit said as much about Josie's profession as Sister Peg's habit said about hers.

Sister Peg tapped on the grinding brakes and lurched to the curb. Josie skittered over on her platforms, leaned in the passenger window, and licked her lips. "Hi, girl-friend," she said. *"Voulez, voulez, voulez vous."* Josie thought the French sounded sexy.

"Are you working?" Sister Peg asked.

"Ain't going to church dressed like this," Josie said. "Whacha looking for?"

"The usual." Sister Peg looked around to see if anyone was watching them.

"You really like that, huh?"

Sister Peg nodded. "I've got a one-track mind," she confessed.

"That's what I'm talkin' about." Josie wiggled her shoulders and looked up the sidewalk, stretching her long back. Josie played this same coy game every time the nun came calling. And every time, the nun played back.

A moment passed before Sister Peg spoke again. "So, are you getting in or what?"

Josie rolled her eyes and cocked her head to one side. "Okay. But just for a minute. We gotta make it fast." She opened the door and slid onto the ragged seat patched with duct tape.

"You look great," Sister Peg said. She reached over to feel the stretchy purple fabric on Josie's leg. "That's nice, shows off your features."

Josie waggled her head. "Use your knack, darlin', that's the rule." She looked at Sister Peg. "You lookin' tired. You sure you can stay awake for this?"

Sister Peg smiled wearily. "Try me."

Josie sighed. "Okay with me, Sister. Let's do it."

"Not here," Sister Peg said. "Let's go somewhere more private. Wouldn't want people to get the wrong impression." A minute later they were behind a drugstore in a dark parking lot. Sister Peg killed the engine and turned away from Josie. "You don't know how bad I need this," Sister Peg said. This wasn't their first time together, and if Sister Peg had anything to do with it, it wouldn't be their last. She needed simple human contact and this is where she found it.

Josie reached over and put her hands on Sister Peg. As Josie performed her magic, Sister Peg moaned. "Oh God, yes. That feels so good." Josie knew exactly where the sister wanted it. "Oh yeah, right there." Sister Peg closed her eyes. "Harder," she said. "I won't break." Sister Peg arched her back and leaned into Josie's skilled hands.

Josie, it turned out, was a part-time masseuse in addition to being a hooker. "Girl, you sure are tensed up," Josie said. "Something you wanna talk about?"

"What I want is the knots out of my shoulders. I'll talk later."

Josie worked the tight muscles like bread dough. After about ten minutes Sister Peg was so much nun putty. She lifted her head and spoke quietly. "They're going to foreclose, I can just tell." Her head dropped a little. "And I'm scared."

Josie had known Sister Peg long enough to know she didn't scare easily, and when she was scared she usually wouldn't admit it. So the confession meant things at the Care Center were worse than usual. "What about that lady you said was helping you out? The one at the bank."

"They fired her. Too much customer service apparently." Sister Peg turned around to face Josie. She rolled her head to one side and something in her neck popped. "Ahhhh."

"Don't mention it." Josie propped her sequined platforms up on the dashboard. "I wish I could help, but I've got to take care of myself. Know what I'm sayin'?"

Sister Peg put her hand on Josie's. "You could help both of us if you got off the street," she said. "Come work at the Care Center. I need your help. Think about those kids."

Josie nodded. "And give up all this?" She laughed nervously.

"I know it doesn't pay as much," Sister Peg said. "But you'll get beaten up less and there's almost no chance you'll get any STDs."

"That's a helluva sales pitch, Sister." Josie reached into her spandex waistband and produced several condoms. "But you know I'm careful." Josie folded one of her long legs under the other and sat sideways. "Besides, I'm not the flimsy little thing I was when we first met." She flexed her biceps. "I'm tougher, harder, and a lot smarter."

Sister Peg reached over and brushed Josie's lemony

bangs to the side. "Well, with all due respect, Professor, the hardness shows." Sister Peg and Josie met almost seven years earlier when Josie was a fresh runaway in the clutches of a pimp with an anger-control issue. Josie, with two black eyes, had approached Peg on the street and begged for her help. Peg took Josie to the Care Center, where she stayed a while before returning to the life. Ever since then, Sister Peg had been after Josie to quit for good. "Did you get tested like I asked?"

"No need," Josie said, holding up one of the condoms. "Shower caps, remember?"

"Please," Sister Peg begged. "Do it for me. The clinic doesn't charge anything."

"Yeah, yeah. I know," Josie said. She hated thinking about AIDS. She'd seen it kill a dozen friends and she knew the chances were good that she'd been exposed, since some guys absolutely refused to wear a raincoat. "I gotta get back to work," Josie said. "And you look like you need some sleep."

Sister Peg drove back to Sepulveda Boulevard. Josie hopped out to the sidewalk, then leaned back in the window. "That'll be twenty bucks, girlfriend."

"Okay," Sister Peg said. "Let's see, I charge forty for my good advice, so you owe me twenty."

"Damn." Josie pulled a twenty from somewhere in the Lycra. "I don't want you buying no cheap wine either, you better be feedin' the kids with that."

Sister Peg took the twenty. "Thanks, Josie. You're a saint."

Dan was ready for the day to end. After resolving the hostage situation with his mother, making it to Oren's emergency meeting, and stealing Scott's idea, Dan had spent the rest of the afternoon polishing the "More Is More" material. It was getting late and Dan still had to come up with the spoof spot for COD. He also had to devise a strategy in case Scott Emmons took exception to the theft of intellectual property that happened to be his. Dan had no ethical concerns about his actions vis-à-vis the "More Is More" idea—this was strictly business, and anyone who didn't know how things worked in the bigs would be improved by the education.

His career notwithstanding, Dan's main concern right now was hooking up with Beverly, the sexually adventurous commercial director. He had reached her at her hotel and she had invited him over for drinks later that night, after her client dinner. All he'd have to do was buy a couple of rounds of drinks and be able to perform. Since Dan hadn't been laid in three months, he was confident, performance-wise. With visions of gymnastic sex making it impossible to concentrate on work, Dan called it a day and headed for his car.

He put the Fujioka materials in the trunk, put the top down on his brand-spanking-new Mercedes, and headed west on Olympic Boulevard toward the ocean. He could have taken the freeway, but he preferred the slower drive down the wide boulevard because it gave him the chance to be seen in his fancy German car. Of course, technically it wasn't *his* car. It was a lease. In fact, it was a lease Dan couldn't really afford, but image being what it was in Los Angeles—not to mention in the advertising business—Dan opted for ego over fiscal responsibility. Besides, he figured after he sold the Fujioka idea, he'd get a corner office, an enormous bonus, and an offer for partnership. He'd certainly be entitled to as much. And then his problems would be over, or at least paid for.

Dan stopped for the light at Cloverfield and began to fantasize about Beverly when he heard a woman's voice. "Excuse me." It was a woman panhandling from the median. "Got any spare change?" She held out her hand, neither meek nor aggressive. She was just worn down and repeating the phrase. "Spare change? I need something to eat," she said.

Charity. Dan had a problem with charity in general, but charity of this sort made him especially uncomfortable—not because it infantilized the recipients or undermined their motivation to go out and get a job, but because it reminded him of his miserable childhood and the shame of having to take handouts. Dan never understood this response. He thought he should be sympathetic, having once been in, or at least very near, their shoes. Sadly, Dan's emotional baggage outweighed his altruistic instincts, resulting in an internal conflict that simply made him ill at ease with the poor. Dan had decided that sympathy wasn't a learned response, so there was no use trying if it didn't come naturally. And besides, he thought, it wasn't as if he was rude to these people.

The driver behind Dan honked his horn when the light turned green. Dan quickly scooped a quarter from the change tray and tossed it to the woman. "Have a nice day," he said as he drove off. The woman read Dan's bumper sticker. *He who dies with the most toys wins.*

Ten minutes later Dan pulled into the secured parking garage of his tony Santa Monica apartment building. Like his car, Dan's three bedrooms and the terrific ocean view were beyond his means, but Dan's sense of entitlement was a powerful thing and so he lived by the bay.

Dan reached the door of his apartment. He could almost taste the peaty single-malt scotch. As he stood at the door juggling his keys and the Fujioka materials, Dan felt a presence behind him. He heard a noise and noticed a man standing in the shadows. Dan hurried to get the door open, but he dropped his keys. The man cleared his throat. "Behold I stand at the door and knock," he said.

The voice sounded familiar, yet Dan still felt threatened. He turned, brandishing his papers. "Don't mess with me, pal."

"Revelations," the man said. "That's correct." The man shifted on his feet in the darkness.

Again the voice struck Dan, almost as if he were speaking to himself. "I'll tear you a new asshole." Dan hoped the strong copy would sell him as tougher than he really was.

"Thanks, bro, but I've got all the asshole I need." The man stepped into the light. Simple black pants topped by a black shirt and a white collar with religious overtones. A priest. He was the same height as Dan but slightly thinner. If he grew a beard and put on a suit, he could have walked into Dan's office at The Prescott Agency without turning a head.

Dan broke into a broad smile. No wonder the voice was familiar. It belonged to his identical twin. "Michael!" he blurted. "I'll be damned. The patron saint of deadbeats. What are you doing here?"

"It's good to see you too," Father Michael said. He went to hug his brother, but Dan hesitated. He didn't hug a lot of men in his line of work, so he extended his hand to shake, then pulled it back. Michael smiled like a saint and embraced his emotionally impaired sibling, pulling him close.

"I thought you were in Africa," Dan said from behind his brother's ear.

"Just got back."

Dan broke the embrace and put his hands on Michael's shoulders. "Well, it's good to see you." Dan turned to unlock the door. "I don't suppose you're here to make a loan payment?" His tone was halfway between *you still owe me the money* and *I'm just giving you a hard time.*

"That was a long time ago." Michael waved a hand to imply how many years had passed.

"A thousand bucks, bro. Whatever happened to thou

shalt not steal?'' Dan arched his eyebrows before opening the door. He bowed and made a doorman's gesture. ''After you.''

''Why, thank you.'' Father Michael walked in and set his small suitcase on the floor.

Dan and Michael had been raised Catholic. The Church's structure and moral guidance filled a void created by their disorderly home life. They were altar boys during junior high, even though they attended public school. Whenever they moved to a new town, Dan and Michael would go straight to the local parish to join the CYO in the hope of making friends. After high school they went to different colleges and earned their undergraduate degrees, but they entered the seminary together. After one semester Dan began to have his doubts, while Michael, having found his calling, slipped into a state of bliss. After a second semester, Dan couldn't take it anymore. He got his own calling, one for a steady and significant income. He went back to school, took some marketing and advertising classes, and got a job.

During Michael's last year of seminary, Dan loaned him a thousand dollars for tuition and so he could fix up his old VW bus. Michael swore he'd pay back the loan, but he never even started to, assuming that his well-employed brother would let it slide. However, Dan refused to forgive the debt. He said there was a principle involved, not to mention the interest.

Michael looked around Dan's spacious living room, then flopped onto the plush sofa. ''I understand why you're mad,'' he said, ''but you're the schmuck who loaned money to a guy bound by an oath of poverty.''

''I figured you'd skim from the collection plate until you repaid me.'' Dan crossed to his extravagant entertainment center as automatically as breathing. He flipped on the television, muted it, then hit Random Play on his one-hundred-disc CD player. ''I didn't think you'd disappear into Africa." As the music began to flow from hidden speakers, Dan headed for the bar. "How 'bout a drink?"

Father Michael perked up a bit. "Got any scotch?"

"Only the best." Dan pulled out a handcrafted wooden box with an etching of the Glenlivet Distillery and its founding year prominently displayed on the inside lid. He held it up as if it were a holy relic. "This is a limited-edition collection of five vintage-dated single-malt Scotch whiskies produced by the world-renowned Glenlivet Distillery." Carefully, almost religiously, Dan pulled the 1968 vintage from the box. "This is as good as it gets," he said as he uncorked the bottle. He nosed the opening, inhaling deeply. "Deep and complex nutty aromas enhanced with a dryish fruitiness." He poured some into a crystal tumbler and tasted it. "Soft, rich flavors and aromatic fragrances, balanced by a gentle sweetness." Dan held the glass up to the light. "Say Seagram's and be sure."

"Sounds terrific," Michael said. "Can I get a shot of that or are you just going to stand there doing an ad for the stuff?"

"All right," Dan said. "Just a shot. Then we're switching to a blend."

Michael pointed a finger at Dan. "Sharing was always one of your issues, wasn't it?"

"I shared the womb, didn't I? All that amniotic fluid and whatever." Dan poured a couple of fingers of scotch into thick crystal tumblers. "That doesn't entitle you to half my income. Community property laws don't apply in utero, or at least they shouldn't." He crossed to the sofa and handed Michael his drink. They toasted and drank. "So how are things on the dark continent?"

"Dark," Michael said. "And getting darker." He rubbed his stiff neck as he trotted out a dozen horror stories about the refugee camps in Africa. He talked about the hundreds of children he saw die every week. He talked about how local military groups routinely stole their supplies. He painted a grim picture that he said was only getting worse. He said it didn't matter how many toothless condemnations the UN issued against the local governments; decrees simply had no fiscal or nutritional value. "What the people really need is food and money."

Dan shook his head. "When are you going to learn that no amount of charity is going to help? These people have to learn to help themselves. Teach a man to fish, that sort of thing."

"Blessed is he that considereth the poor and needy," Father Michael said.

"Yeah, yeah, and you deserve a break today," Dan said. "Have you considered yourself lately? In the light, you don't look so hot. Are you all right?"

"That's one of the reasons I'm back. I've had some health problems. One of the Red Cross doctors said I needed some rest and a decent diet."

"I bet I can fatten you up," Dan said. "Got a place to stay?"

"I was hoping to crash here for a couple of days while I look."

"Sure, no problem," Dan said. "Just don't get too comfortable. This ain't a flophouse for wayward priests." His verbal jabs notwithstanding, Dan was glad to see his brother. He was Dan's only real human connection and the bond was strong. Dan couldn't say it, but he felt it.

Father Michael raised his glass. "And now abideth faith, hope, charity, these three; but the greatest of these is charity."

Dan leaned over and clinked his glass against Michael's. "Speaking of charity," he said. "Remember Mom?"

Father Michael downed his drink. "Mom? The name doesn't ring a bell."

Dan leaned back in his chair. "Sure, you remember."

He held his hand three feet off the ground. "About yea high. That sweet little nutcase I've spent forty thousand a year on for the past five years. How's your math?"

Michael made a face at his brother. "She's not a nutcase, Dan. She's free-spirited."

"Uh huh. Just wait 'til she shoots you with a paint gun before an important meeting."

"Okay, she's a free-spirited manic-depressive. How's she doing?" Father Michael moved his jaw from side to side, stretching the rigid muscles.

"She's fine, long as she gets her medication. But even then she's not exactly June Cleaver."

They talked about Ruth for a while, and before long they started to recall some of their childhood stories, the good ones mostly. They drank some more and the conversation branched from one tangent to another, as conversations about shared past tend to. They knew each other's buttons and they pushed them just for fun. After a couple of hours they had come full circle and were back to talking about their mother.

Father Michael sat up on the sofa. "She's the other reason I came back."

Dan got up and poured another round of drinks. "Oh?"

"You've done your part," Michael said. "I'm here to do mine."

Dan smiled. "Well, pardon the expression, Father, but it's about goddamn time. How exactly do you plan to pay for it?"

"A Monsignor Matthews from the L.A. diocese hooked me up with a place called the Sylmar Care Center. I'm going to work there and take Mom with me."

Dan eyed his brother with suspicion. "You mean I'm off the hook?"

"Free as a bird," Father Michael said, flapping his hands.

Dan couldn't believe it. This was like a 30 percent raise.

Combining it with the bonus he expected for the Fujioka campaign, Dan might actually be able to get ahead now. "So what's this Care Center like?"

"Not sure," Michael said. "All I know is it's run by a nun named Sister Peg and they're underfunded like all charitable organizations trying to take care of the poor."

Dan looked into his glass, rolled the ice around, and shook his head. "Why do you do this to yourself? Why don't you get one of those fat-cat Vatican jobs instead of mucking around in the squalor all the time?"

Michael tilted his head toward Dan, looking almost bewildered. "I do it because my soul demands it."

"Your soul?" Dan sounded as bewildered as his brother looked. "I don't believe you sometimes," he said. "What makes you think you even have a soul?"

"I can feel it." Michael smiled sweetly. "And I can feel yours too."

"This is pointless." Dan didn't want to discuss metaphysics, or charity, or the poor, so he turned the discussion toward himself. He spent twenty minutes bragging about his writer/producer position on COD and the advantages of a double income.

Father Michael looked around the well-appointed apartment. "I suppose that explains your pleasure palace here at the Sodom and Gomorrah apartments."

"Don't let appearances fool you." Dan snorted. "I'm in hock up to my hairy little ass."

"Congratulations. What about romantic entanglements?" Michael asked.

"Fuck!" Dan bolted from his seat and dove at the telephone on the bar. "No no no no no no," as he punched wildly at the keypad. He had completely forgotten about Beverly. "Come on, come on, come on," he urged the phone. "Pa-leeezze!" He was ninety minutes late already. Still, maybe he could get some phone sex. "Pick up pick up pick up!" He felt sick as fleeting images of Beverly's imagined kinks winked out like a dead TV. "Yes, room 703! Fast!"

Father Michael watched this desperate display for a moment before closing his eyes. He took a deep breath and tried to relax. He enjoyed the spell the scotch was casting. The tension in his jaw eased slightly. Still, he felt like something was wrong with him. He tried to dismiss it as a psychosomatic response to the "episode" in Africa with Cardinal Cooper. Michael self-diagnosed that he had transferred his temporary mental instability to a physical one that would pass once he had rested up and resumed a good diet. It was hard to believe that his mind could do this to his body, but his psyche wouldn't allow any other explanation. Psychosomatic would have to do.

Instead of phone sex, Dan got voice mail. He launched into a desperate, stammering message but soon realized he was wasting his time. He dropped the receiver into its cradle and looked at Michael. "I hope you're proud of yourself. You'll never know the multitude of sins you prevented," he said. "And what's worse is I'll never know them either." Dan drained his glass and poured himself a double. "Dammit! This girl is why they invented sin in the first place." Dan couldn't help himself. If he couldn't participate in any depraved sexual activities, he would at least get the satisfaction of telling another man about how close he had come to doing so.

Michael listened patiently, and not without interest, about Dan's setup with Beverly. When Dan finished, Michael looked at him thoughtfully. "I take it then that you're not exactly close to settling down and having a family?"

Dan snorted his reply. "Oh, that's rich," he said, walking to the closet at the near end of the hall. "Until very recently I had a crazy mother who cost me forty thousand bucks a year and a brother who took a vow of poverty."

He pulled a pillow and some blankets from the closet. "I need more family like I need prostate cancer."

"No, you need a family," Michael assured him. "Somebody who depends on you, makes you want to get up every day and get out there." He pointed at his doubtful brother. "You'll see, someday . . ."

Dan thought about his Fujioka presentation, then tossed the pillow and blankets at Michael. "With all due respect, Father, I've got a hundred million reasons to get up tomorrow, so I'm hitting the rack."

The next morning at six Dan was sipping coffee while standing on his balcony overlooking Santa Monica Bay. He was trying to convince himself that all wasn't lost with Beverly. He'd send her roses and hope for the best. Dan's optimism was buoyed by his ocean view and his imagined future. The sky was clear. The water's calm was disturbed only by dolphins surfacing for air as they made their way up the coast. It was the perfect beginning to Dan Steele's perfect life.

In a couple of hours he would give his boss a slam-dunk presentation for a one-hundred-million-dollar account. And, as if that wasn't enough, Dan suddenly hit upon the perfect idea for his COD law-firm spoof. He wrote the spot in thirty minutes. *Damn*, he thought, *it doesn't get any better than this*.

Dan made some phone calls to set the day in motion. Locations would be scouted and sets would be built. The COD casting people would audition the actors and have them hired and rehearsed by two. After making the Fujioka presentation, Dan would spend the rest of the day shooting and editing the COD spot. The next day he and Oren would present the "More Is More" campaign to Fujioka and Dan would join the Advertising Hall of Fame.

Scott Emmons was the only potential turd in the punch

bowl. Dan had stolen Scott's idea because of his financial desperation, but with Michael taking Ruth off his hands, his finances would improve significantly. Dan started to consider sharing credit with Scott; that way he wouldn't have to worry about Scott going postal on him. Besides, Dan figured if COD's popularity continued to climb, his future was limitless. Still, if he could just come up with a way to take full credit for the "More Is More" idea . . . The decision was a tough one for Dan.

He got to Oren's office at eight and made the presentation. Dan waited for Oren's response. If he hated the idea, Dan could—at least partly—blame Scott. If Oren liked it, maybe the best thing was to share the credit.

Finally Oren looked up from the materials. "Damn," he said.

"Damn good or damn bad?" Dan asked.

"Damn good," Oren said. "I love it! More Is More. It's a goddamn bull's-eye." Oren slapped his desktop. "I'll set the Fujioka meeting for tomorrow. Put some teams on this now. Don't change a thing. I want kick-ass visuals!" Dan didn't respond. He just stood there looking out the window thinking about Scott. "Is there a problem?" Oren asked.

The problem was that Dan really didn't like to share. "No, no problems," Dan said. "I was just thinking about the COD spot I'm shooting this afternoon." Maybe he'd tell Oren about Scott's contribution later. Right now he had to keep Emmons from getting wind of the Fujioka news. He called Scott and told him to come along on the COD shoot.

An hour later they were on a sound stage in Burbank shooting the first segment of the spot. They spent the rest of the day together. Scott, taking full advantage, dutifully stroked Dan's ego every thirty minutes or so. Before long, Dan started to like him. Maybe he'd call Oren later and tell him that Scott had come up with the idea. Maybe.

The shoot went flawlessly. The spokesman had his character down cold. He was a jowly old stage actor who could have passed for an Ivy League law school professor with his dark suit and bow tie. As he peered over his glasses in old-money disdain, you could almost hear him say, "We make money the old-fashioned way. We *earn* it." Between every take and setup, Dan called Beverly, but he always got voice mail. Dan and Scott spent the rest of the day in an editing suite. Finally it was ready to watch, stem to stern.

The spot opened with an exterior shot of a rain-slicked city street. Police cars with flashing lights blocked traffic as the cops struggled to subdue an obviously intoxicated man who was wearing only his birthday suit. Once the scene was established, the spokesman walked into frame, gravely intoning the commercial message with perfect Kingsfield inflections.

"You're drunk, you're stoned, and you're *naked*," he said. He turned to survey the scene as he narrated a quick montage of images. "There is a twelve-year-old with several pounds of *heroin* handcuffed to your *wrist*."

Cut to a wide shot as the police interrogated the suspect. "You're in possession of a smoking *gun*, and the police are beginning to ask *embarrassing* questions that *you* can't answer."

Cut to an extreme close-up of the spokesman looking over the top of his glasses directly into the camera. "*You* may need legal help," he said.

The spokesman walked down a hallway toward an impressive walnut door with gold lettering on it, spelling out the name of a law firm. "When you're in a *tricky* situation and the *standard* avenues of legal recourse seem inadequate—call Shaftem, Dickem, Hosem, and *Marx*. We'll get you off, *regardless* of the cost to you."

The spokesman opened the door to reveal a happy customer writing a check and shaking hands with an attorney. "At Shaftem, Dickem, Hosem, and Marx, justice is as close as your *checkbook.*" The happy customer turned, revealing himself as the suspect who was arrested in the first scene. Quick cut to a court file being stamped "Dismissed."

"Shaftem, Dickem, Hosem, and Marx—staying *above* the law, *just* for you."

The spot ended with the firm's logo, which included a large, rotating gold screw.

Dan got high fives from everyone present. Scott said he felt particularly honored that he had been there for the entire process. Dan leaned back in his chair, feeling like a dime-store James Cameron, his day nearly perfect. Moved by all the laughter and congratulations, Dan began feeling charitable, or at least vaguely honest. He was about to call Oren to give Scott partial credit for the "More Is More" idea. However, as he reached for the phone, a sound engineer burst into the editing suite and told them to switch the monitor to one of the local television stations.

The first image came from a news helicopter's camera. It showed an eighteen-wheeler being followed by several police cars, their lights flashing. The helicopter pilot said the truck was picking up speed as it headed south on Balboa Boulevard. They cut from the helicopter shot to a reporter on the ground who was standing by an old Chevrolet, the front of which had been completely smashed. The reporter then narrated video footage from earlier in the chase.

"Not long after this chase started," the reporter said, "as the giant truck turned from Chatsworth onto Balboa, the back wheels rolled over the hood of this low-rider Impala, crushing it under eleven tons of semitrailer and leaving the driver scared and angry, but unhurt."

Dan and the others in the editing suite hooted. They began flipping from station to station to see who had the best pictures. From what they could gather, the truck had already left quite a trail of damage in its wake. Looking at the truck's erratic path, some of the reporters began specu-

lating that the truck hijacker was wild on PCP or metham-
phetamine or, possibly, both.

The reporters said that LAPD had two dozen cars con-
verging from all corners of the San Fernando Valley and
the CHP was mobilizing to put up roadblocks at all the on-
ramps to the 405 between the 101 and the 118 freeways.
Between the television and radio stations, there were ten
helicopters, two fixed-wing aircraft, and six news vans following the events. All regularly scheduled programming had
been interrupted for the spectacle that was the high-
speed chase.

Dan leaned over to Scott and said, "The only thing that
could improve this, from a ratings standpoint, would be
some gunplay." Scott smiled and felt like he had made an
important friend.

News directors refer to greater Los Angeles as a "sea-
soned breaking-news market." What they mean is that the
town is full of lunatics willing to commit all sorts of crimes
in public with the full knowledge that if they get caught
or killed, it will be on live television. Knowing this not
only didn't deter these people, but recent studies showed
it actually served as encouragement. Thus, on a per capita
basis, the Eyewitness and Action news crews covered more
high-speed and low-speed chases, botched bank-robbery
shoot-outs, and freeway-overpass suicides than any other
news crews in the world.

As the chase continued, the news anchors, lacking any
substantial information, could only speculate about the mo-
tives behind what was going on. The anchor for one of the
TV stations stated there was the possibility that the truck
was loaded with biological weapons—possibly anthrax—and
that the driver might be a member of a militant Islamic
organization. The only hard facts he had to support such
wild allegations were these: A driver had left the truck
idling in an alley behind an industrial park that housed,

among other businesses, a couple of biotech outfits. When the driver came out from getting his paperwork signed, his truck was gone.

BAM! The huge truck cut a corner and crushed a brand-new Porsche Boxster. "Whoa!" the editor said. "That's gonna cost somebody."

The reporter put a hand to his earpiece. "It looks like the truck's heading for Van Nuys Airport," he said. A quarter mile ahead of the truck, LAPD officers laid down a spike strip, pulled their cars back, and drew their weapons. The truck continued straight toward them, its airhorn blasting all the way. The hijacker saw the spike strip too late. Tires blew and the driver lost control of the big rig, sending it careening into a sod farm where it bogged down in mud and St. Augustine. The cops quickly surrounded the cab of the truck, guns trained on the two doors.

The guys in the editing suite started making bets about gunplay. "Twenty bucks says he's dead before his feet touch the ground," Dan said.

Before anyone could take the bet, the hijacker's hands poked out of the driver's side window, waving in an unusually friendly manner. A reporter said the police were communicating with the hijacker via bullhorn. A second later the driver's-side door opened. The hijacker reached out to the chrome grab handle and eased onto the big step over the fuel tank.

The editor couldn't believe his eyes. "Holy shit!" He started laughing.

"It's a sweet little old lady," Scott said.

Dan's head landed on the video switcher with a thud. "No, there's nothing sweet about her," he said. "Not a goddamn thing." Dan's perfect day was suddenly and irreparably marred. After this, he could no longer afford to tell the truth about the Fujioka idea. He was going to need the whole damn bonus—and then some.

Although it wasn't Ruth's intention, just as sure as she had crushed that expensive German sports car, she had also just crushed Scott Emmons's career.

Mr. Smith's eyes were empty, his voice hollow. He was eighty-nine and would not see ninety. His sense of smell was gone. He couldn't see, and sounds were only vague noises. He could no longer apprehend the world in which he existed so miserably. He lay stiff and slack-jawed, his black lungs discharging sour fumes. Had he been able to afford a doctor, the doctor would have explained that, among other things, Mr. Smith's sweat glands had atrophied, drying his skin to the texture of salty crackers. A lawyer would have said it was well past time to get the will in order.

But Mr. Smith had nothing to leave. Sadder still, he had no one to leave anything to. His wife and both of his children had preceded him in death. There were no siblings, no cousins, no old friends. There was one grandchild who lived somewhere in Arkansas, but he didn't give a damn about the old man. He had problems of his own. Mr. Smith, whose life was as common as his name, was alone in the world except for one woman, a woman who had been through this sort of thing before.

Sister Peg was born Peggy Morgan. She was raised in a contented middle-class family in San Bernardino, California. Her father was a sweet, quiet man who owned a small electric contracting company. Her mother was the company bookkeeper. Peg was an only child and a straight-A student. She went to Sunday school and, a couple of times a year, she went to Catholic church with a friend of hers. She thought the stained-glass windows were beautiful.

In May of Peg's junior year in high school, her father was diagnosed with cancer. Peg spent every day of that summer at the hospital holding her father's hand, reading to him, watching him deteriorate. His treatment was expensive and they were forced to sell the family business to pay for it. Despite the doctors' best efforts, Mr. Morgan died in early September.

It was three in the morning and Sister Peg was at Mr. Smith's bedside, upstairs at the Care Center. She was holding his frail, spotted hand, but she was thinking about her father. Mr. Smith's palsy had slowed in the last few days and Sister Peg knew he was about to die. His opaque eyes stared at the ceiling. He didn't blink and he couldn't cry, though he wanted to do both. He ran his parched tongue across his lips and whispered. "It's cold."

Sister Peg already had three heavy blankets on the bed. She pulled the top one up around Mr. Smith's neck and softly tucked it in. "There you go," she said. Her voice was sweet and peaceful. "That's better." She touched his forehead, then stroked his hollow cheek. She wanted him to know that someone was there, that someone cared.

It was quiet now. The children were asleep and the police helicopters had gone looking for trouble in other parts of the Valley. Sister Peg picked up the book at the foot of the bed and tilted the dim lamp so she could read. She leaned close to Mr. Smith's ear so that he might hear. "For all those things hath mine hand made, and all those things have been, saith the Lord; but to this man will I look, even to him that is poor and of a contrite spirit, and trembleth at my word."

Despite his blindness, Mr. Smith could see the end. He began to tremble slightly, not at the Lord's word, but because the death rattle demanded it as his last few breaths struggled through his mucus-choked throat. Sister Peg looked at this shell of a human and prayed she had given him some sense of dignity and worth in his dying moments. She sensed how terrible it was to be so alone in such an awful world. And, as Mr. Smith let go of her hand, she wondered if this was all there was.

"She forgot to take her medicine," Dan said. "So, legally, she's not responsible for her actions, right?"

The cop at the desk looked up from her computer screen. "Don't worry," she said. "If your mother's non compos, she's not in any trouble."

Dan was relieved. "Great," he said. "Thanks."

"Of course, someone's gotta pay for all that damage," the officer said. "And I assume that will be you." The officer smiled and resumed her work.

During questioning, Ruth said she just wanted to watch the planes take off and land at Van Nuys Airport. Since no one from the nursing home would take her there, she decided to walk, but she got tired after a mile or so. That's when she saw the idling eighteen-wheeler. Next thing she knew, the thing was going thirty miles an hour and she couldn't make it stop. "I'm sorry if I caused any problems," she said.

Ruth was up a judicial creek without a paddle. She was looking at charges of felony evading, hit-and-run, and grand theft big-rig to name just a few. Before any of the charges could be brought, Ruth had to submit to a 5150 evaluation to determine her competency. She also had a bail hearing in front of her, but none of that could be done until tomorrow. Meanwhile she'd be enjoying the taxpayers' hospitality.

Dan made it back to Santa Monica at two in the morning. He found Michael sitting in the kitchen eating aspirin. He said he was feeling achy, like a flu bug or something was starting to get the better of him. Dan told him to get well quick and get Mom the hell out to the Care Center before something else expensive happened.

The next morning Dan made two phone calls before going to his office. He called Scott Emmons and told him to go to the production house to wait while the editor made a few last cuts to the Shaftem, Dickem spot. Then he was to take the tape to COD's main offices and be sure the executive producer got it. Dan then called the editor and told him to take his time with the cuts.

With Emmons out of the way, Dan headed to work to check on the production studio's progress. Dan arrived to find the office wrecked. It was littered with take-out food cartons, empty soda cans, beer bottles, coffee cups, a mirror with some white powder on it, and lots of overflowing ashtrays. The entire department plus a couple of freelancers had stayed overnight working on the materials for the Fujioka presentation. It was hard to say who looked worse, the graphics people who hadn't slept in twenty-six hours or Dan who had spent a fitful night fretting about the bill his mom had run up the night before.

Dan's funk lifted slightly when he saw what the studio had produced during their all-night session. It was functional yet witty, and it incorporated the company's logo organically. He just hoped it had enough cross-cultural appeal to lure the Fujioka executives.

The presentation started at three. Oren and Dan made a flawless pitch and an hour later they emerged from the conference room with a one-hundred-million-dollar account in their pockets. They made immediate arrangements for a catered cocktail party to celebrate the kickoff of the "More Is More" campaign.

Several hours later the Prescott Agency conference room had been transformed. The walls were plastered with Fujioka logos and dozens of the new "More Is More" posters. In the center of the conference table, the caterer, guided by the campaign motif, had created a miniature—yet fabulously expensive—reflecting pool made of premium beluga caviar. Sitting cross-legged at the edge of the pool was a large marzipan Zen master. The rest of the table was covered with themed appetizers including little goat cheese stereo systems and big-screen TVs fashioned from pâté.

The bars at both ends of the room were stacked three deep with thirsty executives. The mood was high and the room was filled with much toasting and self-congratulation. The bar was generously stocked with the finest Seagram products, including five vintage-dated single-malt Scotch whiskies produced by the world-renowned Glenlivet Distillery, Crown Royal, Boodles gin, Captain Morgan's Private Stock rum, Perrier-Jouet.

"Can I help you, sir?" the bartender asked.

"Yes, please," a handsome executive said. "Do you have any cognac?"

The bartender smiled. "Not just cognac, sir, Martell Cordon Bleu."

The handsome executive nodded knowingly. "Perfect."

Dan put on a great face, selling his excitement and enthusiasm like so much breakfast cereal, but he was starting to fade. Tired of mingling, Dan stood off in a corner watching the celebration but not enjoying it. Dan knew he couldn't keep Scott in the dark forever, and when he found out what had happened, well, Dan didn't want to think about it. All he was thinking about right now was getting some sleep. He stifled a yawn and lifted his Armanis to rub his eyes.

"I can help you out with that," a voice said. It was André from the production studio. André was an adequate artist and a hard enough worker, but he was kept around mainly because of his reliable cocaine connections which allowed the production studio to respond to rush orders like the one they had done the night before. André smiled slyly, brushed a finger past his nose. "It's the quicker picker-upper."

Dan hesitated. He hadn't had a bump since he couldn't remember when, and right now it sounded like a great idea. He just wondered if it was good stuff or if it had been stepped on a dozen times. "Stronger than dirt?" he asked.

André winked. "A little dab'll do ya."

"What are we talking?" Dan asked, rubbing a thumb against fingertips.

André put a hand on Dan's shoulder. "On the house," he said as his free hand slipped the small amber vial into Dan's coat pocket. "Congratulations, big guy. Just remember me when you get that corner office." André turned and headed for the men's room.

Dan was more alert already. He went to the bar, freshened his drink, and was about to sneak off for a jolt when Oren stopped him. "So, did you already write the press release?"

Dan looked confused. "About the account?"

Oren smiled and put his arm around Dan. "About The Prescott Agency's newest partner." He gave Dan's shoulder a firm squeeze.

Dan's roller coaster of a life was suddenly going up. "Partner? Are you shittin' me?"

"I don't kid about that sort of thing," Oren said. "You just doubled our goddamn billings. I figure if I don't let you in, you'll go start your own shop and take Fujioka with you."

Dan rubbed his beard as he soaked up the moment. It was the moment he'd been waiting for, the one he felt he had earned. "Oren, just let me say—"

"You motherfucking thief!"

That is not what I was going to say, Dan thought. There was a commotion at the door and Dan saw something out of the corner of his eye. It was Scott Emmons in midair, flying at him like a round-eyed refugee from a Hong Kong action movie. *Oh, shit!*

"You stole my fucking idea!" Scott crashed into Dan and sent him reeling backward into the conference-room table. His glass flew from his hand and decapitated the marzipan Zen master before skittering off the table. "I'll gut you with a goddamn chain saw!" Scott screeched.

Oren, shrinking from the battle, thought Scott looked as though he meant it.

"Get him off of me!" Dan yelled. "Somebody help!"

It turned out that after delivering the Shaftem, Dickem spot to the executive producer at COD, Scott had called in to see if Dan needed him to do anything else before he went home. Dan's assistant, not knowing any better, told Scott about how Dan had landed the Fujioka account with this great "More Is More" campaign idea. Further she told him they were going to be having a big party in the conference room to celebrate. She invited Scott to join the party.

So he did. "You rat bastard son-of-a-bitching thief!" Scott shrieked.

Oren was terrified, and even though he would have hated to see his ace creative guy gutted with a chain saw, he wasn't about to wade into the fray and risk getting goat cheese on his shirt. But he had to do something. "Somebody call Security," he yelled.

While Scott was banging the rat bastard son-of-a-bitching thief's head into the caviar reflecting pool, Dan managed to have an idea. He wrestled Scott to the floor where they proceeded to roll around furiously while Scott threw wild punches and spewed invective. Scott was so intent on trying to gouge Dan's eyes out that he didn't keep track of what Dan was doing with his hands. With everyone else focused on the fight, the Fujioka executives took the opportunity to get fresh cocktails.

A moment later Security arrived. They were a couple of beefy boys from the UCLA football program who were working part-time until they could find an agent or a booster to give them illegal cash under the table. Oren, wanting to help in any way possible, pointed the security guys in the direction of the fight. They pulled Scott off of Dan and subdued him. Dan was still lying on the floor. He pointed wildly up at Scott. "He's crazy!" Dan yelled. "He's on drugs or something! Get him away from me!"

"I'm going to feed your testicles to my fucking dog!" Scott swore.

The security guards bent Scott violently over the conference table and cuffed him. He continued to struggle and make wheezy threats, so one of the security guys stuffed a handful of the pâté televisions into Scott's mouth. As Scott gagged on the goose liver, the security guys rooted through his pockets. They found car keys, a wallet, some ChapStick, and a small amber vial filled with a rocky white powder. "Looks like meth," one of them said.

The other one shook his head. "Blow."

Scott looked over his shoulder. "What? That's not mine!"

"He's a goddamn drug addict," Dan yelled. "He's crazy. Call the police! Get him out of here! He's a fucking dope dealer!"

In his entire cringing existence, Scott had never even smoked pot, much less snorted any cocaine. It wasn't that he disapproved, he was just too scared to do things like that. Scott knew the security guards didn't have any reason to plant it on him, so the only one left to blame was Dan. Now, Scott was already pretty worked up about the Fujioka thing, but this sent him over the edge. He was so pissed he couldn't begin to articulate his rage. He turned a deep red and looked, quite simply, psychotic.

The security guys lifted Scott by the arms and started to carry him out of the room. Scott finally regained the gift of speech. "The bastard's framing me!" Pâté issued from Scott's nostrils as he continued hurling accusations. "It was my idea! I'm going to kill you, Steele! Count on it! You are a dead man!"

Oren watched as Dan, still sitting on the floor, combed the caviar from his dark hair. It seemed likely that Dan had stolen Scott's idea. He couldn't be sure about the cocaine allegations, but he suspected that somehow Dan had planted the toot on the poor schmuck at some point during the mayhem. *This is my new business partner?* Oren crossed his arms and beamed a magnificent smile. He looked like a proud parent.

Father Michael still felt like he was coming down with something. He'd had a couple of painful spasms in his abdomen and thought he should go see a doctor, but first he had to go to Van Nuys to attend Ruth's 5150 evaluation and bail hearing. Dan talked about just leaving her in jail, but Michael finally shamed him into coughing up a check to cover her bond.

A court-appointed psychiatrist testified that Ruth had no control over her actions when she stopped taking her medication. He cited the "hostage incident" and several other examples to support his position. The judge agreed that Ruth wasn't criminally responsible, but there was nothing the judge could do about the civil suits that had been filed by plaintiffs wanting to recover financial damages. At the end of the hearing, criminal charges were dropped and Ruth was released into Michael's custody.

This was the first time in five years that Michael had seen his mother. He had hoped for a joyful reunion, but Ruth was exhausted and depressed after her night in jail, and no matter what Michael said, his mom wouldn't speak to him. He didn't know if she was withdrawn due to a mood swing or if she was still angry with him for going to work in Africa in the first place. Michael knew she had felt abandoned when he left, but he hoped she had gotten over that. All he really wanted was to hear her say, "I love you." He needed that right now.

Michael stretched the muscles in his neck as he led Ruth out of the police station. He wondered why they were so stiff. "I'm parked around back," he said. They walked slowly across the parking lot toward Michael's ancient VW bus, which he had left with a friend while in Africa. "We're not going back to the nursing home," he said. "We're going out to a place in Sylmar where I'm going to work. They're sending your stuff over later." He opened the car door for his mother.

Ruth climbed into the VW. Michael leaned across to put on her seat belt. Ruth looked into his eyes. "You look terrible," she said. "You should see a doctor."

He was glad just to hear her voice. "Nah, I'm okay. It's just, we didn't eat very good in Africa. Probably need vitamins or something." Michael got into the driver's seat, cranked it up, and pulled out of the parking lot. He tried engaging Ruth in more conversation, but she wouldn't respond to anything. She just stared out the window as Michael drove across the Valley toward Sylmar in the northeasternmost border of the L.A. city limits.

Sylmar was a largely Hispanic community on the other side of the tracks that run parallel with San Fernando Road.

It sits where the foothills of the Santa Susanna Mountains meet the San Gabriels. It's bordered on three sides by freeways. It's dirty and dusty, and while there is a lot of plant life, it's dirty and dusty too. Over the years, the area had evolved into a hodgepodge of low-income homes and light industrial facilities. Old ranchland and citrus and olive orchards had been converted to a ratty suburban purgatory, not really hell but certainly not Pacific Palisades.

Father Michael pulled off the freeway at Polk and turned right at the First Adventist Church. A couple of blocks later, past Our Lady of the Immaculate Conception and then Holy Family Catholic Church, they arrived at the Care Center. It was a large two-story boardinghouse built in the thirties, desert tan with a faded brown roof and trim. It sat at the back of a half acre of crabgrass, gravel, and dirt. There was a tired carport leaning against the east side of the building, tattered blue vinyl tarps stretched across the back doing their best to turn the structure into a garage. Bertha was parked underneath.

Sister Peg came out to meet them. "You must be Father Michael," she said. "Welcome to the Care Center."

Father Michael tried not to stare, but he found Sister Peg's eyes irresistible. They were brown, sweet as angel's breath, and perfectly framed by her habit. "It's nice to meet you, Sister," he said. He was surprised by the effect her eyes had and after a moment realized he was in the middle of an awkward pause. "Oh, uh, this is Ruth, my mother," he said. "She's not feeling well. I think she just wants to get some rest." Ruth never looked up, never spoke. She felt like damaged goods being shuffled from one storage facility to another.

"I understand," Sister Peg said. "I've got her room ready." She looked at her watch. "Let's take her up and then I'll give you the nickel tour if we've got time."

"Perfect." Father Michael gently urged his mom toward the house.

Sister Peg was encouraged by Father Michael's sweet demeanor and tender smile. The way he walked by his mother's side instead of walking ahead of her revealed the sort of patience and kindness and respect that most people didn't bother with anymore. She was glad to have him here.

Sister Peg showed Father Michael and Ruth to Mr. Smith's old room. It was the smallest bedroom in the house and the only one with privacy. While Father Michael unpacked her small suitcase, Ruth sat on the edge of her new bed, looking out the window in silence. "Get some rest, Mom. I'll check in on you later." He gave her a kiss on the head.

Outside, Father Michael told Sister Peg about the stolen-truck escapade but assured her that his mom was back on her medication. Sister Peg told him not to worry. "Your mom's in good hands," she said with a reassuring smile. She looked at her watch again. "I've got to be across the Valley in half an hour, so I'll show you around real quick, then I've got to go." She showed him the rest of the second floor. There were eight bedrooms off the hallway, most of which were occupied by elderly residents. There was a community bathroom at the end of the hall. Next to that was a small room outfitted with a card table and two old jigsaw puzzles.

At the bottom of the stairs they paused at another bedroom. Inside was a young girl, about seven. Sister Peg tapped on the door. "Hi, Alissa. This is Father Michael."

Alissa looked up with wary green eyes. She had feathery blond bangs draped across her forehead. The bruises healing on her face were ghastly blue-gray patches. Her arms looked like evidence photos. She was sitting on the floor with her back to the wall. She had been playing with an old doll until these two adults showed up in the door-way. She put the doll in her lap and eyed them skeptically.

Father Michael started into the room, but Sister Peg stopped him. Alissa tensed noticeably, her face suddenly conveying a toughness that said she could take any abuse that came her way. "It's okay," Sister Peg said. "We're not going to bother you." Sister Peg led Father Michael down the hall. "Her father," she said. Her tone was uncompli-mentary and explained the bruises. "I've got custody until he gets out of County."

"Mother's in jail too?"

"Don't even know who she is," Sister Peg said. She looked at Father Michael and didn't need to say anything else. She had seen this story a thousand times before, and he had seen much worse. They walked the rest of the way down the hall in silence. Father Michael, wondering if that sort of thing would ever end. Sister Peg, thinking of the Old Testament, the part about an eye for an eye.

Sister Peg quickly showed Father Michael the kitchen, the dining room, her office, and, finally, the TV room where many of the Care Center's older residents spent their days and nights living vicariously better lives through television. The only one there at the moment was Mr. Saltzman, a gnarled seventy-eight-year-old who looked like he had suf-fered more than most. He was sitting on the front edge of his chair, his thick arms folded tight against his chest. A few strands of white hair drifted over his liver-spotted scalp. He was watching *Eyewitness Action On-the-Spot News*, cov-ering the latest high-speed chase on L.A. freeways. "Stupid bastards," he muttered to no one.

Sitting on the far side of the room, near a window, was a big Hispanic kid. He was a sixteen-year-old in an eighteen-year-old's hard body. His dark hair was short. He wore baggy pants and a T-shirt stained with a rainbow of paints. His torso was a landscape of green ink on nut brown skin.

He was hunched over a sketch pad, pencil in hand. He didn't look up when Sister Peg and Father Michael came in. "That's Ruben," Sister Peg said. "Our in-house artist."

"Hi, Ruben," Michael said, his hand in the air. Ruben didn't look up from the sketch pad. Father Michael waited a moment. "Must be mid-inspiration."

Sister Peg shook her head. "He's deaf. He came here a few years ago to get out of a gang. Now he's one of my underpaid employees. He's the one who does any heavy lifting that needs to be done, so he'll be glad you're here." Sister Peg stamped a foot on the floor and Ruben looked up. He smiled and showed her what he was working on. It wasn't a drawing. He'd been filling out a lottery form. The jackpot was up to thirty-two million dollars. He put his hands together in mock prayer.

Using sign language, Sister Peg slowly, if gracefully, introduced Father Michael. Ruben responded with fingernails raking up his neck and off his chin. Despite the fact that it looked like an Italian threat, Ruben's generous smile conveyed the sense that he was happy to have a fellow underpaid employee. He acknowledged Father Michael with a short upward nod of the head, then returned his attention to picking numbers for Saturday's Lotto drawing—the state's version of hope and salvation.

"What sort of painting does he do?"

"He's a wizard with a can of spray paint," Sister Peg said. "He does some sculpting too. I think he's got talent, but I'm not a judge of that sort of thing." She turned and headed for the hallway.

Father Michael stopped abruptly. He felt another sharp spasm in his abdomen. He bent slightly at the waist and sent two fingers to probe under his ribs, easing the discomfort. This was the worst one yet. If this didn't clear up on its own, he'd definitely have to see a doctor.

Father Michael caught up with Sister Peg who had

stopped to watch the end of the high-speed chase on the news. They stood there long enough to see the next story. The desk anchor threw it to a reporter who was standing inside a huge warehouse somewhere in Los Angeles. "Thanks, Bob," the reporter said. "You know, they used to say the moon was made of green cheese. Well, if you've ever wondered how much cheese it would take to do that, the contents of this warehouse ought to give you a pretty good idea!" The camera pulled back to a long, wide shot of an enormous warehouse. The reporter explained that the 600,000-square-foot warehouse was filled to the rafters with cheese and other dairy products. "And all of this is anything *but* hard cheese for California's dairy farmers. This warehouse is just a small part of the government's complex overall strategy to keep the state's dairy industry immune to the price fluctuations that can be caused by cheaper imported products. Oh, and one more thing," the reporter said. "I think if I were to come back in another life, I'd like to come back here . . . as a mouse!" The reporter chuckled. "Back to you in the studio, Bob."

"Christ, that pisses me off!" Sister Peg turned to walk away.

Father Michael followed her. "The waste or the inane chatter?"

"I'm sorry, Father. I don't mean to make a bad first impression. But that sort of . . . crap makes me crazy."

"Believe me, I understand." He thought of all the absurd church and government policies he'd encountered in Africa, policies that prevented tons of food and medicine from reaching the sick and starving refugees. "But what can you do?" he asked rhetorically.

"Give me a minute," Sister Peg said. "I'll think of something." She looked at her watch. "All right, I've got to take off. But I'll see you tomorrow morning?"

"First thing." Father Michael was about to go back upstairs to check on Ruth when he had another spasm. He doubled over and decided he had to see a doctor.

Scott Emmons was in an unemployed funk. He was lying on the sofa in his robe watching television. It was during a break between talk shows that he saw the commercial for the first time. It opened with the Zen master sitting at the edge of a reflecting pool. When Scott saw the red neon Fujioka logo mirrored in the black water, he sat up so fast he nearly herniated a disk. It was just as he had imagined it. He leaned close to the screen, taking in every detail.

There was a small boom box on the ground in front of the Zen master. Once the scene was established, the Zen master reached out and pushed the Play button on the cassette player. The meditative strains of a koto wafted in like liquid silk. The Zen master looked up peacefully. "A wise man once said, *less* is more." He paused, as if considering the notion. "But after further contemplation, wise man corrected himself."

The Zen master pushed the Stop button on the small boom box and the strains of the koto vanished. Suddenly there was a disturbance on the calm surface of the reflecting pool. The Fujioka logo shimmered as something began to emerge from the pool's inky depths. A huge big-screen TV and a bank of ominous black stereo equipment with massive speakers rose silently from the water, towering over the Zen master, who looked up at it with a grin. The Zen master pulled a remote control from his robes, pointed it at the glistening wall of electronics. He smiled, then punched the Play button.

The TV screen and the stereo exploded to life with an insane acid-jazz-metal-rap-rock music video. The Zen master smiled knowingly and nodded his approval in rhythm with the beat. An announcer's voice tagged the spot with a simple phrase. "Fujioka Electronics. *More* is more."

Scott tried to scream, but nothing came out. He tried harder, calling on all the strength of his frustrations, but his voice remained silent. The veins in his neck stood out like fat blue snakes as he strained to push the air from his lungs into his vocal cords. Scott began to tremble as he thought about what Dan had taken from him and then, with his crimson face swollen and threatening to explode, Scott blacked out and whacked his head on the coffee table.

Dan gave Michael twenty bucks and the keys to his car. "Do me a favor," he said, "stay out late."

Beverly had finally returned Dan's call late on Friday. She thanked him for all the roses and said she was going to be in town Saturday night. "I want to see you," she said. "You were a bad boy to stand me up. I think you need to be disciplined."

"I was very bad," Dan said. "But I'm willing to take my punishment like a man. Just tell me where and when."

"Tomorrow night, your place, so you can't stand me up so easily," she said. "I'll be there at eight with some new toys, assuming you're into that sort of thing." Click.

Dan had no idea what these toys were, but he was definitely game. He spent Saturday at the market. He bought multiple packs of AAA-, AA-, C-, and D-size batteries in case Beverly's gadgets were energy hogs. Then, fearing his old ones were past their expiration date, Dan threw out his condoms and replaced them with a new box. Feeling cocky, he bought the large size, ribbed and purple.

Back home, Dan cranked the stereo and started cooking. He sang along to a favorite old song, "All I ask of you . . . is to make my wildest dream come true . . ." He released two beautiful sea bass steaks into a pond of sweet ginger and soy marinade in preparation for steaming with scallions and shiitakes. Then he spent an entire hour preparing his favorite pan-Asian appetizer. The wine was a buttery California chardonnay. Beverly was dessert.

Dan's timing was perfect. He was out of the shower, dried, and dressed with ten minutes to spare. He poured a glass of the chardonnay, put on "Countdown to Ecstasy," and relaxed on the sofa, thinking, *God is good.*

Beverly arrived like a storm front in a see-through blouse and studded leather collar. Her beautiful bare legs dropped from a clingy short skirt. Satanic green eyes burned underneath her shiny brown bangs. She carried a small cosmetics case inside of which Dan assumed were Beverly's bizarre sex toys. Dan started getting hard just thinking about it. "Appetizers are almost ready," he said as she slinked in. "Szechwan dumplings."

"We'll eat later," Beverly announced, taking Dan by the belt buckle. "You have to be punished first." She led him to the bedroom and unzipped him. "How fast can you get out of those pants?" Dan was buck naked before she could say "depraved inclinations." "Do you want to touch me?" Beverly asked as she put Dan's hands on her breasts and closed her eyes. "Do you want to do things to me?" Too stupefied to use words, Dan started fumbling with the buttons of her blouse. Beverly stopped him and shoved him toward the bed. "Lie down," she said firmly. Dan complied. "You were very bad. I don't like to be stood up. It's humiliating."

"I'm sorry." Dan had never engaged in any S&M, so he wasn't sure what to say. "Are you going to spank me?"

"You're going to get exactly what a bad boy deserves," Beverly said. "And it's going to be so hot." Beverly opened her cosmetics case. She reached in and removed a pair of shiny chrome handcuffs and some rope. Dan swallowed hard. He was ready to submit or dominate or get on his knees and bark like a Norwegian elkhound, whatever she asked.

A moment later, Dan's legs were spread-eagle, tied to the bedposts. Beverly climbed onto the bed and stood over Dan, straddling him. She walked slowly toward his head. "Do you like what you see?" Dan looked. *My God, she's not wearing panties.* Premature ejaculation became a legitimate concern. Beverly lowered herself until she was squatting warm on Dan's chest. "Give me your hands," she said.

A moment later, Dan was secured to the headboard, watching excitedly as Beverly pulled a tube of some sort of cream or lubrication from the cosmetics case. He couldn't wait to see what it was. "Close your eyes," she said. "Bad boys don't get to watch."

Dan complied. He wondered how long he could hold out. The air filled with the scent of mint. Dan assumed it was a flavored lubricant of some sort and was eager for its application.

Beverly stroked the inside of Dan's thighs. "This is going to be so hot," she repeated.

Dan believed her with all his heart and soul. He began to tingle when Beverly took him gently in her hands. She massaged the cream onto his third leg and then, with a feathery touch, his balls. Dan could now die a happy man.

"Now," Beverly said. "Aren't you sorry you stood me up?"

Uh oh, Dan thought. Something was wrong with that tone of voice. His eyes popped open as Beverly climbed off the bed. He saw her screwing the top back onto a tube of Ben-Gay. "This is going to be so hot," she said with a smirk.

Dan immediately realized he'd been the victim of a classic bait-and-switch ad. At first he apologized. Then he begged. Finally he tried bribery, but Beverly wasn't interested. She picked up the cosmetics case, then gestured at Dan's hot yet withering apparatus. "Oh, by the way," she mocked, "less is less."

Dan whimpered when he heard the apartment door close behind her. *I did not think a girl could be so cruel.*

Michael returned a few hours later with no intentions of looking in on his brother. However, the cries for help were too urgent and literal to ignore. He entered the room and saw Dan lying there, his most prominent feature a sweaty look of disappointment. Dan held his head up and looked at Michael. "Forgive me, Father, for I tried to sin." When Michael stopped laughing he untied his brother and eventually managed to pick the lock on the handcuffs.

"I'd give you some penance," Michael said, "but I suspect it would be redundant."

It took her a while, but Sister Peg eventually found the man she was looking for. He was in downtown Los Angeles, hidden deep within the federal office complex that housed the various divisions of the California Department of Agriculture.

Sister Peg had an appointment with a Mr. Churchill who was the assistant to the Deputy Associate Commissioner under the Deputy Director of the Division of Operations, Planning, and Management within the Office of Regulatory Affairs and Strategic Initiatives for the Division of Economic Policies and Implementation. Mr. Churchill was in his late fifties and was going with the whole Larry King look. He wore a crisp blue shirt, braided leather suspenders, and a red and gold power tie. The black frames of his wildly oversized glasses had a clownish effect in the way they eclipsed his face and magnified his eyes. The fish-eyed bureaucrat was doing his best to be patient as Sister Peg once again asked for an explanation. "But if the cheese is just sitting there, why can't you give some to the poor?"

Mr. Churchill let out a sigh to let the nun know she was testing his forbearance. "Because if we give the cheese away, the people who get it for free won't need to buy any, and that would undermine the purpose of the price-support program, wouldn't it?"

"But I'm talking about people who don't have any money," she said patiently. "So they couldn't buy the cheese even if they wanted to, which they do, but they can't because they're poor. Do you understand my point?"

Mr. Churchill ran into this sort of thinking all the time and it made him absolutely crazy. He didn't know why the general public was so ignorant of basic economic principles. But he didn't seem to be making any headway with words alone, so he decided to use a visual aid. He opened a desk drawer and pulled out a clean sheet of graph paper and a black marker, then he drew a large L on the page. He pointed at the graph. "This horizontal axis represents Tons of Cheese Demanded," he said. "This vertical axis represents the Price of Cheese, okay?" Mr. Churchill then drew two parallel sloping lines within the graph which he labeled RR and YY, for no obvious reason. "Now, a rise in consumer income shifts the demand curve this way, so RR becomes YY." He pointed at the outer sloping line. "In other words, at any given price, assuming a growth in income, consumers will demand more cheese because they can afford more. Now, since we don't have control over consumer income, we're forced to artificially decrease cheese supply which has the effect of making the existing cheese demand higher, relatively speaking, thus maintaining the necessary price of the goods." He handed the graph to Sister Peg. "Now, does that answer your question?"

Sister Peg laid the graph on Mr. Churchill's desk and gestured for the black marker. Mr. Churchill handed it to her. "Let me see if I understand," she said as she drew a graph of her own. "This axis represents Income and this axis represents Tons of Cheese. Now, if income is here"— Sister Peg drew a line indicating an income of zero—"and there's this amount of cheese"—she drew a line indicating lots of cheese—"what does this represent?" She made a tiny black dot on the graph.

Mr. Churchill looked at the tiny dot and shrugged. "You tell me," he said.

"That's your heart, Mr. Churchill. Of course, it's enlarged somewhat so you can actually see the damn thing."

Well, this was just the sort of abuse up with which the assistant to the Deputy Associate Commissioner under the Deputy Director of the Division of Operations, Planning, and Management within the Office of Regulatory Affairs and Strategic Initiatives for the Division of Economic Policies and Implementation did not have to put. Mr. Churchill narrowed his eyes. "Sister, perhaps a little economic disincentive will motivate these people of yours to go out and get jobs. Then they can eat all the cheese they want."

Sister Peg thought back over the past ten minutes or so and concluded that she had shown all the restraint the situation warranted, so she lunged for Mr. Churchill and grabbed his red and gold tie. She pulled him halfway across his desk and looked into his shallow eyes. "You're a heartless piece of shit," she said, accurately. Sister Peg then took the black marker and drew a bold little Hitleresque mustache on the bureaucratic cheese nazi. "Now, are you going to help me or what?"

"Christ Almighty!" Mr. Churchill said. "Let me go!"

Sister Peg pulled tighter. "Give me some disincentive," she hissed. Sister Peg had strong feelings about the equitable distribution of wealth, even if it was in the form of cheese. She believed the notion of noblesse oblige extended to the government and was more than happy to help persuade others to share in her beliefs.

Mr. Churchill couldn't believe it. This lunatic nun had come in off the street blaming him for her constituency's meager income bracket as though market forces and pure economic theory and policy could be burdened by things like compassion.

"I'm waiting," Sister Peg said, doubling her grip on the power tie.

Like a bad dog pulling against a choke chain, Mr. Churchill tried to get away from the righteous and enthusiastic sister. But his struggling just made things worse. He labored to get a breath so he could speak. He finally managed to get the words out. "Just let me make a call . . . see what I can do."

Sister Peg let go, sending Churchill crashing back into his chair. She smiled across the desk. "Bless you," she said.

Mr. Churchill backed away from his desk as he loosened the noose from around his neck. He grabbed a tissue and smeared the little Hitler mustache into a lopsided Groucho Marx affair. "Does the Church know how you operate?" he asked between gasps.

"No, they say they're not their sister's keeper."

Mr. Churchill got on the phone and mumbled something to someone before hanging up. "Help's on the way," he said. And in no time at all two security guards arrived, as if this were the sort of thing they had to do rather frequently. They escorted Sister Peg from the maze of cubicles where Mr. Churchill committed his acts of policy and they deposited her on the dirty sidewalk outside the building. Somewhere in the tussle on the way out, one of the guards had broken her rosary. He tossed it at her feet before going back into the building.

Sister Peg made a mental note to say some prayers for Mr. Churchill that night, then she changed her mind. She figured God had more important things to worry about than a little dickhead who wouldn't share his food with the poor. She gathered her stray rosary beads and thought about what to do next. And then she received her inspiration. She marched over to a pay phone on the sidewalk and searched herself for change. She had none. She stopped a man who was passing by. "Excuse me, could you loan me a quarter?"

The man looked at her. "Why should I loan you a quarter?"

Sister Peg leaned into his face and screamed. "Because I'm a nun! Now, give me a goddamn quarter!"

And lo, the man gave her a quarter. And with the quarter, Sister Peg made a call. "Hi, Josie. It's me, Peg. I got a favor to ask."

The people at the San Fernando Free Clinic couldn't have been nicer. No one asked for proof of income or insurance coverage; they simply took Father Michael at his word and sent him in to see the doctor. Fifteen minutes later Father Michael was in the examination room waiting for the diagnosis.

The doctor came in and apologized. He said he had no idea what was wrong with Father Michael. "Unless you've been ingesting strychnine," he said, adding something about antagonized glycine. "I suggest you go to County Med Center."

So he went. It was a madhouse of bloody gunshot victims, impoverished pregnant women surrounded by multitudes of sick children, and people on the fringe of show business who didn't earn enough to buy medical insurance. Armed guards were stationed by the doors in case gang bangers dropped by to finish off someone they had only wounded in a drive-by. Children were screaming, ringing phones went unanswered, low moans drifted out from the trauma slots in the nearby ER, and the paging system never stopped calling for doctors to answer codes red and blue.

In the midst of all this, Father Michael leaned toward the admitting window, trying to hear the nurse through the tiny slot in the bulletproof glass. The nurse was looking at his application. "So you worked in exchange for an all-expense-paid trip to Africa plus food and lodging?"

"Well, no," Father Michael said, rubbing his stiff jaw. "I think that mischaracterizes—"

The nurse shook her head. "See, that counts as income, which you failed to report here." She pointed at line twenty-three (g) on the form. "That means you don't qualify for public-assistance treatment at this facility. Sorry. Next!"

Father Michael managed an understanding smile as he slipped away from the window. He wandered over to the waiting area and dropped into a hard plastic chair. He needed to sit for a minute and gather himself. He had another spasm, this one severe enough to obstruct his upper airway for a moment. He was sick and he knew it. Where would he turn now? He would have gone to the Church for help except that nasty bit of business with Cardinal Cooper back in Africa precluded that option. It seemed to Father Michael that those who were willing to help were unable, and those able were unwilling. He bent over trying to diminish the pain. He was in bad shape and, worst of all, he realized Dan was his only hope.

Willy had been a security guard for nearly a year, but it seemed like an eternity. Night after night watching a small black-and-white TV, interrupted only by the routine of checking the locks on the warehouse doors. Willy occasionally prayed that something would happen to break the monotony—a fire, a terrorist attack, anything.

So when a tall blonde in an impossibly short, clingy skirt emerged from the darkness as he was making his rounds one night, Willy silently thanked the Lord. The blonde was carrying something in a plastic grocery sack. "Hey," she said, still twenty yards away. "I need some help."

"What's the problem?" Willy asked. He moved closer to the gate to get a better look at the damsel's two distress signals.

"I was on my way to a party and my car broke down," she said. "Can you believe it?" Quite frankly, Willy couldn't. He figured the girl was in her twenties. Looked like a tall size six. Real tall, he thought, and bouncy. "Do you have a phone I could use?" she asked.

"Yeah," Willy said. "No problem."

"Great!" The blonde giggled. She seemed a little drunk.

And that got Willy to thinking. He slipped off his wedding ring while taking the big key chain off his belt. No need to let a thin band of gold stand between little Willy and a tall, drunk blonde. When he saw that she wasn't wearing a bra, he started to feel lucky. "This is a bad neighborhood for a breakdown," Willy said. "Good thing I was here, huh?" Willy opened the gate and let her in.

"This is sooo sweet of you." She tossed her hair from one side to the other.

Willy made small talk as he led her to the security office.

She flashed a grateful smile as she dialed. Then she scooted up on top of the desk, giving Willy a reminder of Sharon Stone in *Basic Instinct*. He just wished he had a pause button. The bouncy blonde got someone on the phone, arranged for a ride, then hung up. "My friend'll be here in about thirty minutes. Mind if I just hang here?" She hopped off the desk and looked around the office for a minute, letting Willy's imagination run wild. "Hey, would you like a beer?" She pointed at the grocery sack.

"Well, I'm on duty," he said. "But . . . okay, maybe one." He pulled a couple of the sixteen-ounce cans from the sack and opened one for each of them. "My name's Willy, what's yours?"

"Josie," she said. "Like *Josie and the Pussycats*. Remember that show?" She sang the opening line of the theme song and did a little dance right there in front of Willy.

Man, is she bouncy. Willy drained his beer and went back for another. In no time at all he was feeling handsome despite the fact that he was known as Toad-boy in high school. "So who's throwing the party?" he asked. He turned the TV off and turned on the radio.

"I dunno," Josie said. "Just some people. I didn't really wanna go, I was just kinda bored." She gave Willy a once-over. "You know, you remind me of somebody." She looked into his eyes long enough to take control. "I just can't think of who it is." Then, after a minute she smiled and pointed at him. "I know! One of those Baldwins. Do you do like modeling during the day or something?"

Willy broke into a thirty-two-ounce smile. "Yeah, you know, I've thought about doing that, but I'm too busy." He opened a third can and waved it around the office. "I gotta find some time to look into that." After another gulp of beer Willy started telling Josie lies about the dangers of his job and all the rough characters he had subdued.

"You have a gun?" Josie asked.

"Don't really need one," Willy said with a wink. "I got a pretty big nightstick."

"Oh yeah?" Josie licked her lips. "You wanna show me?"

A minute later Willy was leading Josie deep into the refrigerated warehouse, through long corridors of endless crates marked "Cheese." Willy was out of uniform in record time, and while his nightstick wasn't as grand as advertised, Willy was going to try to make up for that with enthusiasm.

The chill of the warehouse made Josie's nipples hard as a wedge of Romano. In the course of her career, Josie had had sex in a lot of places, but it was safe to say this was the first time she had done it while leaning against a large block of cheddar. But Josie was a professional, so despite the fact that she was cold and surrounded by curds of soured milk, she did and said all the right things. "Oh baby," she moaned. "Just like that. Give it to me. Yeah, oh yeah. Ohhh!" She glanced at her nails behind Willy's back.

Willy, meanwhile, was doing yeoman's work, and after several minutes his eyelids started to flutter. "Here we go," he said. "Hold on to something, baby." Willy shifted into high gear. "Oh yeah. Oh yeah. Oh—"

"Hello!" The voice came from behind Willy, startling

him, to say the least. He stopped midstroke and prayed that Josie was a ventriloquist. "Excuse me," the voice said. "Sorry to interrupt."

Willy spun around and saw a nun standing there with a camera. "Say 'Cheese'!" she said. FLASH!

Willy was horrified. First of all, he'd been caught screwing on the job. Second, he'd been caught by a nun, of all things. And finally, the nun had a camera and wasn't afraid to use it. Sister Peg moved to one side. "How about a profile shot?" FLASH!

"What the hell—" Willy's nightstick softened like Brie in a microwave.

FLASH! Sister Peg took another. "How about the full monty?" Sister Peg said, zooming in on her target.

"Hey! Stop it!" Willy made an aggressive move toward Sister Peg. That's when Ruben stepped from the shadows, brandishing a large gun. He fired into a crate of Monterey Jack which exploded behind Willy. Willy stopped cold and put his hands straight up in the air. "What the hell is going on?"

Josie slipped back into her skirt. She hopped onto the block of cheddar as she made introductions. "Willy, this is Sister Peg and Ruben. Peg, Ruben, this is Willy."

With his free hand Ruben signed something to Sister Peg, ending with the first two fingers of his hand quickly brushing his forehead.

"Is he talking about me?" Willy looked to Sister Peg. "What's he saying?"

"He said, 'hollow point,' Willy. Do you have any idea what that means?"

Willy nodded his head and raised his hands even higher.

Ruben loved being Sister Peg's spear-carrier. She had taken care of him when he needed it and he intended to take care of her in return. Ruben gestured at Willy's nightstick, then wiggled his little finger. Sister Peg and Josie laughed. "Now, Ruben," Sister Peg said. "Judge not lest ye be judged." She nodded at Willy. "You can put your hands down now."

Willy covered his giblets. "What do you want?"

"Well," Sister Peg said. "I think I speak for all of us when I say we want you to put your pants back on." Willy grabbed his pants and got dressed. "Willy, let me ask you," Sister Peg said. "Would you like this roll of film or should we deliver it directly to Mrs. Willy?"

Willy could see the merits of the nun's argument and agreed to help. Willy and Ruben got Bertha loaded with around six hundred pounds of cheese in just under half an hour. As they were finishing, Sister Peg walked Josie over to her car.

"You know I can't pay you for this," Sister Peg said.

"No problem." Josie gestured to her backseat. "I grabbed enough Gouda to last me six months."

"I know it's hypocritical of me to ask, since I talked you into doing this," Sister Peg said, "but why not make Willy your last one? Come live with us."

"What kind of invitation is that?" Josie asked. "I thought you were about to be evicted."

"I'm working on that. But in the meanwhile, we could really use your help."

Josie got into the car. "I'll think about it," she said. Sister Peg gave her a look. "I know you don't believe me," Josie said as she started the car. "But guess what. I made an appointment to get tested like you asked."

"Thanks. Let me know what they say." Sister Peg slapped the roof of the car as Josie drove off.

Ruben closed the back doors on the Suburban while Sister Peg climbed into the passenger seat. Willy stood by, looking defeated. His prayer had been answered, all right. Next time he'd be more careful. Sister Peg removed the roll of film from the camera and tossed it to Willy. "I suggest confession for you, young man," she said.

Dan was cranky when he got home. He'd been on the phone with lawyers all day after being named in a host of civil lawsuits stemming from Ruth's big-rig demolition derby. Most of the damage wasn't covered by insurance and several plaintiffs were talking about serious pain-and-suffering claims. Depending on the judges and juries he drew, Dan was looking at cash settlements and legal fees totaling in the neighborhood of two hundred thousand dollars, which was about a hundred ninety-nine thousand more than he had.

Father Michael, meanwhile, was dealing with his own problems. Since he had given Mom his room at the Care Center, Michael had to find a cheap apartment in the Sylmar area for himself. After a hot day weeding through the seediest dwellings in the vicinity, Michael finally settled on a two-room hovel not far from the Care Center. It would cost him two-fifty a month. It was small but crappy. It would suit his humble needs just fine.

Now the thing Michael needed most was medical attention. His malady—whatever it was—wasn't responding to prayer. And just as there was no denying the fact that a good doctor was going to cost money, it was equally certain that Dan was the only person to whom Father Michael could turn for funding. From the moment Dan walked in the door, Michael dropped hints about his deteriorating condition. But Dan was too preoccupied with his status as a defendant to pick up on the clues. He thought Michael was just being a whiner.

Finally Michael looked Dan in the eyes and said, "He healeth those that are broken in heart, and giveth medicine to heal their sickness."

Dan looked at Michael for a moment before speaking.

"You know, if I tightened that up, it could be the slogan for the new HMO campaign we're doing." Dan sensed his brother was about to pass the plate and he wasn't in the mood to make it easy.

Father Michael sat on the sofa and probed at his abdomen. "I don't feel very good."

"Who does these days?" Dan replied.

"Do I have to just come out and say it?" Father Michael hated having to ask, but he knew that charity sometimes had to be tweezed like nose hair from the giver. He held his hands out as if asking for gruel. "I need to borrow some money to see a doctor. There, are you happy?"

Dan walked to the bar. "Now, Michael, it's in the Good Book," Dan said. "Neither a borrower nor a lender be." He poured himself a stiff drink.

"That's from *Hamlet*," Father Michael said.

"Good Book, good play, doesn't matter. It's a solid policy." Dan took a gulp of the peaty scotch. "One I should have had in effect years ago," Dan said, alluding to the thousand dollars he had loaned his brother. "Don't they have, like, complimentary medical assistance in poor parts of the city?" He chewed a piece of ice and spit it back in his drink. "Maybe you should try something like that."

Father Michael told Dan about the Free Clinic and about being turned down by County Medical. It was embarrassing to have to go through this with his brother, but the shame of it was nothing compared to how sick he felt. Even though the spasms had diminished in frequency, he still sensed that he was infected with something awful.

Dan could see that Michael wasn't well. And as much as he wanted to make a point about responsibility and obligations, he knew he had to take care of his brother. "Look," Dan said, "being the soft touch that I am, I'd loan you the money if I had it, but I don't. I'm so in debt it's not funny, and now I'm being sued by a dozen people, thanks to Mom's joyride."

Father Michael assumed Dan was just holding out on him. It certainly wouldn't be the first time. "C'mon, what about that big raise? I bet you've got a ton in the bank."

Dan slammed his drink down. "You have no idea what the real world is like, do you? You think just because a person has a nice place and a nice car, you think they're rolling in it. Well, in the real world—"

Father Michael cut him off. He was pissed. "You don't know the first thing about the real world," he said. "You know, there's a reason they call this La-La Land. The real world's not about luxury cars and ocean views. It's about children starving to death and dying of diseases we can cure. It's about rebels armed with machetes chopping the hands off every man and boy in randomly chosen villages—" Father Michael went on a rant about the horrors of Africa, about mercenaries routinely invading refugee camps to kidnap children who were then beaten and tortured and "reeducated" and turned into an obedient army of rapists, murderers, and thieves.

Dan quickly surrendered. "Okay, okay, I know. Different worlds. But the fact is, in *this* world, I'm dead fucking broke."

Father Michael took a deep breath and let it out slowly. He figured the only way he was going to separate Dan from his money was to turn up the heat. He stood and pulled up his shirt. "Look at this." Michael pointed at a nasty purplish scar on his right flank. It was eight inches long and healing badly. It didn't exactly look infected, but it didn't look right either.

"What the hell is that?" Dan asked.

Father Michael touched the wound gingerly. He wasn't sure why, but he couldn't bring himself to tell Dan the truth. "I got sick while I was in Africa. This, uh, this doctor had to do some surgery."

"What, like a witch doctor?" Dan leaned in to get a closer look. "Mangy cats leave cleaner scars than that."

"It was field surgery, not the Mayo Clinic. I think it's infected or something. I really need to see a doctor." He was nervous and full of regret.

"Don't you have insurance through the Church?"

"They canceled it."

Dan needed a minute to think. There was no need to tap into the last few bucks in his checking account if he could come up with a better idea. He stood at the balcony door looking down at the moonlight shimmering on Santa Monica Bay. He wondered why this kind of shit always landed in his lap. First his mother, now this. His family seemed determined to prevent him from getting ahead in this life. He wondered what would happen if he didn't bail them out every time they got in a bind. Maybe they'd learn to swim. Then again, maybe they'd drown.

Father Michael had another spasm, causing him to double over. "This isn't getting any better," he said. "My jaw really hurts. It's hard to move."

Finally it came to Dan. It was unoriginal, but it had a good chance of working. That, plus the fact that Dan didn't think he'd get caught, convinced him. He turned around and looked at his brother. "I tell you what," Dan said. "You probably just need a shot of penicillin or something, right?"

Father Michael sat up; a sense of hope returned to his voice. "Yeah, probably."

Dan nodded agreement. "All right. Let's go." They got into Dan's car and headed for the hospital. On the way, Father Michael felt an odd combination of relief and pain. The relief was understandable given that he knew he was finally going to receive some treatment. Ironically, that allowed Father Michael to acknowledge to himself just how bad the pain was. They arrived at St. Luke's Hospital and parked near the top of the crowded parking structure. Walking toward the elevators, Dan pulled out his wallet and held it out to his brother. "Here, take this and give me yours," he said.

Father Michael looked at Dan's wallet, a regular serpent in the tree. Then he looked at Dan. "And herein do I exercise myself, to have always a conscience void of offense toward God, and toward men. Acts twenty-four:sixteen."

Like the tempting snake's tongue, Dan wiggled the wallet at his principled brother. "Correct me if I'm wrong, Father, but I believe it was St. Schulberg, in a letter to the Friars, who said, 'Living with a conscience is like driving with the brakes on.' " Dan raised his eyebrows as though he had made an irrefutable point. "Now, take the damn wallet."

Father Michael, in a moment of weakness, took it and followed Dan toward the elevator.

"Okay," Dan said. "Now, my insurance card's in front, right by my driver's license. I think you look enough like the photo. If anyone asks"—Dan rubbed his chin—"tell them you shaved." They were almost at the elevators when Dan suddenly grabbed his brother and dragged him aside. "Whoa! What the hell am I thinking? Take your clothes off!"

"What?"

"You can't be using my insurance dressed like Father Flanagan." They ducked between a minivan and a Volvo wagon to change clothes. Dan put on the black shirt and white collar. "C'mon, hurry up," he insisted. "Take your pants off!"

"Oh my Lord," a woman said. She had never witnessed such a sordid scene, though she had heard such things happened.

With his pants around his ankles, Father Michael looked up and saw the disappointed faces of a Catholic couple in their sixties who were looking for their car. The man put his hands over his wife's eyes and hurried her away.

Having inadvertently reinforced the popular stereotype of the aberrant cleric, Dan and Michael finished changing clothes and headed for the emergency room.

"All right," Dan said. "This is a piece of cake, yes? No point in feeling guilty until it's over. Then you can go to confession and wipe the slate clean." Dan knew that wasn't really how it worked, but what the hell, it was close.

"Don't worry," Michael said. "I won't fall apart on you." He said this despite the fact that he was having difficulty breathing.

"Attaboy." Dan slapped him on the back.

They entered the lobby of the emergency room and approached the Admissions window. That's when Michael had a terrible spasm. He grabbed his gut and doubled over, groaning. He crumpled to the floor. He went into full respiratory failure.

The woman at the desk looked at Michael. She pulled out a form and looked at Dan. "Name?" Her voice lacked any human emotion.

"Jesus!" Dan said. "Get some help!" He bent over and lifted Michael's head off the floor.

"And the last name?" She was calm and efficient in the face of a medical emergency. A doctor passing by saw the man on the floor being attended to by a priest. Thanks to his years of rigorous training, the doctor knew this was a bad sign, healthwise, so he called for help. There was a flurry of activity as medical personnel hurried to get Michael onto a gurney.

The woman at the Admissions window called to Dan. "Excuse me, Father, did you bring this man in?" Dan stood by, dazed by what had happened so suddenly. "Father?" the woman repeated. Dan looked at the woman for a moment before realizing he was the Father in question.

"Yes. Yes, he's my brother."

"Is he insured?"

Not for this, Dan thought. Before he could think of something that would get him out of what was turning into an ugly, and probably very expensive, situation, one of the nurses attending to Michael picked his pocket and held up the insurance card. "Yes!" she cried. "California Life, Platinum Coverage."

"But—" Dan could only watch as they wheeled Michael through the swinging doors.

The Admissions woman came out from behind the window, smiling all of a sudden. She put her arm around Dan's shoulder. "Relax, Father. He's insured. They'll take good care of him. Now, I just need a little information." She sat him down and gave him some forms. "Would you like a cup of coffee?"

Dan filled out the paperwork, then went to the designated waiting area. He read three issues of *Newsweek*, two *Entertainment Weekly*s, and a *People* before a doctor came out. "Your brother is presenting some unusual symptoms," the doctor said. "Dysphagia, hyperreflexia. There may be some sort of infection. We've got him on emergency ventilation while we're running tests." The doctor stood and pointed to the door. "You can see him now, if you'd like, Father. But only for a few minutes."

Dan found his way to Room 605, a semiprivate suite that spoke well of Dan's insurance coverage. Michael was in bed with IV lines trailing from both arms. He was sharing the room with an older man, apparently comatose, and on life support.

Dan went to Michael's bedside. "What the hell is going

on?" There was an urgency in his voice. "I thought you just needed a shot of penicillin."

Father Michael shrugged weakly. "They think it's more than that," he said from under his oxygen mask.

Dan looked at the clipboard hanging at the end of the bed. He made an odd gagging sound when he saw his own name listed as patient. "Holy Kuh-rist! This was supposed to be a quick fix, a shot in the butt. The second those bastards saw you were insured, they called every specialist in the hospital. I bet you're not even sick. They're just running up a big tab." He slapped Michael's shoulder. "C'mon, let's get out of here."

"I want to stay," Father Michael said.

"Oh, jeeeeezz." Dan sounded like he had a slow leak. He slumped onto the edge of Michael's bed, panic setting in. Dan began to worry about getting caught, about being charged with felony insurance fraud, about going to prison. He had to get Michael out of there. "C'mon," he said. "We're leaving." Dan started exploring the how-tos of undoing the tubes and wires attached to his brother.

"Dan, stop it," Michael said.

Dan ripped the adhesive monitors from Michael's chest. "Oww!"

"This is insane!" Dan snarled. "You're not staying here. We'll go to a drugstore, get you something over-the-counter so nobody goes to jail."

"Father! What are you doing?" a woman asked, out of nowhere.

Dan spun around and saw a very large old nun coming toward him. It was Sister Mary Anthony, a sixty-nine-year-old bowling ball of robes and rosaries. Dan couldn't tell by her habit if she was a Sister of Charity or a Lady of the Sacred Heart. All he knew was that she looked like she outweighed him and that she might produce an eighteen-inch ruler at any moment and do him some harm. "I asked

what you were doing, Father." The question was ac-
cusatory.

"Uh, he, uh, this looked a little loose." Dan said, pointing at the IV. "Can't take any chances, right?" He turned
back to look at Michael. "How's that feel . . . Dan?" He
smiled and patted his brother's hand.

Sister Mary Anthony gave Dan the evil eye as she
checked the IV and reattached the heart monitor. With
that taken care of, she snatched Dan's arm and forced him
to the door. "Thank you, Father, but we don't need *your*
help." She seemed quite bitter about something. "Now, go
on back to your rectory. I have to get Dan here in for
some tests."

Fernando's Dance and Social Club was in the basement of
an old office building not far from the San Fernando Mission Cemetery. It opened in the late 1950's and a flood
of Mexican immigrants quickly made it the most popular
nightspot in the Valley. Its popularity waned as the years
passed and now it was just a refuge for older men who had
come to California from Mexico decades ago.

Like the clientele, the interior was in decline—faded,
shadowy, sad. The decor evoked another time and place as
well as the memories of people long forgotten. One dimly
lit wall was dedicated to the art of the bullfight. It was
covered with old black-and-white photos of famous mata-
dors, picadors, and cape-men—gauchos all. There was a
small and neglected shrine to Benito Juárez in one corner
of the room. Day or night, it was equally dark inside the
club. A string of small red and amber lights was embedded
in the entire length of the bar. As customers leaned over
to order drinks, the lights lent an uncanny blush to their
faces and caused chins and noses to cast peculiar upward
shadows.

It was a typical weekday afternoon, five older men and

one woman, each sitting alone. The bartender pushed a fine shot of Mariachi tequila across the bar to the old gentleman who had come to Los Angeles from Oaxaca fifty years earlier. The man shook his head and said he did not order a shot of tequila. The bartender told him the woman at the end of the bar had sent it. She said she wanted to dance to a slow song. *"Creo que ella siente sola,"* the bartender said.

This struck a chord with the old man. He knew all about loneliness. He looked down the bar and acknowledged the woman with a mannerly nod. He sipped the tequila, then went to the jukebox and considered his options. He saw *"Aquellos Ojos Verdes"* and smiled. He fed the machine some coins and the song drifted into the room, sweet and nostalgic. The man smoothed the front of his shirt, then checked his hair in the reflection of the glass. He wanted to be presentable. He went to the woman and bowed in a courtly style. *"Le gustaria bailar?"*

"Sí." Ruth smiled demurely, then took the man's warm, weathered hand. She had left the Care Center earlier that morning feeling unwelcome and unwanted. In view of the fact that she hadn't seen Michael in two days, Ruth feared he had simply left her among strangers. She had been abandoned before and wasn't going to suffer that fate again, so she left the Care Center and set out for her old nursing home where she had friends. But she got lost along the way. She wandered the streets for hours before ducking into Fernando's. Something about the place called her inside, maybe the promise of meeting someone else who was alone.

As they moved slowly around the dance floor, Ruth returned to her youth, when lots of men had asked her to dance. She wondered where those men, and those days, were now. She closed her eyes and appreciated the feel of the man's hand against her back, of her hand in his. It had been too long since she had been held this way, or any other.

Dan couldn't sleep. Too many thoughts were crashing around inside his head. His whole world was collapsing. All he could do was lie in bed and try to figure out a way to prop it up.

At eight Dan called his office to say he was sick and on his way to the hospital. He wanted to leave a paper trail of some sort about the hospital visit. He figured a phone message to the head of Human Resources would cover him on the off chance that the insurance company ever called to verify the claim.

As Dan was about to leave for the hospital, it occurred to him that he ought to be wearing clerical garb. As he changed clothes, Dan thought of how he should act while dressed as a priest. He wanted to be prepared in case anyone approached him about something spiritual. Assuming he wouldn't be called upon to perform any of the sacraments, Dan figured he could get by with a small set of Catholic facial expressions. He posed in front of the mirror and tried, without much luck, to conjure a look of benevolence. He had more success with his look of judgmental disdain. Dan wondered if he would need a look that said he really cared about others. The priests from Dan's youth never looked that way to him. They always looked mean and serious and unamused. Dan figured he'd go with that.

He tugged at the clerical collar, trying to get some breathing room. He looked in the mirror and, for the briefest—most unlikely—moment, he thought he felt like a priest. The power vested in the uniform made him uncomfortable. It was as though he had been given serious responsibilities regarding other people's souls. He didn't like the way it felt. Not one bit. He preferred being responsible for just his own. Dan wondered why anyone would choose this life. It wasn't exactly what you'd call a glamour profession. People always asking for forgiveness, begging for miracles, demanding selflessness on your part. And the celibacy. Forget about it. These were the exact reasons Dan had dropped out of seminary in the first place.

Dan was on his way out the door when the phone rang. It was Karen, his attorney, calling to say he had been served with some more papers. Dan violated the Second Commandment and told Karen he'd call her later.

He got to the hospital and snagged a wheelchair from the maternity ward in case his brother was too lazy or too weak to walk. As soon as visiting hours started, Dan was in Michael's room. This time Dan wasn't taking no for an answer. He began issuing orders the moment he walked in the room. "C'mon, bro, saddle up, time to get going." He wanted to get out as quickly as possible, and he certainly didn't want to run into Sister Mary Anthony again.

Michael's comatose roommate was still there, lingering. Dan walked to the curtain separating the old man's bed from Michael's. He yanked the curtain back, scaring the hell out of a man in a full body cast. Dan looked at him for a moment. "Excuse me," he said. Dan turned to the comatose roommate. "I don't suppose you have any insights on this."

Given how things were going, Dan figured they'd moved Michael to a private suite on the top floor, something with a city view and a $10,000-a-day price tag. He looked for someone who might have some information. He cornered an orderly in the hallway and asked where Michael was. The orderly refused to make eye contact. Dan attributed that to the priest outfit and guilty feelings on the orderly's part. The orderly directed Dan to an office at the end of the hall.

The nameplate on the door read "Dr. Wu." Dan knocked once and walked right in. "I'm looking for Dan

Steele. He was in room 605 yesterday. You know where he is now?"

Dr. Wu tensed at the question, but he relaxed when he looked up and saw a priest. Priests were so understanding, he thought, so at peace with everything. This would make Dr. Wu's job much easier. "Come in, Father," Dr. Wu said.

Dan instinctively target-modeled him as a "Doc in Hock." He was a thirty-eight–to–forty-two–year–old, student-loan-paying, credit-card-balance-carrying, steak-eating A&E viewer who had considered Rogaine. "Please, sit down." Dr. Wu gestured at a chair.

"I'm not in a sitting mood," Dan said.

Dr. Wu nodded. "Are you the family's spiritual adviser?"

"No, I'm the family itself. Could you just tell me where he is? I'm in kind of a hurry."

Well, Dr. Wu thought, *that certainly put things in a new light*. Still, it was better to have to tell a brother who was a father than a loving mother or wife—much less chance of one of those big emotional scenes that made the doctor so uncomfortable.

"Can you hear me, Doctor? I'm still here," Dan said. "Waiting. Dan Steele, remember?"

"What? Oh, yes," Dr. Wu said. "Forgive me, Father. Just gathering my thoughts." He leaned forward onto his desk and looked at a document, then looked up at the priest. "Uh, Father . . . Dan's gone *home*," Dr. Wu said. He nodded slowly as if that said it all.

"No, he's staying with me," Dan said. "I'd know it if he'd gone home."

Fortunately Dr. Wu had been trained to deal with denial. What he didn't want to do was hit the poor man right in the nuts with the hard facts, so Dr. Wu again tried the soft approach. "Father, I'm sorry," he said. "Dan left us."

"I heard you," Dan said. "But I don't think he'd leave without me."

Dr. Wu gazed at Dan with understanding eyes. "Well, Father, we don't always get to choose when we coil up our ropes, do we?"

Dan cocked his head toward the ceiling and looked at the light fixture. Then he looked back at the doctor. "Ropes?" The doctor smiled sadly when he realized the priest simply wasn't fluent in euphemism. "What the hell are you talking about . . . ropes?" Dan asked.

"I'm sorry, Father. I thought you knew. Dan's dead."

If you talk to God, you are praying; if God talks to you, you have schizophrenia.

—LILY TOMLIN (ALSO ATTRIBUTED TO THOMAS SZASZ)

"There must be some mistake," Dan insisted. "He was fine yesterday."

Dr. Wu acknowledged that, although doctors sometimes made mistakes, diagnosing death was something at which they were fairly adept. There was no mistake. Dan was dead.

It didn't hit Dan all at once. There were too many variables to consider, too many implications, and Dan was too upset to consider all that at present. The only thing he could think about was his brother. Michael was dead. Gone. Forever. Dan just sat there, his eyes unfocused and staring into space. After a minute he looked up at the doctor. "He's dead?"

Dr. Wu nodded and began to explain. "As you know, when you brought Dan in yesterday we ran a GI series as well as CT and MRI scans and a WBC nuclear scan. That led us to a small intra-abdominal abscess and sepsis. We consulted with Surgical and Infectious Disease Services and they put him on an experimental antibiotic to fight the infection." Not wanting to add insult to injury—or in this case, to death—Dr. Wu neglected to mention that the hospital was charging five thousand dollars per cc for the newly patented antibiotic.

Dan was stunned. He didn't hear a word Dr. Wu said. He just sat there thinking about Michael. A million thoughts and images—mostly from childhood—raced through his mind. He thought about how he and Michael had protected each other, as best they could, from all the fears and insecurities that their miserable childhood handed them.

Dr. Wu knew that Dan wasn't listening, but he continued nonetheless. "Since the infection didn't respond to the antibiotic, we did an exploratory laparotomy," Dr. Wu said. "It took about twelve hours to resect his colon and distal pancreas." The doctor looked back at the document on his desk and marveled that they were able to charge $1,500 an hour plus some weighty professional fees for that surgery.

Dan started to cry when he remembered the day he learned his father had abandoned them. He'd been gone for a week without any explanation. Then one afternoon, the phone rang. Dan picked it up at the same time his mom did. Dan didn't say anything; he just listened. It was his father saying he'd had all he could take. He wasn't coming back. "But what about the boys?" Ruth had asked.

"You can keep 'em," he said. "I sure as hell don't want 'em." And then he hung up.

That was the last thing Dan ever heard his father say. And he never repeated those words to Michael. He kept that to himself. All he told Michael was that their father wasn't coming back. The two boys made a vow to be better men than that and to take care of their mother.

As Dan wiped the tears from his face, Dr. Wu continued. "After the surgery, Dan's oxygenation dropped badly. We suspected a pulmonary embolus. So we did a nuclear VQ scan, an arteriogram, and an emergency cardiopulmonary bypass to remove the clot." Expensive procedures all.

Dan remembered one time when his mom was so crippled by depression that she couldn't get out of bed. After missing a few meals, Dan and Michael realized they'd have to cook their own, so they pretended to run their own restaurant. Dan designed a menu while Michael cooked bacon and eggs sprinkled with instant chocolate powder. They gave themselves a four-star rating and swore to keep the secret ingredient strictly between themselves.

Dr. Wu was as lost in his own world as Dan was in his. "Unfortunately," the doctor said, "they couldn't separate Dan from cardiopulmonary bypass, so he required ECMO support which led to some uncontrollable bleeding. He used every unit of his type blood we had." Dr. Wu pointed at the document on his desk. "And somewhere during all this they had to do an emergency tracheostomy because of a ventilation problem. He was in ICU for a while with multiple IV inotropic drugs maintaining his blood pressure."

Dan rubbed at his bleary eyes as he remembered the night their mom had told them they had to move out of their house. She said they couldn't afford to live there anymore. As the two boys packed their belongings in the dimness of their sad little bedroom, Dan started to cry. "I'm scared," he had said. "Why do we have to move?"

Michael stopped packing his box and sat down next to his brother. "I don't know," he said, "but it's going to be all right." He put his arm around Dan. "As long as we're together we'll be fine."

Dr. Wu turned the page and continued reading. "Then the damnedest thing happened." He looked up momentarily, almost embarrassed. "An intern who had spent some time in the Third World diagnosed *tetanus*, of all things. Of course, that would explain the stiff muscles, dysphagia, hyperreflexia, and opisthotonos, but none of the rest of us had ever seen it. We never even considered tetanus because Dan's medical records showed he'd been immunized. Unfortunately, the diagnosis came a little late. Your brother went into serious convulsions during which his glottis and respiratory muscles went into spasm. He was unable to breathe and cyanosis ensued. He lapsed into a coma and we eventually ran several brain scans and angiograms which confirmed brain death, so we harvested what we could and called it a day." Dr. Wu's eyes lingered on the bottom line. "We did everything we could," he said. "Honestly."

Dan sniffed his running nose. Things weren't always bad as kids, he thought. He and Michael had shared the happiest moments of their lives together. They had played all the tricks that twins play, on parents, teachers, and friends. Each of them always knew what the other was thinking. They finished each other's sentences. They had laughed and played and conspired. They were confederates in their own war against the evils of their world. But now Dan's accomplice, his best friend, his brother, was gone. Forever.

Dr. Wu stood and walked Dan out to the hallway. "Father, I know this is a difficult time for you," he said. "Apparently Dan's employers were quite shocked as well."

"His employers?" Dan squeaked slightly when he asked the question.

"Yes. We notified them, to save you the trouble."

"I see." Dan felt faint.

Dr. Wu stopped at the elevators and punched the Down button. "They sent over half a dozen lilies," Dr. Wu said. "And they offered to design and print the funeral announcements. Obviously caring people."

As they stepped onto the elevator a panic suddenly seized Dan. He grabbed Dr. Wu by the arm. "Did he get the last rites?" The doors closed.

Dr. Wu looked at the floor. "I don't think so, Father."

Dan feared that Michael had lapsed into the coma before he could ask forgiveness for the fraud. If that was true, then Michael couldn't have atoned for his sin, and depending on whether insurance fraud was a venial or a mortal offense, Michael's soul could have been suffering the temporal punishments of purgatory, or worse, the tortures of hell. All of Michael's good work just flushed down the toilet, and it would all be Dan's fault. He shook Dr. Wu. "Why didn't you get him a priest?"

Dr. Wu shrugged. "The admission form said Dan was agnostic."

Dan slumped. He hadn't thought about that.

The elevator doors opened and Dr. Wu urged Dan out. "Well, here we are," Dr. Wu said. He delivered Dan to the front desk so he could take care of the paperwork. "Call if you need anything."

The woman at the desk flipped through a dozen pages of a computer printout, pointing out the various procedures and drugs that had been applied to Michael in his final hours. She handed Dan a copy of the document. Like a dazed diner at an overpriced restaurant, Dan glanced at the various items and their cost. Then something caught his eye. "You amputated his legs?" He pointed at a series of enormous charges on page six.

"Oh, that . . ." The woman smiled. "That's what we call an inadvertent surgery," she said without batting an eye. "It was supposed to be a Mr. Stone, but somehow they got your brother instead. Stone, Steele, it happens." She flipped to page eight and pointed at the top. "See, here's where we credited you," she said. "So there was no charge for that. Like I said, it was inadvertent. No harm done, really, when you think about it." She then turned to the last page and pointed to the bottom line. "I need you to sign here as next of kin."

Dan took the pen and froze momentarily when he saw "Total charges due: $329,442.09."

The woman folded Dan's copy of the document and

stuffed it into an envelope. "Good thing he had insurance on this one. Paid a hundred percent."

Dan slowly signed his name, "Michael Steele." Then he went back and inserted "Father" and drew a small cross, just for good measure.

Scott managed to rise above his unemployment funk by listening to his motivational tapes. He had listened to them a hundred times since being fired and they were finally starting to pay off. First they got Scott up off his couch and out looking for a new job. However, since no one in advertising would return his calls, Scott was reduced to the lowest possible level of employment—retail sales. In fact, Scott had just returned from an interview at Transistor Town, a huge stereo warehouse outlet that was in the throes of its second "once-in-a-lifetime Fujioka sales event." As if that weren't demoralizing enough, Scott didn't know if he would even get the shitty little job. The interviewer, a Mr. Ted Tibblett, told Scott to go home and wait for his call.

Fortunately, Scott wouldn't just have to sit in his crummy, cramped apartment staring at the phone. That's because Scott's motivational tapes had led him to take up a new hobby. He hoped the repeated pumping action that was involved would eventually bring him some much-needed release. According to the pamphlet he had read, Scott's new hobby was both challenging and rewarding and "by no means high risk" (though in the next sentence the pamphlet did recommend wearing safety glasses so as to avoid going blind).

Encouraged by his tapes, Scott had purchased a Bully-Boy 200 Handloading Press and a brand-spanking-new Ruger Super Redhawk .44 magnum with the handsome stainless steel finish. He bought the gun and the loading press at a gun show up in Ventura. The helpful folks there explained that for maximum stopping power, Scott would want to hot-load some semijacketed hollow points, the sort of thing that mushroomed on impact and did obscene things to "any sort of animal tissue."

Scott was hunkered down at a card table that he had pushed up against a wall in his tiny apartment. The wall was covered with Fujioka logos from the current campaign. His campaign. In the middle of the wall was a picture of Dan that Scott had cut out of The Prescott Agency's annual report.

With a shiny brass case in the shell holder, Scott carefully seated the large primer anvil-side-up in the primer pocket. Employing the aforementioned pumping action, he carefully lowered the press handle, pushing the primer arm all the way into the slot of the shell-holder ram. Next, Scott deviated from the standard reloading manual, opting instead to follow the tips he had picked up at the gun show. Using the loading kit's sensitive scales, Scott measured double the recommended amount of gunpowder into the small bowl, then poured it through the small plastic funnel. Then, just to prove his point, Scott tapped several extra grains of the powder into the large brass casing. "More is more," he repeated for the hundredth time that day.

After hot-loading a half dozen rounds, Scott prepared the stainless steel Super Redhawk for duty, sweetly kissing each cartridge before slipping it into the cylinder. An hour later Scott was sitting on the sofa admiring his weighty tool when the commercial came on the television. He stiffened when he heard the silk strings of the koto. He looked up and saw it wasn't the real commercial but part of an "Eyewitness News Break." The news anchor was at his desk with the Fujioka commercial superimposed over his shoulder. The spot was suddenly replaced by Dan's photo—the same photo that was pinned to Scott's wall.

"The creator of Fujioka's popular 'More Is More' ad

campaign, Dan Steele, died today at St. Luke's Hospital,"
the news anchor said. "The thirty-six-year-old ad executive . . ."

That's all of the news report that Scott heard. His head
filled suddenly with an apocalyptic cacophony of throbbing,
screeching, grinding noises of indeterminate nature. Scott
had been psychologically violated by the news. It was bad
enough that the bastard had stolen his idea, Scott thought.
But now he up and dies, thus securing his legend in the
annals of advertising history and, at the same time, depriv-
ing Scott of the sweet revenge that was the only worthwhile
thing he had left to live for. Raw nerves and humiliation
came crashing together in a hot flash and Scott went completely ATF. He raised the .44 magnum and blew the television tube into fifty thousand tiny pieces. Urged by the
extra gunpowder, the .44 kicked like a senator going before
an ethics committee. The hammer spur smashed into
Scott's forehead, causing a hairline fracture in his frontal
cranial bone. Blood trickled down between Scott's eyes, but
he didn't seem to notice. He just stared through the stars
at the smoldering pile of boob tube.

Then, as quickly as the madness had descended upon
Scott, it disappeared. The apartment was suddenly quiet as
death. The television had been silenced. The dissonant clat-
ter in his head vanished. The thunderous report from the
.44 had purged the room of all sound. As the smoky blue
haze drifted peacefully toward the cottage-cheese ceiling,
Scott sagged, the wind sucked from his sails. He looked
like a small child who had told the truth, but whom no
one believed.

"It was my idea," he said.

Dan was exhausted. He hadn't slept for thirty-six hours.
He was too upset and angry. At the same time, he was
slowly coming to terms with the fact that Michael was

dead, though he still hadn't admitted to himself what that implied about his own future.

He was back at his apartment in Santa Monica trying to figure out what to do next when he suddenly remembered that *Comedy On Demand* was about to come on. Dan hadn't seen the final edit of the Shaftem, Dickem spot, and he was curious about how it came out. Unsure of what else he ought to be doing, Dan flopped onto his sofa, flipped on the TV, and waited for the show to start.

The spot opened with the exterior shot of a rain-slicked city street. Police cars with flashing lights blocked traffic as the cops struggled to subdue an obviously intoxicated man who was wearing only his birthday suit. Only this time, the naked man was Dan and the cop was Scott Emmons. "You're drunk . . . you're naked . . . and you've committed felony insurance fraud," Scott said.

There was an abrupt cut to a courtroom. WHAM! The judge smashed his gavel. "Guilty!"

Another abrupt cut to an overcrowded jail cell. WHAM! The door slammed. A large and dangerous-looking man sidled up and put his arm around Dan. "Let me show you the showers," he said. "We've got Dove."

Another inmate leaned in close. "The soap that creams your skin while you wash."

Dan woke abruptly, snapped from his nightmare and keenly aware that he was up to his neck in it. He looked at the TV and saw that COD was running children's programming, which meant Dan had slept through the night and part of the morning. He got up, had some coffee, and reflected on his legal situation before returning his lawyer's call from the previous day.

An hour later Dan was in the office of Karen Vaughey, Esquire. Karen was a Stanford grad, top of her class. She was a sharp blonde, capable in all aspects of the law. Dan target-modeled her as "Elite Esquire." Mid-forties-attorney, first-class-flying, yogurt-eating, theater-attending, treasury-bond-holding three-VCR owner.

Dan had shed the priest outfit in favor of jeans, a T-shirt, and a baseball cap. He sat across the desk from Karen, sucking on a lemon drop he had grabbed from the bowl in the reception area. He told Karen that he was thinking about telling the authorities what had happened.

"Bad idea," Karen said.

"Why? What am I looking at?"

Ms. Vaughey looked over the contents of a manila folder as she spoke. "Well, since the hospital's already been paid, the insurance carrier would come after you for the three hundred thirty thousand. Then the DA would file a criminal complaint for felony insurance fraud. And finally you'd get hit with a civil suit that would cost you as much to defend as to lose, which you would surely do."

Dan's head dropped into his hands. "Great," he said. Dan wondered what he ever did to deserve this. "Just t-fucking-rific."

"It gets better," Karen said, trying to suppress a laugh. "Since it's an election year, the DA will want to nail you to a cross for some extra votes."

Dan attempted some indignation. "He was my brother, for God's sake! It's not like I made money on the deal."

Karen shrugged and tossed the folder onto the desk. "Doesn't matter," she said. "Juries hate people like you."

The thought slapped Dan in the face. "People like me? What's that supposed to mean? I was just trying to take care of my brother!"

"All they'll see is the guy who makes their insurance rates go up," Karen said. "Now, if you had *killed* your brother, I could probably get you off. But this is serious. We're talking other people's money. You're looking at three to six for the fraud, plus a stiff fine, forty-fifty grand, plus the hospital bill."

"Three-seventy and jail?"

"More like four hundred and prison," Karen said. "I don't work for free."

Dan hung his head, shaking it slowly.

"You know, there is one alternative," Karen said.

Dan perked up. "What? I'm open. Talk to me."

"Your brother's wardrobe and the statute of limitations may be your, uh, salvation."

Dan sucked on his lemon drop and squinted at his lawyer. "I don't get it." Actually he was starting to get it—he just didn't like what he was getting.

"How does seven years of celibacy strike you?" Karen winked at Dan.

"Celibacy?" Dan stared at every single one of Karen's soft parts as she crossed the room to a bookshelf. *No, not that*, he thought. *Anything but that.*

"Think of Michael as your altar ego," Karen said. "Get it? A-l-t-*a*-r ego." She chuckled as she pulled a Bible from the shelf. "You want my advice?" She tossed the Bible to Dan. "I suggest you bone up on your new employee handbook."

Sister Peg was busy as the devil in a high wind. She was making lunch for the residents while simultaneously working the phone. Among her other calls, she was calling Father Michael's apartment every hour or so, hoping to find him and get him back.

As usual, Ruben was helping. Sister Peg had thanked the Lord for Ruben more than once. He was the hardest-working, least-complaining person she'd ever met. He'd been raised on the fringe of gang culture, and when the time came he had joined a neighborhood clique of the San Fers, hence the Gothic-lettering tattoos on his neck, arms, and back. As with most gang bangers, it was the "family" aspect of the gang that appealed to him. His own family had disintegrated by the time he was twelve, so the San Fers provided an important sense of belonging. A few years later, when his younger brother was killed in a drive-by, Ruben quit the San Fers and moved into the Care Center where he found a new family. He held a grudge about his brother's death, but he wasn't vengeful. Ruben showed great respect for life, at least for those who deserved it. He honored the elderly residents and was protective of the kids who came through, and he never shrank from any duty, no matter how unpleasant.

Ruben had been a tagger with the gang, a regular Jackson Pollock with a can of spray paint. Since his education consisted of three years at a school for the deaf and two years in special-ed classes in the L.A. public school system, he had no formal art training, but he was gifted, there was no question about that. Ruben sensed that he could somehow make a living with his skills, but without a mentor to guide him, he had no real hopes in that regard. His hopes were in the lottery, twice weekly.

There was still no answer at Father Michael's apartment. Sister Peg considered going over there but knew she didn't have the time. She hung up and looked at her list to see which funding application she needed to follow up on next. She dialed, reached her party's extension, and was put on hold. She watched Ruben as he grated a giant wedge of cheese. When he was finished, Sister Peg squeezed the phone between her ear and shoulder, then plunged her hands into the mound of shredded cheddar. A second later someone came back on the line. "Yes," Sister Peg said, "we're registered with the Department of Health Services as an in-home congregate care facility." She dumped the cheese into a steaming vat of macaroni and stirred. "I submitted the funding request two months ago. Could you please look again?"

They looked again, then came back on the line. "I can't

find it, Sister," the voice said. "It's lost if it was ever here to begin with. You'll have to start over, sorry." Click. Sister Peg listened to the dial tone for a moment and wanted to explode. She clenched her teeth and whispered something coarse into the phone. She hung up, made a note to resubmit, then dialed Father Michael again. Still no answer.

When it came time to serve lunch, Sister Peg and Ruben formed a short buffet service. The phone cord stretched tight to the wall as Peg moved from serving the mac and cheese to the pot full of string beans, all the while wheeling and dealing with a plumber. "Trust me, it's a tax write-off," she improvised. "Donation of services." Ruben passed her a plate with a piece of Wonder bread on it. "Of course I'll pad the invoice, I need your help." She thought about the backed-up toilet as she slapped some string beans onto a plate. "Say, do you like cheese?" Sister Peg hammered on the guy until he finally relented. He said he'd come by that afternoon.

Sister Peg was set to dial again when something caught her eye. It was an empty plate rising slowly from the other side of the counter. Sister Peg could see some little fingers holding the plate, but she couldn't see who belonged to the fingers. When she peeked around the edge of the plate she saw Alissa looking up at her. "Hello there," Peg said.

Alissa didn't say a word. Her expression never changed.

Sister Peg smiled. "Would you like the beef Wellington or the crab bisque?"

Alissa had no idea what the nun was talking about. She just nodded and hoped for the best as she held her plate up a little higher.

Sister Peg served her lunch. "It's okay, sweetheart," she said. "You're going to be fine." She watched Alissa walk to a table in the corner. She was still limping. It brought back bad memories. Sister Peg had lived in Los Angeles all her life and had seen some awful things. And lately, things seemed to be getting worse.

Over the previous five years, in Los Angeles County, the number of abused children had increased by 63 percent, dwarfing the national average increase of 16 percent. More than 100,000 of the people who called the county's abuse hot line hung up before speaking to anyone because they were on hold for so long. Sister Peg didn't know which statistic was more disturbing—that so many people hung up or that there were so many calls to deal with in the first place.

Sister Peg knew the frustration of dealing with this bureaucracy. A couple of years earlier she had called to report that a five-year-old child she knew was being abused. She was put on hold. Thirty-two minutes later an overworked social worker came on the line. Sister Peg told the woman about a little girl named Sonia. The girl's mother, who was supposed to be under the supervision of Child Protective Services, had a long history of abusing her eight children. She disciplined them with burning cigarettes or by locking them in a closet for days without food. The social worker apologized and said there was nothing her department could do.

"Why not?" Sister Peg asked.

"We don't have the funding or the manpower," the social worker said. "And trust me, we have a lot of cases worse than this." The social worker wasn't unsympathetic, she was just numb from her workload. She took Sister Peg's information and said—without a trace of cynicism—"If nothing else, Sonia will be an important statistic."

Sister Peg was so infuriated that she set out to fix the problem. She wrote to her elected officials and she badgered someone at the L.A. *Daily Times* into investigating the matter. The paper eventually ran a two-part story criticizing the department for failing to investigate as many as 25 percent of the calls reporting abuse.

Local officials were suddenly facing a serious problem. Since none of them could get reelected with the press tossing around statistics like that, the only prudent thing to do was to raise the legal threshold of what constituted child abuse. So the City Council and the Board of Supervisors quickly passed the necessary measure, and just like that, the Department of Social Services was investigating all but 2 percent of calls reporting abuse.

Several months later, the paper published a follow-up article about Sonia. She was found dead, having been tortured with a butane lighter before her mother dropped her onto the freeway from an overpass. In the article someone from Social Services lamented the child's fate, laying blame at the feet of whoever had cut the department's funding. Someone from a twelve-step program was quoted as saying that crack cocaine had killed the girl, not the mother. And finally, in a fine example of one of the unusual ways in which the word *lucky* was used in Los Angeles, the newspaper writer said that, all things considered, Sonia was lucky to be dead.

Most people would have surrendered in the face of such madness and acknowledged that they were wasting their time trying to change things. But Sister Peg couldn't surrender. She felt responsible for Sonia's death. She could have done something. Sonia was one of the reasons Sister Peg wouldn't give up on the Care Center. She didn't know how, but the next time—and there would certainly be a next time—Sister Peg was going to do whatever it took to ensure there were no more Sonias in her world. The night she read about Sonia's death, all Sister Peg could do was pray. So she prayed for Sonia's soul. Then she asked that God forgive her for agreeing that Sonia was, somehow, lucky.

*   *   *

After reflecting on the scenario laid out by his attorney, Dan opted for what he felt was the lesser of two evils. *I guess I'll change my name,* he thought. So he went to the bathroom, pulled out his electric clippers, and lost the beard. He rooted through the medicine cabinet and bathroom drawers, until he found his old contacts hidden behind some expired ointments and old throat lozenges. He dropped his Armani frames into the trash and inserted the hard lenses. He blinked and squinted and teared up before regaining focus.

Finally Dan put on Michael's clericals and stood before the full-length mirror. As he adjusted the collar, something came over him. It was an odd, not altogether unpleasant, sensation. It was seductive and had something to do with the outfit. Dan got the feeling that the clothes came with certain expectations and demands. They also commanded some degree of respect, both by the person wearing them and by those who encountered him. It was an interesting dynamic, he thought, and a familiar one as well. This was the reason advertisers used "authority figures" in commercials. The right outfit implied endorsement by the corresponding ruling organization. If a man wearing a white coat and a stethoscope smiled and held up a box of laxatives, the little pile-driving pills suddenly had an unauthorized nod from the AMA. Disclaimers like "I'm not a doctor but I play one on TV" didn't matter; the picture was far more powerful than the copy. Or, as one advertiser smugly put it, "Image is everything."

Another aspect of the psychology of clothes that Dan thought about was the hierarchy of garments. Why did high-ranking military and religious people wear more conspicuous clothes than those of lower rank? Did they do it simply to identify their rank? No, that could be accomplished in far simpler ways. Ornate outfits were simply a bald show of power intended to intimidate, convey superiority, and demand obedience.

But why did people assume that anyone they saw in a uniform was really what the uniform said they were? Simple. Because they usually were, which was why wearing a uniform was so effective in pulling a con, whether it be advertising or convincing people that you had a direct link with the supreme deity. The appearance of authority was usually as good as actually having it—as long as you didn't get caught.

Dan turned and looked at himself sideways in the mirror. It struck him that the clericals not only carried responsibility, they were also rife with potential. The potential to do good, to help, to save, to offer redemption and forgiveness and hope. Dan recognized the sensation as the one that had urged him to theological study in the first place. He hoped it would pass quickly.

Dan glanced over to the dresser and saw the Bible that his attorney had given him. He picked it up and read out loud the first thing he saw. "I am the Lord thy God," he said. Dan liked the way he sounded. His voice resonated as he continued, "Thou shalt have no other gods before me!" Dan raised his chin and looked down his nose at his reflection in the mirror. He tried to look as if he had God's direct line. Suddenly the earth began to shake. Dan dropped the Bible and prepared to fall to his knees when he realized it was just a small temblor, probably an aftershock to the Northridge quake. Then again, maybe it wasn't. Dan picked up the book, looked up, and apologized. As he was about to put the Bible back on the dresser, he noticed a dog-eared page. He opened it to Matthew, chapter eight, verse twenty-two. "But Jesus said unto him, Follow me; and let the dead bury their dead." Dan slowly closed the book, thinking of Michael. *Oh, yeah*, he thought. *That reminds me. I need to call the funeral home.*

* * *

Sister Peg was still thinking about Sonia when a loud noise brought her back to the kitchen. Ruben was banging a big metal spoon against the vat of macaroni. He was trying to get Sister Peg's attention so he could hand her a plate. Ruben sometimes worried about her. She worked so hard and had so many frustrations. He knew how that sort of thing took its toll, little by little chipping away at whatever hope you may have had. She got so busy that she sometimes forgot to eat. Ruben did what he could to make sure it didn't happen often. He handed her a plate.

She spooned some soggy string beans next to the macaroni and cheese, then scooted up on the counter to eat while making another call. She took a bite of bread, dialed, then waited.

"Hello?" The voice was distant and slightly echoed, the speaker-phone effect.

Sister Peg hated that. "Monsignor, it's Sister Peg. I'm trying to find Father Michael. I figured you knew where he—"

Monsignor Matthews grabbed the phone. "Sister!" he said. His tone was nervous and agitated. "I wouldn't have any idea where he is and I'm sure you know he's not to be called 'Father' any longer." He paused. "Not after Africa."

Sister Peg smirked into the phone. "Let me guess," she said. "Someone's in the office with you."

"Yes, that's right," he said.

"Well, that should teach you not to use that damn speaker phone. It's rude."

"It's merely a convenience," he answered. "Can you hold a moment?" Monsignor Matthews put his hand over the mouthpiece and asked to be left alone, then he returned to Sister Peg. "Look," he said, lowering his voice. "I gave him your name and number and washed my hands of it.

Don't get me any more involved if you want me in a position to help in the future."

"I know," she said. "I'm sorry. But I need help here. Father Michael showed up a couple of days ago, moved his mother in, then disappeared. I thought you might know where he is."

"I don't know," Monsignor Matthews said. "But I'll ask around."

"Thanks, Matty." Her voice softened. "Would you like your reward in this life or the next?" Sister Peg could almost hear him blush over the phone.

"Now, Sister, let's not go there," he said. "I'm hoping you'll honor our agreement."

"Relax," she said. "It's not in my best interest to cause trouble." Sister Peg popped a piece of macaroni into her mouth. "You sound a little tense. How're things going at your end?"

"I'm doing what I can," he said. "But I'm hearing rumors. Someone's called a meeting. Word is the higher-ups are dissatisfied with the diminishing diocesan assessments that have been flowing their way the past three quarters." Monsignor Matthews paused and swallowed hard. "If it's true, it could mean cutbacks."

That was the last thing Sister Peg wanted to hear. Things were hard enough as it was. Cutbacks would do her in. She knew Monsignor Matthews was on her side, but every now and then he got nervous and needed a prod. Sometimes he needed only a nudge. Occasionally he required a threat. Fortunately she knew his weak spot.

Monsignor Matthews was one of the youngest Monsignors in California history. He was Ivy League educated but surprisingly pleasant. He was also a subversive of sorts. He had an undergraduate degree in business, with a minor in accounting. He graduated from Harvard Divinity School, suffered his curacy, then began a quick rise through the ranks. He landed a parish in record time, did some good deeds, and was now working his way through the labyrinthine Catholic hierarchy. The Monsignor felt the Church was doing far less good than it was capable of and he felt working from the inside was the best way to use the Church's resources to help those in need. Unfortunately, the resources at his end of the Catholic food chain seemed to be drying up.

"I can't accept any cutbacks," Sister Peg said. "If I have to, I'll—"

"What do you want from me?" He sounded far more worried than most Monsignors when threatened by a nun. "I can't do a loaves-and-fishes thing with money. There's only so much."

Sister Peg wasn't in the mood for this. "Now, you know how much I care about you, Matty, but this is not going to be *my* problem," she said. "You short me so much as a dime, the problem is going to be yours."

Mr. Butch Harnett saw himself as a man of faith. He didn't attend church, but he remembered a lot of what he had learned in Sunday school when he was young. He always liked Romans the best. Although he completely misunderstood Paul's epistle about achieving salvation through faith, he liked many of its powerful verses. It seemed to Butch irrefutable that the wages of sin was death, or at least that's the way it ought to be.

Butch was six feet tall and thicker than average. He had a rough complexion and an oval head, shaved and shined. He looked like Mr. Clean without the earring or the wink. He wore simple dark suits and a flat expression. He didn't care for shows of emotion. He found such things ungodly and inefficient. Butch had a job to do, and emotions simply clouded the picture.

He was on an elevator heading to the top floor of the

Mutual of California Insurance Corporation headquarters. He looked displeased as he flipped through the file folder in his hands. The elevator doors opened and he walked silently down the carpeted hallway, not looking until he reached the double doors at the end of the hall. He knocked.

"Come," came the reply. Harnett's boss was hunched over his desk trying to ferret out a pattern of fraud from a series of claims on his desk. He looked up at his ace investigator. "Whatcha got?" he asked.

Butch sniffed at the file he was holding. "This one stinks," he said.

"To the tune of what?"

"Three hundred forty large."

"Anybody we know?"

Butch shook his head. "Looks like a rookie," he said. "One Dan Steele, deceased."

"Deceased, huh?" Harnett's boss loved the fact that Butch didn't believe anything until he put his hand in the wound, so to speak. "Whaddya think?"

"I think all men are sinners in God's eyes," Butch said.

6

Dan didn't want to be cheap on this, but his situation was dictating. He was at Smyth's Funeral Home near the interchange of the San Diego and the Simi Valley freeways. "Dignity and value where the 405 meets the 118."

Funeral homes had always given Dan the willies. Despite efforts to decorate with warm dark woods and heavy soothing drapes, Dan never felt warm or soothed when he attended funerals or visitations. Smyth's Funeral Home was an exception only to the extent that they had made no obvious attempt to offer consolation through interior decorating. The place was cinder block painted baby-shit brown. The thing Dan noticed the most was the smell. Dan fanned the air with the brochure he was holding. There was no getting around the fact that the place smelled funny, not ha-ha funny, but are-you-sure-that-body-was-embalmed-properly funny.

Dan flipped through the brochure until he saw the "Alternative Container Price Range." Looking at the cheap end of the spectrum, Dan wondered what you got sent home in for $84.06. Given what Smyth's was charging for a pine box, Dan figured eighty-four bucks might get you a mayonnaise jar with the label peeled. The small print at the bottom of the page caught his eye. "There is no scientific or other evidence that a casket with a sealing device will preserve human remains." Dan wondered what sort of false promises had prompted the government to require that disclaimer. "Let's say you spring for the Deluxe Dust-to-Dust III with the advanced hydroseal, okay? Ten years from now, if medical science finds a cure for whatever killed your beloved husband, we can exhume him and . . ." Dan put the brochure down and wiped his hands. Even after his years in advertising, Dan was put off by the lies these people were willing to tell in order to make a sale. It was one thing, he thought, to make bogus claims about laundry detergent—"now with ultrabrightening enzymes!"—it was something else altogether to take advantage of the grief-stricken. Dan paused. He wondered where this sudden bout of moralizing had come from. He used to be a strict caveat emptor kind of guy.

A few moments later a salesman materialized. Dan had been expecting someone out of a Charles Addams cartoon, but the guy turned out to look more or less normal. His name was Walter. He had interesting eyebrows but little else that Dan noticed. Walter hated his job, but he tried not to let it show. He had bills to pay and no ambition to find other work. So he pushed the high-end stuff at everybody who came in.

This month, the biggest commission was with the Promethean Bronze caskets with the Pomp and Circumstance Services. So, after feigning compassion for Dan's loss, Walter put his hand on the small of Dan's back. "Father," he said. "If you'll come with me, I'll show you a casket that says you really care." Walter steered Dan over to a garish, three-tone coffin shrouded with gaudy filigree. "This is the top of the line," he said. "We're talking a forty-eight-ounce, solid bronze full couch with decorative marquetry finish, powder blue ultravelvet interior, and twenty-four-karat gold-plated hand staffs." It looked like a small, rectangular Graceland with handles. Walter pointed to a thick strip of soft rubber that ran the circumference of the coffin. "This is what I call the casket gasket. It's an advanced hydroseal feature that prevents the body from decomposing."

"How much?" Dan asked.

Walter stroked the powder blue ultravelvet interior and tilted his head slightly upward. He appeared to do some mental calculation. "With the Pomp and Circumstance Service, funeral coach, flower car, facilities for visitation, organist, filing of death certificate, transportation of grave monument to cemetery, imported Italian prayer cards with gold trim, I'd say in the range of thirty-eight thousand. A terrific price, really. I'm sure your brother deserves nothing less."

Startled at the terrific price, Dan glanced around the showroom for something in pine.

"You know," Walter said. "There's no better way to say good-bye than with the Promethean Bronze."

Dan stared at the casket for a moment. He'd gladly spend forty thousand to put his brother to rest in a quality casket, but he just didn't have the money. Besides, he thought, Michael was dead. He wouldn't know if he was laid to rest in powder blue ultravelvet interior or burlap. Finally Dan shook his head. "No," he said. "My brother's tastes were, uh . . . simpler."

"I understand," Walter said, "something less—"

"Elvis," Dan said.

Walter smiled sadly as he thought of what to say next. The words "cheap bastard" came to mind, but instead he said, "Let me show you a little something we call the Oro Del Divino, brushed and shaded thirty-two-ounce bronze half couch with champagne velvet interior."

Dan wasn't listening anymore. The budget just wasn't

there for champagne velvet interior. He looked around the room. "Got anything on sale?"

At the end of another eighteen-hour day, Sister Peg retired to her small room, physically and mentally exhausted. She and Ruben had spent the last two hours scrubbing the kitchen and bathroom floors, interrupted only by her calls to Father Michael's apartment, which went unanswered. The muscles in her back were thick cords of gristle. She was dismayed by the hopelessness in the eyes of the Care Center's elderly residents and the mistrust in those of Alissa. Late in the day, Larry Sturholm had called to gently remind Sister Peg that foreclosure was as certain as Judgment Day, and much closer.

Sister Peg walked to the foot of her bed, where she lowered herself slowly onto her knees. She looked up at the wall where Jesus hung on the cross, then she closed her eyes and bowed her head. "Dear Heavenly Father," she said. "Please look down on us and show us the way to fulfill Your will. These people have come to me for help and in Your name I have promised to help them, but I seem to be falling short and I need Your guidance to help me understand . . ."

There are those who speak of a virtuous life as an uninterrupted prayer, appealing to the Latin adage *laborare est orare*—"to toil is to pray." If there was any truth to that, no one prayed more or harder than Sister Peg.

Most people are under the impression that prayer is a simple act wherein a supplicant asks God for help in some temporal or moral matter. Most people, of course, are wrong. There's nothing simple about it. There are strict rules and regulations to follow if you want your prayers to get through. In fact, a thumbnail outline of the official doctrine on praying takes up eight full pages in *The Catholic Encyclopedia*.

The complexity of Catholic theology makes the Federal Tax Code look like a first-grade primer. This results from Pope Pius IX's notion that the doctrines, edicts, and other papal bulls that Popes hand down are infallible. The problem comes when one Pope makes a decree that contradicts a doctrine handed down by some previous Pope. Since infallibility can't be questioned, and because the Church can't admit to moral relativism, this sets Church theologians scurrying to obscure the inconsistency, usually in Latin. The result is a system of beliefs that, if studied sufficiently, is found to be less than wholly defensible. Fortunately, the faith was built on such solid ground that no amount of theological tinkering seems able to screw it up. In fact, as long as you don't wander too far from the Ten Commandments and the old chestnuts from the Sermon on the Mount, you're not likely to find yourself facing off with the College of Cardinals at an excommunication hearing.

Now, Sister Peg was no Thomas Aquinas, theologically speaking, but she had faith. Faith in God and His goodness. That wasn't to say she never suffered doubt; she was human, after all.

Sometimes, in fact, Sister Peg found while praying that she was simply expressing gratitude for the bad things that *hadn't* happened rather than being thankful for all the good things that had. Still, she prayed every day through her labors and every night on her knees. She hoped that someday her prayers would be answered in the affirmative.

According to the authorities, prayers must be for the right things, be they temporal or moral. The rules strictly limit to whom you may pray—you can pray to God the Father, or the Son, or even Christ the man because he is a Divine Person. However, the rules do not allow praying to Christ's human nature as such, since prayers are never to be addressed to something so abstract. You can pray to saints, asking that they intercede on your behalf, but not because you expect them to actually deliver. For all the good they did on earth, in heaven saints are simply message-delivery systems. God is the One Who delivers. Or not, depending on circumstances and His will.

"Merciful Father," Sister Peg continued, "I pray that in Your wisdom You deliver Alissa from the torments she suffers and that You open her heart to the love and the hope that You have bestowed upon all of us . . ."

The just can pray, as can sinners (though there was some controversy about sinners until Pope Clement XI cleared up what he decreed was Pasquier Quesnel's heretical position on the matter). They say prayer is impossible in hell, and besides, at that point, it's too damn late.

"Show me the way to meet the earthly obligations I have assumed so that I might better serve You . . ."

There are several further conditions of prayer. The object of prayer must be worthy of God. Faith and humility are required. Sincerity is a must. Earnestness and fervor are important; lukewarm beseeching won't cut the cheese. You must be resigned to God's will, *resigned* being used in the positive sense of the word. And you have to pay attention while praying. In fact, attention is said to be the very essence of prayer. As soon as your attention ceases, so does the prayer. There's vocal prayer and there's mental prayer, the difference being self-explanatory. And—hard as it is to imagine God passing judgment on such a thing—posture is a consideration. A proper display of reverence and outward manner is essential. In other words, appearances are important. Image is almost everything, even in prayer.

All things considered, Sister Peg had what it took to pray. From a presupposed faith in God and hope in His goodness, right down to her posture and focused attention. She meant every word she said. "Holy Father, please bless all those whose paths lead to the door of this humble dwelling and forgive all those who impede the work I do in Your name, especially the lost souls of Mr. Sturholm and Mr. Churchill." Sister Peg looked up at her Savior suffering on the cross. She hesitated before asking, wanting not to sound selfish. "Lastly, dear Lord, please find Father Michael and return him to our doorstep. We could really use his help. I ask this humbly in the name of Your Son, our Savior, Jesus Christ. Amen."

It occurred to Dan that his desire to spend forty thousand dollars to put his dead brother in a hole in the ground was not dictated by love but rather because he was a well-trained consumer. Hell, he'd spent the last fifteen years training others to be consumers. "When you care enough to send the very best." What could that mean other than failing to buy the most expensive item means you don't care enough? Implied was that if you didn't buy the very best for your loved one, he or she was going to go out and find someone who would. Fear sold a lot of goods.

The American brand of consumerism had rendered the act of giving a simple gift inadequate. Dan lived in an age when the it's-the-thought-that-counts philosophy was scoffed at; it was the ideology of losers. Winners bought diamonds.

Like the rest of America, Dan had seen nearly a million ads over the course of his life, and despite the fact that he understood the behavioral-science aspect of the business, he still wasn't immune to the effects. Advertising was like the Chinese water torture—one ad wouldn't make you go out and buy an unnecessary product, but after you've been hit in the head a million times with the idea of buying, the message starts to compel.

So, while he wanted to go Promethean Bronze, Dan knew he didn't have enough money for it. Michael would have to take his dirt nap in something simpler than the powder blue ultravelvet interior. He settled on a less-is-more cremation plan. That Dan didn't have the money for the Pomp and Circumstance ceremony made him feel like a tightwad, a jerk, a Judas. He owed Michael more than a cheap funeral and a headstone with the wrong name on it; unfortunately he couldn't afford better.

As Dan sulked out of Smyth's Funeral Home and over to his leased Mercedes, he wondered where all his money had gone. He knew a lot of it went to his mom, and even though he had pissed and moaned about that, he knew he owed her as well. She'd done her best, after all. She could have abandoned them just as easily as their father had— but she hadn't. She did right when she could have done wrong, and that counted for something.

Dan was heading south on the 405, toward the L.A. Basin. As he crept over the Sepulveda pass he tried to figure out what the hell he was going to do next. Tell Mom? Tell her what? The truth? That seemed injudicious. Did she even need to know? He owed her a lot, but this didn't seem to be part of the debt. He'd deal with her later. Right now Dan had more important problems. Like employment. One thought was to move to the East Coast and send out his reel under an assumed name. But in such a small industry, where names were tied to campaigns, that was too risky. Besides, he couldn't just leave Ruth.

On the other hand, if he stayed here, he'd have to keep up the religious ruse and . . . and what? Find a job? As what? Freelance priest? What would he do, rent a space in a strip mall and perform sacraments? Maybe do something on the Internet? He paused. *Not such a bad idea.* An on-line confessional had real possibilities in a hurried age when spirituality was making a minor comeback. *WWW.Indulgences.com! It's the All Saints Day Sale! 50% off venial sins!* Of course, the whole thing would require some seed money, and where the hell was he going to get that? There had to be a good answer somewhere. Dan would mull it over with a drink.

He arrived at his building and parked. He slipped up to his apartment without running into any neighbors or Mr. Moore, the building manager. Dan grabbed a beer and sat on the balcony, grateful for the view overlooking the bay. He sat there a minute before he thought he heard voices. He leaned back in his chair to listen. Yes, definitely voices. Dan jerked to his feet and moved toward the door. Sounded like two people—and they were coming in. Dan began to panic. The only other way out of the apartment was to jump off the balcony to the concrete fifty feet below. Bad option. Dan heard a key in the lock. Jesus Christ! He had to hide. Dan dove into the foyer closet just as the door opened.

"Trust me," Mr. Moore said, "this is the only ocean view you'll find for less than four thousand a month."

Dan peeked out through the slats of the louvered door. All he could tell for certain was that Mr. Moore was showing his apartment to a woman wearing beige pumps. "Does it come furnished?" the pumps asked.

Mr. Moore hadn't thought about that. "Uh, yeah," he said, "everything but the electronics. The TV, stereo, that stuff."

"I'll take it." The woman handed over a check. "I'll move in tomorrow," she said.

Dan expected Mr. Moore to follow the woman out, but when she left, he moved toward the entertainment system. Dan pried the slats in the door a little wider so he could see what the man was doing. He unplugged Dan's one-hundred-disc CD player. Dan couldn't believe it; the bastard was looting his place, and what was worse, Dan could only watch.

"Knock, knock." It was onomatopoeia, a man's sterile voice.

Dan saw Mr. Moore stiffen momentarily, as if ashamed. He relaxed just as quickly—apparently realizing that no one would know the stereo wasn't his to take in the first place. He casually resumed his looting.

"I said, knock, knock," the voice repeated.

"Sorry," Mr. Moore said over his shoulder. "The place is already rented."

A pair of cheap but highly polished wing tips came into Dan's view. "I'm not here about the apartment," the voice said. "I'm Butch Harnett. I'm an investigator for Mutual of California. I'd like to speak to you about Dan Steele."

Dan had all the traditional physiological reactions to a moment of extreme fear. His amygdala rioted. His heart rate and blood pressure soared. His adrenal glands discharged a load of glucocorticoids, his hypothalamus released enough endorphins to swoon a moose. When his body finally caught up with his mind, panic spread across Dan's face.

"Dan Steele's dead," Mr. Moore said.

"I'll be the judge of that." Harnett cocked his head and sniffed the air. Dan thought he saw Harnett turn toward the closet as if he could smell him. Dan quickly pulled his fat, pink fingers out from between the louvers and stopped breathing. Harnett sniffed again before turning his attention back to Mr. Moore. "I understand he had a twin brother."

Mr. Moore took Mr. Harnett back to his office to look through Dan's files for information that might be of help to the insurance company. Dan stayed in the closet for ten minutes before creeping out. He packed a suitcase, then stepped onto the balcony to take in the view one last time. He was sure going to miss the ocean.

Dan had as much reason to be depressed as he did to be angry, but he opted for the latter. *Goddammit! I don't deserve this. Do. Not. Deserve it. Any of this, all of this.* Ten days ago Dan was on the cusp of being a "name" in L.A. The More Is More / "Commercials on Demand" man. Da man! Dan Steele, demigod in the cult of celebrity. Now he was just a badly lapsed Catholic wearing a priest outfit, standing in a stranger's apartment. The only thing Dan could take any comfort in was the fact that he had been declared dead.

Dan needed to get out of the apartment pretty quick, since he figured Mr. Moore would be back soon to get the rest of the entertainment system. Dan took one last look around, trying to decide what else he would take to his new life. He could carry one more thing in addition to his suitcase. The decision was easy. He went to the bar and grabbed the limited-edition collection of vintage-dated single-malt Scotch whiskies produced by the world-renowned Glenlivet Distillery. With his precious cargo tucked under this arm, Dan went back to the balcony.

Looking down at the sidewalk, Dan saw Mr. Moore walking Harnett out to his car. As soon as the insurance investigator drove off, Dan slipped down to the parking garage with his belongings. When he rounded the corner to his parking spot, he saw his beloved Mercedes attached to the business end of a tow truck that was pulling away. Dan dropped his suitcase and raced to the truck driver's window, still clutching the box of scotch. "Hey!" Dan yelled as he chased the truck out of the garage and onto Colorado Boulevard. "Hey!" He banged on the driver's window.

Normally the tow-truck driver would have slammed on his brakes and opened his door on the guy's face. But instead, he rolled his window down and smiled. "What's the problem, Padre?" Turned out he was a Catholic.

"What the hell are you doing?" Dan demanded.

"I got orders to hook the car, Father," the grease monkey said. "The guy's way behind on payments. Plus he's dead. You know him?"

"Yes. I'm his brother. The car is . . . in my care."

"My condolences, Father." The driver looked at his clipboard. "Ya got twenty-two hundred bucks?"

"Uh . . . no."

"Sorry, Father. It's not up to me. God may forgive, but the bank don't." He gassed the engine. Dan stood there watching as his bumper sticker faded from sight: He who dies with the most toys wins. As the truck turned south on Fourth Street, Dan's eyes followed and ended up on a billboard that screamed at him, "More Is More!"

"Son of a bitch!" Dan was standing in the middle of the street feeling forsaken when he heard the sound of tires screeching on asphalt. He turned just in time to see a gleaming BMW 750*il* heading right for him. Dan dove into the gutter and heard the BMW owner yell something about getting his Catholic ass out of the damn road. El Niño not-withstanding, the gutters in Los Angeles are dry ten months out of the year, and today was no expection, until now. Dan had landed on top of the limited edition collection of vintage-dated single-malt Scotch whiskies produced by the world-renowned Glenlivet Distillery. All the bottles had shattered and the rare, elegant spirits seeped into the gutter on their way to Santa Monica Bay. Dan mourned the loss for a moment before he stood and brushed the gravel from his pants. He headed back to the garage to get his suitcase. What else could he do?

He crossed Ocean to the public park on the bluff over-looking Santa Monica Bay. This was, understandably, a park popular with the homeless—a terrific view, an ocean breeze, and easy access to good panhandling. Dan sat on a bench and took stock. He'd lost everything—his job, his car, his home, his identity, his brother. Then something occurred to him. He realized Michael had left him something. He opened the suitcase and rooted around until he found it. A set of keys—one of which opened the door to an apartment in Pacoima, another which would start Michael's ancient VW bus, assuming he could find it.

Dan wandered the streets of Santa Monica, stopping at every VW bus that looked more than ten years old. Twenty minutes later, he found it. It was covered with bumper stickers of the "Practice Acts of Random Kindness" variety. There were two parking tickets tucked under the cracked wiper blades. The old microbus wasn't Dan's idea of the ultimate driving machine, but it beat the shit out of walking. He drove down to Ocean Boulevard for a last look at the bay; then he hopped on the Santa Monica Freeway heading for the 405, which he would take north into the valley of the shadow of Universal City.

Father Michael coughs and covers his eyes. The truck that brought him to this troubled place rattles off in a smutty cloud of dust and diesel fumes, the driver hell-bent on reaching the Didinga Hills before day's end. The man standing in the bed of the truck holding the rifle is a Toposa tribesman hired to ward off hijackers. He knows a dozen of the four hundred languages spoken in this part of Africa. Father Michael speaks only English, so the two of them have exchanged nothing more than glances during the entire seven-hour ride. Still, after so much time in such close proximity, Father Michael feels some camaraderie, so he waves good-bye. The Toposa tribesman stares blankly at the white man dressed in black who has come to peddle his God.

Father Michael sets his small suitcase on the ground and tries to get his bearings. He turns toward the sunrise. He had studied the updated maps before coming here, but he's not sure how much he remembers. Ethiopia is to the east; that much he is sure of. He used the e as a mnemonic device. Zaire, Uganda, and Kenya are to the south, he thinks. Chad, Libya,

*and Egypt are north and/or west of where he is. The Red Sea
and the Nubian Desert are far to the northeast.*

The word desolate *occurs to Father Michael. The truck is
long gone. He looks around and takes in the measureless space.
This is Africa. It's exotic, certainly, but that's not the same as
romantic. But Father Michael knew this. He was told this was
a severe, relentless place. It was the sort of place that could
test one's faith, someone had said. Father Michael had to laugh
at that. He had never doubted his faith. He believed in God
the Father; His Son, Jesus Christ; and the Holy Spirit. He
believed in the Church, and most of all, he believed that God
had brought him to this place to help the poor and to spread
the word.*

*In the vast expanse Father Michael sees what he thinks
are giraffes. It seems odd to him that none of them is moving.
It's dawn. Perhaps they sleep standing? He hasn't studied anything about the native wildlife. He approaches them and dis-
covers they are anthills. Huge, red, and churning.*

*Father Michael is not sure what to expect. He was simply
told that when he arrived at the place near Babanusa, he
should wait. Someone would pick him up to take him to the
refugee camp when it was safe. There is no way to know how
long it will be. Things in Africa happen whenever they happen;
time and schedules don't apply, not here.*

*A few hours after the sun comes up the heat is absurd.
Father Michael parks himself in the haggard shade of a dying
tree and imagines the good he will do. Now and then he ven-
tures out to the knobby rut that passes for a road. He looks
left and right for signs of life but sees little. Given the continent's vast population, Father Michael expects to see someone.
There are six hundred ethnic groups in Sudan alone. Where
are they? Where are the Dinkas, the Turkanas, the Nuer? The
only movement he sees is a small troop of baboons heading
north.*

Father Michael finishes the water from one of his two can-

teens. His shirt is soaked. He hasn't expected to wait so long. The heat forces him to sit. Three more hours pass. He is eager to get to the refugee camp and start his work. He takes off his shirt and hangs it on a branch to dry. He takes off his undershirt and wrings out the sweat. He folds it into a neat rectangle and places it on the ground in front of him. He kneels on the shirt and prays, thanking God for delivering him to this place where he is needed.

When Scott shot his television, the slug blew through the set and the wall behind it en route to the apartment across the courtyard, where it shattered a lava lamp before coming to rest on page 310 of the San Fernando Valley East Yellow Pages. When the apartment's owner returned and found the damage, he called the cops. They arrived an hour later and wrote it up as a stray bullet from a drive-by.

Scott was peeking nervously through his curtains at the police when his phone rang. It was Mr. Tibblett, the manager of Transistor Town Electronics, where Scott had interviewed earlier that day. Scott got the job.

Now, three days later, Mr. Tibblett laid his hands on Scott's shoulders and looked into his eyes. "Are you ready?" He asked this as though Scott were about to parachute into the jungles of Cambodia on a black-ops mission.

"Yeah," Scott said, flatly. "Whatever." He was wearing an ill-fitting, brightly colored polyester outfit, complete with an idiotic-looking vest.

Mr. Tibblett primped Scott's bright blue bow tie. "Attaboy!" He gave Scott a pat on the back and shoved him through the swinging doors and onto the showroom floor, where he nearly knocked over a large promotional display that read, "More Is More!"

And then, in the blink of an eye, Scott's life took a profound turn.

* * *

According to the radio traffic reports, a big rig carrying a load of tofu had overturned on the Golden State Freeway, causing what they referred to as "some delays." This was traffic-speak meaning no one was going anywhere. Over on the Hollywood Freeway someone was threatening to jump off the Barham overpass, backing traffic up six miles in both directions. And the downtown four-level was "wide open" with traffic racing along at the speed of inertia.

Fortunately, Dan was heading north on the 405, which, from the sounds of it, was in great shape. He was somewhere near the top of the Sepulveda pass when he saw the brake lights. There were no accidents, no brushfires on the roadside, and no suspicious devices being detonated by the bomb squad, yet traffic had come to a complete halt. Dan had lived in L.A. for twenty-some years and had never heard an explanation for this phenomenon. As far as he could see, there were five lanes of interstate filled with idling cars and trucks. As usual, the traffic reports said nothing about this, mere traffic stoppage being insufficient in this godforsaken sprawl to warrant mention. The nearest exit was three miles north, at Ventura Boulevard, so Dan was trapped.

But at least he had a view. From the top of the pass, smog willing, a northbound driver had a sweeping vista of the San Fernando Valley, 250 square miles of what used to be farm- and ranchland. The Valley was paved over long ago and transformed into suburbs, shopping malls, multiplexes, and McRestaurants. The Santa Monica Mountains (which were the Hollywood Hills a little farther east) stood between the Valley and the L.A. Basin like a producer's assistant blocking access to her boss. The mountains prevented the cooling effects of the Pacific Ocean from working on the Valley, so come summer, the Valley averaged ten to twenty degrees hotter than "the west side," where Dan used to live. Like most Westsiders, Dan had referred to the Valley derisively. As part of his relocation strategy, Dan was rethinking his position in that regard.

Dan and Michael had been born in Flagstaff, Arizona. When their dad disappeared, Ruth packed them up and moved them to Los Angeles in hopes of finding work. She found it, but could never keep it. Over the years, they moved from Azusa to San Dimas to Monrovia to Van Nuys, never staying in any one place long enough to make real friends. As kids, Dan and Michael told themselves it was better not to have friends, since they would have been too embarrassed to invite anyone to their house for fear of how their mom might be acting.

Growing up, Dan hated that he didn't live in a better neighborhood. There were so many to choose from. The people on TV always lived in better houses than he did. Dan had seen Beverly Hills and the Pacific Palisades and he wondered why he couldn't live there. He just knew if he lived in a nicer area, his life would be better.

When Dan got out on his own and started to make enough money, he moved to Santa Monica and waited for his life to improve. It didn't improve immediately, so he bought a terrific entertainment center and leased the Mercedes and he kept waiting. Once or twice he thought he might be happy, but he couldn't say for sure. And now he was headed back to the Valley, specifically to Sylmar, where happiness seemed highly unlikely.

Sylmar was in the northeast corner of the Valley. It was an occasionally dangerous neighborhood near the city of San Fernando. Being well versed in the demographic makeup of Los Angeles neighborhoods, Dan knew this part of the Valley was largely Hispanic. Or was it Chicano, or was Latino the correct term this month? He'd try to avoid all three.

Just past the exit for Ventura Boulevard, traffic inexplicably resumed the speed limit—no rhyme, no reason, that was just how traffic worked. Dan took the 405 to the 118 and twenty minutes later he pulled off the freeway and onto the dusty streets of Sylmar. At the second light he noticed a totally slammed Chevy S-10 pickup in the mirror. It was chopped and lowered, and it was hard to say whether the paint job or the windows were a darker shade of black. It had a stereo too, a loud one. It boomed tautologically. From what Dan could see through the tinted window, the driver and his passenger were violent-looking young men with very little light in their eyes.

Dan had entered a new culture. He wondered how he would deal with it. After a few wrong turns Dan pulled the VW bus into the parking lot of his new home, a ratty two-story, sixteen-unit apartment complex. He got out to admire the place and was standing there when the black Chevy S-10 glided silently to a stop across the street. Then the volume began to rise, louder and louder until it was thunder. The doors opened and the two young men stepped out with a boom. It was Razor Boy and Charlie Freak, gang bangers who had earned their bad reputations.

Sidestepping the Chicano/Hispanic/Latino/whatever question, Dan pegged these two as unpleasant mutations of the "Urban Cores" demographic cluster. Under-twenty-four, some-grade-school, rap-listening, money-order-using, gun-owning malt liquor drinkers. Razor Boy wore a blue work shirt buttoned to the neck, a hairnet, and baggy jeans one tug from being around his ankles. Charlie Freak complemented his pair of baggy pants with the classic white sleeveless undershirt known as the wife-beater.

Dan assumed the one with the work shirt had as many tattoos as did his associate. Dan also assumed they were gang members. That Dan arrived at this conclusion based on prejudice and stereotypes didn't make him any less correct.

Surrounded by his thunder, Razor Boy smiled at Dan,

revealing some gold teeth. It wasn't a Welcome Wagon smile. It was pure menace, cultured in violence and intimidation. This was his hood. He controlled this little corner of the Valley.

Dan hoped his priest outfit might make him bulletproof in some sense. He grabbed his suitcase and went looking for his apartment, which turned out to be on the ground floor, around the corner of the building. Approaching the door, he could hear the phone ringing. However, before he got inside, it stopped. *Just as well*, he thought. He wasn't ready to play Michael on the phone just yet.

Inside, Dan could hardly breathe; there was only one window in the entire apartment and it had been closed for the better part of five days. Dim sunlight filtered through a dirty brown sheet that was hung as a curtain. An exhausted sofa upholstered in what looked like soiled green burlap served as the centerpiece of a design motif best described as Olde Crap. A tattered plaid blanket thumbtacked to the ceiling acted as a partition to create a bedroom at one end of the tiny apartment. The kitchen featured a noisy old refrigerator, a couple of cockroaches, and a crucifix on the wall. There was also a sturdy little table with a Bible on it.

Dan stood there for a moment soaking up the gloom. The sonic booming from outside continued to vibrate the entire apartment and Dan was soon reminiscing about his quiet balcony overlooking Santa Monica Bay. He emptied his pockets onto the table and counted up the change. A buck twenty. "Terrific," he mumbled. He sat at the table pushing the coins around into different patterns. It wasn't as much fun as it sounded, but since there were no forms of electronic entertainment, he hoped it would at least postpone the inevitable despair. It wasn't long before Dan felt entitled to feel sorry for himself. *What did I do to deserve this?* he wondered, not for the first time in the last few days.

He picked up the Bible and thumbed the pages back to front until he came across a photo somewhere in the Book of Nehemiah. It was a picture of Michael in Africa, surrounded by refugees and hopelessness. Michael was dirty and frazzled and had managed only a tired smile for the photographer. But the child at his side, on whose shoulder Michael's hand lay, looked absurdly happy. The child—Dan couldn't tell if it was a boy or a girl—was looking up at Father Michael as if he were Christ Himself. Was this a testament to faith or simply a starving child hoping to curry favor with the food giver? Regardless, it cast Dan's situation in a new light and he decided he wasn't yet entitled to any self-pity.

Dan continued thumbing through the Bible while considering his next move. He was reading about someone begetting someone else when a third someone began banging on the door and yelling as if to say he had an arrest warrant. Dan nearly jumped out of his skeletal system, but he had nowhere to run. He peeked out the window and saw it was the mailman, not the cops. "What do you want?!" Dan yelled through the thin door.

"I got a package for a Father Michael," the man replied.

Dan opened the door. The mailman said he'd tried knocking, but with the booming across the street he figured he had to make some serious noise to get anyone's attention. "Don't want to leave a package on a doorstep in this neighborhood," he said. Dan took the box. The return address was St. Luke's Hospital. He brought the box into the kitchen and opened it. Inside was a plastic bag filled with Michael's personal effects. Of course, since Michael had checked in (and for that matter, had checked out) under Dan's name, the package actually contained Dan's stuff. His suit. His shoes. And, most important, his wallet. The wallet opened to a hallelujah chorus of credit cards. Dan looked heavenward. "Thankewgeezusss!" he said.

The Care Center was open to anyone it could accommodate. In the past there had been an equal mix of young and old, but right now most of the permanent residents were elderly. Mr. Saltzman, Mr. Avery, and Captain Boone shared the house with Ruth, Mrs. Gerbracht, Mrs. Ciocchetti, and Mrs. Zamora. Alissa was a recent addition. Sister Peg and Ruben also lived there. The gathering made for a ragtag family of three generations and several ethnic backgrounds. And right now none of them was smiling.

They gathered three times a day for meals. Since the kitchen was the largest room in the house, it also served as the dining room. There was one table, just big enough to seat everyone elbow to elbow. Nine mouths and no smiles, not a tooth in sight, just glum faces staring at stale bread. It didn't help that Sister Peg was serving cheese sandwiches again.

Sister Peg hadn't told anyone about their precarious financial situation, but they all seemed to know. They were used to their homes and their lives falling apart. They'd come to expect it.

But there was good news, at least for Ruth. She had emerged from her depression. She was cycling up and life seemed good. It was only now, when she felt so positive, that Ruth became aware of how depressed everyone around her was. Something had to be done, she thought, especially about Alissa.

Alissa was sitting at one end of the table, her doll tucked in her lap and her small arms close by her sides so as not to bother anyone. Ruth sat down next to her. "I don't think we've been prop'ly introduced," she said in a funny Cockney accent. "My name's Roof, what's yours, love?"

Alissa turned to look at the old lady who talked so funny. Her eyes were wide and curious but not without fear. She didn't respond except to clutch her doll more tightly.

Ruth nodded as if listening. "Alissa, is it? 'At's a luvly name," Ruth said. "I'd 'ave named me own li'ul girl Alissa if I'd 'ad one, but I only 'ad boys, two of 'em, in fact." Ruth had Alissa's undivided attention. She figured if she was going to make Alissa smile, she needed to make her move now. Ruth opened her sandwich. She pointed at it and leaned over to Alissa, whispering conspiratorially. "I'm tellin' ya, guv'nor, if I 'ave to eat one more piece a cheese, I'll turn into a bloody mouse!" Ruth scrunched her face up and did her best mouse imitation, emphasizing her teeth and making what must have been little mouse sounds. Alissa's mouth moved toward a tiny smile. "I dunno 'bout you, luv, but I'd ravver not be a mouse. Wha' abou' you?"

Alissa tentatively shook her head, never taking her eyes off the funny lady. Alissa liked the way she talked.

"I didn't fink so," Ruth said. "I'd say you're the mourning dove type, a ravver pri'ee bird in my opinion. 'At's what I fink." Ruth cooed a few times and tried to look like a mourning dove. Alissa thought that was very silly, though she didn't show it. "Now," Ruth said, "the fing I like most

abou' birds is 'ow they can fly." She picked up the slice of
cheese from her sandwich. "Loik this!"

Sister Peg was quite startled when the slice of cheese
landed on the funding proposal she was trying to decipher.
She tensed. Then, after a moment, she found herself sup-
pressing a laugh, something she hadn't done since she
couldn't remember when. She looked up in the direction
whence the cheese had come. She saw Ruth making a
funny face and pointing at Alissa. And for the first time
since she had met her, Sister Peg saw Alissa smile as she
shook her head and pointed back at Ruth.

Everyone at the table waited to see what would happen
next. Sister Peg took the only option available to an authority figure in a situation like this. She loaded a spoonful of
Jell-O and launched it toward Ruben, who hadn't been paying attention. It landed in his lap, surprising him so that he
flipped over backward in his chair, sprawling on the floor.
He scrambled to his feet and retaliated with his own dessert, catching Sister Peg squarely on the nose. She crossed
her eyes and burst out laughing, prompting an all-out
food fight.

Everyone was screaming with delight. People who
hadn't laughed in years were red-faced with joy. Seventy-
two-year-old Mrs. Ciocchetti began shooting cheesy little
spitballs through her straw, with surprising accuracy. Alissa
ducked under the table and launched individually wrapped
slices of cheddar like little square Frisbees. Mr. Saltzman,
the resident curmudgeon, was taking unexpected pleasure
from being the primary target for so many of the other
residents. Mr. Avery, still spry at sixty-seven, pushed Mrs.
Zamora's wheelchair, forming an aged yet effective mobile
infantry. Captain Boone, a proud World War II veteran,
wanted to join in, but he was too arthritic to do anything
but watch and laugh.

It was a sight, blood-pulsing life where moments before

there had been only torpid despair. They were laughing, throwing food, rubbing it into each other's faces. Sister Peg was caked with cheese and Jell-O and a warmth she hadn't felt in a long time. She watched Alissa sneak up behind Ruth with a handful of the wiggling dessert. Ruth saw her too but didn't let on. Alissa tugged on Ruth's dress. Feigning innocence, Ruth turned around and took it like a Stooge, right in the face. At that moment—one of the rare moments in her short life—Alissa looked like the happiest person on earth.

It crossed Sister Peg's mind that good food was going to waste, but she decided the trade-off was worth it. The way she saw it, the soul needed the sort of nourishment that a good food fight provided. When she looked over at Alissa, giggling uncontrollably, Sister Peg glanced up and thanked God for laughter.

The temptation was simply too much for a man as weak as Dan. All his life, Dan's head had been filled with those things the Church called "reiterated evil interior sugges- tions." Over and over the voice reiterated, *Go ahead. Just do it!* When he thought about it, Dan realized this aspect of temptation was the equivalent to what those in the ad- vertising business called *frequency*.

One of the basic tenets of advertising is that *reach* (the number of households exposed to a message) plus *frequency* (the number of times a household is exposed to a message) equals *gross rating points* (a number important to media planners). The frequency with which a message is conveyed has a direct bearing on how well the message is integrated by the consumer. In a media-saturated world, frequency was crucial if you wanted to capture a share of the consum- er's distracted mind. The greater the frequency, the greater the probability that the message would lead to action, be it sin or consumerism—or in this instance, both. That's why

Satan can't simply tempt everybody once and move on. Inducements must be repeated to be effective, elected officials being the possible exception to this rule.

In his brief foray at seminary, Dan learned that temptation was an invitation to sin caused by persuasion or by the offer of some good or pleasure. When he joined The Prescott Agency, Dan learned that advertising was an invitation to buy, using persuasion and the offer of some good or pleasure. It's true that the message in any given advertisement was "go and buy," not "go and steal." The problem came when you found yourself without money. Then you just might find those reiterated evil interior suggestions tempting you to violate the Seventh Commandment.

Dan knew all of this, but again, knowing it didn't make him immune to the effect of temptation. Ever since Dan's father had abandoned the family, Dan had wanted material things—the things that promised to make him happy, just like the people in the ads. Dan's pursuit of these things had become habituated. He needed the happiness that consumption brought. He had come to believe that he deserved it.

Dan looked at it this way: He had tried to help someone in need and for his trouble he had been declared dead. Making matters worse, he was now being pursued by an insurance investigator who wanted to put him in prison. The only good to come out of this was that Dan finally understood what was meant by the adage "No good deed goes unpunished."

Dan decided the issue of right versus wrong didn't apply to the credit card situation any more than it seemed to apply to the forces that had put him where he was now. If he was going to have to suffer for doing his good deed, at least he was going to suffer in style. Besides, a few months ago a telephone marketing associate from his credit card company had badgered Dan into buying insurance for his account—insurance that would pay any outstanding balance if Dan were to die. In that regard, Dan rationalized he was getting back at his credit card company for the unethical sales techniques they employed. His argument wasn't exactly unassailable from an ethical standpoint, but Dan was under quite a bit of stress at the time.

In addition to his musings on the nexus between temptation and advertising, Dan had to consider the potential danger of using the credit cards. After mulling it over, Dan decided he was safe. All the charges would predate his funeral. Besides, the credit card company would have no reason to come after him, since the insurance would pay the outstanding balance.

From his liturgical studies, Dan knew that God didn't initiate temptation. God simply allowed temptation to happen. So, in a sense, God was simply giving Dan an opportunity to practice virtue and self-mastery. Unfortunately, Dan was a weak man. Not only that, but now he was a weak man with credit cards. He bought a pile of CDs and some casual outfits and was on his way to purchase the electronic altar at which most Americans prayed—the almighty entertainment center.

The moment he walked into the store he was set upon by a saleswoman. Dan knew exactly what he wanted, so he pointed at the huge shrine of black electronic devices in the middle of the store. "I'll take the full Fujioka package," he said.

"All right!" the woman blurted. "More is more!" She immediately called back to the stockroom and told them to get the thing loaded into Father Michael's VW bus while she rang it up. She swiped the credit card and waited for clearance. Dan gave his car keys to the kid from the stockroom and told him where he was parked.

On the far side of the store, about thirty yards to Dan's left, were two large swinging doors leading to the employee lounge and locker area. Behind that door, the store manager, Mr. Ted Tibblett, laid his hands on Scott Emmons's shoulders and looked into his eyes. "Are you ready?" he asked solemnly.

"Yeah," Scott said, his voice lacking affect. Scott's ill-fitting polyester outfit was bunching in the crotch, compounding his misery. "Whatever."

Mr. Tibblett primped Scott's bright blue bow tie. "Attaboy!" He gave Scott a pat on the back and shoved him through the swinging doors and onto the showroom floor, where he nearly knocked over a large Fujioka promotional display. The first thing Scott saw after he recovered his balance was the priest at the checkout stand. Since Scott didn't know any priests, he thought it was strange that the priest looked so familiar. Scott began walking toward the man, staring.

Dan took the credit card receipt from the cashier and turned to leave, giving Scott a good look at his face. It sort of looked like Dan, Scott thought, but without the beard and glasses—and he was certainly dressed differently. Scott had to be sure. "Hey!" Scott yelled. "Dan!"

Instinctively Dan looked in Scott's direction. He immediately realized the error in his ways. "Oh, shit!" Dan recognized Emmons and the disturbed look in his eyes. Dan turned and ran for the front door, removing all doubt in Scott's mind. As Dan headed out the front, Scott turned and ran back to the employee locker area.

The stock boy was still loading the boxes when Dan hit the parking lot. "Go, go, go!" Dan yelled from fifty feet away. "Emergency sacrament! Big hurry!" The kid shoved the last boxes into the microbus and slammed the door. Dan dove in and keyed the ignition. The engine sputtered but didn't start. "Oh, Christ!"

Scott, meanwhile, reached into his locker and pulled out a paper sack. A moment later he charged through the swinging doors and trampled over the Fujioka sign while tearing his Ruger Super Redhawk .44 magnum out of the bag. As he raced through the store, gun held high, customers and employees screamed and parted like the Red Sea.

Dan was praying hard that the VW bus would start this time. "C'mon, baby!" He rubbed the little statue on the dashboard. "For Christ's sake!" *Bam!* A lead mushroom crashed through the side window before tearing a jagged hole in the metal dashboard. "Sweet Jesus!" Dan turned the key again and the engine finally cranked. He gassed the old microbus and ripped across the parking lot in a zigzag pattern, trying to be a difficult target.

Scott raced after him, firing his gun until he had emptied his cylinder. Click, click, click. "You're a dead man!" he yelled. Emmons finally came to a stop, out of breath. He lowered his gun as he realized the truth of his statement. "That's right. He is a dead man." Scott looked down and saw a consumer cowering between two cars. "I can't go to jail for killing a dead man, can I?"

The consumer shook his head vigorously. "No way," he said.

Scott watched the VW bus disappear down Lankershim Boulevard. He tucked the gun into his waistband and returned to the store. Mr. Tibblett stuck his head up from behind the checkout counter. "Emmons, you're fired."

"No problem," Scott replied, and he meant it. In fact, he was smiling. His reason for living had risen from the dead after three days and had come to offer him salvation. Thanks be to God.

Josie stared at the needle in her arm and wondered about her past sins. She'd been a bad girl and, for all she knew, she'd committed sins that not even God would forgive. The syringe jutting from Josie's vein didn't bother her as much as seeing the blood. Was it diseased? She was certain of it.

Off and on, over the past few months, she'd felt something was wrong with her.

After running away from home, Josie ended up in Hollywood, where more often than not a young girl runs into the wrong people. She was luckier than most, though, and more attractive. She wasn't so attractive that someone from the William Morris Agency saw her on the sidewalk, pulled over, and signed her, but she did get a film role after being in town for less than a month. It wasn't a speaking part, though she did have to open her mouth.

Josie watched the nurse fill a tube with her dark red pestilence. Josie held the cotton ball tight to her wound as she wondered how many times she'd had unsafe sex. She'd used condoms most of the time, but she knew "most of the time" wasn't good enough. It only took one.

During her first three years in El Lay, Josie had performed in several dozen adult movies while simultaneously working as a call girl for a madam who serviced the studios and other high rollers. But the hard life became a feature on Josie's face and she was soon deemed too old and haggard. This at the ripe old age of twenty-six. So she ended up turning tricks on the streets, where she looked good relative to the other girls.

After all that sex, and sharing a needle now and then, Josie figured the odds were seriously against her. She'd probably been with thousands of men. She'd seen the religious people and the conservative politicians on TV saying how people like her deserved to get AIDS and die. "We're better off without them," they said. Every year Josie had less self-respect and her safe-sex policy would suffer for it. If only she'd listened to Sister Peg and gotten off the street that first night.

The nurse capped and labeled the test tube and told Josie she'd get a call in a few days. Josie wondered if this was the best way to atone for her sins. Or would knowing simply make it easier to continue selling herself? Either way the test came out, she had a reason to continue—if it came back negative, she would be encouraged that it was safe and she could carry on. If it came out positive, she figured she didn't have anything to lose.

How long have you been here?''

Father Michael hasn't thought about that for a long time. He looks bemused, then shrugs. "I'm not even sure." His laugh is nervous. He is like a man suffering from nitrogen narcosis— something dangerous is happening, but the event itself prevents him from caring. His mind is slipping. "A couple of years, I suppose." Father Michael doesn't want to think about it in terms of time. The awareness of having accomplished so little after so much effort is too jarring in his fragile state. "Were you in Bahr al-Ghazal? It was very difficult."

The woman from the Red Cross puts her hand on Father Michael's shoulder. "Maybe you should talk to someone about going home. I think you need some time."

"No, there's too much to do yet. We're making progress, slowly, but still . . ." Father Michael cranes his neck to see if any supply trucks are on the horizon. "Our work here is too important to walk away." He raises his voice above the clamor of ten thousand refugees. "I've written to Catholic Relief Services. I'm sure help is on the way . . ."

Though Father Michael is unaware of it, the worldwide emergency relief business has grown in recent years from a three-hundred-million-dollar-a-year enterprise to an eight-billion-dollar-a-year industry. The civil wars in Sudan and Chechnya; genocides in Kosovo, Burundi, and Rwanda; factional fighting in Liberia and Afghanistan; the civil unrest of Somalia; the famine in Bahr al-Ghazal—these and dozens of other events around the world have left millions of sick, wounded, and starving refugees in dire need of assistance.

Indicative of its capacity for charity, mankind responds to

*this need with staggering sums of money. And, of course, when-
ever such sums of money are gathered together, mankind also
reveals its vast capacity for profiteering.*

*Rwanda in 1994 is an excellent example. After several
national governments and large charitable agencies sent two
billion dollars in emergency money to deal with the refugee
problems, 170 relief agencies hustled in to get a cut of the loot.
According to the Federation of Red Cross and Red Crescent
Societies, $173 million mysteriously disappeared over the fol-
lowing three years, apparently pilfered by fly-by-night outfits.*

*Despite the eternal frustration inherent in such work,
organizations like Doctors Without Borders, CARE, Oxfam-
America, and the Red Cross continued to try to help. And it
isn't just the people employed by these large charity organizations who are moved to do this sort of work. Certain individu-
als—people like Father Michael—refuse to surrender even in
the face of this Sisyphean task, so they step into the fray and
deal with it.*

*Father Michael bends down to a young boy, prone on the
ground. He is bloated and dying and covered with skin ulcers.
"Kala-Azar," he says, using the common term for the protozoal
infection that has severely enlarged the boy's spleen and liver.
"It's the damn sand flies," he says, "but then, they're God's
creatures too." Father Michael takes a rag and wipes the boy's
bleeding nose and gums. "He is wasting, like all the others."*

*The woman from the Red Cross nods as she looks out
over the sea of dead and dying. "I hope those supplies get
here soon."*

Father Michael crosses himself. "You hope, I'll pray."

It took him a couple of hours, but the owner of Fernando's
finally got Ruth to tell him who she was and where she
lived. He tracked down the Care Center's number and
called Sister Peg, who came over and picked her up. Sister

Peg had been worried about Ruth ever since, so she made a point to go to her room every afternoon to have a little talk.

"Have you heard from Michael?" Ruth's eyes showed little hope.

"No, I think he's doing something for Monsignor Matthews." Sister Peg had no idea where Father Michael was, but she didn't want to worry Ruth. "I expect him back soon."

Ruth nodded, but in truth she wasn't optimistic. For some reason men had a tendency to disappear on her. But Ruth didn't want to dwell on that, so she and Peg traded small talk for a few minutes before Ruth asked Sister Peg where she was from.

Peg told her about growing up in San Bernardino and how her father had died of cancer. "My mom was in pretty bad shape after that, emotionally and financially. I think that's why she remarried so soon." Sister Peg shrugged. "Unfortunately I didn't like my stepfather. We didn't get along at all," is how she put it. "So I ended up moving to Hollywood to live with a friend of mine." She shook her head as she recalled those days. "We were young and crazy and it was fun, for a while anyway. We had a great apartment in the hills and we went to clubs all the time, but it all cost more than I made as a waitress. After a while I just got tired of all the money hassles and I started to feel like I needed something else in my life, you know, another direction." She gestured at her habit like she never expected to become a nun. "And eventually I found it."

Ruth reached over and patted Sister Peg's hand. "Well, thank goodness for that." Ruth had a vague sense that Peg had left some details out of the story, but she didn't think it was her business to pry. "I think this must be what God intended for you."

"I think so." Sister Peg didn't like to lie about her past, but she didn't see any point in going into the gory details either. The truth was that within a month of moving in, Peg's stepfather began coming to her room late at night after her mother had gone to sleep. Peg's grades slipped and she began feeling guilty and depressed. The abuse went on for nearly a year before Peg finally told her mother. Her mother became violent, screaming and accusing Peg of lying and trying to destroy their family. She grabbed Peg and slapped her repeatedly in the face before Peg got away from her. She moved to Hollywood and had a string of crummy jobs. After the money situation got really bad and they were about to get tossed out of their apartment, Peg's friend said she'd found an easy way to make money. And for a while Peg went along with it.

"You know, it's funny," Ruth said. "It's different with Michael, since I watched him grow up and become a priest. But it's hard to imagine that you were ever anything but a nun. Do you know what I mean?"

"Yeah." Sister Peg smiled. "It's hard for me to imagine too."

Dan was glad to be alive. He was in his Sylmar apartment, propped up in his new vibrating leather recliner, surrounded by three thousand dollars' worth of television, DVD, and audio equipment. The kitchen was full of food and fine wines from Sterling and the Monterey vineyards, and his closet was filled with some serious wool. But like an increasing number of Americans who had discovered that buying everything in sight didn't guarantee happiness, Dan was miserable. Oddly, his dissatisfaction had nothing to do with wanting a larger TV. Dan realized, as he flipped through two hundred channels of satellite-delivered entertainment, that there were only two things he really wanted. He wanted another shot at his own life and he wanted his brother back.

Unfortunately these were things over which Dan had

no control, and as his expensive new watch began to chime, he realized these were also things he didn't have the time to be worrying about. Dan turned off the chime and pulled himself from his chair. *I better leave now or I'll be late for my own funeral.*

In light of his shopping extravaganza, Dan felt guilty about the less-is-more service he had purchased for Michael, sort of a reverse-buyer's-remorse phenomenon. But the credit cards had come when they had come, and there wasn't any credit left on them to upgrade to the next level of ritual, and for that matter, there wasn't any time. Not wanting to run into Butch Harnett at the cemetery, Dan had put a notice in the papers that his funeral was tomorrow, so any delay to upgrade would probably lead to Dan's arrest. He'd stick with the cheap funeral.

Dan drove to the cemetery, his guilt compounding like credit card interest because Ruth wouldn't be there for her son's funeral. Ruth probably didn't know Michael was dead, though it was possible she'd seen the news on television. If that was the case, she would be under the impression that Dan was the dead one. She wouldn't have called his apartment looking for him if she heard he was dead, would she? How much sense would that make? Dan couldn't worry about what his mom knew at this point. Right now he had to lay his brother to rest.

To the lone gravedigger who was leaning against his shovel in the shade of a nearby mulberry tree, it looked like a sad little memorial service. A single priest standing by the small hole in the ground he had dug an hour earlier. The gravedigger assumed the priest was the dear departed's confessor, which meant the stiff had either died alone or alienated every friend and family member he had. The gravedigger couldn't decide which would be worse.

Dan wasn't sure how to proceed, never having presided

over a funeral. He had prepared a few things to say, but he didn't know where to put the ashes while he said them. It was too soon to put Michael in the ground, so Dan held the urn in his left hand while holding his script in his right. He glanced at the words he had scribbled down, stuff cobbled together from memory. It was the usual graveside script about how it pleased Almighty God to take the soul of the brother here departed. There was talk of hope for the resurrection to eternal life, through Jesus Christ. There was the clause about committing his body to the ground, ashes to ashes, dust to dust, that sort of thing. It was fine, time-tested material, and when Dan had scribbled it down, he thought it was what needed to be said.

Now that the time had come, however, Dan realized he had more to say. His mind was choked with guilt and he needed the words to express his emotions, but words failed him as his guilt grew. It was bad enough that he had popped for a cheap funeral, worse that he hadn't told his mom, but to top it off, Dan's scheme might have sent his good brother straight to hell. Try living with that.

Instead of reading what he had written, Dan considered just speaking off the cuff. *Goddammit, you son of a bitch. Why did you have to die? Why were you off in the godforsaken Third World taking care of others instead of taking care of yourself or your own mother? What were you thinking? Why did you leave me alone to deal with all this?* But he couldn't say that. It was bad enough that the thoughts had entered his mind. Dan wiped the tears from his eyes and carried on.

The gravedigger kept watching from under the mulberry tree. He had to wait until the priest was finished before he could go shovel the dirt back into the hole.

Dan tried reading from the sheet of paper, but it wasn't coming from his heart, so he put the paper away. He cradled the urn in his hands and looked at it, hoping something profound would spill from his soul, but all he came up with was *plop, plop, fizz, fizz, oh what a relief death is.* Fortunately he had the good taste not to say it.

He brought the ashes to his chest and he held them close. After a moment, Dan knelt and slipped the urn into the ground. Then, using his hands, Dan scooped up the dirt and buried his brother, all the while thinking: *The Lord giveth and the Lord taketh away.*

The gravedigger shrugged and walked off.

The office of the Catholic Archdiocese of Los Angeles is in an ordinary-looking office building on Wilshire Boulevard halfway between Beverly Hills and downtown. There are a few photos on the lobby wall, a local Bishop here, an old Pope there, but it's nothing fancy. The current issue of *The Tidings*, Southern California's Catholic weekly, is stacked on a small wooden table just inside the door. The office is populated by good, hardworking Catholics of both the ordained and the lay variety who, for the most part, handle the administration of nonspiritual matters.

Although no one will acknowledge it—indeed, there are few who even know about it—the Church has another office, this one in a polished forty-two-story container on The Avenue of the Stars in Century City. This furtive location had a better decorator with a much larger budget than the office on Wilshire Boulevard.

Monsignor Matthews was one of the many who were previously unaware of this location. As he rode the elevator to the thirteenth floor he began to worry about being called to a meeting with no named purpose held at this mysterious place. When the elevator doors opened and the cool air rushed in, Monsignor Matthews feared he had been found out.

Matthews was a financial analyst for the Church and, over the years, he had done some poking around in the books. Although he was never able to get an exact figure,

Monsignor Matthews once calculated that only twenty-eight cents of every dollar given to the Church ever reached the poor. The Monsignor had the nutty idea that Jesus had something else in mind; consequently, for the past few years he had been diverting Church funds from certain accounts and turning the money over to Sister Peg. He did this because he knew things about the Church that he couldn't reconcile with his understanding of Scripture. Monsignor Matthews felt the Church wasn't living up to its potential, so he was doing his best to right the wrong—to help those in need. He was working from the inside.

He stepped into the reception area and felt as if he'd been transported to another time and place—the Inquisition came to mind. The floor was a spectacle. It was Italian pink marble inlaid with three-hundred-year-old ceramic tiles which formed the seal of Vatican City in the center of the large room. The windows were covered with heavy fuchsin drapes, completely blocking the bright Southern California sun. The space was gently illuminated by muted, recessed lighting.

Monsignor Matthews was holding his small briefcase. Inside was some unfinished paperwork and a copy of David Mamet's *Speed-the-Plow*. He always carried reading material with him in case he got stuck in traffic, as had happened on the way to Century City. Matthews had become a big Mamet fan after seeing *House of Games*. He found Mamet's use of colloquial dialogue authentic, plus he knew some higher-ups in the Church who reminded him of the real estate agents in *Glengarry Glen Ross*.

Matthews was as tall as your average Monsignor. His straight brown hair was cut short. He had quick eyes and a resourceful aspect. But in this calculatedly ecclesiastical place Monsignor Matthews felt small and inept. He stood in the center of the room, looking and listening, though there was nothing to hear. After a moment, he folded his arms against the chill. The room was cold, the atmosphere like a climate-controlled museum.

Monsignor Matthews had arrived early and no one was there to tell him what to do or where to go, so he looked around while he waited. He was drawn to a large portrait on one of the walls. It was Pope Gregory IX, an imposing, grim-looking cleric from the eleventh century. Matthews marveled that the Church had ever fallen into hands such as his.

Over the next fifteen minutes the elevator delivered several more priests and Monsignors to this foyer. They were all from the larger parishes of Southern California and none of them had the vaguest idea why they were here. Every man kept to himself, unsure if trust was the best policy. Monsignor Matthews wondered if the other men were guilty of the same thing he was, or of something different. Time, he feared, would tell.

Another five minutes passed before a nondescript woman entered the foyer and escorted the group down a hallway to a conference room. They were told to wait. The conference room was even more Gothic than the reception area. The weirdness of the place and the mystery of the conference began to pull the men together. They started to talk. "Nice artwork," one of them ventured. He was Monsignor Spadini, a round, monk-faced man. He examined a fresco on one of the walls and announced it was from the catacombs of Domitilla, third century, authentic. A series of illuminated manuscripts lined the other walls. *"The Scribe Ezra Rewriting the Sacred Records,"* Spadini said, pointing. "And that's *The Transfiguration Scene as Seen by St. Apollinaris.*"

Monsignor Matthews asked if Spadini had studied art. He shook his head. "I've been doing some research," he said. "Working on a screenplay. Do you know of any Catholic literary agents?"

Before Matthews could respond, a voice came from above, from speakers hidden in the ceiling. "Take your seats." The men moved to the conference table and did as they were told.

"Anyone know what this is about?" Monsignor Matthews asked. Heads shook. No one had a clue. The mood was uncertain, with each man contemplating his worst indiscretion. Another few minutes passed before the large double doors at the far end of the room opened to reveal a priest. He entered the room pulling an overhead projector behind him like a cross. He looked tired, burdened by something.

Monsignor Matthews recognized him. They had worked together briefly in the administrative office of the archdiocese in Boston. This guy was a serious financial wonk.

The priest said nothing as he plugged the projector in and turned it on. "And there was light," he mumbled. He turned to face his audience. "My name is Father Carter. I'm with the Church's accounting office. I'm here to give a presentation on current fiscal matters." He pushed a button and the room's lights dimmed. "Oh, by the way, we're meeting here instead of the diocese office because they're repainting that conference room." Father Carter placed a transparency on the projector. "Now, if you will turn your attention to graph A, which I'm projecting now . . ."

Thus began the most tedious monologue on Church finances to which Monsignor Matthews had ever been subjected. "Let's start with a discussion on marginal analysis," Father Carter intoned. Monsignor Matthews slipped his copy of *Speed-the-Plow* from his briefcase and tried to read it by the light of the overhead projector, but after ten minutes, his head began to set like the sun. When his chin touched his chest he snapped back from his brush with sleep. Father Carter's voice remained languid and dreamy. "Marginal analysis says that full costs are less important than marginal costs and we must be careful when calculating average cost . . ."

Monsignor Matthews struggled against the drowsiness, but the dimmed lights and the priest's presentation made it a challenge. He refocused on Mamet, hoping to stay awake, but the droning priest was aural opium and again the Monsignor's head lolled. Things remained dull as a High Mass until the door behind Father Carter suddenly opened. This time a man wearing a miter appeared, filling the doorway. He was a powerful, austere-looking fellow. He carried a small wooden box under one arm. He was not smiling. He looked incapable.

Father Carter quickly turned off the projector and scurried to the side of the room. Everyone at the table stood, soldiers at attention. "I am Cardinal Glen Goddard," said the man in the miter. He looked to be in his early sixties. He entered the room and placed the wooden box at the end of the table. "I have an undergraduate degree in business management from Notre Dame." He removed his pointy headgear and laid it next to the box. His hair looked like iron styled in the Julius Caesar fashion, which didn't work for the Cardinal any more than it had worked for anyone since George Peppard. "I earned my M.B.A. at Loyola."

Monsignor Matthews had never heard of Cardinal Goddard, but ever since Pope John XXIII opened the floodgates established by Pope Sixtus V (who had set the number of Cardinals at seventy), you needed a program to know who was who at that level of the Church. There were Cardinal Bishops, Bishops of the seven sees around Rome, and the Eastern-rite Patriarchs. But this guy was different, Matthews thought. This guy was half disciple, half drill sergeant.

Cardinal Goddard leaned onto the head of the table, assessing his audience. "I have a Ph.D. in economics from the University of Chicago," he said. "So trust me, I know whereof I speak." Monsignor Matthews nonchalantly reached for the water pitcher in the center of the table. "Don't even touch it," Cardinal Goddard said. "Water is for saviors only."

Monsignor Matthews froze. *Did he say, water is for saviors only?* He turned his head to look at the Cardinal as if he was joking.

Goddard stared him down. "You think I'm kidding?" he asked. "Well, think again, Padre." He paused. "I am here from Rome." The Cardinal never broke eye contact with Matthews as he pointed at the ceiling. "I get my orders from upstairs, and I am here on a serious mission." He raised his eyebrows and tilted his head slightly until Matthews withdrew his hand from the water pitcher. Cardinal Goddard began to circle the table. "Okay, so you're sitting there asking yourself, what is this all about? Well, it's about the future of the Church, my friends, and I'm afraid that means it's all about mammon." Cardinal Goddard reached the head of the table. "That's right, the almighty dollar. In God we trust, all others pay cash. Jesus saves, but the Church invests and has a highly diversified portfolio." Once again the Cardinal leaned onto the conference table, his hands wide apart. "It's as simple as this," he said. "You have got to stop thinking of yourselves as religious men, because to the Church you are something else. You are branch managers in a multinational corporation that is in the business of saving souls." He cocked his head to the side and opened his eyes wide. "And saving souls . . . Don't. Come. Cheap. Revenues and expenditures, gentlemen. Income and expenses. When you're in business—even the business of saving souls—you need more of the former and less of the latter or you go straight to H-E-double-toothpicks."

Monsignor Spadini suddenly cracked. He didn't appreciate being lectured about how much money he was expected to deliver on a quarterly basis. "Hey, I don't need to hear all this." He said this with, perhaps, too much zest. Someone in the room actually gasped.

Cardinal Goddard turned quickly, like a wolf taking sudden notice of a wounded lamb. "Ahhh, so *Mister* Spadini has something to say about all this." Goddard walked over behind the chubby Monsignor and put his hands on his shoulders. "You call yourself a Monsignor, you pissant?" Quick as a spark he slapped Spadini on the side of the head.

"Hey!" Monsignor Spadini tried to stand, but the Cardinal shoved him back to his seat.

"Sit!"

Spadini was incensed. "The hell . . ." He rubbed the side of his head, which was already showing the red imprint of Goddard's hand. "I don't have to put up with this sort of crap." Spadini used to teach junior high school, so he was used to being the slapper, not the slappee.

"You certainly don't, my fat friend," the Cardinal said. "And you know why? Because as of this moment, you're fired. Every blessed one of you. You can turn in your collars, dust off your résumés, and hit the bricks." Disbelief spread from face to face like the Angel of Death going door to door in Egypt. "Orrrrrrr, you can suck it up and get your job back." He paused, smiling. "The choice is entirely yours."

The men at the table were stunned. They looked to one another as if to say, *he can't fire us . . . can he?* Of course, they knew he could. A Cardinal could drop-kick these guys like an overinflated soccer ball. There was no due process, no administrative hearing, just pack your bags and check you chalice on the way out. Cardinal Goddard stared at the men, still smiling. "Ahhh, now I have your attention," he said as he began to pace. "That's good, because you're all going to want to listen to what I have to say. Starting right now, you're in a competition." He turned

to face the conference table again. "What sort of competition? you ask. To save souls? To forgive sins?" He closed
his eyes momentarily and shook his head. "No." He opened
his eyes. "It's a collection contest. See, back in Rome,
they've noticed the diocesan assessments have been dwin-
dling, and they won't have that. So here's the deal."
Cardinal Goddard opened the wooden box and removed
some papers which he handed to Monsignor Matthews.
"Pass those around."

The Monsignor did as he was told. "These are your
goals and your potential rewards," Cardinal Goddard said.
"As you can see, first prize is a trip to the Vatican." He
arched his eyebrows. "Anybody want to see second prize?"
Goddard pulled something from the box and held it up.
"Second prize is a Virgin Mary night-light. Third prize is
you're excommunicated." He dropped the night-light back
into the box. "Starting to get the picture?"

One of the priests pushed the Cardinal's paper away as
if it were a document from Satan. Goddard walked over to
the priest, fingering the jewel-encrusted cross hanging from
the gold chain around his neck. "You see this cross?" The
priest didn't acknowledge the question, so Goddard
smacked him across the head. "You see it, huckleberry?"

Cowed, the priest nodded. "Yes, Your Eminence."

"This cost more than your car." Cardinal Goddard
paused to let that sink in. "You see, my frocked friend,
that's who I am—and you're nobody." The Cardinal walked
back to the head of the table and reached into the box. "It
takes only two things to win that trip to Rome, fellas."
Goddard stepped from behind the box to reveal a pair of
ornate brass balls dangling from strips of leather. "It takes
these," he said. "The money's out there, gentlemen. All
you have to do is collect it. Fail to do so and I will make
everlasting damnation seem like a pancake supper. Any
questions?" There was a pause as the gathered clerics

looked to see if anyone was bold enough to voice an objection. Something caught Cardinal Goddard's eye. He walked slowly over to Monsignor Matthews. "What about you, Monsignor?" He waited for a response. "Monsignor, are you with us?"

Matthews looked up, startled back from his daydream. "Uh, Mamet," he sputtered. "I mean, mammon. It's all about mammon."

Father Carter looked at him oddly. "Yes, well, to the extent that we need to see the ten percent increase in your diocesan assessments, that's true," he said. "Thank you, gentlemen." With that, Father Carter shuffled out of the room with his projector.

As the rest of the men gathered their belongings and drifted toward the elevator, Monsignor Matthews gathered his thoughts. On the one hand, he was relieved that he hadn't been busted for his subversive activities. On the other, he now had a serious problem with Sister Peg—which problem could easily lead to his being . . . busted. He hated that sort of thing. Matthews knew that the quickest way to improve his diocesan assessment payments was by cutting off his Care Center funding. That wouldn't be a problem except that he wasn't supposed to be funding the Care Center in the first place. In fact, several years ago Monsignor Matthews had received a tersely worded memo specifically ordering him not to fund Sister Peg's charitable enterprise for reasons not divulged in the memo.

Of course, Monsignor Matthews knew the reasons and had dismissed them as irrelevant. He had known Sister Peg for years and he knew that she could help more people with a hundred dollars than most charities did with a thousand. If he cut her off now, there was no telling what song she'd start to sing. She knew at least two tunes that would bury him.

Monsignor Matthews looked across the room at a glass

display case containing a sacred ivory diptych, a hinged writing tablet from the second century, decorated with the image of the Virgin Mary flanked by angels, probably worth twelve million dollars on a good day at Christie's. It sickened him to think of how much good that money *could* do, but never would. Instead, it would sit in this conference room for the enjoyment of a few men. This was a perfect example of the sort of thing that angered the Monsignor. Still, he knew how to pick his fights and there was no point agitating the pea-brained prelates in Accounts Receivable. Monsignor Matthews had a far more dangerous foe to deal with.

Dan had a bottle of scotch in the van; unfortunately it wasn't one of the five vintage-dated single-malt Scotch whiskies produced by the world-renowned Glenlivet Distillery. Still, it was good whisky, Chivas Regal twelve-year-old. As the sun went down, he sat there with his dirty hands and had a few while looking out over the cemetery. He thought about the good times and he took some comfort in the sentimentality and the sadness, but mostly it came from the Chivas. Dan felt bad about the service he'd performed and wanted to make up for it. After another drink Dan warmed to the idea of a wake. Of course, it would be a small wake—party of one—but it would be good for him, something to wash away his bitterness and anger, something to honor his other half. So he cranked the old VW and drove home.

On the way back, Dan remembered that he had a nice steak in the fridge. That would be a good start. He could open a Sterling Vineyard cabernet and make toasts to his brother's memory. It would be a nice gesture and far more Catholic than Dan's service, which was closer to Church of England than anything else. He'd load up the new Fujioka with CDs that Michael would have liked, some Bob

Dylan maybe, or Paul Simon. Then, after dinner, he'd sit in the big recliner, finish off the wine, and have a good cry.

Dan pulled into his parking spot. Across the street he saw Razor Boy and Charlie Freak and their ominous black S-10 pickup. They were posturing against the truck, all tattoos, malt liquor, and menace. They laughed when Dan looked their way and the one with the gold teeth lifted his shirt to show the chrome handle of the gun in his waistband.

Dan didn't care. He simply locked the van and walked around the corner of the building. He heard his phone ringing again, but he still wasn't ready to answer it, especially now. He was in a bad place and he could feel it getting worse. The moment he got to the door, his emotions started to get the better of him. And when he walked into the apartment—the apartment that used to be Michael's—he was unable to contain himself any longer. Dan began to cry again. *Why me?* he thought. The anguish overwhelmed him and he fell to his knees, but it had nothing to do with Michael. He'd been robbed. No more Fujioka, no more nothing. The place was stripped bone-clean.

It was one thing, Sister Peg thought, for the head of a multinational corporation to be paid millions of dollars each year, but ever since the United Way scandal, Sister Peg had kept a jaundiced eye on the salaries of those who ran the nation's largest charity organizations and foundations. It seemed fundamentally wrong to her that someone sweating in a soup kitchen sixty hours a week would earn twenty thousand dollars while someone putting in twenty-hour weeks running a charitable foundation would make as much as $600,000 in salary and benefits, which many of them did. It struck Sister Peg as, somehow, hypocritical. She was funny that way.

When Sister Peg read the newspaper article about the

heads of the nation's largest charitable foundations gathering in Los Angeles for an awards banquet of a self-congratulatory nature, she decided to call in a favor.

The Beverly Eldorado was a five-star hotel on Rodeo Drive in the heart of the city of conspicuous consumption. Elegant architecture and spacious interiors reflected the enormous sums of money that went into the creation of this luxurious attraction frequented by celebrities and royalty alike. It was resplendence manifest at six hundred bucks a night—for the cheap rooms.

Outside, the valet had just returned from parking a Lamborghini Diablo VT, a jewel of automotive design. Even in Beverly Hills, one didn't see these frequently. The valet was still basking in the afterglow when the old Suburban lurched to a stop. He assumed the suspension was shot as it was riding so low to the ground. When the nun opened the doors and more than a dozen people piled out of the creaky beast, however, he understood why it had been hugging the ground so. What he didn't understand was what these bedraggled people were doing at his fine hotel. However, since he'd been trained not to pass judgment on guests based on their vehicles, he simply handed the nun her ticket and pointed her toward the door.

Inside, everything was cool and rich and golden and quiet. The beautiful people in the lobby and the bar seemed to whisper their words while the tasteful percussion of silverware on china issuing from the Golden Calf Restaurant was softened by heavy drapes and thick carpeting. This costly calm was violated when Sister Peg led the charge into the marbled main hall. She was accompanied by a television camera crew and the timid, and hungry, residents of the Care Center. The large blue-and-white sticker prominently displayed on the side of the camera spoke to the seriousness of Sister Peg's mission. It said, "CNN." With the media at her side, Sister Peg guided her platoon of have-nots down a sumptuous hallway graced by a priceless collection of handmade tapestries and carpets and replicas of eighteenth-century furniture.

Peg's posse was headed for the opulent and classically designed five-thousand-square-foot ballroom, which was the ideal venue for large, lavish gala social events. The elegantly dressed crowd was inside the ballroom swilling cocktails to the strains of a tasteful piano, bass, and drum trio. A man in a tuxedo was stationed at the door to welcome late-arriving guests and to keep out the rabble. The moment he saw Sister Peg and the camera crew round the corner, he feared he was in over his head.

Sister Peg walked directly up to the man and put a stopwatch in his face. "Think fast," she said. "The camera is on." The man panicked and reached for the phone. Ruben, silent as ever, put his strong hand on the receiver, shook his head, and frowned. "See, the thing is," Sister Peg said, "we've been eating cheese for damn near forty days and forty nights and we're tired of it. So you've got two choices. The first and the best choice, I might add, is to find the event coordinator and tell her there's a nun out here with a CNN camera crew and fifteen hungry people. Advise this person to allow us in to be warmly received and fed in exchange for being featured in a very favorable human interest story to be broadcast on national television."

The man in the tux listened intently. He wasn't sure what to make of the terrorist-nun.

"The second option," Sister Peg said, "is to call Security and have us thrown out, which I think you would agree would also make for some very good television. Do you understand?"

The man looked past Sister Peg and, over her shoulder, saw the frightened faces of old people and a few small children. They were huddled behind their protector. The man could see how they trusted this woman and he took this to mean she had earned this trust and was not to be trifled with.

Sister Peg snapped her fingers in front of the man's face. "I said, do you understand?"

"Yes, Sister," the man said.

"Excellent." Sister Peg started the stopwatch. "You've got sixty seconds. If you're not back by then, we'll just let ourselves in. Go." Tick, tick, tick . . .

The man disappeared. Ruben sniffed the air. It smelled like filets and lobster and melted butter. He smiled at Sister Peg, crossing his arms across his chest, his hands in soft fists. Then he made funny snapping claws with his hands. He loved lobster.

Sister Peg winked and gave a quick nod. The man in the tux came back with twelve seconds to spare, a svelte socialite in tow. The woman extended her hand. "Hello," she said. "My name is Eleanor Colvin, and you are?"

"Sister Peg. I run a place called—"

Eleanor gently held up one hand, dismissing the explanation. "Why don't you tell me about it over dinner?"

Sister Peg was momentarily at a loss for words. She had expected some resistance, certainly some disdainful looks, snide remarks. Finally she said, "That's very generous of you."

"Don't be silly," the woman replied. "I'm seated at the most pathetic table in the history of social galas. I've been listening to the most tiresome screenwriter droning on about his lack of adequate representation. I can't thank you enough for rescuing me." And with that, Eleanor ushered the Care Center residents into the ballroom.

Although some in the crowd were dismayed that they would have to share their opulence with "these people," the majority were liquored up enough to let it slide. The wait staff quickly set up a table for the Care Center residents. Alissa was absolutely captivated by the splendor of the ballroom. She told Ruth she felt like Cinderella. Ruth, who was savoring the cabernet, told Alissa to keep her eye out for Prince Charming. Ruben paused between bites of lobster to cut the meat for some of the older residents. During the soup course, the CNN camera crew covered the event and got comments from some of the attending celebrities.

Eleanor Colvin was across the room, speaking with a gentleman who was a heavy hitter on the charity circuit. When she saw Sister Peg looking her way, Eleanor smiled and gave her a gracious nod. Then she turned back to the gentleman and finished what she was saying. "The woman had a news crew with her, for God's sake. I didn't think we needed the bad publicity."

As Sister Peg enjoyed the best meal of her life, her friend the cameraman leaned over and thanked her for calling him. "This is a great steak," he said.

Sister Peg reached over and patted his hand. "I appreciate your help. I couldn't have done it without you."

The cameraman winked. "I think the CNN sticker was the key," he said. "I got into the Emmys using that last year."

Sister Peg had to laugh. Her friend was a gofer at a cable-access station in Van Nuys. When Peg called with her idea, he simply checked out the Betacam unit with the CNN sticker and got his roommate to be the phony sound man in exchange for a free dinner. For the moment Sister Peg was quite pleased with herself. Pulling off these scams had always given her a bit of a thrill, and she wasn't worried about the ethics. She was willing to take the moral bullet if it meant feeding her charges. But she knew this was only a short-term solution. Her long-term solutions, primarily grant applications and requests for public-sector funding, were constantly being shot down. As the eviction noose tightened around her neck, Sister Peg was starting to consider more extreme approaches, but she hoped to find funding without actually having to use her gun.

Father Michael looks to the sky but not to pray. He wishes it weren't so hot. His faith wanes with each hour. He has seen the money and relief supplies diverted by whichever rebel group controls a given area. Frustrated, he has written letters to his superiors in hopes of effecting change in that regard. He is told that someone from the Church will come to investigate the matter. Three months pass and nothing changes.

It's a Friday and Father Michael has gone without food or water for forty-eight hours. He is weak and disoriented as he administers the last rites to a group of recent converts. When he stands to stretch his back, he notices a commotion on the horizon. There is a small convoy coming his way. Even from a distance Father Michael can tell it is neither a military nor an aid convoy. There is too much dust to make things out until they get closer, so he waits, hopeful that it is help of some sort. When they get closer, the drivers begin honking their horns. The refugees—some stumbling, others being dragged out of the way—clear a path. Father Michael watches in confusion as the refugees scramble to their feet and wave at the line of trucks as if it is a parade—which, in a sense, it is.

The last vehicle in the convoy is the strangest truck Father Michael has ever seen. It is a Range Rover, the back of which has been modified into what looks like an oversized phone booth or perhaps a giant terrarium. The truck and the frame of the Plexiglas container have been painted a custom shade of bone. Inside the booth, sitting in a sumptuous cream-colored leather wing-back chair, is Cardinal Cooper. He is wearing an alabaster chasuble trimmed with silk cord. His shoulders are draped with a short cape embroidered with ecclesiastical symbols sewn from glittery golden threads, all festooned with a jewel-encrusted crucifix dangling on an elegant silver chain. As a topper, Cardinal Cooper sports a Paris white miter with mother-of-pearl brocade which tests the height of his enclosure. He is a feather boa away from looking like a religious Liberace as he waves at the starving refugees like a Sweet Potato Queen in a harvest parade. Father Michael thinks he is hallucinating.

The Cardinal's conveyance comes to a stop in front of Father Michael. As he stands there, coughing in the dust, Father Michael peers through the tinted Plexiglas. Inside, on a teakwood end table next to the leather chair, he sees a bowl of pistachios, a golden chalice, and a can of caffeine-free diet soda. There is a cooler filled with more soft drinks against the wall. When the dust finally settles, an electric window rolls down and the Cardinal pokes his jewel-encrusted hand out for the humble priest to kiss. Standing in the absurd heat, Father Michael feels an air-conditioned breeze cool his face. Cardinal Cooper clears his throat as if to say hurry up, you're letting all the cold air out.

Father Michael stares at the Cardinal's finery and jewels, then at the mass of skeletal remains that are the refugees, and suddenly, for reasons unknown, something inside of him snaps. He grabs the Cardinal by the hand and yanks hard. "Whoa!" The Cardinal bangs his head on his way through the window. His immaculate white miter lands in the dirt. A struggle ensues as Father Michael attempts to pull the diamond rings from the Cardinal's fingers. "I can sell this," he screams. "We can feed these people!"

The bodyguards quickly pull Father Michael off and restrain him. Cardinal Cooper is helped to his feet, where he stands like a king as his attendants brush the dust from his vestments. He doesn't appear to be thinking about forgiveness.

Father Michael isn't sure what happened. He tries to clear his head, but he can't make sense of anything. He doesn't know if he has gone crazy or if it's the rest of the world. It doesn't take him long to realize that such distinctions are moot.

After dusting off his soiled miter, the Cardinal steps onto his portable speaker's platform and, with a vague sweep of his hand, he blesses the starving crowd. He then turns to Father Michael, smirks, and exercises his power to excommunicate. A moment later Cardinal Cooper is back in the comfort of the air-conditioned booth. The convoy goes on its way, leaving behind little more than an empty soda can.

Like everyone else who had ever been burglarized, Dan felt violated. He also felt a certain helplessness, an impotence stemming from the fact that he couldn't even report the burglary because the investigation might turn up the fact that the merchandise that had been stolen had been purchased using a dead guy's credit card in the first place. After reflecting further on his circumstances, Dan felt yet another sensation—hunger. He had gotten himself all worked up for that steak dinner only to find the cupboards laid bare. The thieves had taken everything but a can of tomatoes, some soy sauce, and an ancient rotary phone.

Driving force that it is, hunger drove Dan to a large Lucky Store a few miles away. Dan hoped that he hadn't lost his feel for the five-finger discount at which he had been rather adept as a boy. He picked up a plastic hand-basket as he entered the store. He went directly to the produce section. While browsing there, he casually looked around to find the mirrored windows and the half globes of black glass in the ceiling that concealed the cameras. The fact that Dan was hungrier than he was nervous also helped.

Somewhere near the wall containing sixty-seven different salad dressings Dan noticed something odd about the way people were looking at him. Whenever he made eye contact with anyone, they smiled at him rather sweetly. They weren't smiling in the simple-acknowledgment way people do when they're merely being pleasant. This smile was respectful, almost thankful, and in any event, it wasn't the sort of smile Dan was accustomed to getting. That's when Dan realized he wouldn't get caught. He was safe because people were responding not to him, but to his clothes. He was a priest in their eyes. And given fifty random people in a store, Dan thought, who is security *not* going to watch?

He started at the bulk candy containers, eating yogurt-coated malt balls. Then he put a roll of toilet paper in his basket before filching a can of tuna. Things were going smoothly as he wandered over to the meat section. He didn't like the looks of the pork and he didn't think he could get away with a whole chicken, so he moved down to the end of the cooler and grabbed what he thought he could get away with. He headed to the front of the store and stopped at the magazine rack. He put down his basket and distanced himself from it as he leafed through a magazine. Then he casually headed for the exit.

Wearing the clericals, Dan felt like a man with diplomatic immunity. He was home free. The automatic doors opened like the gates to heaven. A second later he was safely on the sidewalk outside the store, feeling haughty about his shoplifting skills. Dan's pride took a fall, however, when the security guard tapped him on the shoulder. "Excuse me, Father," he said. The guard reached into Dan's shirt pocket and produced the can of tuna. Then he gestured toward the bulge in Dan's crotch.

Dan smiled immodestly. "Impressive, isn't it?"

"I'm afraid I'll have to see it."

Dan reached into his pants and liberated the stolen kielbasa. Then, with a swift backhand, Dan whacked the guard across the head with the sausage and disappeared into the parking lot.

Typically, when one is fired from a job for attempting to kill a customer, it becomes difficult to find employment in that same field. Mr. Ted Tibblett, however, could think of no good reason to provoke the moody bastard with the Ruger Super Redhawk .44 magnum, so he made a point of telling Scott that he would give him a glowing reference should anyone inquire.

Scott knew Dan was out there. He also knew it wouldn't be easy to find him. It would take time, which was all right. Scott had plenty of time, but like everything else, it would also take money, so Scott began his job search first. With Mr. Tibblett's generous reference, Scott felt good about finding work that would fund his search for Dan. After that, nothing would matter.

While he waited for his interviews, Scott had time to think. He couldn't figure out why Dan had faked his own death, but he did have an idea why Dan was posing as a Catholic priest. Scott knew Dan had attended seminary before starting his advertising career. He knew this because Dan had used the fact to help land the Mormon account a few years earlier. The Church of Jesus Christ of Latter Day Saints was the GM of organized religions in that it had a significant ad budget as part of its proselytizing campaign. But why fake his death? *Hell, why ask why?* he thought. The "why" of it didn't matter. The priest angle was a good lead, and Scott was going to follow it up.

Scott was in his apartment pumping furiously on the BullyBoy, hot-loading some new rounds for the hunt. He had become quite adept at handloading his own ammo over the past two weeks and he found that the process relaxed him, so he kept loading and loading until he had enough cartridges to fill a bandoleer. When he ran out of primers and brass casings, Scott started working out his strategy. He grabbed the Yellow Pages and looked up Churches, Catholic. There were several subcategories: Byzantine, Eastern, Latin Rite, Liberal, Roman, and Traditional. He decided the simplest approach would be the best, so he tore the page from the book and began plotting the church locations on a map of the Valley. He would start at the west end and work his way east until he found the priest he was looking for. He would go to confession over and over until he heard a voice he recognized. Then he'd give Dan his penance.

Dan played hide-and-seek with the security guard until he could sneak back into the microbus and escape. Despite being only a mile from the apartment, it took him nearly an hour to get back. Cal-Trans was doing some unnecessary midday work in the middle two lanes of the San Diego Freeway and there was a Sig-Alert on the 118 due to a six-car pileup caused by idiots in the westbound lanes rubbernecking at a police stop on the eastbound lanes. This forced roughly fifty-eight thousand cars onto surface streets, gridlocking that portion of the Valley. The whole thing was compounded by a fearsome excavation on Magnolia Boulevard, which otherwise would have been the best alternative route.

By the time Dan got home, he was starving, which went a long way in explaining why he thought the pan of soy sauce and canned tomatoes smelled so mmmm-mmmm good. As he stirred the dark red concoction, the heat from the stove charmed his eyes. He stared at the bubbling liquid, thinking about what to do next. He needed a job; that much he knew. A moment later it dawned on him that he already had one waiting for him. Now all he had to do was remember the name of his employer. *What was her name? Sister Somebody. Teresa? No, that was Mother, not Sister. Bertrille? Bernadette? Mary Clarence?* Dan was sure Michael had mentioned her name, but for the life of him, Dan couldn't remember it.

After the tomatoes bubbled for a while Dan poured them into a bowl. He looked at his dinner and, for the first time in many years, he paused to give thanks. And while he was at it, he prayed that God would remind him of the name of the nun who was out there waiting to write him a paycheck. After grace, Dan scooped up a steaming tomato. As he blew on it to cool it down, the phone began to ring. Without thinking, he popped the tomato into his mouth and grabbed the phone. The tomato was so much napalm on his tongue. Dan spit it out with phenomenal force. "Jesus!" The tomato shot across the room and exploded against the wall. "Shit! Yiiiiiiiiiii!"

"Excuse me?" came the voice from the telephone.

Dan dropped the receiver and dove for the sink. He flushed his mouth with cold water for a minute before returning to the phone. "Huu-ooo?" he said, the letter *L* being too painful to pronounce at the moment.

"Father Michael?" It was a woman.

"Uh huh," Dan said, suddenly wondering why he had answered the phone in the first place. "Who is this?"

"It's Sister Peg." She paused, wondering best how to proceed. "Uh . . . where the hell have you been?"

Dan's mind raced. How much was he supposed to know about this woman? Should he have recognized her voice? Had Michael told him anything about her that he could use? *Quick*, he thought, *put her on the defensive.* "Oh, hi, Sister. I'm sorry I've been out of touch, but"—he paused and made what he hoped was a pitiful sniffling sound— "my brother died."

Sister Peg gasped. "Oh my God," she said. "How . . . I had no idea. When . . . I mean, what happened?"

Phew, Dan thought. He made the transition from burn victim to grieving next of kin and laid it on thick. He talked about the shock and how he had to decide not to tell his mother because of her emotional profile and about how there was no money for a good funeral and about all the inner turmoil that caused and on and on. It was a pathetic story convincingly told, but then Dan had always written good copy.

"I understand," Sister Peg said. "Is there anything I can do to help?"

"No." He sighed. "No, the worst has passed," Dan said, wondering if he'd crossed into melodrama. "I think I'm ready to get back to work." Dan stuck out his tongue and felt for blisters.

"If you're sure," Sister Peg said. "We really do need you out here."

"I understand," Dan said. "And again, I'm sorry I didn't call, but, well, you know, it's funny, I was going to call you at one point, but I couldn't remember the phone number out there or even where your, uh, place is." Dan realized how lame that sounded. "My grief counselor said it was post-traumatic stress amnesia. Said it's fairly common in this sort of situation."

Monsignor Matthews had told Sister Peg that Father Michael was prone to stress-related reactions, though he hadn't been specific and, at any rate, she didn't care. She just needed his help, so she gave him the phone number, the address, and a description of the place. She just hoped that he could deal with the stress of the Care Center. "So I'll see you tomorrow?"

Dan hesitated, wondering what the hell he was getting into. "I'll be there in the morning."

Butch Harnett occupied a moral universe that lacked shades of gray. Things were either right or they were wrong. Either you had sinned or you hadn't. The very finest moments of Butch's life were spent trying to find out into which category the subjects of his investigations fell.

Butch was guided by his own interpretation of Romans 3:23. "For all have sinned, and come short of the glory of God." Of course, by "all" Butch understood the verse to mean all the people who attempted to defraud his employer. Butch sensed that Dan Steele was one of the people who had sinned and come short of the glory of God.

Righteously motivated, Butch had obtained a copy of Dan's medical records in an effort to find the truth. Butch loved medical records because, as he liked to say, "you can't hide from what's inside of you." That Butch had obtained these records under false pretenses was immaterial. There was a greater good to be served and one did what one had to in order to serve it; Butch was dedicated to this credo.

Other than CPR training, Butch had no official medical education, but after ten years of poking through people's private medical files he had picked up a point or two. The thing that jumped out of this particular file was the fact that as a child, Dan Steele had received an active immunization with tetanus toxoid, and ever since then, he had received regular booster shots, his most recent a mere two years ago. Now, Butch would have been the first to admit that he didn't know all there was to know about tetanus, but he was pretty sure Dan shouldn't have had it, much less should he have died from it. But he had to make sure. That was his job. So he did some research and discovered that tetanus was an acute intoxication by the neurotoxin elaborated by *Clostridium tetani*, the spores of which were universally present in soil. When *Clostridium tetani* was introduced into a wound in the presence of necrotic tissue and impaired circulation, the spores germinated. Untreated, the bacteria elaborated tetanospasmin, a toxin that blocked the action of inhibitory mediators at spinal synapses and interfered with neuromuscular transmission. The incubation period ranged from eight days to as long as fifteen weeks. Immunization and booster shots were known to prevent the disease with nearly 100 percent efficiency, yet according to the hospital records, Dan was deader than Lazarus—the second time he died.

That could mean only one of two things. Either Dan was one of the unluckiest bastards in the world or he had, indeed, sinned.

Dan found the Care Center with no problem. It was only ten minutes from his apartment. The neighborhood was poor, like all the neighborhoods where Dan had grown up, but this was a notch or two down the food chain. This was truly grim.

Perhaps understandably, the area had a disproportionate number of churches, Sylmar being the sort of place where the promise of a reward in the next life had tremendous appeal. But that was a relatively new phenomenon. It used to be that people out here went to church to be thankful for what they had. For decades Sylmar had been a perfectly nice place to live where—for the most part—people didn't really want for anything. They were close to the mountains, not far from the amenities of a big city, and the ocean was only an hour or so to the west. But as television and radio spread, so did discontent. All those sitcoms and advertisements showed viewers all the things they didn't have, all the things that would make them happier if they did. Later, cable and satellite dishes came along, delivering not only more of the same information but also the brilliant hybrid of entertainment and advertisement known as the infomercial. And finally, with the arrival of the shopping channel, one didn't even have to get out of one's La-Z-Boy to keep up with the Hernandezes.

The message was clear and the medium was effective and after a while people who once thought they had it all began to feel something was missing in their lives. Consumerism rapidly became a lifestyle. Shopping became a form of entertainment instead of something you did when you needed something. Now people simply *wanted* stuff. They began to feel entitled to it, and they went into debt to get it. But the easy payment plans designed to help the American consumer acquire the trappings of luxury turned out to be an albatross, especially in poorer neighborhoods. Despite an economy expanding at a record pace, per capita savings was down to zero while personal bankruptcies were reaching historic levels. Before long, people were drowning in debt, hounded by debt collectors, and were told they simply couldn't afford the American dream. Sorry.

That's when the Church's age-old product began to look attractive again. From a manufacturer's point of view, the notion of eternal happiness in the next life was the perfect commodity. "Its the only product you will ever need!" Its perfection lay in the fact that the consumer—exploiting the original layaway plan—paid for it every Sunday but had to die in order to find out if the sales pitch was true. "It never needs ironing!" No one in the history of mankind had ever returned the product for a full refund. Not even Microsoft managed that.

Dan pulled into the dirt driveway and parked in the shade of a fruitless orange tree. Stepping out of the old van, Dan waved at the dust kicked up by his arrival. He was nervous. He feared that this Sister Peg would nail him as a fraud the moment he walked in the door, and then where would he be? He took some comfort in the fact that Michael had seen Sister Peg only once and then not for long. But even if he managed to fool the nun, his mother was a different story. What would she do when she found out? The possibilities seemed endless and none were in his favor.

Dan brushed the dust from his black pants and shirt, then checked himself in the side mirror. He straightened his clerical collar, then turned to look at his future. It was a large tan ramshackle building, its paint sloughing off like skin from a snake. Broken windowpanes had been replaced with cardboard and the roof shingles were all but red dust. The place lacked a lot of things, chief among them hope.

It reminded Dan of his past—hell, it *was* his past. And just as he began to conjure unpleasant memories from his childhood, Dan felt something. It wasn't a shiver or a shock, it was something he'd never felt and it wasn't altogether unpleasant. Then, as quickly as it had come, it was gone. Dan shrugged it off as mild anxiety.

As he approached the front door, Mrs. Ciocchetti came out. She wore a black veil draped over a crown of gray-black hair as though she were mourning. Her face was despair personified. *Oh Lord*, he thought, *I hate dealing with old people*. It was too late to turn around. She had seen him already and, oddly, she had brightened like a star. She straightened up and beamed a silver smile. "Good morning, Father," she said, crossing herself. Her tone was sweet and respectful, not at all what Dan had expected.

"Good morning," he said, surprising himself with a smile of his own. The exchange was simple but no less striking for its simplicity. His mere presence seemed to have enriched this woman's day. He had made a genuine emotional connection with a stranger without the aid of a gently manipulative long-distance phone call commercial, something Dan didn't think was possible. It was the same thing that had happened at the grocery store, and it made him consider the responsibility that came with his new station. Ever since he'd put on the clericals, everyone Dan encountered looked at him as if he had something they longed for. Guidance? Hope? Wisdom? Well, something. It was something Dan wasn't sure he could deliver.

Dan became aware of a slight tingling on the crown of his head. He didn't know if it was the painful itch of eczema, the heartbreak of psoriasis, or something more divine in nature. In any event, it itched, so Dan scratched.

Dan went inside and wandered down the hall looking for Sister Peg. His anxiety had vanished. He suddenly felt like he belonged here. The place was no longer a squalid tenement of hopelessness but a haven in need of repair—repair that Dan could supply. Walking down the hallway, Dan could hear a television and he thought he smelled cheese. "Sister Peg?" he called out, but no one responded.

Near the foot of a stairway, he poked his head into Alissa's bedroom. At first he didn't see her, but as he turned to leave, she caught his eye. She was sitting in the corner on the floor with her ragged cloth doll. Dan tried to look benevolent. "Hello," he said.

Alissa looked up, giving Dan a view of her face. It was still slightly discolored from the healing bruises. Dan was struck cold. It was a terrible reminder of precisely why advertisers used images to convey their messages. The sight of this small damaged child was more powerful than Christ on the cross. It also reminded Dan of his childhood. He stepped into the room and crouched down. He hoped his clericals would ease the girl's mind. "I'm not going to hurt you," Dan said. "Are you okay?" Dan's attempt at a tender smile resulted in lips that looked more like a disconsolate oyster.

Alissa pulled her doll closer and watched Dan with distrust.

"My name's"—there was a long pause—"Father Michael." It was the first time he'd told the lie and it stuck a little on the way out. The fact that he was lying to an abused child a mere ten seconds after first setting eyes on her may have added to the delay. "What's yours?"

Alissa looked down at the floor and said nothing.

"Well, you don't have to tell me if you don't want," Dan said. "I understand. I've been scared before too." Dan suddenly felt emotions he'd locked away decades ago, feelings of abandonment and vulnerability. The fear of being small in a large world with no one to protect you. He wanted to comfort this little girl, but he had no idea how. He'd had no practice. Still, he had to do something. "I tell you what," he said. "I'll be around for a while and whenever you want something, you come to me and I'll get it for you, how's that?" Alissa looked up just the slightest bit. She seemed leery.

The tingling sensation suddenly returned. It started on Dan's scalp and worked its way down his body. He looked at his hands hoping to see whatever it was, but it wasn't visible. It was as if his soul had opened up suddenly and, in one clarifying moment, revealed to Dan that this was his chance to re-create himself—to be born again. The new, improved, holier-than-ever Dan Steele, as it were. "Don't worry," he said to the little girl. "It's going to be all right."

Dan backed into the hall and eased the door shut. He looked down at his outfit and, like a newly minted superhero coming to terms with the powers imparted by a change of clothes, Dan was reminded of the potential for doing good that came with his new outfit. It wasn't the sort of good that came from convincing people that they needed whiter, brighter teeth, or fresher-smelling breath. This was real, sincere, honest-to-God good.

I've been put here to help these people, he thought. It was so . . . not Dan. Yet at the same time, Dan couldn't believe he had ever felt otherwise. Dan didn't know whether to be euphoric or terrified. Naturally, he was suspicious of the whole thing, but even his natural skepticism couldn't dampen this . . . this thing that had chosen him. It was the strangest thing, and he embraced it.

"Well, hello there." The voice snapped Dan back from his rapture. He turned and saw a woman in blue jeans, a dirty work shirt, and a baseball cap. She was about his age, maybe a bit younger. She had wisps of brown hair, slick with sweat, stuck to the side of her face and she had the slightest crow's-feet pointing to gentle brown eyes. After a moment, Dan realized he was staring. "Oh. Hello," he said, blushing. As he came back down the stairs he noticed the thing on the woman's head wasn't a baseball cap at all. It was a wimple, and that could only mean one thing. The woman wearing it was a nun—presumably *the* nun. "Oh, I'm sorry, Sister," Dan flustered. "It's good to see you again." He extended his hand. "I'm glad to be back."

Sister Peg gazed at him sympathetically. "You poor man," she said. She reached over and took both of Dan's hands. She looked into his eyes, her head tilted just so. "I am so sorry about your brother," she said.

Her sincerity put Dan at ease. "Thank you, Sister." Dan had been so struck by what was happening to him and by the image of Alissa that he'd forgotten he was supposed to be playing the role of the grieving brother. Despite his spiritual rebirth, Dan wasn't convinced that "honesty is the best policy" applied in this situation. His practical side argued it was better to accomplish some good under pretense than confess and risk jail. "I appreciate that, Sister. He was my"—Dan nearly said "twin," but he stopped—"my only brother. I don't know how I'll tell Mom."

Sister Peg shook her head slightly. "It's never easy," she said. "But I'm sure you'll find a way." She motioned for Dan to follow her. "Let's go to my office." As they walked, Sister Peg wondered what Father Michael knew about her. They had met so briefly that first time, they were essentially strangers. When Monsignor Matthews arranged for Father Michael to work at the Care Center, he told Sister Peg a few things about Father Michael's past. She wondered if the Monsignor had told Father Michael anything about hers.

As Dan followed Sister Peg down the hall, he made a list of the things he needed to do. The place was gloom central. There were holes in the drywall that needed repair, a door that needed to be put back on its hinges, and the industrial gray paint had to go. They went into Sister Peg's cramped office and sat down. Her desk was a storm of paper. Post-it notes with names and phone numbers were everywhere—these were the latest additions to her network of helpful cops, food-bank managers, and potential volunteers. Social service directories and books on how to write grant proposals were stacked like masonry, forming a wall on one side of the desk. Sister Peg moved a pile of papers from a chair and motioned for Dan to sit. She wanted to lend him a sympathetic ear before putting him to work. "Had your brother been ill?" she asked.

"He never said anything to me. It just came out of the blue." Dan thought about that for a moment. Would Michael still be alive had Dan been more probing about his sickly appearance the day he arrived—or would that have served only to get Dan into the clericals sooner?

Sister Peg rolled her head to one side. "What did he do?" she asked. "For a living, I mean." Her neck made a satisfying cracking noise.

"He was in advertising," Dan said. "But he hated it." This was the first time Dan had acknowledged this. It surprised him, but it was true. All that insane pressure and hustling and energy expended in an effort to differentiate one identical light beer from another. "The creative part appealed to him and he was good at it, from what I gather."

"Sounds like a good guy," Sister Peg said.

"He had his moments." Dan was uncomfortable talking about himself in the dead tense, but he thought it would seem odd not to continue. So they talked about the late Dan Steele for a few more minutes before Dan turned the conversation to his duties and the residents at the Care Center. He wanted to ask specifically about the little girl, but since Sister Peg may have told Michael all about her, he feigned absentmindedness and just asked about her name.

"Alissa," Sister Peg said. "She's improved a little since you saw her. In fact, she smiled a few days ago, thanks to your mom. But she still spends most of her time in her room." Sister Peg rooted through the papers until she found a discouraging letter from the District Attorney's office. "I'm still trying to get a court order to keep her dad away when he gets out, but the courts seem to think children should be with their parents, regardless of their parenting skills."

Dan nodded. In the meager catalogue of things he refused to tolerate, the abuse and neglect of children was at the top, but there was nothing to be done in that regard at the moment, so Dan focused his energy elsewhere. "Sister, if you don't mind, I think I should go see my mom and then maybe I should get to work." As he stood, Dan noticed all the overdue bills among the papers on the desk. "Do you know where she is?"

"I think she went upstairs to play cards."

Every day people are straying away from church and going back to God.

—LENNY BRUCE

Ruth was playing it close to the vest. "Okay, Saltzman." She pointed at him. "Put a dollar in the kitty." He scowled and did as he was told. Ruth peeked at her cards. "Now, who's in?" She looked around the table at the competition. Sixty-six-year-old Mrs. Gerbracht was to her left. As always, she was wearing her giant black bouffant wig, copious wagon red lipstick, and a leopard scarf twisted around her crêpey neck.

"Mrs. Gerbracht, we're waiting."

Mrs. Gerbracht studied her cards as if they were slides under a microscope. "I'm thinking." She'd been losing all morning with decent cards, so she didn't have much faith in her pair of eights. "Fold," she said finally.

Mr. Avery was the youngest of the older set at the Care Center. He wore a sporty checked shirt and had a spray of freckles across his cheeks that made you think he had played in the outfield as a kid. He was the only one at the table who didn't wear glasses. Having gone for the long shot with a one-card draw, Mr. Avery was looking at four clubs and a spade. He looked around at his elderly opponents and wondered if their eyes were bad enough that he could get away with calling it a flush. He considered the stakes, then he flipped his cards into the middle of the table. "Shit," was all he said.

Mrs. Zamora nodded approvingly. She was sitting next to Mr. Avery and had been looking at his hand the entire time. She didn't consider it cheating, since she had folded without benefit of drawing any cards. Mrs. Zamora knew the odds were far too long to improve what she'd been dealt. She reached over and took a cube of cheese from the nearby TV tray.

Mr. Saltzman lifted his wrinkled eyelids and looked at Ruth. He tried to read her, but the lines in her face weren't revealing any secrets. He made a grumbling noise.

"You still alive there, Saltzman?" Ruth asked. "It's time to shit or get off the pot."

Mr. Saltzman glowered at Ruth. He looked like a crusty old prospector who hadn't shaved in a few days; a patchy white growth of stubble covered his bony face. He looked back at his hand. It was the best he'd had all morning. He felt he was due, so he made his play. "Straight to the jack," he said, smearing the cards faceup onto the table.

"Damn," Ruth said, prompting a smile from Mr. Saltzman. "You stayed with a straight?" Ruth chuckled. Saltzman didn't. Ruth neatly laid her cards on the table. "Boat," she said. "Jacks over treys."

The other women at the table hooted and slapped the tabletop. Mr. Saltzman's already unpleasant expression soured further. "C'mon, pay up," Mrs. Zamora said.

"And put on the hat," Mr. Avery insisted.

"Yeah," Mrs. Gerbracht said, "you must do it with the fez on."

Mr. Saltzman, who, at this point, was down to his boxers, stood and glared at everyone. He felt he'd been cheated, but since he couldn't prove anything, he put on the hat. Then he hooked his gnarled thumbs on the frayed elastic band of his boxers and pushed down, revealing himself to be less of a man than he had led some to believe.

"Sweet Jesus! What are you doing?"

Everyone turned and saw the priest standing in the doorway. Ruth did a double take. "Playing strip poker," she said. "Care to join us? That collar's probably good for two hands."

"No!" Dan said. He'd never seen a sight as unpleasant as what lay before him, a half dozen puckered bodies in various states of undress, one of which was his mother's.

Mr. Saltzman pointed at Ruth. "I think she cheats," he grumbled.

Mrs. Zamora put her old elbows on the table. "Quit complaining and dance," she said.

Dan began waving his hands wildly. "No! No dancing!" he yelled. "You people get dressed. The game's over." Everyone groaned and began putting their clothes back on. Despite their combined four hundred years of experience at getting dressed, the process was slow and painful to watch. The shock of all the pendulous flesh momentarily knocked the Holy Spirit out of Dan, much the way a sharp blow to the thorax knocks the wind out of you.

"You're looking better." Ruth stared at Dan as she slipped on a shoe, the only thing she had lost in the game. "I've missed you."

"Yeah," Dan said. "I missed you too." He didn't know where to start. He couldn't just blurt out the truth. *Say, listen, Mom, I'm really Dan. I'm afraid Michael's dead and I've committed a couple of felonies. And I'd appreciate it if you could keep that to yourself.* He had no idea how she'd react. Would she go goofy and blow his cover? He couldn't take that chance. Dan noticed that Ruth was looking intently at him. He worried that she had some secret way of telling him from Michael that he never knew about. He turned slightly so she couldn't see his face full on. "Have you been taking your medicine?" he asked.

She smiled. "I haven't been arrested lately, if that answers your question." She stood and walked to the door.

Dan could tell that Ruth's mind was fixed on something, but she wasn't sharing it. Or maybe he was being paranoid. He decided that unless she asked directly about Dan, he would avoid the subject. He also decided not to tell Ruth any direct lies, his thinking being that a sin of omission was less serious than a sin of commission.

"So," Ruth said as she headed out the door. "Have you heard from your brother lately?"

Goddammit, Dan thought. *What did she mean by that? She said "your brother," not "Dan."* Was it an innocent phrasing or a sly acknowledgment that she knew he wasn't Michael? "Yeah," Dan said. "He's in New York on a business trip. Something to do with that Fujioka campaign." *Okay, so I lied.* Still, it was better than upsetting his mom and running the risk of being exposed. He couldn't save this place from jail, after all.

"That's nice." Ruth tried to get a good look at her son's face. "You know, it looks like you've put on some weight in the last couple of weeks. So tell me what you've been up to."

Dan looked skyward and prayed for guidance.

Scott Emmons had been raised without benefit of religion. His father considered church attendance an unforgivable waste of anyone's time. He didn't forbid his wife from taking Scott to the occasional Unitarian service, but he usually made sarcastic remarks about it. "While you're there you better ask forgiveness for not using your time more productively," he'd say.

The result of all this was a spiritual yearning that Scott completely misinterpreted. While he was vaguely aware that something was missing in his life, he had no idea what it was. Influenced by his father's lack of faith, and the lack of prayer in the public schools he attended, Scott looked elsewhere to fill his spiritual void. He dabbled in a series of pop psychology movements, New Age flightiness, and, most recently, motivational tapes. With each new approach, he felt a brief sense that he had finally tapped into the real thing, the answer to his vague question. But each time the feeling would pass like a cheap high, and Scott would be forced off on his continuing search for meaning and direction.

At the moment, however, standing at the door of St. Bernadine of Siena Catholic church, Scott felt sublimely focused on his life's mission. He entered the church carrying a Bible, thinking, among other things, that it would help him blend in. The Bible was a pulpit-size, jumbo set of Scriptures, hefty enough to use as a weapon. After purchasing it at a used-book store, Scott took it home and edited it. Using a single-edge razor blade, Scott cut a large hole through both Testaments. It was not a coincidence that the hole was in the shape of his Ruger Super Redhawk .44 magnum.

Scott paused at the large baptismal and saw his reflection on the surface of the holy water. Curious, Scott dipped a finger into the water and tasted it—it was salty and somewhat oily. He spit. There were only a few people in the church, some seated in pews gazing at the altar, some kneeling, deep in prayer, a few standing in line for confession. Scott took his place in the line, clutching the Bible tightly to his chest. He wasn't exactly sure what he would do if he got into the little box and heard Dan's voice coming from behind the screen. He'd just have to improvise.

A few minutes later it was Scott's turn. He entered the confessional and stood there with all the uncertainty of a first-timer. It was cramped, dark, and a little scary. He wondered where he was supposed to sit. He groped around until his foot hit something. It was too low and narrow to sit on, so he knelt.

The priest waited patiently for Scott to declare his guilt; however, since Scott was unfamiliar with confessional protocol, he didn't know he was supposed to make the first move. There was a long silence as they each waited for the other to speak. Finally Scott decided to break the ice. He cleared his throat. "More is more," he whispered.

The priest, who was, admittedly, new on the job, wasn't sure what to make of that. After a long silence, the priest decided to guide the sinner. "Have you come to ask forgiveness?"

Scott twitched at the voice, which seemed familiar. Scott opened his Bible and removed his gun. "Yes," he said, hoping the man would speak again.

"How long has it been since your last confession?" The voice had certain qualities that reminded Scott of his former boss. Scott's heart began to race as he raised the gun. Still, he wanted to be sure before he did anything rash. "Could you say that again?" Scott asked. The priest repeated his question. Scott tried to look through the small screen, but all he could make out was a silhouette of a man's face. It *might* be Dan, he thought.

The priest, thinking the penitent was hard of hearing, raised his voice. "I said, how long has it been since—"

Click. It was the unmistakable sound of a large gun being cocked. The priest stopped breathing for a moment. There seemed to be only a couple of explanations for such a sound in a confessional. The best one, from the priest's perspective, was that the man on the other side was so distressed at his sins that he was contemplating suicide. The more worrisome explanation was that the sinner had an ax to grind with the church. "Listen to me, my son," he said, his voice steady. "I hereby absolve you of whatever sins you have committed as well as all sins you may commit in the future." Then he made his move.

Scott felt a sudden rush of air when the priest bolted. Assuming it was Dan trying to escape his past, Scott dove out of his side of the confessional and blindsided the man, sending him sprawling onto the floor. Scott scrambled to his feet and freed himself from the curtain in which he was tangled. The curtain fell to Scott's feet and he stood there—Bible in one hand, gun in the other. He looked down and saw the terrified priest. He was a short guy with red hair in his thirties who was, at this point, prepared to make a deal with the devil if it meant not dying like this. Scott stared at the man, wondering if he'd ever find Dan. "Shit," he said. He put the gun back in the Bible and headed for the door.

"Dammit!" Monsignor Matthews was doing his best to help the poor, but he had just hit an internal fire wall in the Church's intranet while trying to access some directories that, technically speaking, he lacked authorization to access. He wanted to do one of his sleight-of-hand fund transfers for the Care Center, but someone had made that damned difficult.

Frustrated, Monsignor Matthews dragged a hand across his face while considering the virtue of patience. It used to be that the highest level of security was simple password protection, but that was before someone started airing filthy bits of the Church's laundry—various soiled items that were supposed to remain hidden in a large directory of obliquely named files. After the breach, the higher-ups brought in computer consultants who retrofitted the system with some serious fire walls. Now, despite his fluency in several computer languages, Monsignor Matthews doubted his ability to hack past these new features. If he couldn't get in, no funds would get transferred, and if he didn't transfer the funds, there was no telling what Sister Peg might do. He tried a wormhole-tunneling maneuver that had worked for him in the past, but access was denied again. "Dammit!"

Matthews hadn't always been such a dissident. When he became a priest, he wanted—and expected—to spend the rest of his life serving Jesus Christ through the Church, ministering to the sick, caring for a congregation, that sort of thing. But instead of a parish, he got a computer terminal. Sure, he got to sit in on the celebration of a mass now and then, but for the most part he served the Lord by dealing with the sophisticated financial matters of the Church.

For the first few years that was all right. Then he stumbled across some disturbing files detailing the Church's legal and financial strategies for handling sexual abuse cases. One case in particular caught his eye. A priest in a large diocese in the Southwest had sexually assaulted a dozen altar boys over the course of ten years. When parents of the boys complained, the Church covered it up. Then one of the boys committed suicide and the story broke. The Church got dragged—kicking and screaming—into the courts. Before it was over, senior Church officials were found guilty of gross negligence, malice, conspiracy, and fraud for ignoring the warnings about the priest as well as for covering up the parents' complaints.

The jury eventually ordered the Church to pay $119 million to the victims. A Catholic spokesman, who seemed quite put out about the matter, was quoted as saying, "The Church just wants to get the whole thing behind them." He may as well have said they wanted to act like it never happened. A newly appointed bishop offered a sincere public apology to the victims, but the parents of the dead child had the temerity to note that neither the money nor the apology would bring their son back.

It was enough to shake Monsignor Matthews's faith. He

knew as well as anyone that it was impossible to screen out all the rotten apples in an organization as large as the Catholic Church, so he didn't blame the Church for the priest's actions. It was the cover-up that galled him.

Had that been the lone case or if there were but a few more, Monsignor Matthews would have let it go, but it turned out this was just the tip of the pederastic iceberg. There were hundreds of other files on similar cases. The same diocese had been forced into a $5 million settlement involving two different priests and five other altar boys. In another Southwest diocese, an Archbishop disgraced the Church when the details of his sexual misconduct showed up on *60 Minutes*. The subsequent investigation of widespread cover-ups led to the removal of twenty priests and the settlement of 165 clergy sex-abuse cases totaling another $50 million. No damn wonder the diocese was always crying poor mouth.

Almost as startling as the corruption was the fact that the Church was, to an extent, insured against this sort of thing. Given the Church's track record, Monsignor Matthews imagined the rates for that sort of coverage were staggering, like insuring the post office against employee shooting sprees.

As Monsignor Matthews worked his way through the files, he discovered that a great many parishes were nearly bankrupted by paying settlements for these types of cases and—most amazing—that some of the money used to pay for these crimes came from parish fund-raising drives. Matthews wondered how they sold that to the congregation. "Remember, next weekend is the big catamite car wash and bake sale . . ."

Matthews also found what appeared to be a slush fund tucked away in the undisclosed financial records. The money was apparently used to pay parents who were willing to be bought off instead of taking their children's complaints to the proper authorities.

The Monsignor knew that in some instances the guilty priests were quickly removed from their duties. But in many more instances the Church simply denied the charges, covered up the cases, and moved priests to other parishes where they continued to prey on others. Sometimes they were sent to a "retreat center" in New Mexico for some therapy—the Church's equivalent of a child's "time-out"—before being reassigned to a new parish where they could resume practicing their true faith on new children.

Monsignor Matthews was floored when he tallied everything up. He found that the Catholic Church had paid over $800 million to settle sex-abuse cases in the United States since 1985. Eight. Hundred. Million. Dollars. He shook his head. How many children could be fed with $800 million? He could almost see the shame on St. Paul's face.

Monsignor Matthews knew he was in no position to confront higher-ups about the policies and handling of these matters—he felt he could do more from where he was than if he were excommunicated—so he decided to play a game of his own, and that game involved diverting money from the slush fund to various charities. Unfortunately for Monsignor Matthews, the Church's accounts receivable department was breathing down his neck and the newly installed fire wall was impervious to his hacking. It was starting to look like he would have to face the wrath of Sister Peg.

When Dan first arrived at the Care Center, he figured he'd be doing fix-it projects and maybe some cooking and cleaning. Inspired by what he assumed was the Holy Ghost, Dan put in eighteen-hour days fixing every broken window and leaky faucet and light switch in the place. Dan thought he had found his true calling as the handyman to the poor.

Dan was ready for his next assignment, so he went to

Sister Peg's office and asked what she wanted him to do. "I need you to help Captain Boone with his bath and his appliance," she said.

"Appliance?" Dan was clueless.

"His colostomy bag," she said. "It needs to be changed." Dan looked at her as if she'd asked him to crucify the old man.

"Is there a problem?" Sister Peg asked.

"Uhhhh," Dan replied. "No." He forced a smile. "Not a problem." Without thinking, Dan wiped his hands on his pants. His spiritual bubble had just burst. The job itself was bad enough, but worse was the fact that the thing Dan had assumed was the Holy Ghost had disappeared the moment Sister Peg asked him to do it. Dan was disillusioned. It never occurred to him that he'd actually have to work at maintaining his faith. It wasn't that his spirit was willing and his flesh was weak, though certainly the latter was true. It was more that his spirit was wholly repulsed. Dan had never considered helping anyone with their personal hygiene. It was the sort of notion that took some getting used to. It was a test of faith.

Sister Peg was surprised. She assumed he had done far more unpleasant things in Africa. "Let me tell you about Captain Boone," she said. "He earned a Purple Heart in World War Two—and I mean he *earned* it. His unit was in a small town in France, I think, when the Germans launched a mortar attack. Captain Boone heard screams coming from a building, so he went in to see if he could help. He dragged several people out and was going back for one more when he got hit. The doctors kept him alive, but they left him with the appliance. And you know what? I've never heard him complain about it."

Up until now, Dan had been proud of the sacrifices he had made in order to help out at the Care Center. He'd given up his fine car and his view apartment and his fancy job. Granted, they weren't voluntary sacrifices, but still, he had given himself points for his efforts.

"Not only did he not complain, he didn't even tell me about it," Sister Peg said. "I only found out when I went to the VA to find out why he doesn't get any benefits."

Dan's mouth began to form the word "why," but nothing came out.

Sister Peg's mouth twisted into something ugly. "A 'snafu,'" she said. "Situation normal, all fucked up." She looked away quickly and made a gesture conveying her frustration. Then she looked back at Dan. "Pardon my French, Father," she said. "It just makes me mad."

"Forget it," he said. "I think you're showing restraint." Dan looked at her eyes and saw fight and compassion and maybe some loneliness. "What sort of snafu?"

"I've been trying for two years to get an explanation," Sister Peg said. "But the Veterans Affairs bureaucracy is a disaster. They say they can't find the necessary paperwork."

"Have you tried threatening them?" Dan smiled.

Sister Peg smiled back, unsure if Father Michael would approve of her tactics. "I've tried everything," she said. "Though sometimes I wonder why I try at all." She grabbed a stack of overdue bills and looked to see which one she could pay.

As he made his way up the stairs, Dan wrestled his self-consciousness. This was so *not* Dan. Until recently, the most help Dan ever offered anyone was to hold a door open. But he knew he had to change. He had to learn how to do this sort of thing. He had to learn to care. Out of the blue it occurred to Dan that he also wanted to impress Sister Peg. What the hell was that?

Dan paused at the top of the stairs and took a deep breath, hoping to suck some inspiration or, better still, some courage from the air. *I can do this*, he thought. He thought he felt the courage coming on until he heard the gunshot, then he hit the floor so hard he thought he'd broken his nose. Dan assumed that Emmons had tracked him down at the Care Center and was shooting his way in the front door. Dan heard another shot, though this time it sounded less like a gun than a car backfiring. He crawled to the window and peeked out. He saw Ruben under the hood of the Suburban tinkering with the carburetor. Dan knew he'd never be a martyr.

Dan found Captain Boone in his room down the hall. He was eighty years old and wronged by arthritis. He had a round, jowly face and big dull teeth. He still sported a military buzz cut; the short white stubs of hair lent his head the aspect of a round albino cactus. He was wearing a thin cotton bathrobe and slippers. Dan forced a reassuring smile as he walked into the room. He hoped his priest outfit would do most of the work.

Captain Boone saw Dan's awkwardness the moment he walked in. He could tell the young priest was going to need help. "Good morning, Father," he said, all chipper. "Do me a favor and relax, all right?" His voice was gruff, vaguely Southern, and grandfatherly. "I know this is a bit unpleasant, but I do need the help and I appreciate your giving it. I truly do." He adjusted himself in his chair. "And just so you won't accuse me of not helping, I'm going to tell you some war stories that'll make this little job seem like a walk in a rose garden." He laughed like an old army guy and gestured for Dan to come over.

The gesture alone lightened Dan's burden and made him grateful. Still, he felt the itch of embarrassment as he approached his task. "Thanks," Dan said, still uncertain of his capacity to care. "I've got to tell you, I've never done this before."

Captain Boone put the back of his hand to his forehead and feigned a swoon. "Just be gentle with me, kind sir."

He sounded like a crusty old Southern belle. He laughed again. "Come 'ere, it's easy. Just give the old outer layer a quick scrub with a warm rag and then change the bag like an oil filter. Nothing to it." He could see Dan trying to imagine what it would be like. "Okay," Captain Boone said, "there's *something* to it, and quite frankly, it stinks like shit." He laughed again. "There's no getting around that." He nodded toward his bedside table at a box of rubber gloves and a can of air freshener. "Give us a quick spray before you get started," the Captain said. "It's patchouli. Pretend we're in an East Indian whorehouse."

Dan couldn't believe this guy. Damaged on some foreign battlefield, all but forgotten by his government, spending his last days being washed by strangers—and he still had a sense of humor. He was such a fundamentally decent man that his first concern was making Dan feel, if not exactly comfortable, then at least less *un*comfortable. Dan thought Captain Boone would have made a great dad. Especially when compared to his own.

Dan helped Captain Boone into the tub, and with his guidance Dan bathed him. All the while, Captain Boone told Dan distracting stories of war and death and the ghastly sacrifices he had seen men make. Each story was peppered with coarse language and dirty jokes. Dan smirked, then laughed, and soon was no more self-conscious than if he were washing Captain Boone's car. When Dan got around to the man's botched abdomen, he was comfortable enough to say what came to his mind. "If you don't mind my saying so, sir, that is one nasty fucking scar." He looked closely at the tissue. The skin looked like dripped wax.

Captain Boone nodded and told Dan what happened. "Damn mortar hit me clean, right here." He pointed a gnarled finger at the left upper quadrant of his abdomen. "The surgeons had to remove my spleen seein' as how it had ruptured into about a hundred pieces. They fished the parts out of a pool of shit in my gut, did a complete transection of my transverse colon, or so they told me. The only thing they could do to avoid more fecal contamination was to do a diverting colostomy. And it's been shit-in-a-bag ever since," he said, almost with pride. "But it could've been worse. The damn mortar could have hit me here." He pointed at his heart and smiled.

Dan nodded thoughtfully, amazed that anyone could find a bright side to having lost the better part of their digestive tract. As Dan continued washing, Captain Boone talked about his wife and two children who had died years ago and about how he had lost touch with most of his buddies from the war. But he told it all matter-of-factly, without sadness. "Of course, that's not the way you want it to be," he said. "But what the heck, that's the way it is. I just accept that the Lord has a plan and that I'm just not ready to understand it yet."

Dan imagined the man sixty years ago when everything lay in front of him—when he was all potential and enthusiasm and hopes and dreams. And then he was a soldier shedding his blood fighting for others. And then his government lost track of him and his family died and his comrades disappeared and the man was left all but alone, everything lost but his dignity.

Dan felt Captain Boone's hand on his forearm. "Now, do a lonely old army man a favor," Captain Boone said. "Give my crooked old dick a good, sweet scrubbin', okay?" He leaned back in the tub and looked up at Dan.

Dan froze. He had no idea what to do or say. He fumbled for words and tried to avoid eye contact, then he saw the smirk on Captain Boone's face and realized that he'd been had. Dan tossed the washrag into the Captain's lap. "I don't think your arthritis is that bad, sir," he said with a laugh. "Scrub it yourself."

The old man's grin kept spreading. "Oh pleeeease . . ."

Captain Boone whined. "Pretty please . . ." He laughed, full of gusto and enjoying the moment. He pointed at Dan. "I gotcha, Padre! You shoulda seen the look on your face!" He imitated the expression until Dan finally burst out laughing.

Ruth had a funny feeling. She could have gone to her son and asked a few simple questions—he was just downstairs, after all—but if she was right, his answers would most likely be lies. Besides, she'd already tried to corner him a few times since the poker game, but he kept avoiding her. He was too busy to talk when she found him alone, and when they were in the kitchen or the TV room with the other residents, somebody was bound to hear her, and she didn't want that.

Ruth could think of only one solution, so she picked up the phone and dialed. A woman's voice came on the other end of the line, warbling. "We're sorry, the number you have dialed is no longer in service. If you feel you have reached this number in error . . ." Ruth hung up. *That's not good.* She waited a minute before she picked up the phone and dialed again. She thought about hanging up and just living with not knowing, but then another woman's voice came on the line. "The Prescott Agency."

Ruth braced herself. "Dan Steele, please."

There was a pause. "I'm very sorry, but Mr. Steele passed away recently. Can I put you through to someone else?"

"No. Thank you." Ruth hung up.

There seemed to be a very limited number of explanations for the set of facts she had, and no matter how hard she tried, Ruth couldn't keep Michael alive in any of them. He was gone, she was certain of it. She wondered what had happened. Now she had no choice. She would simply have to confront Dan. But how? She didn't want to do it in front of anyone. Dan might be in some sort of trouble. *Why hadn't he come to me?* It didn't take long to figure out. *He was probably afraid I was so crazy that I'd blow his cover.*

It was hard enough to deal with that, but then it hit her that Michael was dead and she hadn't said good-bye. One of her babies was gone. Ruth's hand slid off the phone and she curled up on her bed and began to cry.

Father Michael spends three more years working in Africa before he snaps again. It's a nasty combination of things that pushes him over the edge the second time. In some parts of the country he sees people starve to death because the land can't be cultivated. In other parts, he sees them starve to death because starvation is simply another weapon in the civil wars and the tribal conflicts that define the continent. No matter what the charitable organizations say in their fund-raising brochures, Father Michael knows the truth, and that is what makes him crack. The truth is that most of the food and medicine shipped into these war-torn areas goes to whichever army controls the roads and the airstrips. In other words, the recipients of the charity are the same people who create the need for it in the first place. The supplies in turn strengthen these militias and allow them to continue causing problems, thus bringing in more charity.

The result of this corrupt cycle is death and suffering on a titanic scale. Dealing with that level of misery and sorrow is trying enough, but something else gnaws at Father Michael. His faith is under attack. He had turned to religion thirty years earlier, looking for a way to exist with his childhood. He bought everything they sold. He cultivated a deep faith, joined the priesthood, then went to practice it in a very difficult place. This is where the theology began to fail.

Father Michael has come to realize that organized religion is at the root of the problems he is fighting. Horrible, bloody wars between Muslims and Christians kill untold numbers and displace hundreds of thousands of others, leaving them to wander semiarid wastelands cutting the throats of animals in order to get enough fluids to stay alive. Sometimes it is done in the name of God, other times Allah's name is invoked. In other parts of Africa, Father Michael knows, millions of lives can be saved by handing out birth control along with food, but that sort of thing doesn't fly with the guys back in Rome.

It isn't that Father Michael has lost his faith in God, but he certainly has lost his faith in the Church. More correctly, he has lost his faith in the reactionary fraternity of old men who run the Church as if it is a twelfth-century country club. They are patronizing misogynists utterly disconnected from reality. Their policies encourage the starvation of millions of babies and treat women as second-class citizens whose primary worth is defined by their willingness to reproduce. These are the men who took fifty years to admit that not speaking out against the Holocaust was wrongish. These are the men who denied for several centuries that killing millions during the Inquisition was a somewhat less than Christian thing to do. Father Michael takes no comfort when he hears that the Vatican is hosting a three-day symposium on the Inquisition in a feeble attempt to address the past sins of the Roman Catholic Church. He thinks maybe they should be taking a closer look at their current crop.

Surrounded by so much death and rendered helpless by governments, armies, and his own Church, Father Michael comes to believe that nothing in his world will change unless he changes it himself. Unable to do anything about the larger problems, Father Michael obsesses on the smaller ones. If he can just get food and clean water into the belly of one child, delaying that child's miserable, stinking death by a single day, he feels he will be doing God's work.

It is to this end that Father Michael approaches a man who is known as General Garang. He is a belligerent African rebel leader who makes a good living on the misfortune of some and the charity of others. He has narrow, piercing eyes and a wide, flat nose.

"I have a proposal," Father Michael says.

General Garang is used to making deals with the aid workers. He likes them because they tend to keep their word. Garang smiles. "I am always interested in something profitable."

Father Michael explains that a man has come to him looking to buy human organs.

"And where do I come in?" Garang asks. "I am certainly not interested in selling." He chuckles and looks at one of his bodyguards, who laughs despite not knowing why he should.

"The refugees will sell," Father Michael says. "I just need money to pay them first."

"Why doesn't this man just take what he wants?" Garang asks. "The refugees are too weak to fight back."

Father Michael hesitates a moment. "He says he's a Christian, and that would be stealing. He wants to pay for them. Give me the loan and you will triple your money in a week."

General Garang sits forward and looks into Father Michael's eyes. After a tense moment, he smiles and says, "If you can't trust a priest, who can you trust?" He turns to one of his guards and says something. The man goes into the next room and returns a minute later with a small canvas satchel containing several thousand U.S. dollars.

Dan made a pile of the dirty sheets. He looked at the Care Center's ancient Whirlpool washer and the box of generic laundry detergent and had serious doubts about their ability to get things whiter than white. Dan reached into the box of detergent, deeper and deeper until he hit the gritty bottom of the nearly empty container. He tilted and shook and thumped the box until he had rallied half a cup of soap flakes. When Michael had said the place was short on funding, Dan had assumed that was just poor-mouth posturing, another way of saying it would be nice to have more money. Now, after being there a week, Dan knew the place was in bad financial shape, but the question was, how bad?

Across the kitchen Ruben and Sister Peg were cleaning up after breakfast. Dan watched as they signed to one another between dirty dishes. A curled index finger brushed his cheek, then he slapped one hand backward into the other. She crossed an X over her heart and rubbed a set of knuckles in small counterclockwise circles on her breastbone. Hopelessly locked out of their silent conversation, Dan simply enjoyed the ballet of the thing, fingers dancing in elegant chatter. Dan didn't care what they were talking about as long as he could watch Sister Peg's hands. He

couldn't stop looking at her hands. They were soft as forgiveness despite the hard work.

Dan took an armful of warm, dry towels over to a table
and started folding them. He was trying to think of a fund-
raising scheme when two men walked into the kitchen.
They were in their thirties, wearing nearly identical suits.
One of them brandished a Louis Vuitton briefcase as
though it proved something. The other one conspicuously
displayed a $2,000 Mont Blanc pen in his breast pocket as
a way of saying he wanted to give you the short end of the
stick. Like a jerked knee, Dan target-modeled them as
"Urban Veblenites." The man impressed by the brand of
his own briefcase was Larry Sturholm. "Good morning,"
he said.

Sister Peg turned around. It took a moment for Larry's
face to register. Sister Peg had never seen him in any con-
text other than the bank. "Oh, hello, Mr. Sturholm."

"I bring good tidings, Sister," Larry said with a thick
smile.

For a moment, Sister Peg allowed herself to believe it
was true. "Really? That's . . . that's great." She wiped her
hands as she walked over to greet the men.

"Sister, I'd like you to meet Mr. Benjamin. His company's made an offer to assume your mortgage." Larry gestured at Mr. Benjamin. "They have a very exciting
development concept. It's going to bring significant employment to the area, which I think you'll agree is sorely
needed."

"Maybe," Sister Peg said, "but what's the good news?"

"Well," Larry said, "if they take over your payments,
we keep your credit rating from getting worse than it already is."

Good tidings, my ass, Dan thought. *This guy is a prick.*

Mr. Benjamin shook her hand. "Nice to meet you, Sister," he said. "As Larry said, we're very excited about this location. Our research tells us it's perfect for our project."

Dan knew three things right off the bat. First, he didn't like these guys. Second, whatever their project was, it was bad news. Third, both men were wearing too much cologne. They smelled like a slap fight between Ralph Lauren and Karl Lagerfeld. Mr. Benjamin made eye contact with Dan and nodded a dismissive acknowledgment. "Father," he said. Dan wondered if Michael had known that his place of employment was near foreclosure when he signed on.

Mr. Benjamin walked to one of the load-bearing walls and banged on it with his fist. He figured a bulldozer could bring the old building down in an afternoon. "When Larry showed me the property, I knew it was the perfect place for our new efficiency retail commerce center."

Larry gave an aw-shucks shrug. "Mr. Benjamin's already got a doughnut shop, a liquor store, and a check-cashing service lined up," Larry said. "That's seventy-five percent occupancy before we've even started to build. Of course, there's a zoning matter still pending and we can't proceed until then, but we have relationships with those guys, so we're optimistic." He smiled like a guy who knew how to purchase influence at a reasonable price.

Dan looked at Sister Peg. A shadow of defeat darkened her eyes, giving her the look of a woman who felt she had let someone down. "I thought I had another month," she said.

"You might have more than that," Larry said. "It just depends on the zoning board."

Dan wanted to slap the callous prick. "Well, I can certainly see why you'd be excited about this project," Dan said. "An efficiency . . . retail . . . commerce . . . center." He said the words deliberately, revealing their dishonesty. "Wow. That's quite a concept."

Larry and Mr. Benjamin turned, surprised that the

priest was addressing them. Dan walked toward the men, his hands held up like a film director framing a scene. "I can see it now. Another exceptionally crappy little L-shaped building with inadequate parking." Dan stood uncomfortably close to Mr. Benjamin. "Got a name for it?" Dan tapped his chin with a finger. "Hmmmm, what shall we call it?" He jerked his finger into the air. "Got it! 'Load of Crap Plaza'? Whaddya think?"

Sister Peg smiled. She felt like a girl whose honor was being defended in the schoolyard. Perhaps Father Michael was more of a kindred spirit than she had imagined. "Father," she said. "It's okay. That's really not necessary."

Dan looked at Sister Peg and shook his head. "No, Sister, a strip mall—excuse me—an efficiency retail commerce center is what's not necessary." He spun back to Mr. Benjamin. "But as long as you're building one, let's talk about it. I assume the liquor store will concentrate on fortified wines and malt liquor, am I right?"

"Listen, Father," Mr. Benjamin said. "I—"

Dan thrust an index finger into Mr. Benjamin's face. "Son, it's rude to interrupt." Dan became the stern priest excoriating the moneylender and his crony. "Now, the check-cashing service will take ten, fifteen percent of whatever the already underpaid laborers bring in, right?"

"It's a service, Father," Larry said. "A lot of these people don't have bank accounts. They need—"

"They need what? Liquor, doughnuts, and another bite out of their checks?" Dan shoved Larry. "Who the hell do you think you are? You think you can just throw these people out on the street?"

Sister Peg was heartened by Dan's defiance. It felt nice having someone on her side.

Mr. Benjamin folded his arms and spoke confidently. "Father, I understand your sentiments, but I think you've been watching too many movies. People don't actually end up on the street unless that's where they want to be. There are all sorts of programs out there for these people."

Sister Peg saw Dan's eyes pinch into angry slits, his hands balled up into fists. As much as she would have liked to see Mr. Benjamin stomped like a bunch of grapes, she didn't think it was the answer. She walked over to Dan and put her hand firmly on his forearm. "Let it go, Father," she said. Sister Peg felt the muscles as Dan opened his fist. She secretly thrilled at the touch of her brave knight in shining armor.

"Uh, Sister, we really have to get going," Larry said. "But as I mentioned, I do have some good news." Larry reached into his coat pocket. "I looked over your financial statements and I decided what you really need is a consolidation loan. And right now we're offering a terrific rate." Larry handed her an application form. "Here, fill this out and drop it by any branch."

When Sturholm and Benjamin turned to leave, Dan started after them, but Sister Peg held his arm tightly. He could have pulled away but knew there was no point. Besides, he liked that she was touching him.

Larry paused at the door. "And I'll call you about that rental property if I hear anything."

Dan wondered what Jesus would do in a situation like this. Sister Peg stayed at his side waiting for him to decompress. She let her hand slide down Dan's arm. She took his hand and gave it a gentle squeeze. "Thanks," she said.

"Don't mention it." Dan was pissed. These pricks were messing with his mission. He wondered if Sister Peg was going to clue him in on her plans. Maybe she didn't have a plan. Maybe she was in complete denial about the foreclosure. They probably didn't teach a lot of banking and finance in nun school. Maybe she was waiting for a miracle. Dan felt Sister Peg letting go of his hand, but he held on.

He wanted an explanation. He turned her to face him. "Sister, is there something you haven't told me?"

Back in her office Sister Peg gave Dan a partial confession. "Well, we're having some financial problems," she said, "but I expect some funding from Monsignor Matthews any day now." Her speech left Dan unconvinced, but he didn't press her. If Sister Peg was telling the truth, he had nothing to worry about. On the other hand, if they were about to become homeless, Dan knew the best thing he could do was to come up with a new funding source. He spent the rest of the day trying to brainstorm ideas while doing laundry, cooking dinner, and cleaning the kitchen. He came up with several solutions. The problem was that each of the solutions required him to be Mr. Dan Steele, who, unfortunately, had been declared dead as the proverbial doornail. He couldn't think of a way to solve the problem as Father Michael, but he was working on it.

Before leaving that night, Dan looked in on Alissa. She was curled up in her bed, her doll held close. Dan wanted to get her to trust him, even a little. He sat on the edge of her bed. "If you want, I could read you a story," he said. Alissa shook her head like she didn't want to cause anyone any trouble. "Okay, maybe tomorrow." She reminded Dan of childhood nights he had spent curled up in fear about what the next day might bring. Dan smiled and, as gently as he could, he touched Alissa's forehead. "You sleep tight," he said. He crossed to the door and turned out the light.

Dan walked out the front door and headed for the VW. For the first time since the funeral, Dan was going to go visit Michael's grave. Something had been bothering him and he wanted to get it off his chest. As he walked around the side of the building, Dan noticed the one room in the Care Center with a light still on. He saw Sister Peg's silhouette moving against her partially drawn curtains. Even in silhouette there was no mistaking her movements. She was undressing.

Lead me not into temptation. Dan knew he should look away and go straight to his car, but he didn't. From where he stood, Dan could see Sister Peg from the waist up. If he took just one step forward, he'd be able to see between the curtains, but in a twisted display of decorum, he stayed put. She removed a couple of hairpins and placed her wimple on the dresser. Then she began to unbutton her shirt. As if nudged by Satan, Dan took a step forward for an unobstructed view. Dan's id argued with his superego. *She's a nun, for God's sake. You can't stand here and watch a nun undress*, his conscience said. *She's a woman*, the id countered. *What harm is there in catching a glimpse of her skin?* Dan saw merit in both arguments, but he knew the furtive nature of his viewing position made him a creep, so he decided to walk away.

Before Dan could get his body to cooperate with his mind, however, Sister Peg removed her shirt and made herself a revelation unto Dan. She was beautiful, living proof that God knew exactly what He was doing. Her skin was creamy, her habit having protected it from too much sun. Her body was lean from her stingy diet and toned from all the hard work. And her breasts, upturned in praise of— *Good Lord*, Dan thought, *I'm staring at a nun's . . . tits.* And they were good. No, great. She looked at her body in the mirror and tilted her head as she ran her hands lightly down her torso. Dan had a woody hard enough to nail something to, and that just had to be bad, didn't it? Before he resolved the question, Sister Peg disappeared from sight and a moment later her room went dark.

Dan walked quickly to where he was parked. He sat in the driver's seat thinking, *forgive us our trespasses.* It was a good thing he was on his way to see a priest.

*   *   *

Filtered moonlight cast a milky glow on the field of marble markers, allowing Dan to find Michael's plot. "Sorry I haven't been out to visit," he said. "We've been kinda busy." Dan looked around the cemetery. It was more peaceful than spooky. It seemed like a decent place to spend eternity, the chittering crickets masking the freeway sounds that drifted in from all sides.

Dan sat down next to Michael's headstone. "Listen, I suppose this might fall into the category of too-little-too-late, but I hope I didn't keep you from getting into heaven. It's hard to imagine a guy like you getting sent to hell, but all that doctrine about how failing to do penance for sins in this life results in punishment in the next and how you have to be perfectly pure and free from even venial sins to come into God's presence, well, it seems like you could have been sentenced to some time in purgatory, and if you did, that's my fault and I'm sorry."

Dan knew that Church dogma allowed him to offer to God all of his works at the Care Center as a means of freeing Michael from purgatory, sort of like paying a fine in lieu of doing time. There was no way for Dan to know if there was truth to any of that, but given Pope Gregory I's words about how those dying with sin will expiate their faults by purgatorial fire and how the pain would be more intolerable than anyone could suffer in this life, Dan thought—on the chance that it was true—that he should do whatever he could to get Michael out of the trouble Dan had gotten him into.

While the Church spoke with great assurance that the prayers of the living could benefit the souls in purgatory, Dan knew it was less certain about whether the prayers of the souls in purgatory could benefit the living. St. Thomas argued against the notion, saying such souls weren't in a position to pray for us. On the other hand, Bellarmine in *De Purgatorio* said the reasons alleged by St. Thomas weren't all that convincing, and St. Alphonsus, in his work *Great Means of Salvation*, argued forcefully that the souls in purgatory, being beloved by God and confirmed in grace, had absolutely no impediment to prevent them from praying for us. So it was a toss-up. No one knew the answer to that any more than they knew how many angels could stand on the point of a pin.

Dan rubbed his eyes. It was late and he was getting cold. "I tell you what," he said. "I'm putting my money on St. Alphonsus." Dan ran his hand over the tips of the blades of grass, then dabbed the dew onto his face like holy water. "I'll pray for you if you'll pray for me."

That Father Michael never considered what General Garang would do if he failed to repay the loan was indicative of his deteriorating mental capacity. Father Michael never intended to buy or sell human organs. He simply took Garang's money and bought rice and hydration packs on the thriving black market. He just wanted to feed the hungry, and thanks to the borrowed money, he does so for three days. Then it is all gone. A week later, when Father Michael fails to repay the loan, General Garang sends his gorilla to do his dirty work.

He is a rude-looking Third World Man with fat Mobutu-like features, dark as baker's chocolate. He is from the swampland of the White Nile and he wears filthy fatigues with pride. He doesn't care if he kills Christians or Muslims as long as he gets paid.

The Third World Man finds Father Michael in a hole in the ground next to a mound of dead bodies four feet high. He is digging a large grave. The Third World Man gets into the hole with Father Michael and pulls his knife. It is covered with dirt and dried blood. "General Garang would like his money."

"I don't have it," Father Michael says, pointing to a shovel. "Help me dig."

"That's too bad." The Third World Man grabs Father

*Michael and slashes his flank with his filthy knife. "If you
don't have it in two days, I will be back to take your kidneys."*

*After the Third World Man leaves, Father Michael sews
his own wound, then flees the refugee camp, unaware that the
tetanus is incubating.*

Monsignor Matthews was terrified. Unable to divert any
new funds for the Care Center, he was afraid of how Sister
Peg would react to his news. He knew she was willing and
able to employ some frightening tactics in pursuit of her
goals. Ironically, that was one of the things that attracted
him to her in the first place. Her willingness to think and
act outside the box combined with her refusal to be passive
in the face of her struggle were powerful pheromones drawing the cleric in, even against his will.

A couple of years earlier, Sister Peg first approached
Monsignor Matthews for help. It was her initial effort to
raise funds for the Care Center, which, at that point, had
been struggling for six or eight years. She came to his office,
nervous and unsure of how to proceed. But he could sense
that she was committed to the task and he offered to help.
Over the next several months they spent a great deal of
time together, working on plans, writing proposals, and
making pitches. They frequently worked late into the night
and, as often happens when two like-minded people spend
so many hours in such close proximity, an attraction began.

Monsignor Matthews reacted swiftly. He told Sister Peg
about his feelings and she confessed to hers. They acknowledged that to succumb to their urges would violate their
vows and, they feared, it might also undermine their quest.
They shook hands and agreed to exercise self-control so as
not to endanger either their cause or their friendship.

For the next two months they worked side by side or-
ganizing a fund-raiser that ended up raising four thousand
dollars for the Care Center. It was an enormous sum of

money relative to their annual budget and it left Sister Peg
and Monsignor Matthews ecstatic and grateful.

The fund-raiser was held at a community center in Van
Nuys with members of local civic groups providing the
food, drink, and entertainment. The party finally ended
around midnight. Sister Peg and Monsignor Matthews
stayed to clean up; both were exhausted and euphoric. As
they swept up, they shared a bottle of champagne. When
they finished cleaning, they sat at the edge of the stage and
polished off their bottle. Then they opened another. As
they drank, they talked about when and why they had dedicated themselves to the Church, about their disappoint-
ments, and their dreams. The champagne and the
fellowship were an irresistible aphrodisiac and before they
knew what had happened, they had broken their vows. Several times.

The incident nearly crippled Monsignor Matthews—
from a guilt standpoint more than from tender testicles,
though there was that too. No amount of penance would
assuage his remorse. Sister Peg was less troubled by it and
she did what she could to get the Monsignor to forgive
himself, to admit to his humanity and to his frailties, but
he would have none of it. The more she pressed the issue,
the more he resisted, and an argument ensued. They didn't
speak for six months, but when the finances at the Care
Center got tight again, Sister Peg knew what she had to
do. She had to break the silence. She didn't want to do it,
but it seemed better than letting the Care Center residents
become homeless. So she called Monsignor Matthews and
made it clear that if he didn't find some way to provide
regular funding to the Care Center, she might have to make
her confession to a certain Archbishop.

Thus motivated, Monsignor Matthews began skimming
funds and diverting them to the Care Center. He realized
immediately that his subversive accounting activities eased

his mind about his tryst with Sister Peg despite the fact that it seemed almost like making a late payment for sex. His system worked beautifully and he was planning to expand it until the recent meeting in Century City.

Now he was carrying all that baggage down the hall toward Sister Peg's office to tell her that the gravy train had been derailed. Thus was he terrified as he knocked on the door. "Good morning, Sister," he said.

Sister Peg looked up from her desk. "Good morning, Monsignor," she said. "What brings you to our little corner of paradise?"

Matthews pulled up a chair. "I have a rather delicate situation to discuss, Sister."

She slapped a hand against the side of her face. "My God, you've gotten someone pregnant, haven't you?"

Monsignor Matthews closed his eyes and massaged his temples. "Worse, I'm afraid."

Sister Peg sensed his anxiety. This wasn't a joking matter. "What is it?"

"The meeting I told you about was worse than expected." He looked her in the eyes. "I'm sorry, I can't fund you anymore."

Sister Peg leaned back in her chair and let out a long deep breath. She didn't think she had the heart to lose another fight.

"What are you going to do?" Monsignor Matthews asked.

"You mean am I going to go all Judas and turn you in?" She let the question hang for a moment before shaking her head. "I'd never do that, Matty. That would be blackmail."

"Did you ever intend to?"

"I'm not that kind of girl," Sister Peg said. "I just wanted to give you some inspiration."

Monsignor Matthews reached across the desk and put

his hand on hers. "So, what are you going to do about the Center?" He saw the tears welling in her eyes.

"I don't know, Monsignor. I honestly don't know."

Mrs. Zamora was sitting in her wheelchair in the sunlight just the way Ruben had posed her. The window was to her right. The sun was coming in at an angle hitting her from the front. "Is this dress all right? I think the colors look nice." It was a floral pattern, faded and rural-looking. Mrs. Zamora smoothed the fabric in her lap and felt closer to worthwhile than she had in fifty years. She stared straight ahead at the bare, cracked wall of her room, happy to be the artist's subject.

Ruben studied Mrs. Zamora's profile and the way the light worked on her face. Something about her reminded Ruben of his grandmother on his mother's side. The gray hair pulled into a bun at the back of her head, her small fragile frame, her light brown skin, the way her ears kept to her head. That's why he asked Mrs. Zamora to sit for him. She would be the stand-in for his dear, departed *abuelita*.

Mrs. Zamora could walk, but her balance wasn't good and her eighty-year-old bones were brittle, so the wheelchair was precautionary, but it hurt her pride. She took a breath and sat up straight and proper. "I was born on a ship in 1919," she said. "That's the year they signed the Treaty of Versailles, you know. I was always good with history." Her voice was clear and sure of itself.

Not that Ruben could tell. He was born deaf. He had never heard sounds and he made them only when extremely agitated, like when a referee made a bad call against his beloved Raiders. He would stand and bellow at the television while using sign language that even the hearing could understand. He hated to see the Raiders return to Oakland, but he knew that's where they belonged. L.A. was too soft a place for the silver and black. They belonged in a dirtier, industrial spot. The day they announced the move, Ruben had the team's logo, the eye-patched pirate, tattooed on his right arm.

Mrs. Zamora knew Ruben was deaf, but she didn't think he'd mind if she talked while he drew her. She enjoyed the reminiscing. "My parents were from Spain originally. I believe we moved to Bakersfield in 1921. My father was a farmer. He grew olives mostly, but it was hard for him. The local people didn't welcome outsiders back then." Mrs. Zamora hadn't been back to Bakersfield in sixty years, but her memories of the place were vivid. She could remember exactly how the air smelled in the summer and how good her father's olives tasted. She wondered what it was like now. She wondered if any of her childhood friends were still alive, what their lives had been like, if any of their dreams had come true. She kept wondering about things, but only in her head. Otherwise she just sat in the warm sunlight, staring at the bare cracked wall of her room.

Ruben tilted his head and squinted. He made a mental note to go to the store later to get the results from last night's Lotto drawing, since he had missed it on the television. Then he made a few deft strokes with his pencil and shaded in around Mrs. Zamora's jawline.

Ruth was still in bed, curled into the fetal position. She was confused and deeply depressed. Sister Peg had brought food sometime in the last day or two, but Ruth couldn't remember if she had taken her medicine. Maybe she had, only this time the chemicals were inadequate to the task. Maybe this time the depression would finally claim her. Ruth prayed it would. She had been waiting so long.

Ruth thought about the razor blade she kept hidden in the drawer of her bedside table. Her doomed eyes stared at nothing as she thought about how the rusty edge would feel when she used it. If only she could muster the strength or the courage or whatever it was she lacked. How long had she been in here? she wondered. What had happened to Michael? Was he in trouble? No, she remembered now. He was dead. But how? Why? She knew something bad had happened. She could feel it. They said Dan was dead, but she knew otherwise. Dan was pretending he was a priest. Mothers can just tell these things. Had Dan killed his brother? Cain and Abel came to mind. No, Dan wouldn't do that. But knowing that didn't explain what had happened to Michael. Whatever the explanation, it had to be bad. Didn't it?

Just like the rest of her life. All the bad things had happened to Ruth and she never had control of any of it. Why did these things happen? Her churchgoing friends said it was God's will. What kind of God would do that? Maybe the Old Testament God. What was the point of such a terrible and empty life? Was she just a lesson for other people to learn? She had been sentenced to a life term without the possibility of anything. Without at least potential, there was no reason to struggle. Without promise, there was no hope. Why wasn't her life more like the happy people in the television commercials her son made? *I was meant to suffer.* Where was her other son and why weren't the pills working? *It doesn't matter.* Where was her guardian angel? *I must not deserve one.* Her eyes hurt. She wanted to die. Maybe then she'd find her son or maybe the Son of God. She could ask Him for forgiveness in person.

She needed just enough energy to get the razor blade, then she could open her wrists to let the pain and frustration out. No one else would do it for her. Maybe the questions would make sense if she were gone. It seemed like the only way out. It was the right thing to do.

*   *   *

God is good. The thought repeated again and again in Oren Prescott's mind. *Yes, God is fabulous.* Oren was admiring himself on the cover of *Advertising Age* magazine and reveling in the glory generated by the Fujioka campaign. "More Is More" had become the hottest catchphrase since "Where's the Beef?" What had started as a mere advertising slogan had become an unprecedented marketing phenomenon. Sales of "More Is More" T-shirts, baseball caps, and other merchandise best described as crap had already passed the $20 million mark. By every conceivable measure, the campaign was a huge success both domestically and overseas.

Sam Chan, the actor who played the Zen master in all the ads, had recently signed a huge sitcom deal. *Zen Daddy* was the story of a widowed Zen master who moves to Beverly Hills with his two kids. Hilarity ensues when the Zen Daddy buys his kids a wisecracking cat named Stan only to discover that the funny feline is the reincarnation of his dead wife! Focus-group tests indicated that the show had terrific across-the-board appeal. *Zen Daddy* was bound to be a hit.

Not wanting to miss the wagon, Burger Doodle, one of the nation's largest fast-food chains, designed a merchandising tie-in with something they called their "More Is More Meal Deal," which was as emblematic of America's bloated sense of consumption as anything ever to come down the pike.

Sitting on Oren Prescott's desk were the results of a recent advertising industry survey. The research showed that the mere fact that people were hungry was way down on the list of why they ate fast food. Thanks to the advertising industry, eating in America had become more about entertainment than about satisfying hunger. It was about fun meals and happy meals, not good meals. Chuck E. Cheese was to kids what Planet Hollywood and the Hard

Rock Cafe were to adults—cholesterol-delivery systems dis-guised as live-action music videos. The promise of an enter-tainment experience with every hot sack of grease was the best way these restaurants could differentiate themselves from their competitors.

Another way was by selling products in increasingly larger sizes. Bigger is better! More Is More! Whereas the original serving size for Coca-Cola was a six-ounce bottle, the advertising industry was now marketing the one-liter size as a single serving. The same was true for the food: an effective ad campaign could make a plain hamburger and an order of fries seem inadequate—even embarrassing—when compared to a satisfying charbroiled double bacon cheese-burger and the jumbo-whopper-super-size fries.

Of course, no one in the advertising industry gave a second thought to the negative impact their work had on the health of consumers. That wasn't the ad industry's job. Still, they were well aware that a typical fast-food ham-burger contained 260 calories, while a double bacon cheese-burger had 475, most of which were fat. They also knew that the percentage of Americans deemed clinically obese had nearly doubled since the early 1960's. These were the sorts of facts they would tout in their ads for weight-loss products.

Still, interesting as these facts were, the fine folks in the advertising business felt that the most important thing to know was that people preferred to have their bad habits encouraged rather than condemned, and that probably went a long way toward explaining the vast popularity of the "More Is More" campaign.

Some advertising campaigns lacked cross-cultural appeal. Something important tended to get lost or distorted in a bad translation of a tag line or a product name. For exam-ple, when Ford introduced the Pinto in Brazil, it flopped because on the streets of Rio de Janeiro *pinto* is slang for "tiny male genitals." In Mexico the American Dairy Council's "Got Milk?" campaign got translated as "Are You Lactating?" And in Saudi Arabia, the Jolly Green Giant became the Intimidating Green Ogre. But the "More Is More" slogan didn't suffer overseas. In fact, in the South American markets, the tag line was understood to mean "Makes Your Dick Bigger!" Needless to say, sales soared.

In the final analysis, the most important measure of the success of the campaign was that sales of Fujioka electronic equipment had doubled and the value of Fujioka stock had jumped by 47 percent during the same period.

In a perfect world, all of this would have resulted in Scott Emmons's grinning visage being pasted on the cover of *Advertising Age* magazine, but this was by no means a perfect world and thus everyone in the ad business was looking at Oren Prescott's capped teeth on the cover instead.

Despite this fabulous turn of events, Oren suddenly stopped praising the Lord and slammed his hand down on his desk. "Goddammit!" It occurred to him that Fujioka, far and away his largest client, would soon want to know how Prescott planned to evolve the "More Is More" campaign. They would demand that Dan Steele be in charge of the campaign and it wouldn't matter one whit to them that the man was dead as an irregular Latin verb. It was either Dan Steele or Mr. Prescott himself, and Oren Prescott hadn't generated an original idea in ten years.

He sat at his desk and dropped his head into his hands, fully aware that the only way he could maintain his reputation was to come up with something more successful than the most successful campaign in modern advertising history. It was a fool's errand, and he knew it. After a few minutes his hands slipped to the sides of his head and Oren began to apply pressure to his skull. He squeezed harder and harder, as if an idea might drip out like so much juice.

Wait a second. Didn't Dan have a twin brother? Yes! Oren looked up, hope flashing across his face like a falling star. He wondered . . . Maybe he could talk Dan's twin brother into pretending he was . . . Nah, that was a crazy idea. He'd have to think of something else.

It was midnight. Dan finished wiping down the kitchen countertops as Sister Peg cleaned the last of the dirty pans. Dan tossed his dish towel into the laundry pile, stretched his back, then headed for the door. "I guess I'll see you tomorrow," he said.

Sister Peg stifled a yawn. "You want a cup of coffee?"

The invitation caught him off guard. "How old is it?"

Sister Peg held the pot under her nose. "Plenty, but I think milk and sugar can save it."

Dan walked over and sniffed. "I think whiskey'd save it better, but if milk and sugar's all we got . . ."

Sister Peg grinned. "A man after my own heart." She dragged a chair over and stood on it to reach the top shelf of a cabinet. "Cheap bourbon do?"

Dan beamed. "You bet." He thought about his last drink, Chivas Regal twelve-year-old. Still, cheap bourbon sounded surprisingly good. As Sister Peg climbed down with the bottle, it occurred to Dan that the two of them had never just sat down and had an ordinary conversation. Their discussions always revolved around Care Center problems. Peg's difficulties getting funds or Dan trying to deal with his mother's depression, or Alissa's future. Dan held his cup out to Peg as she opened the bottle. "I'll have mine without the coffee."

Sister Peg was wearing a pair of tired gray sweatpants, a long-sleeve black pullover shirt, and a Dodgers cap. Dan was in his clericals. They sat at the long table in the kitchen, propped up on their elbows, and agreed not to talk about the Care Center. Sister Peg took off her shoes and rolled her ankles in soothing circles. "Let's just talk about stuff," she said.

Dan studied her face for a moment and wondered what would happen if he leaned across the table and kissed her. *Probably get my face slapped halfway across the Valley, and rightly so.* Still, he couldn't help but wonder if the celibacy rule included kissing, or excluded it, depending on your point of view. Regardless, Dan wasn't about to test the question. "Here's lookin' at ya." Dan held his mug out for a toast. Sister Peg tapped her mug against his and held his gaze for a moment. Then, smiling, they drank. It had been a while since Dan initiated small talk with anyone, let alone a nun, so he struggled with where to start. "So, where'd you learn sign language?"

Sister Peg put down her cup and signed as she spoke. "Ruben taught me. He had some books that taught the basics and he showed me the rest. I've been doing it for about a year."

Dan mimicked the motions as he spoke. "Did you ever see *Children of a Lesser God?*"

Peg smiled. "Yeah, I liked it."

"What's your favorite movie? And you can't say *Citizen Kane* or *Sister Act.*"

Sister Peg scrunched her face up in thought. "Let's see." She poked her lower lip out and made some other searching-the-database expressions. She sipped her bourbon, then suddenly looked very pleased with herself. "*Pretty Woman,*" she said. "Best thing Julia Roberts ever did."

Dan nodded. "Yeah, but c'mon. In the real world, hookers aren't that good-looking, right?" He whirled his whiskey around inside his mug. "She just seemed too, I don't know, too clean and bubbly for a hooker."

Sister Peg sat up, all but bristling. "What, you think they're all skanky drug addicts?"

Dan was surprised by both the vehemence and the vocabulary of her response. "Skanky?"

"Hey, I've worked with some of those girls," Sister Peg said. "A lot of them are attractive and smart and . . ." She let go of the thought abruptly. "And I just think Julia Roberts was terrific, that's all." She finished her bourbon and poured another.

Dan wondered what that was all about. He'd never seen her spark like that before, not even about the Care Center. He thought it odd that she would get inflamed about a Richard Gere movie. Sister Peg cupped her hands around her drink, funneling the evaporating alcohol toward her nose. She knew she'd overreacted and decided to change the subject. After a moment she looked at Dan. He was rubbing his face with both hands. "Why did you become a priest?"

Dan opened his eyes behind his hands and peeked out between his fingers. "Uh, well, at the time I didn't feel like I had much of a choice," he said, reaching for the bottle. "It was something I thought I had to do." Dan refreshed his drink.

Sister Peg nodded as if that described her decision to become a nun. "Was it like a 'big moment' sort of thing?"

"You could say that." The alcohol caused Dan to embellish his story. He mainly stuck to the facts, though he rearranged the order in which they happened. "I was raised Catholic and got a B.A., lots of humanities, plus a few marketing courses. At one point I actually considered going to work at an ad agency."

"And that led to being a priest?"

"I wrote a paper for an advertising class. It was a critical study on Neil Postman's notion that the best television commercials are essentially religious parables." Sister Peg's look of bemused interest encouraged him to continue. "The style's a little dated," Dan said. "It was mostly used for personal hygiene and household cleaning products." He began to recall the finer points of his paper. "Postman argued that an effective spot conveyed four important points. The first was that the failure to know about any given product, for example, dandruff shampoo, was the cause of discord in life. In other words, 'Technological Innocence,' as he called it, was the sin in these commercials. This particular sin resulted in the shame and stigma of having dandruff, which in turn resulted in, say, a lack of companionship or the loss of a business deal, a sort of hell, right? Secondly, the theory goes, the way to salvation is in learning about, and using, the product. The third point of one of these spots is that using the product results in some version of heaven, for example, a honeymoon in a beautiful place or the riches of consummating a big business deal. The final point is that the obligation of the righteous is to spread the gospel about the product."

Sister Peg reached across the table and poked at the band around Dan's neck. "Sort of like the 'Ring Around the Collar' ads, right?"

"Exactly." Dan smiled, pleased that she'd chosen the perfect example. "I got an A on the paper, but in the process I realized I could do more good spreading the real Gospel instead of the Madison Avenue version." Dan sat back in his chair. "What about you? You grow up wanting to be a nun? Or did you just wake up one day and decide to give it a try?"

It hadn't occurred to Sister Peg that this was the inevitable flip side of the question she had asked Dan. She didn't want to lie about it, but she also didn't think telling the truth was the best thing she could do. She stood up and stretched, her hands raised high in the air as she arched her back. "Let's just say I took a roundabout way to get where I am." She walked to the sink and rinsed out her cup. "I'm sorry, Father, I just hit a wall," she said, faking a yawn.

"I'm going to call it a night. I'll see you tomorrow." She made a quick exit.

"Good night," Dan said. He sat there for a minute wondering what stops had been on Peg's circuitous route to nunhood. She certainly wasn't like any nun Dan had ever met, but then he figured he probably wasn't like any priest she'd met either. He gulped down his bourbon and headed home.

The bourbon made Dan more contemplative than he'd been in quite a while. Back at his apartment Dan found himself amused as he reflected on his financial situation. The funniest thing, he thought, was not being able to figure out which part of his poverty he enjoyed the most. Since assuming the role of Father Michael, he had lost weight, gained perspective, and found something he assumed was inner peace. He had to laugh. He was in a tiny apartment, sitting in a five-dollar, garage-sale armchair thinking it was the best piece of furniture he'd ever owned. After another eighteen-hour day at the Care Center, Dan felt more satisfied than he had ever felt after orchestrating a twenty-million-dollar ad campaign. Dan had to laugh because six months earlier, this might have been his definition of hell.

Dan used to come home from a day at The Prescott Agency and automatically turn something on—the TV, the stereo, usually both. As long as there was noise—noise that passed as entertainment, noise that passed as news, noise that tried to sell you stuff. The noise was distracting. It demanded one's attention. It kept one's mind off anything substantial. Far easier to spend sixty seconds wondering if that wacky lizard was going to get the frog's job selling beer than to spend it pondering life. Dan imagined Socrates pitching beer: *The unexamined life is worth living, but only if you drink enough Budweiser . . .*

But now Dan was free of all that. He was no longer subjected to the constant babble of electronic sales pitches; better still, he no longer had to spend his days creating the damn things. It was a relief he could never have imagined. Now, at the end of his long days, Dan returned to his little apartment and reveled in the simplicity of it all. He had come to recognize the pleasure of quiet. He enjoyed the peace of mind that came from not having to schedule his night's television programming—watching one thing while taping another, surfing seventy channels in search of the perfect arresting image, making sure he didn't miss any must-see TV.

Dan had to laugh because it occurred to him that over the past several weeks he had made a radical lifestyle-segmentation transformation. He had converted from being a retailer's dream come true ("Gold Card Swinger") to a retailer's worst nightmare ("Downshifter"). Dan had known about the "voluntary simplicity" movement for years. It had made a small blip on the advertising industry's radar but had been dismissed as a threat to consumerism because it was inherently un-American—or at least could be made to seem that way. Contrary to what many were saying, however, "voluntary simplicity" wasn't about living in poverty; it was about living in balance. Instead of seeking fulfillment in the things you bought, downshifting was about seeking fulfillment in the things you did. It was about frugal consumption, ecological awareness, and personal growth. It was about spending less and enjoying more. It was a reaction to life that offered more conveniences but less time. It was a healing response to the fact that we had multiplied our possessions but reduced our values. Dan had definitely downshifted, though he'd be the first to admit that his consumptive simplicity hadn't come about voluntarily. Dan had been so busy pursuing a lifestyle that he had failed to grasp life.

Sitting in his ratty chair, Dan took the opportunity to gather his thoughts. He knew he was doing important work. He also knew if he didn't find a way to save the Care Center, he'd have no place to continue doing it. He knew that Alissa, the sweet little angel, faced a bleak future if she got sucked into the foster care system. He knew Captain Boone would die slowly among strangers at a grim state-run nursing facility, and he knew his mother deserved better than wandering the streets with her son the fraudulent priest.

Dan had always performed well under pressure. It was a point of pride for him and it had served him well over the years. But now he was afraid he had lost his touch. He had tried a thousand times to come up with ways to raise money for the Care Center, but the best he could come up with was bake sales and car washes, and neither of those would cut the financial mustard. Maybe if he closed his eyes he could conjure a brainstorm. Snapsnapsnapsnapsnap.

The problem is that revenues for the Catholic Church are slipping and thus the funds to the Care Center are being cut, right? So if I can find a way to increase Church revenues . . . A dark cloud began forming on his mind's horizon. *How to increase Church revenues?* Then, suddenly, lightning!

Dan bolted from his chair and grabbed the phone. He called the archdiocese and asked for the biggest muckety-muck available. The receptionist told him the Bishop was out to dinner at Wolfgang Puck's newest restaurant. Dan got in his old VW van and drove straight over.

The Bishop was halfway through his duck terrine with hazelnuts and green peppercorn appetizer when this priest arrived at his table, pulled up a chair, and announced that he was going to save the Catholic Church. This priest was so enthusiastic and sure of himself that the Bishop couldn't ignore him. "We've got an image problem," Dan said. "Too much blood and guilt, the whole medieval thing's gotta go."

The Bishop saw Dan's point. He'd seen the fear in the faces of children as they peered up at the tortured body of Christ nailed to the cross. He'd seen them shrink away as they listened to terrifying descriptions of hell and eternal damnation. He'd seen their confused expressions as they tried to fathom the difference between cannibalism and eating the body of Christ. Maybe there was something to this idea of softening the image. "Okay, so, what's your approach?"

Dan smiled. "Two things to focus on," he said. "Market segmentation and branding."

"Branding?" The Bishop wasn't up on current marketing theory.

Dan waved his hands vaguely. "A brand is simply the promise of an experience," he said. "One thing we have to do is understand and communicate what experience the Catholic brand is promising. You have to ask yourself, 'What are the emotional drivers inherent in the church-going process' and, most importantly, I think, we have to start offering a wider range of experiences in order to reach the different kinds of Catholics in the marketplace. In other words, we need different brands of Catholicism."

The waiter set two plates in front of the Bishop. One was a filet of beef in puff pastry with béarnaise, the other was a lobster with tarragon butter. "What do you mean, different kinds of Catholics?" The Bishop cracked one of the lobster claws, baptizing Dan with a spritz of salty water.

Dan started counting on his fingers. "You got pro-life Catholics and you got pro-choice Catholics. There are Catholics who refuse to accept Vatican Two and others who want women free to become priests. There are gay Catholics and antigay Catholics and—"

"Okay, okay, I know, they're all over the damn road," the Bishop said. "How are we supposed to appeal to them all?"

"These days you'll never get 'em all under one roof, so the answer is niche marketing, just like magazines and cable," Dan said. "You have to design the product to meet the specific desire. It's like cola. There used to be just one kind, right? Now you've got regular cola, diet cola, caffeine-free cola, sodium-and-caffeine-free diet cola, and so on. It's all about choice. And people want a choice in their Catholicism just as sure as they want a choice in their soft drinks. Hey, you want it in Latin, we'll give it to you in Latin!"

The Bishop couldn't argue. He had to admit, he liked a good Latin mass every now and then himself. He picked up a roll and gestured. "Pass the butter, please."

"Salted or unsalted?" Dan winked.

A drop of the béarnaise dribbled down the Bishop's chin. "Go on."

Dan passed the butter. "So we do some focus groups, then we design the products based on the research. Finally, we do a national TV ad campaign to spread the word." Dan scooted his chair over next to the Bishop. He made a frame of his fingers. He held the frame out so the Bishop could look through it. "Picture this," Dan said. The Bishop leaned over and looked through the frame. "The spot opens with a simple Gregorian chant over a long shot of Calvary . . . a terrific image that gives you some brand familiarity right from the start."

The Bishop nodded thoughtfully as he chewed his roll.

"The three crosses are backlit by a redemptive sunset," Dan said. "The camera pushes in on Christ's head, which is lolled to one side, bleeding. He looks bad. The camera holds on his tortured face for a moment. Then, suddenly, Christ lifts his head and looks straight into the camera. He winks, then smiles.

" 'Hi!' Christ says. 'I just wanted to tell you about an exciting new product from your friends in Rome . . .' " Dan put one arm around the Bishop and gestured with his free hand as he continued. "Christ pops his hands and feet free from the cross and hops down. He begins walking down Calvary, speaking to the camera. 'Over the past ten years or so, a lot of you have left the Catholic Church because, well, because we zigged when you wanted to zag.'

"Cut to Christ walking on a busy street in Galilee, okay? He stops to lay his hands on a cripple, but he keeps talking. 'So the guys in Rome put their heads together and, well . . .' Christ looks at one of his hands and pulls out a big nail, holding it up for inspection. 'I think they hit the proverbial nail on the head.'

"In the background, the cripple stands and dances a jig as Christ walks out of frame," Dan said. "Cut to a scene on a lakeshore. Christ walks through a throng of peasants, pulling unlimited loaves and fishes from his robe, handing them to the rabble as he walks. A small boy tugs on Christ's robe. Christ slaps a large, wiggling mackerel in the kid's grateful arms. The kid smiles deliriously. It's a lightly funny but touching image," Dan assured the Bishop, who was beginning to look doubtful.

"So," Dan said, "Christ keeps talking as he approaches a big lake. 'Hey, times change. Believe me, I know. That's why we came up with new Cath-o-Lite.' When Christ reaches the lakeshore he just keeps on going. As he walks on the water, he continues his pitch. 'We've cut ninety percent of the damnation to bring you the religion you want.' "

Dan paused and made eye contact with the Bishop. "That's the key, you have to give them what they want." Dan nearly knocked over the Bishop's water glass as he gestured toward the far side of the restaurant. "Christ reaches the far shore of the lake and walks onto the beach, still pitching.

" 'We're still doing things better than all the other major religions. And when it comes to what counts the most . . . we deliver.' Christ walks past a line of four Hindus. He stops and looks at the camera. 'So many religions are gimmicky or, worse, they're just plain cults. But with us—at the end of the day—we offer you what they don't . . . eternal happiness . . . not just constant recycling.'

"Christ watches the four Hindus. The first one morphs into a cat. The second one turns into a warthog. The third becomes a monkey. The fourth becomes Newt Gingrich. Christ turns back to the camera with an amused smile. 'Need I say more?'

"Cut to Christ arriving at the Last Supper. He bumps fists with several of the Apostles before taking his place at the center of the table. 'New Cath-o-Lite, give it a try.' Christ gives a big toothy smile. 'You'll be glad you did.' "

Dan stood slowly, raising his hands toward the ceiling. "Christ ascends offscreen giving the 'okay' sign as the Apostles watch in awe. We fade to black, then bring up a stylized logo for the new brand. We hear Christ's voice with a slight echo. 'New Cath-o-Lite, less guilt, more forgiveness.' "

The waiter brought two frozen Grand Marnier soufflés as Dan waited for the tag line to sink into the Bishop's mind. It seemed to sink in quickly, for in one swift move the Bishop stood, pulled a large heavy crucifix from his robe, and smacked Dan across the head, waking him from his dream and spilling him from his chair onto the floor of his ascetic apartment. Dan lay there for a moment, gathering his wits. He hated to see a good idea go to waste, but at the same time, he damn sure didn't want to be the one to pitch this in Rome.

*　　*　　*

Ruth reached for the drawer. She imagined the relief that would come when her brittle skin yielded to the razor's rusty edge. She was sorry in advance for the trouble this would cause. Someone would have to clean it up. She hoped it wouldn't be Dan. He didn't deserve that. But what did "deserve" have to do with anything? she wondered. She didn't deserve her life the way it was. There didn't seem to be any logic to it. Her pointless existence was a random event. She was just a drain on a system she didn't understand. She was a waste of space.

Ruth's hand crept across the bedside table, closing in on her way out. She began to cry as a part of her prayed for intercession. *Give me a reason to stop.* But none came to her and a moment later she opened the drawer and touched the blade. The cold shock of death crept into Ruth's heart and then a strong voice came from within her. *We should pray to the angels who are given to us as guardians.*

The terror that accompanied Ruth's struggle toward self-sacrifice was as nothing compared to the moment she heard that voice. It was the voice of a stranger, yet it had come from within. It was the same thing that had happened to Zacharias when revelations were bestowed upon him. Ruth was conscious of an interior voice that was not her own. She knew the voice was not that of God but that of His messenger. This gave Ruth pause, and in that moment came the hope she had lacked.

She lifted her hand from the table and turned toward the door of her room as though she knew something was coming. There was a noise in the hall; then the door slowly opened. An amber light shone in Ruth's eyes, but she never blinked. *This must be my guardian angel.* The angel's golden hair shone despite the gloom. Ruth wanted to speak but didn't know where to begin. Maybe she would ask why the angel had no wings.

The angel was young but could sense Ruth's sadness

from across the room. The depth of the matter escaped the sweet cherub, but there was something elemental about it and the angel was drawn to Ruth's bedside. Her head tilted to one side and she looked at Ruth's doomed eyes for a moment. "Are you an angel?" Ruth asked.

Alissa smiled. "I don't think so." Alissa climbed up into the bed and curled up next to Ruth and the gloom began to lift.

Butch Harnett was sitting at his computer terminal trying to gain access to some financial information that was supposed to be private, yet he was unburdened by ethical matters. His thinking was that a man in search of the truth should not be hindered by petty considerations, that plus it was Mutual of California policy.

After obtaining Dan's medical records and discovering the truth about tetanus, Butch knew he was on the right track. He massaged his hairless scalp as he moused his way around a credit card database. After a few swift keystrokes he found what he was looking for. He compared the numbers on the screen with those on a piece of paper from the file at his side. He made a disapproving clucking sound by sucking some air through his teeth, then he clicked the print command.

A minute later he was standing in front of his boss, expressionless. He opened his folder and gently pinched the sheet of paper that was still warm from the printer. He held it aloft for his boss to see. "Seek and ye shall find," Butch said, momentarily forsaking Paul for Matthew.

"Our deceased Mr. Steele?" his boss asked.

Butch nearly smiled. "He that seeketh findeth." Although he was not a true devotee of St. Matthew, Butch had adopted as one of his aphorisms this excerpt from the Gospel according to the former tax collector. It was a fine credo for an insurance investigator. "Odd though it may seem," Butch said, "Dan Steele apparently did some shopping in the days after he was laid to rest."

"I'm shocked," the boss said with little expression. "What sort of tastes does he have?"

Butch looked at the printout of charges. "El Rey del Mundos, Brooks Brothers, and Fujioka electronic equipment."

His boss suddenly slapped his hand down onto his desk. "More is more!" he shouted, showing more emotion than Butch had ever seen him reveal. "I love the Zen guy in those ads!"

"Yes, sir," Butch said, apparently put off by the ungodly emotional outburst. "Me too."

Sister Peg had started to tell the older residents about the Care Center's financial trouble. She assured them that she would find them new homes and she apologized for letting them down. She felt like she had lied to them all. Mrs. Gerbracht tried to comfort her, saying Sister Peg had done her best and that no one would hold it against her; times were just tough. "We're all used to that," she said.

Dan had just returned from the food bank. He was in the kitchen unpacking a box when Sister Peg walked in. "Father, I forgot to tell you. You've got to do Reconciliation this week." She looked in the box to see if there was anything to snack on.

Dan had no idea what Peg was talking about. Wasn't *reconciliation* an accounting term? Was he supposed to help everyone balance their checkbooks? As far as he knew, nobody at the Care Center even had a checking account. "Say again?"

"The residents are waiting for you to hear their confessions." Sister Peg pointed toward the television room.

Dan looked as though she had said the residents were waiting for him to set himself on fire. *When did they start calling it Reconciliation?* Dan wondered. "Don't they usually go to Holy Family for that?" he asked.

"I'm sorry," Sister Peg said. "Father James is ill and can't do it this week."

Dan wondered if they had changed anything besides the name. He hoped the script was the same. He wondered how upset the Lord would be when Dan started offering forgiveness without a license. He imagined the assortment of sins the residents might have committed. He figured them for a venial crowd, but you never knew who might confess something mortal. *This might actually be interesting,* he thought. Dan straightened his collar and prepared to dish out some absolution.

Ruben had fashioned a makeshift confessional out of a couple of cardboard refrigerator boxes and a roll of duct tape. Ruben made it the best he could and he dedicated his labors to the Virgin Mary. It sat off to one side of the television room. While Mrs. Zamora and some of the other residents waited in line to confess, they watched game shows with the sound turned off. When Mr. Avery saw the pretty girl pointing at the new sports car, he was forced to add a couple of sins of a covetous nature to his list. Inside the box, Ruben taped a thin dish towel over the "window" through which the supplicant and priest would speak.

Dan was nervous at first but relaxed after the first couple of confessions. In fact, he began to enjoy it. His approach was unorthodox, certainly, but the sinners seemed to appreciate his style. Mr. Avery confessed that he had cursed the Lord when Sister Peg told him the Care Center was going under. "Can't say as I blame you," Dan replied.

"But the Second Commandment says—"

"Trust me," Dan said, "I'm familiar with the rules, and until you start violating five through ten, I don't see a real problem. But I tell you what, if you really feel bad about it, say a couple of Hail Marys and watch your damn mouth.

Now, get outta here, you knucklehead.'' Mr. Avery thanked Dan and left the confessional feeling relieved. Mrs. Ciocchetti was next. She shuffled in to bare her soul.

Sister Peg stood in the corner watching. She was thinking about making an honest confession herself. One thing in particular was bothering her, though she hated to think of it as a sin. Sister Peg had considered waiting until Father James returned to Holy Family, but she knew all he could offer was forgiveness—and she wasn't sure that was what she really wanted. In any event, she decided to confess to Father Michael. *Just tell the truth,* she thought. *Get it out in the open.* But how would she say it? "Forgive me, Father, I've been having impure thoughts about you''? A bit too direct, perhaps, but true. She'd had more than one dream about Dan that left her itchy and feeling human and wondering why nuns had to take a vow of celibacy. *I mean if a bunch of nuns jumped off a bridge, would I do it too?*

Sister Peg had finished first in her nun class, but that was only because she was a self-taught nun. Class of one. As such, her thoughts on celibacy were uninformed by traditional Church teachings about self-denial. She knew nothing about canon xxxiii as enacted by the Spanish Council of Elvira, nor could she debate the pros and cons of Bishop Osius's attempts at the Council of Nicaea to impose a law similar to that passed in the Spanish Council. All Sister Peg was sure of was that—unlike the Fathers of Nicaea, who were content with the prohibition expressed in the third canon, which forbade *mulieres subintroductas*—she sometimes wanted to be held and kissed by a man.

Had she a better grasp of the history of Church-imposed celibacy, Sister Peg in her dreams might have screamed, "Forget canon x from the Council of Ancyra in Galatia. Damn the Apostolic Constitutions. And double damn the stricter views of the Council of Trullo, in 692, I'm horny as Old Scratch!'' But Sister Peg lacked such historical grasp, so she'd never utter such words in her dreams or elsewhere. Still, on the rare occasion she let herself think of such things, she wondered about the supposed virtues of celibacy. It certainly wasn't natural, and wearing a habit did nothing to diminish her human nature. She had the same urges and desires that any woman would, but still, with the exception of that night with Monsignor Matthews, she had for years been sublimating those urges into her work at the Care Center. What she was discovering was that a girl could sublimate only so much before the dreams began to surface.

Sister Peg knew she ought to be ashamed for even thinking about it. Her head was filled with those reiterated evil interior suggestions, though they didn't seem evil to her. They seemed natural. *Oh God*, she thought, *it's a Monsignor Matthews scenario all over again.* Working side by side with a man dedicated to the same cause she was had led to . . . feelings. Was it infatuation? She had caught herself coveting his butt more than once, but it was more than that. She had come to care about him; in fact, she was afraid she had fallen in love. But should she tell him? What good would that do? He'd also taken a vow of celibacy, right? No, telling Father Michael would just make things awkward and, worse, it might force him to leave so as not to tempt fate. And then where would she be? No, she'd just have to sublimate a little harder.

After hearing her confession, Dan told Mrs. Ciocchetti that she was the least sinful person he'd ever met. "You not only don't get any penance now," Dan said, "but I'm giving you credit toward your next confession. Now go in peace." Mrs. Ciocchetti thanked him and left feeling much better about herself.

A moment later the next sinner entered the confessional and knelt. "Forgive me, Father, for I have sinned."

Dan blanched. "Mom?" He had failed to anticipate this eventuality. "What are you doing in here?"

"I've come to confess my sins," she said. "It's been a long time since my last confession."

"But . . . but . . ." Dan sputtered. "I think there's a conflict-of-interest clause somewhere that doesn't allow this sort of thing." What if she wanted to tell him things he didn't want to hear? There are certain things boys might assume their mothers do—if they ever stopped to think about those sorts of things, which they don't—but the last thing a boy wants is to hear his mother talk about them.

"Don't worry," Ruth said. "I just wanted to say I'm sorry I was such a terrible mother. I've wanted to tell you that for a long time. Can you forgive me?"

Dan didn't know what to say. It broke his heart to know his mother had been carrying that with her for all these years, that she'd been blaming herself. "It wasn't your fault," he said. "It was Dad's." Dan was suddenly battered by a storm of emotions. His love and empathy for his mother were as powerful as his hatred and contempt of his father. "You did fine, Mom," Dan said. "You loved us. You don't owe me an apology." He tried to blink back the tears, but there was more to it than that.

Ruth paused a moment to let Dan collect himself. "I'm sorry," she said. "I didn't come in here to make you cry." It was true. She had come to get answers to her questions. She also thought she could have some fun teaching Dan a lesson about lying to his mother. She wasn't really mad about the lie he'd been living, but since he seemed unwilling to volunteer information about what had happened to Michael, she was going to make him confess. And what better place than a confessional? It was just dumb luck that Father James was sick this week.

"You know, I was angry at you for going to Africa. I wanted to figure out what made men abandon me, but I couldn't. Dan was the only one who never left. He was

always there for me. But he hasn't visited in so long I'm
beginning to think I've lost him."

Dan's mind reeled. He never knew she felt that way
about him. He had always figured Ruth had been angry
with him for shuffling her off to nursing homes instead of
taking care of her himself. Sure, he had put up the money
to have her taken care of, but he had done it for his own
convenience and never with a smile. And the only time he
saw her was when she caused trouble. *Maybe it's time I
start telling the truth. But how will she react to the news about
Michael? What if she goes goofy and blows my cover? Maybe
I'll start off with the truth about the Care Center and work
my way up to the really bad news.*

"You know, I just had the best idea. I think we should
go visit him. Wouldn't that be fun? Just show up at his
office one day and yell, 'Surprise!' Wouldn't that be a
shocker?"

"Uhhh. We can't do that."

"Why not?"

"Uh . . . well . . ."

"Is something wrong?"

"Listen, I think I need to hear the rest of the confessions. We'll talk about this later."

"Do you remember the Fourth Commandment?"

*Dammit, why is she quizzing me on catechism all of a
sudden?* "Uh, give me a second to think. Did you say the
Fourth?"

"Take your time."

Dan counted on his fingers. *No other Gods, name in
vain, keep Sabbath holy . . .* "Uh, honor thy mother and
thy father."

"Good. Now, you know what that means, right? That
means lying to me would be a sin."

"Right," Dan said. "Can we talk about this later?"

"Okay, with that in mind, it's your turn."

"My turn?"

"To confess," Ruth said.

"Confess?" Dan said in a little voice.

"What happened to Michael?"

"Uhhhhh, the saint or the archangel?"

"Your brother," Ruth said like an exasperated mom. "He's dead, isn't he?"

"You know?" Dan was struck. "How could you know?"

"Your mother knows everything."

"When did you know?"

"I could tell Michael was sick when he brought me out here. Then he disappeared and two weeks later, you showed up in a priest outfit and started avoiding me. So I called your office and they said you were dead. Well, I knew you weren't dead, so I figured it had to be Michael." She could hear Dan hyperventilating. "Would you relax? I'm not going to blow the whistle. You're all I've got left. I just want to know what happened."

Dan told Ruth the whole story, from the insurance scam to the burial. "Why didn't you say something earlier?" he asked.

"I figured you had enough on your mind, regardless of what had happened. I assumed you'd tell me sooner or later. When it got obvious you were avoiding me, you sort of forced my hand."

"I'm sorry," Dan said. "I should have told you."

"Forget about it," Ruth said. "What's done is done. I've cried and said my prayers for Michael and now we've got other problems to deal with. Rumor has it we're about to get kicked out of here."

"Yeah, well, I'm working on it."

To millions of people, Los Angeles was the promised land. Much to Scott Emmons's dismay, he was not one of those people. Instead of the land of milk and honey, Scott found little more than jealousy and mayhem. The poor were lost in the barrio while the children of the wealthy schemed and ran wild and made movies of themselves. But at least he had a job.

Thanks to Ted Tibblett's glowing reference, Scott was currently doing ten-hour days at Stereo Central, one of the few stores in Southern California that didn't sell Fujioka products. Scott was glad to be away from all the "More Is More" displays.

Ever since being fired from The Prescott Agency, Scott had been subjected to a steady stream of ridicule by his father. "I guess they throw back the little ones," he would say. The derision simply fueled Scott's determination to find Dan Steele—the man who had robbed him of the only opportunity he would ever have to show his old man he wasn't a loser. That was the sin for which Dan had to atone.

Ironically, Scott was the one going to confession. In fact, he had gone sixteen times in the past three weeks. With each reconciliation Scott found himself lingering in the confessional, revealing the unmatched pieces of his emotional baggage to the priests he determined weren't Dan. Not all of them were patient and comforting. One particularly testy priest cut Scott off after about two minutes. "A," the priest said. "You haven't mentioned a single thing that qualifies as a sin. And B, if you want some goddamn psychotherapy, you ought to go see a goddamn three-hundred-dollar-an-hour shrink and stop eating into my time!"

Every day after work Scott did the same thing. He got into his car and opened his hollowed-out Bible. Inside, folded up next to his gun, was the yellow page he had torn from the phone book. Scott had been to most of the churches listed under "Catholic." There were only nine left in the Valley. St. Richard's was next. Scott knew this one from growing up. It was right down the street from his old school.

Scott hopped onto the 101 and headed west. After about a hundred yards, traffic came to a complete standstill. "Dammit!" Scott pounded on the steering wheel. He dialed in a radio traffic report. "Well, westbound lanes of the Ventura Freeway are backed up about a mile because of a headless torso in the fast lane," the traffic reporter said with a chuckle. "Sure got a lot of lookee-loos on this one . . ."

Scott's anxiety surged as he crept down the freeway at half a mile an hour. Assuming he ever got to St. Richard's, Scott thought about what he would say to the priest, assuming the priest wasn't Dan. He was looking forward to dealing with his tangled issues in the comfort of the dark Catholic cubicle. He wanted to get some more of this stuff off his chest before it crushed him. He really just needed someone to talk to.

Scott punched in one of his motivational tapes and listened. He wondered how long he'd have to wait for traffic to start moving. Suddenly a hideous noise erupted from the speakers as the cassette player began eating the cheaply made tape. Scott punched hysterically at the eject button, but too late. The tape was already crumpled around the capstan and pinch roller, ruined. Scott wrenched the thing from the tape deck and hurled it out the window. "Aagghhhhh!"

Scott suddenly felt very small. He was surrounded on all sides by an army of huge vehicles, spewing fumes and wasting nonrenewable resources. A red Lincoln Navigator loomed behind him. A white Chevy Silverado raised crew-cab dually was pushing in on his right while a blue Ford Excursion crowded him from the left. Blocking Scott's frontal view was a black GMC Yukon. As the sense of claustrophobia tightened its noose, Scott craned his neck to look around the unnecessarily roomy vehicle in front of him. He hoped to see some light at the end of the tunnel, but other than a mile of brake lights, the only thing Scott could see was a billboard with the Fujioka Zen master smirking down at him, shouting, "More Is More!"

Since at least as far back as the Sacred Congregation for the Propagation of the Faith in 1622, Christians have been systematically seeking converts around the world. Africa, with its so-called primitive religions, has long been a popular continent for these conversions, and the Christians seem to have done well spreading their beliefs here. Of course, it's hard to tell, just by looking, whether the natives have embraced all of the Church's tenets, but it does appear that they have taken strongly to the one about not using contraception.

As far as the eye can see in this particular stretch of Africa, there are new believers. They're all starving to death, but God bless 'em, they have faith. And somewhere in this mass of converts, there is the well-fed, rude-looking Third World Man who has come to take care of some business. He's in a bad mood, having to run errands in stinking hundred-degree heat, so he's taking it out on whoever gets in his way. Presently he is kicking and shoving his way through this sea of sick and starving refugees, a handkerchief held fast to his nose and mouth. He is wearing his filthy fatigues and he is well armed. In addition to several jagged-edged knives and some hand grenades, he carries an expensive Italian-made Spectre 9mm machine gun, capable of firing fifteen rounds a second—or, if sold, capable of feeding hundreds, at least for a little while.

This refugee camp redefines squalor. Disease-carrying flies lick at the salty lacrimal ducts of the eyes of starving Christian children who are too weak to blink them away. Diarrhea is killing hundreds of converts each day, leaving behind more than the stench of rotting bodies. The air is cluttered with the din of screeching vultures, crying babies, and the buzz of a million gnawing insects. Sand and dust blow relentlessly into the hollowed faces, leaving a crust of mud in the corners of otherwise empty mouths. It's worse than any plague conjured in the Bible and it makes a Sally Struthers charity infomercial look like home movies of a church picnic. This is hell on earth.

And again, though it's hard to tell just by looking, one feels certain these refugees are all of joyous spirit, knowing that since they have been baptized and cleansed of original sin, they will be in heaven just as soon as they starve to death.

But none of this matters to General Garang. He just wants his money, or some answers, so he has sent the Third World Man to bully his way through the fetid mass of desperate refugees to get what he can. About a hundred yards off to his left, the Third World Man sees some adults moving suddenly, as if clamoring for food. He turns and heads in that direction. At the center of this insanity the Third World Man finds who he is looking for. He is a haggard, half-mad priest, Father John, who is doling out cups of pasty gruel and some hydration packs. The Third World Man steps up to the priest and jabs him with the stubby barrel of the machine gun. "Where is Father Michael?" he demands.

Staring, as he does, into death's skull every day, Father John is well past being intimidated by a gun-toting yahoo. He wipes his sweaty face with his sleeve and yells over the din. "Put down your gun and help me feed these people!"

The Third World Man doesn't hesitate. He smacks the priest across the face with the frame of his gun. "I said, where is Father Michael?" Father John spits a tooth into his hand and looks like he might collapse. The Third World Man, impatient for an answer, hits the priest again, this time in the stomach. "Where is he?"

Father John falls to his knees with one hand on the ground, gasping for air. "I don't know. He's been gone awhile. He may have been killed by the SPLA. Who knows?"

The Third World Man grabs Father John by his hair and pulls his head up. He forces the barrel of his gun into the *priest's mouth. "I will count to three." The Third World Man leans down into Father John's face. "One." Father John closes his eyes and begins to pray. "Two."*

Still spitting blood, Father John reaches out and grabs his tormentor's leg. The Third World Man pulls the gun from the priest's mouth. "I swear to you, I don't know where he is."

The Third World Man squints down at the terrified priest who holds his gaze. After a long pause, the Third World Man smirks and lowers his gun. "I'll be back," he says in a dead-on Schwarzenegger imitation. He then turns around and disappears into the swarm of refugees.

Father John closes his eyes in a moment of doubt. He finds it disquieting that while he is unable to get food to the poor in this part of the world, others are getting satellite TV.

Sister Peg got in line behind Mr. Saltzman, who was grumbling something about not even being Catholic. Sister Peg was still unsure about the nature of her own confession, though she was leaning toward admitting her feelings and asking for guidance.

A second later she was startled by the sound of the front door slamming, followed by what sounded like a troubled sea lion. It was Ruben uttering loud, excited noises. Since he had gone to check his lottery numbers, Sister Peg hoped against the odds that he had actually won something. A moment later Ruben raced into the room, breathless and agitated, not the face of a lottery winner. He pulled Sister Peg's sleeve with one hand while trying to sign with the other. His gestures were so fast and exaggerated that she couldn't tell what he was trying to say. She calmed him down so he could explain what the hell was wrong.

"Razor Boy and Charlie Freak," he signed. He tugged again on the sleeves of Sister Peg's habit, then signed something else that she couldn't understand.

"The children stole what?" she signed back to him. "I

don't understand. Slow down." Sister Peg had heard enough about Razor Boy and Charlie Freak to know they were capable of anything. Both had done time for violent crimes and had come out harder than they had gone in. They were soulless bastards, malicious and indifferent to suffering.

Ruben collected himself and signed more slowly. He said he had run into an ex–gang banger he knew. He told Ruben what Razor Boy and Charlie Freak were up to. Sister Peg listened, increasingly amazed at mankind's capacity for brutality. When Ruben finished, Sister Peg just stood there, numb. She thought of Sonia, the little girl who had died at the age of five, killed by her own mother after the state—and Sister Peg—had failed to protect her.

Ruben waited as long as he could. He finally shook Sister Peg to get her attention. "Come on," he signed. "We have to do something!"

She looked at him. "Stay here," she signed. "I'll be right back."

Josie glanced at the envelope and poured some more vodka. The letter had arrived several days ago and Josie still hadn't screwed up the courage to open it. She expected the worst and she was scared. The vodka usually helped her be brave. It had certainly helped the first time she sold herself, though since then it had been helping less and less.

The letter contained the results of Josie's blood test. She might be fine. She might be dying. All she had to do was open the envelope.

Looking back, Josie knew she'd had a lot of opportunities to take her life in different directions. She wondered why she had always taken the wrong fork in the road. How had she ended up in this dumping ground for marginalized women? She'd been given lots of advice that might have led her down better paths. How come she never took it?

Teachers, cops, fellow flat-backs—everybody told her she
was going in the wrong direction. It's easy to point out the
problem. It was something else to suggest a solution.

Only one person had actually offered to take her down
a better road. From the first night they met on Ventura
Boulevard, Sister Peg had tried to save her. Josie knew she
was the one person who really cared. She hated herself for
letting Sister Peg down so many times. Peg deserved better
than that.

Josie tore open the envelope and pulled out the letter,
but she didn't look at it. Instead she interlaced her fingers
and looked out the window at the sunset. She tried not to
cry. "God," she said, "I've never done this before, but I
figure it's worth a shot. I'm going to make a promise, but
You've gotta help me. Okay, so here's the deal. I swear, if
it's negative I'll quit and I'll go out there and spend the
rest of my life helping Peg. But if it's positive . . ." Josie
didn't know how that sentence ended, so she just gulped
the last ounce of her courage and opened the letter.

12

"That's it? The sign of the cross?" Mr. Saltzman sounded miffed. "What sort of penance is that?" He felt Dan had undervalued his sins.

"Trust me," Dan said.

Sister Peg barged in and grabbed Mr. Saltzman by his thick forearm. "Hey!" the sinner protested. "I'm—"

"You're done," she said, tossing the old man out. "Say your prayers, you'll be fine."

Dan cleared his throat. "Uh, you must have done something really bad," he said.

"You any good with a gun?" Sister Peg asked.

"Come again?" Dan pulled back the curtain separating the two sides. He saw Sister Peg slipping rounds into the cylinder of a blue-steel .38. "Judas H. Priest! What are you doing?"

"Ruben just told me something that, as a good Christian, I simply can't ignore."

"And, as a good Christian, you think the solution involves a thirty-eight?"

Sister Peg spun the cylinder and closed it. "Are you familiar with the San Fers?"

Dan thought for a second. "As in the gang?"

"As in," she said. "Two of their looser cannons have apparently graduated from crack dealing to kidnapping and slave trading. Ruben tells me that one of Razor Boy's crack-head customers traded his eight-year-old son for a fifty-dollar rock. Now, instead of being in second grade, the kid is on a street corner selling crack."

"Jesus," Dan said.

"Oh, it gets better," Sister Peg said. "His homey, an idiot named Charlie Freak, thought that was such a great idea that he went and found a crack whore willing to trade her seven-year-old daughter for some rock. When the girl didn't work out as a crack dealer, he sold her to a child pornographer."

"My God." Dan couldn't believe it; even by gang standards this was outrageous.

"Since then, they've traded a quarter ounce of crack for three more children, and I don't want to wait around to find out where those kids end up." Sister Peg held the gun up. "So I ask you again, are you any good with a gun?"

"Don't get me wrong," Dan said, after more of a hesitation than seemed manly, "I'm behind you all the way on this, but don't you think the cops might do a better job against these guys than a priest and a nun?"

"LAPD can't do anything without investigating first or the ACLU would have a federal lawsuit filed before the cops could get those animals in a cage. Personally, I'm not concerned about violating Razor Boy's civil rights." Sister Peg stood. "If anyone asks, we're on a mission from God."

If Stephen Leacock was right when he described advertising as the science of arresting human intelligence long enough to get money from it, then the Fujioka account was Oren Prescott's Nobel Prize. Oren Prescott's problem, however, was that he had begun a personal spending spree based on the assumption that his shop would win the award for years to come.

However, with the tragic death of Dan Steele, the assumed architect of the "More Is More" campaign, Oren Prescott's long-term ability to sustain his extravagant lifestyle was coming under heavy fire. TBWA/Chiat/Day, Cliff Freeman, Wieden & Kennedy, and two dozen other agencies had begun circling within days of Dan's funeral. One by one they'd trekked to Fujioka headquarters to express their condolences about the loss of the man who had put the Fujioka brand on top of the heap. And, as long as they were there, they pitched their ideas of how best to follow up on the "More Is More" campaign.

But the Fujioka board of directors showed more loyalty than anyone expected. The chairman of the board, Mr. Ihara Fujioka, was enamored of the American expression "dance with the one who brought you," and he was going to do just that, assuming, of course, that he liked what The Prescott Agency came up with next. Otherwise he'd be sticking with the old Japanese expression *sayonara*.

Oren Prescott had been dodging Ihara's phone calls for weeks, but the day of reckoning had finally come. Mr. Fujioka was on line one. Oren took a deep breath and grabbed the phone, prepared to blow enough smoke to blind the entire board of directors.

"Hello, Ihara, I was just—"

"Mr. Prescott," a thin, stiff voice interrupted. "I know what a busy man you are as you are unable to take so many of my phone calls, so I will make this quick. I expect your presentation within fourteen days. Otherwise, we are considering the proposals of The Sinnert Group and Chiat/Day."

Oren was suddenly nauseous. "No sweat," he croaked. "In fact, I've got a terrific idea I'm polishing up right now. I'll set the pitch next week, okay? Ciao!" In one swift mo-

262 • Bill Fitzhugh

tion, Oren hung up, then banged his head on his desk. "I'm doomed," he said.

Earlier in the day Butch Harnett was looking at his copies of the hospital records. He was interested in the name in the "next of kin" box. According to the records, it was Dan's brother, who appeared to be a priest, a Father Michael Steele. But there was something funny about the signature. The "Father" part looked as if it was signed as an afterthought, sort of wedged in ex post facto. What Butch needed was a true Father Michael signature to compare to this one, so he headed to the diocesan offices to see what he could find.

Butch approached the woman at the front desk and told her what he needed. The woman said she had worked for the diocese for twenty-two years and knew most of the clergy working in the L.A. area, but she denied knowing a Father Michael. "Perhaps you should speak to Father David. He can access the database."

So Butch went to the third floor to meet Father David. "I'm looking for Father Michael Steele," Butch said.

Father David went to a row of filing cabinets. "Do you know in which diocese he was ordained, or if he's ever changed diocese?"

"No idea," Butch said.

"That would make it easier. I could just search the letters dimissory of the appropriate Bishop." Father David had his back to Butch. He was reading something in a file that seemed to catch his eye. "Do you know if—" Father David suddenly stopped. He closed the file and the file drawer. "Well, I guess it doesn't matter," he said. "I have nothing here on any Father Michael, sorry."

Butch smelled a Catholic rat. "Are you sure?" He gestured at the filing cabinet. "It looked like you saw something in there."

"I'm telling you, I don't know the man," Father David replied rather defensively. "Good day." Father David locked the filing cabinet, then disappeared into a back room.

Butch was getting the ecclesiastical runaround and he knew it. He was surprised such a simple piece of information was so hard to come by. He began to wonder if thirty pieces of silver might buy him what he was looking for. Obviously it was too late to test Father David's price, but another opportunity lay just down the hall. There was a man looking up at something, his hands clutched behind his back. As he approached, Butch could see that the man was admiring a painting of St. Matthew, weeping bitterly. The man looked like a Bishop in his splendid black robe with red piping and buttons to match. "Excuse me," Butch said, pulling a wad of bills from his pocket. "I'm trying to find a Father Michael. I was wondering if you might know him." He peeled a twenty off the stack and dangled it like a green carrot.

The man in the robe appeared insulted, as if to say a man of his rank couldn't be bought so cheaply. He returned his attention to the weeping St. Matthew without saying a word.

Butch peeled a few more carrots and waved them at the Bishop. "This Father Michael I'm looking for, he's in his mid-thirties, average height, brown hair. Are you sure you don't know him?" The Bishop glanced down at the money and held his hand out like a shabby maître d'. Butch withheld it until the Bishop considered the question.

"Let's see, Father Michael," the Bishop mused. "Oh yes, I remember hearing something about him . . ." He scratched at his empty palm and looked up at Butch.

Butch shook his head. "You have to earn it," he said.

"Yes, well, if I remember correctly," the Bishop said, "he was in Africa and Cardinal Cooper—" The Bishop paused a moment and looked as though he had just remembered something important. Something he wasn't supposed to share with strangers. He clasped his hands together behind his back and turned back to St. Matthew. "No, I'm mistaken," the Bishop said. "I've never heard of him."

He started to walk away, but Butch grabbed his arm. "Are you sure? He's from around here."

The Bishop pushed Butch's hand away. "I'm telling you, I do not know the man!"

Since her habit was both conspicuous and unwieldy, Sister Peg changed into jeans and a dark long-sleeve shirt for her mission. Dan simply plucked the stiff white thing from his collar and loosened his top button. In his all-black outfit he looked like a Catholic ninja or maybe a studio development executive. They were in Dan's VW van, headed southeast on San Fernando Road. Sister Peg was driving. Ruben rode shotgun. Dan was in the back, holding on to Sister Peg's .38.

It was only now that Dan realized what a great opportunity this was for him. Sure, the idea itself was insane—confronting violent convicted felons who were probably armed and high on something could scarcely be considered bright—but on the other hand, this was a great chance to show off for his girl. Of course, Dan knew it was ludicrous to think of a nun as "his girl," but it was a well-established medical fact that love tended to make people stupid. And now, with adrenaline and testosterone gushing into his system like an oil spill, all reason had been suspended. Anything was possible in such a heightened glandular state. As they passed Polk Street, Dan leaned forward like a hardened SWAT team member. "So what's the plan?" he asked.

"I plan to get the kids out of the house, Father." Sister Peg flashed her eyes in the mirror. She meant business. "I don't know how."

Dan nodded. "I'm with you, Sister," he said. "It's just, some people are more comfortable with a plan, but whatever. We'll just play this by ear. We'll be good." He wasn't sure if he believed it, but he knew he had to sound positive.

Ruben signed directions to Sister Peg, then he pulled a second gun from the glove compartment. This was no six-shooter, either. It was a converted semiauto, essentially a machine gun. Ruben checked the gun's clip to see that it was full. Then he slid it back in until the magazine catch clicked.

Dan felt this improved their odds somewhat, but it raised a question that had crossed his mind once before. "If you don't mind my asking, Sister . . . where'd you get the guns?"

Sister Peg thought about telling him the truth but decided now was not the time. "My old convent was in a tough neighborhood," she said. Before Dan could inquire further, Sister Peg reached into her pocket and pulled something out. "Here." She tossed something into Ruben's lap and handed one back to Dan.

It was a stocking for masking his face, standard armed-robbery gear. Dan rubbed the fine nylon mesh between his fingers. "Nothing beats a great pair of L'eggs," he said. He stretched the thigh end to see how it fit over his head. That's when he noticed it wasn't a pair of cheap panty hose. This was a fine stocking with the imprint of a garter snap on it. "Hey, this is very nice," he said. "Is this Austrian?"

Sister Peg glanced at the rearview. "You seem to know a lot about women's hosiery for a priest."

"Hey, you leave a bunch of guys alone at a monastery . . ."

Sister Peg looked over her shoulder at Dan and raised an eyebrow.

Dan smiled. "You brought it up."

Ruben indicated for Sister Peg to take a right. He had the stocking on top of his head ready to roll down. His face was hard as steel plate.

"What do we know about this place?" Dan asked.

"Ruben said it's just a two-room house. A front door, a back door, and bars on the windows. We don't even know if anyone's there," she said. "Like you said, we'll play it by ear."

A few minutes later Ruben pointed at a house. Sister Peg killed the lights, then pulled over and parked. The black S-10 wasn't there. The lights were on inside, but there were no silhouettes in the windows. After a minute Dan spoke up. "Let's go get a closer look." He hoped he sounded brave.

Guns tucked in waistbands and masks pulled over their faces, the three of them crossed the street and slipped into the edge of a row of neglected shrubbery. They paused for a moment looking for their next step. Dan pointed at a side window that didn't have a curtain. Sister Peg went over and peeked inside. Dan admired her from the bushes. *How many people would do this?* he wondered. Her determination was sexy as hell. She showed no fear. Dan loved that.

Sister Peg couldn't see the whole room, but she could see four children sitting on a sofa. They didn't appear to be tied up or anything, but since there was no sign of Razor Boy or Charlie Freak, she wondered why the kids didn't just leave. She returned to the shrubs and sent Ruben to the back door. She and Dan went to the front and found the door padlocked from the outside. They removed their stocking masks. "The stupid bastards locked the kids inside," Sister Peg said. "What if the place caught fire?" Ruben came around the side of the house. He signed to Sister Peg, who nodded and pointed at the padlock. Ruben's face tensed. A flurry of signs ended with his first two fingers bouncing off his forehead angrily. He said he had looked around and couldn't find anything useful for breaking the padlocks.

Dan had nothing in the van either, no crowbars for prying them off and no rope or chain for pulling the bars off the windows, and they couldn't chance shooting the locks off, since there was no way to predict what might happen with a ricochet.

Sister Peg heard the notorious booming of a gangsta car somewhere in the general vicinity. "We better do something before these yahoos come home," Sister Peg said, looking up and down the street. Suddenly, "Car!" She grabbed Ruben. They dove into the shrubs and kept low. The sound was there long before the car was, menacing and vulgar.

Ruben shook his head and signed to Sister Peg. "It's not them," she said. The car slowed at the house and the pitch black window glided down. "What if it's a drive-by?" She reached into Dan's waistband and grabbed the gun.

Dammit, Dan thought. *I should have drawn the gun.* On the other hand, she had practically reached into his pants. He felt that was a step in the right direction. After a moment, the car's window glided back up and the car drove on.

Dan took the gun back from Sister Peg, then went over to the window and looked in. "Son of a bitch," he muttered. The television was on. It was a big-screen Fujioka, exactly like the one stolen from Dan's apartment. In fact, the room was filled with all the stuff Dan had bought when he maxed out his credit cards. The solution hit Dan like a set of stone tablets. "Sister, you and Ruben get the kids' attention," he said. "Get 'em over to this window and keep 'em here."

Dan raced to the van and waited for Sister Peg's signal. When she waved, Dan backed the van over the curb, then suddenly gassed it, heading straight for a corner of the house. He was pretty sure this would impress her. He was going about thirty when he crashed into the living room. The cheaply made entertainment center collapsed like the tower of Siloam. The big-screen Fujioka disintegrated in a flashbulb of sparks. From the driver's seat, Dan looked over and saw one of the children staring at him, his mouth wide open. The kid could think of nothing else to do, so he waved. Dan smiled and waved back before pulling the van back out onto the yard.

Sister Peg and Ruben rushed in through the breach and started clearing the debris so they could gather the kids. "Let's do this fast," Sister Peg said. She didn't want to be there when the owners returned. Dan got out of the van and went back to the house, unaware that neighbors were peering out their windows, taking in the details. Ruben pushed the splintered Sheetrock out of the way while Dan cleared a path out of the house. Sister Peg called to the kids, reassuring them that everything was going to be all right. Still, they seemed uncertain. Dan stood behind her, watching, waiting to take the kids. He was mesmerized by the way she moved. Her sweet, calm voice was dazzling and—God help him—he couldn't help but notice how well her jeans fit.

Ruben suddenly punched Dan's shoulder. "Hey! What the hell was that for?" Dan said. Ruben scowled and signed like a psychotic first-base coach giving signals. Dan didn't know whether to swing away or take the next pitch, so he threw his hands up in surrender. "Whatever."

Sister Peg, watching the whole thing, broke into a broad smile. "Hey, Father, nice job getting us in here," she said.

"Anything for you, Sister," he said. Dan turned and jabbed Ruben's shoulder in retaliation.

"Here!" Sister Peg handed Dan one of the kids. "Get her in the van." Dan took the little girl. She was scared and she struggled against Dan's grasp. Dan tried to calm her down, but the child was beyond soothing talk. Sister Peg handed another kid to Ruben, then took the remaining two by their hands and led them out of the house. "Let's go," Dan shouted. "Buckle up!" With everyone secure in the van, Dan gunned it down the street, lights off. None of them noticed the rustling curtains of the neighboring houses. A couple of blocks later, with tensions eased, Ruben nudged Dan and signed something. Dan turned to Sister Peg. "What is he saying?"

"He said Razor Boy's going to be pissed about his TV," Peg said.

"I should hope so," Dan said.

Sister Peg smiled. "Oh yeah, and earlier he said you shouldn't be looking at my butt that way."

Oh, jeez . . . Dan suddenly felt light-headed. "What? No, I was . . ." He knew he was busted. There was no point. "Sorry, Sister. It's the way you were standing, I—"

"It's okay," she said sweetly. "As long as your thoughts were pure."

The priest is bound, gagged, and naked, save his ratty pair of briefs. He's sitting on a toilet in a filthy bathroom stall, a camouflage military uniform wadded up in his lap. Aircraft exhaust wafts in through the open window behind him. The humid African heat draws sweat from every pore of the priest's body and he's beginning to wonder if this is really part of God's plan.

The Third World Man is in the next stall adjusting his new collar while trying to decide whether he should kill the priest before he leaves. A few days earlier the Third World Man had talked to a reticent Red Cross worker who knew Father Michael. The Third World Man pulled his knife and nearly cut off the woman's thumb. When he got to the bone, she finally said where Father Michael was rumored to have gone.

Now, after three days of hard travel, the Third World Man is at the airport in Addis Ababa preparing to take a series of flights that will eventually land him in Los Angeles. While sitting at the airport, the Third World Man can think of no better disguise for tracking the elusive Father Michael than that of a fellow priest. The nearly naked man in the next stall was simply in the wrong place at the wrong time.

The Third World Man finishes dressing. Before leaving the rest room he squeezes into the booth with the sweaty priest and latches the door. "Your prayer has been answered. I have decided not to kill you." The Third World Man holds up his new Bible and poses for a moment like a cartoon missionary. "Now you better start praying for Father Michael." The Third World Man slithers out from under the door, then stands and brushes the dirt from his clothes. He looks at his ticket. His flight will leave in ten minutes.

It was a long night. The four children—unsure if they'd been rescued or rekidnapped—were frightened, and nothing Peg or Dan said seemed to assuage their fear. In the kitchen at the Care Center, the children clung to one another, a huddle of uncertainty. Not knowing whom they could trust, they trusted no one. Finally Sister Peg had a thought. "Father, you and Ruben get them something to eat," she said. "I'll be right back." A few minutes later, Sister Peg walked back into the kitchen wearing her best habit. She was a holy vision of elegance and piety. The children looked as amazed as if Mother Mary Herself had suddenly appeared before them. She smiled beatifically and kissed each of them on the head. It was all the reassurance they needed.

After some cheese sandwiches, they got the kids to sleep. Sister Peg put two of the children in her own bed while Ruben and Dan made up the sofa for the other two. Sister Peg finally fell asleep at her desk at three in the morning.

Ten hours later, Sister Peg was still at her desk, wishing that Josie were there to rub her back. She twisted her neck until it made a loud pop that sounded more satisfying than it really was. She had been on the phone since eight-thirty, trying to find foster homes for the children. So far, the only places willing to take them were some famously substandard group homes. Sister Peg would turn to them only as a last resort. If nothing else, they were preferable to having the children traded on the street like items at a swap meet.

There were more than 100,000 children in foster care in California, more than half of those in Los Angeles County. Among the many things you didn't want to be in Los Angeles was a child in the foster care system. The problem was the shortage of qualified caretakers. According to a grand jury report Sister Peg had read about in the L.A. *Times*, some group homes were so overcrowded that children ranging from three to twelve years old were routinely drugged to make them easier to handle.

A friend of Sister Peg's—a woman who ran a child-advocacy group within the public defender's office—called this the chemical straitjacket approach. She said their office had found more than two hundred cases of children who were given adult doses of antimanic and antiseizure drugs on a daily basis without legally required consent. They had also discovered a dozen group homes where all the toddlers were kept narcotized on sedatives. A caseworker told Sister Peg that she had came across mildly hyperactive children who had been rendered catatonic by Risperdol and Trazodone. This combination of antipsychotic and antidepressant had been given in dosages appropriate for grown men with full-blown schizophrenia, not overactive children.

Unqualified caretakers routinely gave foster kids Tegretol, Depakote, and Clonidine to treat attention deficit disorder. Unfortunately, those drugs were for treating mania and bipolar disorder, not ADD. Sister Peg knew that the children trapped in this end of the foster care system suffered from uncontrollable tremors, drug-induced psychosis, hallucinations, abnormal heart activity, liver problems, and worse. But at least they were easy to deal with.

However, the news wasn't all bad. Sister Peg knew there were some good homes out there. She knew there were good people who took children in and gave them the love and attention and patience they required. She just hoped she could find some of them, and quick.

"No, I understand," Sister Peg said. "I'll try there. Thank you." She hung up, then scratched another name off an already short list. She was about to dial another number when she looked up and saw a man standing in the doorway. He was a five-foot-ten, 150-pound pile of white trash. He was wearing a raggedy-ass pair of blue jeans and a faded Ozzy Osbourne T-shirt. "You in charge here?" He had a scruffy rodent's face, twitchy and mean with too much tooth for his little mouth. "I'm Carl Deats," he said. "Where the hell's my little girl?"

Sister Peg casually dialed 911 as she stood up. The man wasn't very big, but she knew he was violent. "Hello, Mr. Deats," she said. "Alissa's not here. She's been placed in a foster home." She gestured as if to indicate the place was far away.

Carl squinted his bloodshot eyes. "Bullshit," he said. "Lady at the courthouse said that little crumb snatcher's still here." He tilted his head upward. "Guess I'll go have a look." He walked back to the hallway. "Hey! Alissa! Where the hell are you?"

Sister Peg raced out of the office after him. "You can't take her, Mr. Deats," she said.

"I damn sure can," he said. "She's mine and I'll do exactly as I please with her."

Sister Peg was right behind Carl, her words measured and sure. "I've called the police. You have no business—"

Carl turned and grabbed Sister Peg by the shoulders. "Get outta my fuckin' way, bitch!" He threw her against the wall and continued searching for Alissa. "Where you at, girl?" He looked in each room as he stormed down the hall. He stopped at the open door by the stairway and looked in. Alissa was curled up in the corner, her eyes wide in terror. She was clutching her doll with all her might. "There you are," Carl said, real sweet. He crossed the room and reached down. "C'mon!" He grabbed the doll and tried to jerk it out of Alissa's arms, tearing off its head in the process. "You're too damn old for dolls, girl. Now, get up!"

Dan was upstairs when he first heard the raised voices. He was on his way down when he heard Alissa scream. He took the last ten stairs in two steps and got to Alissa's room just as Sister Peg jumped on Carl's back, trying to keep him away from Alissa. Carl threw Peg off his back, then he reached down and slapped Alissa. "Get up!" he yelled.

Dan was halfway across the room when Carl slapped Alissa again. If Dan didn't already have murder on his mind, he did now. "Hey!" he screamed. Carl turned around just in time to see Dan's fist. He was too slow to duck and Dan caught him square on the nose. Carl staggered backward into the wall, blood spurting from both nostrils onto Ozzy's head.

Alissa ran across the room, grabbed her headless doll, then ran off crying.

Dan wasn't sure, but it felt like he'd broken his hand, and unfortunately, it didn't look like the fight was over yet. Carl came up spitting blood. He charged at Dan, screaming. "Son of a bitch!" He'd taken about two steps when Sister Peg teed off on his balls. It was a square, cracking kick that ended in a hideous squishing sound. Carl dropped to his knees, vomited a little, then fell forward onto his broken nose.

Except for the soft gurgling noises coming from Carl,

the room was suddenly quiet. Dan's heart was pounding, as was Sister Peg's. They looked sheepishly at one another, then shared a smile. Sister Peg felt like one of them ought to say something about what just happened.

Dan was thinking the same thing, so he looked up at Sister Peg. "Helluva kick."

"Thanks." Sister Peg looked down at Carl. "You know, I don't care what it says in the Bible. Vengeance is *mine*," she said.

"Yeah, that turn-the-other-cheek business doesn't always apply," Dan said. "This seems more like an I'd-rather-fight-than-switch moment." Dan nudged Carl with his foot but got no response. "Exactly what order of nun are you anyway?" he asked. "Like, Sisters of Very Little Mercy?"

Sister Peg smiled. "Something like that," she said. "How's your hand?"

Dan flexed it gingerly. It was a little sore, but it seemed okay. "I don't know," he said. "It might be broken." He held it out hoping she'd take a look at it.

Sister Peg took his hand and gently inspected the bones one at a time. She applied some pressure to a metacarpus. "Does that hurt?" Dan acted tough and said it didn't. She wanted to kiss each and every one of his knuckles, but she refrained. She looked up into Dan's eyes. "Thanks for the help," she said.

"No problem." Without thinking, he wrapped his arms around her and she just about melted. It had been too long since she'd felt safe in someone's strong arms. With her head pressed against Dan's chest, something stirred in her, something that wasn't supposed to stir, or something she was supposed to ignore or fight, or certainly stop stirring. But she didn't want to stop. She liked the way it felt, so she hugged back.

Dan's head was a choir of reiterated evil interior suggestions. He remembered that night when he saw Peg undress.

Lord did she have a body, and the only thing separating his from hers was a habit and a priest outfit, oh, and her vows. Dan suddenly flashed back to one of the lectures he attended while at the seminary. "Temptations," the Jesuit had said, "are never *intended* by God, rather they are *permitted* by Him to give us the opportunity of practicing virtue and self-mastery."

Well, the opportunity was certainly knocking right now. Then it cleared its throat. *Wait a minute*, Dan thought. *Someone really is clearing their throat.* Sister Peg heard it too. The two of them simultaneously turned their heads. What they saw was a cop standing in the doorway, a tickled look on his face. "You call 911?" he asked.

Sister Peg suddenly remembered that she was in the arms of a priest. She almost knocked Dan over pushing away from him. "This isn't what it looks like," she insisted.

"Oh? What's it look like?" the cop asked.

"Well, we were . . . embracing," she said, flustered and worried about appearances.

"No laws against that, Sister." The cop sauntered into the room and extended a hand to Dan. "Father," he said with a respectful nod. The cop casually looked down at Carl. "You know, seventy percent of my calls are domestic disputes," the cop said. "Husbands and wives, girlfriends and boyfriends, boyfriends and boyfriends, all trying to hurt or kill each other." He poked at Carl with his nightstick. "I wish I walked in on more people hugging." The cop turned to Sister Peg and shook her hand. "By the way, I'm Officer Gorman," he said. He poked at Carl again with his stick. "I assume this is the reason you called?"

As Dan explained who Carl was and what had happened, Officer Gorman's mood shifted from amused to angered. Each time he shifted his weight from one foot to the other, his shiny black leather belt squeaked like a saddle with a fat cowboy in it. "I can't abide child abusers," he said. "Lowest form I come across as far as I'm concerned." He stepped over to Sister Peg's desk and looked around. "I've heard good things about the work you do here," he said as he shuffled through the papers on the desk. "World needs more people like you." He opened the top drawer of the desk. "Here we go," he said, reaching into the drawer and picking up a letter opener.

Dan exchanged a curious glance with Sister Peg. Officer Gorman squatted down and wrapped Carl's fingers around the letter opener. Then he stood up, holding it by its tip. "So, Sister, Mr. Deats attacked you with this sharp object?" He asked the question all matter-of-fact.

Sister Peg looked at Dan, unsure. She knew what she wanted to say, but she worried about what Dan would think of her if she said it. Dan didn't want Sister Peg to have the lie on her conscience, so he took it. "That's right, Officer," Dan said. "Then he attacked the child, striking her several times."

Officer Gorman pulled an envelope from the trash can and dropped the letter opener inside. "Well, that's assault with a deadly weapon," he said as he pulled his handcuffs from his belt and hooked Carl up. "If this piece of crap's on parole, pardon my language, Sister, that'll violate him plenty."

"No need to apologize," Sister Peg said. "He's definitely a piece of crap." She looked at Dan. Her eyes were grateful for the lie he told for her.

Officer Gorman did his paperwork, then yanked Carl to his feet. "Now you better go find that little girl," he said. "Make sure she's okay."

13

Alissa was nowhere to be found inside the Care Center, so Dan, Sister Peg, and Ruben resumed their search outside. Dan picked up a trail of cotton stuffing and followed it to the carport, where he found Alissa hiding in the back of his VW van, silently clutching her headless doll. Her face was already showing the bruise where her father had hit her. "It's okay," Dan said. "He's gone."

Alissa had seen her father put in the back of a cop car before. She didn't know where they took him or what they did to him while he was gone. She knew only two things for sure. One was that it meant a brief respite from the routine of abuse. The other was that he always came back and did it again. She assumed that was how her whole life would be.

Dan picked Alissa up and consoled her. She was bruised, inside and out. When Ruben came over, Alissa climbed into his arms and laid her head on his big brown shoulder. Ruben rocked her gently side to side, all the while wishing he could get his hands on her father.

None of them noticed the squat black truck that had slithered to a stop at the end of the driveway. Razor Boy and Charlie Freak recognized Dan's VW bus from their neighbors' descriptions. The two had come to respond to the lack of respect they'd been shown.

Sister Peg and Dan followed Ruben as he walked back toward the front of the Care Center. They were thirty feet from the front door when Ruben saw the truck. He continued walking, hoping it didn't mean what he feared. The moment he saw the black windows gliding down, however, he knew it did. He knew what was going to happen, but with Alissa in his arms, Ruben couldn't sign a warning. All he could do was try to get Alissa to a safe place and hope that Sister Peg and Dan recognized panic when they saw it.

The air suddenly moved with the booming thunder of the truck's three-hundred-watt stereo. The deafening roar drew Sister Peg's and Dan's attention, but it would take them a few seconds to understand what was about to happen. Ruben turned to run, intentionally hitting Dan to get his attention. Dan watched as Ruben dove for cover behind a tree.

It happened in a matter of seconds. Sister Peg and Dan knew something was wrong, but by the time they recognized the modern plague that was about to be visited upon them, it was too late. He reached for Sister Peg's hand to pull her to the ground, but the automatic weapons were already demanding respect at a very high rate of fire. Everything became fragments of time, sight, and sound. Sister Peg made a noise like someone had punched her in the stomach. Something warm splashed on Dan's cheek. They were on the ground, dust mixed with blood. They kept moving. He looked over and saw Sister Peg's face. She looked more surprised than hurt. Glass shattered. Alissa was crying. Two more shots were fired and Dan pressed his face hard to the ground. The thunder stopped suddenly and someone yelled something in Spanish. Tires squealed and it was over as quickly as it had begun.

Ruben scrambled to his feet and tried to calm Alissa.

Neither had been hurt. Dan thought Sister Peg was right next to him, but when he lifted his head, he saw her several yards to his left. She was biting her lip; a bloody hand clutched her shoulder. He crawled over to her and looked for the wounds. "I can't get my breath," she said.

Despite the pressure Dan had applied to the wound, Sister Peg had lost a lot of blood by the time the paramedics arrived. She was blinking slowly. Her mouth was dry and she responded to questions with one-word answers. "Hurts." "Tired." "Don't." The paramedics were pumping her full of fluids in an attempt to fend off the collapse of her capillary and venous beds. Dan heard one of the paramedics say something about hypovolemic shock. There was talk of decreased cardiac output and cerebral blood flow. The translation came when Sister Peg lost consciousness and they loaded her into the ambulance.

There were a dozen cops on the scene by the time the ambulance left. Dan told them what happened and he identified the shooters as Razor Boy and Charlie Freak. The shock of the drive-by was bad enough, but he couldn't get over the sight of Sister Peg, bloody and unconscious. The more he imagined her lying on the ground, struggling to breathe, the angrier he got. Dan stopped one of the cops and said something to the effect of wanting the scumbags tracked down and executed on the street. The cop said nothing would please him more, but they didn't know where to find the suspects.

"Why don't you start by looking at their house!" Dan screamed.

The cop shrugged and said a unit had already been dispatched to Razor Boy's last known address. No one was there. "Apparently someone drove a car into their living room the other day," the cop said. "We don't know where they're staying now."

Dan tried to act surprised at the news. "Someone drove a car into their house?" Dan crossed himself. "What's this world coming to?"

The cop took off his hat and wiped the sweat off his forehead. "Father, do you have any idea why they'd target you guys for a drive-by?" He put his hat back on.

Dan shook his head and looked as mystified as he could. "No rhyme. No reason," he said. He threw his arms up existentially. "They're just animals." The cop didn't argue. He just walked off.

A vaguely familiar voice came from behind him. "Father?" Dan turned and saw Larry Sturholm walking toward him, his suit shining in the sun. Dan wondered what brought the would-be king of the strip mall out to the Care Center. He knew better than to think Larry came bearing tidings of joy. Maybe he had come to brag about landing a video porn outlet for his efficiency retail commerce center. "What happened?" Larry asked, more curious than concerned.

Dan told him about the drive-by. "They just took her to the hospital," he said.

Larry listened, nodding and making appropriate facial expressions. "Man," he said, "that's a tough break. She's going to be all right, I hope." He rubbed his hands together. "Anyway, we finally got the good news. We got the zoning variance we needed, so you guys need to be cleared out by the end of next week. I hope that's not a problem." Larry turned and walked to his car. Before getting in, he turned back to Dan. "Oh, Father, I almost forgot. I'm having a tough time finding you a new place, a real seller's market, you know. I'll give a call if something pops."

Josie had been in a lot of beds in her time and she had done things in more positions than a gymnast, but right now, perched precariously on the pillows at the head of an adjustable bed, she was afraid someone might get hurt. "It's not easy doin' it on just one side," she said. "Was that too hard?"

"It was perfect," Sister Peg said. She torqued her neck to the left until it popped. "Ahhhh." She rolled her head around in a circle, wincing when she stretched her wounded muscles.

Josie hopped out of the bed and rearranged the pillows so Peg could lean back. "Relax," she said.

Sister Peg closed her eyes and tried taking a deep breath, but she couldn't. Her right arm was in a sling, and the top of her rib cage was wrapped, binding her and making a deep breath impossible. A tube ran into her left arm and another one was scooted up her nose. Razor Boy's bullet had hit her from behind, around the shoulder blade. It chipped the edge of her scapula and fractured a rib before nicking the upper lobe of her lung. The bullet caused significant soft-tissue damage before exiting through her right deltoid. Sister Peg opened her eyes and looked at her throbbing shoulder. "Take my advice," she said. "Avoid getting shot if at all possible. It really hurts."

Josie smiled unevenly, then pulled an envelope from her back pocket. She looked nervous as she held it up. She looked at the floor, then at Sister Peg. "I got tested, like you asked." Sister Peg lifted her head. She couldn't tell if Josie's crooked smile was ironic or anxious. She assumed the letter contained the results of a blood test. Peg prayed it wasn't Josie's death warrant. "I made a deal with God," Josie said. She seemed embarrassed to admit it. "I swore I'd quit working and come help you if I came back negative." As she talked, Josie saw the fear creep into Sister Peg's sweet eyes. Josie reached down and took her hand. "I hope you're still hiring."

Sister Peg let her head sink back into the pillows. "Thank God," she said, squeezing Josie's hand. "I'd jump

up and hug you if this tube wasn't jammed up my nose."
Sister Peg felt a blessed relief. She had seen too many
strangers die of AIDS. She didn't have the strength to
watch a friend go that way. "Only problem is, we might
not be in business much longer."

Josie nodded. She knew the story. "We'll figure something out," she said. What else could she say?

Sister Peg warmed at Josie's optimism until a cold
thought occurred. "What were you going to do if you
were positive?"

Josie shrugged. "Same as everybody, I guess."

During the silence that followed, there was a gentle
knock at the door. Sister Peg and Josie looked over and saw
a modest bouquet of flowers peeking around the corner.
"You decent?" a voice asked.

"Come on in, Father," Sister Peg said.

He stepped into the room. "This where they bring all
the shot-up nuns?" He looked at Peg and smiled. Then he
saw Josie. He didn't want to stare, but she was wearing
tight jeans and a T-shirt that demanded his attention. Dan
wondered if Josie was one of Peg's nun friends. Perhaps she
belonged to an order that shunned bras.

"Josie, this is Father Michael," Peg said. "Father, this
is my friend Josie."

"Sister?" Dan ventured weakly.

"Masseuse," she said, handing Dan a card. "Call me. I
give clergy discounts."

Dan blinked once, like a stunned frog, then turned his
attention to Sister Peg. "How're you feeling?"

"I'll be okay," she said. "They'll release me in a couple
of days. I'm just praying Sturholm doesn't get his variance
before I'm out of here."

"Amen," Dan said. He decided not to tell Sister Peg
about Larry Sturholm's visit. She'd find out soon enough,

and in the meanwhile, Dan hoped to stumble across a solution.

"How's Alissa?" Sister Peg asked.

"She's okay. My mom's sort of adopted her," he said. "They seem to need each other."

The door opened again and a nurse breezed in carrying a small tray. "Time for your shot, Sister," she said. The nurse doused a cotton ball with alcohol. "Show me that hip." She reached to pull the sheet down, but Sister Peg stopped her. "Is there a problem?" the nurse asked.

Sister Peg looked to Dan, who was watching intently. "Uh, Father, do you mind?"

Dan looked up, smiling sheepishly. "Oh . . . sorry." He turned away and stared at the television set mounted on the wall. The TV wasn't on, but there were images on the screen nonetheless. The reflection gave Dan a perfect view of everything. Talk about your must-see TV. The nurse uncapped the loaded syringe, then pulled back the sheet. Sister Peg rolled onto her side, yielding access to the squishy part of her hip.

Dan couldn't believe his eyes. He wondered if he gasped out loud or if he managed to keep it to himself. He blinked hard, inching closer to the television, hoping for better focus. Maybe the light was playing tricks in the reflection. Surely he didn't see what he thought he saw. Josie noticed Dan staring at the television and immediately realized he could see everything. Her main concern wasn't that a priest shouldn't see a nun's leg, but rather how the priest would react to seeing it. They made eye contact in the reflection. Josie turned away first, but she knew that he knew.

"Better say good-bye now, Sister," the nurse said. "You'll be out in a minute." The nurse put the syringe on her tray and left.

"Okay, guys," Sister Peg said. "You heard the lady.

Time for me to shleeep." She giggled as she felt the Demerol easing her mind. Her eyelids started to droop. "Shister's shleepy, shleepy, shleepy." She giggled dreamily.

Josie wanted to make a quick exit. "All right, I'll come by tomorrow. You just sleep." She patted Sister Peg's arm.

"Okeydokey, nitey-nite." Sister Peg's eyes closed. Her delirious smile remained as she went under.

Dan stood his ground for a moment, unsure of what to do next. Josie made a nervous move for the door. "Uh, Josie," Dan said. "Do you have a minute?"

Josie stopped. *Oh God, he's going to start asking questions,* she thought. *I can't lie to a priest, not after making promises to God.* "Uh, I'm in kind of a hurry, Father."

Dan gestured. "Come here a second." He stepped to the side of the bed and gingerly lifted the sheet, then looked. One word came to mind: *Wow.* There it was, exactly what he thought he had seen, although now it was in full, rich color. It was a foot-long tattoo of a snake crawling up Sister Peg's ivory thigh. It was a thing of surprising beauty, and the tattoo wasn't bad either. He looked at Josie to see if she wanted to offer an explanation. She shrugged unconvincingly. Dan looked again at the colorful snake. "That's a part of Vatican Two I never heard of," he mumbled as he leaned closer. "That's a helluva tattoo." He traced his finger over the snake.

Josie gave Dan a knowing look. "Ohhhh, you're one of *those* priests . . ."

Dan jerked his hand away and drew the sheet back over the leg. He turned to Josie. "So," he said. "Any idea why a nun would have a snake tattooed on her leg?"

Josie was torn between loyalty to her friend and her recent vow to God to turn her life around. She shrugged. "Uhhhh, maybe it's a reminder of that Garden of Eden story. She's very religious, you know."

Dan wouldn't have pressed Josie on this, except that

she had never acted surprised about the tattoo in the first place. He assumed that meant she knew about it. He assumed further that by playing the priest card he could get Josie to spill the beans. He put his arm over her shoulder. "Josie, I can see that you're torn about this, but you know, the truth will set you free."

Josie had never been very good at keeping secrets, so when the Lord's representative started leaning on her like a bad cop, she cracked. "Oh God," she blubbered, "I'm not supposed to tell anybody."

Famous last words. Josie was close to opening up now, so Dan racked his brain for something biblical to use as a crowbar. "In Deuteronomy it says, 'the secret things belong unto the Lord our God.' "

Well, this was more than Josie could take. "Swear you won't tell anybody," she said.

Dan held a hand up in oath. "Nun's the word."

Josie pulled Dan over to the corner of the room and whispered. "Peg's not exactly a nun."

"Okay . . ." Dan looked over his shoulder at Peg, then back at Josie. "So what is she, exactly?"

Josie was avoiding eye contact at this point. She looked at the chipped polish of her fingernails. "Well, she didn't go to nun school or whatever, so I guess it just depends on what you think a nun is. I mean, if it's just a lady with an outfit who helps others, then she's a nun . . . but she didn't start out that way."

Dan put his hands on Josie's shoulders and made her look at him. "Josie," he said, "let's skip this part and get to the kicker, shall we?"

Josie hoped Peg would forgive her, but she had to say it. "She was a working girl."

Dan narrowed his eyes in confusion. Josie waited to see if it would clear up on its own, but Dan's face remained completely blank. Josie halfway rolled her eyes. "You know, a hooker." She might as well have said Peg was a spider monkey.

"A hooker." Dan's tone was flat as a communion wafer. "A hooker," he repeated, nodding his head slowly. "I see." Though he didn't. He couldn't. It was too far-fetched, but at the same time it sort of explained the tattoo. Josie launched into Peg's story. Her father's death, the abusive stepfather, the move to Hollywood, the money problems, and her eventual foray into prostitution. Dan listened patiently. When she finished, Dan felt Josie had left a few pertinent details unexplained. "I'm sorry," he said, "but the nun-hooker connection still escapes me."

"Oh, that." Josie noticed part of her T-shirt had come untucked, so she pulled the rest of it out. "This was, what, about five or six years ago, I guess. I was maybe sixteen and pretty new to it all, had no idea what I was doing. Anyway, I'm out there one night all depressed and I'm thinking about killing myself or something when I see this nun coming down the sidewalk. Now, I'd heard about this place called the Care Center, all the girls had heard about it, you know, a place to get off the street and whatever. So when I saw this nun, I asked if she was the sister from the Care Center. So it's Sister Peg, right? She just laughed and said she had a john with a nun thing. He liked her to dress up and spank him with a ruler, stuff like that, you know. So, anyway, I was all, 'I can't do this anymore' and I started crying and I didn't know what to do."

Josie looked down and didn't like the way her T-shirt looked, so she started tucking it back in as she talked. "At first Peg thought I was tryin' to scam her with the crying and everything, but then she could tell I was really losing it. Peg's all, 'I'll take you home.' And I'm all, 'No, Donnie'll kill me if I go back to the apartment.'" Josie looked up. "Donnie was my pimp. Peg knew who Donnie was and knew he'd beat me half to death if I quit working, so she drove me out to the Care Center, you know? It was kinda late, but this old nun answered the door." Josie smiled as she remembered this part. "She had the sweetest face. I'm pretty sure she knew Peg wasn't really a nun, but she never said anything. She just took me in and gave me a room, no questions asked. Peg came out to help with stuff for the next few days. Sometimes she brought food, other times she worked in the kitchen. A few weeks later, the older nun died.

"Peg stuck around a few more days, just helping out, waitin' 'til another nun showed up or something, but no-body else came. All the people there were depending on her, so she just moved in, just gave up tricks and never took off the habit. Pretty soon everybody called her Sister Peg." Josie looked at Dan, all serious. "Are you going to turn her in?"

"Nah, I'm a priest," he said. "Your confession's confi-dential." Dan sat on the edge of the bed and tried to gauge his feelings about this revelation. Given his own deceit, Dan wasn't in a position to be angry about being duped. Let he who is without sin cast the first stone and all that. He certainly didn't have anything against bighearted hookers, but it did feel a little odd suddenly to discover that he was in love with one. Especially in light of the fact that he thought he was in love with a nun, which was weird enough in sort of the opposite way.

"It'll kill her if they close the Care Center," Josie said.

"I know." Dan stood and headed for the door. "Don't worry about it. I don't plan to let them close us down," he said. "I've got an idea." He exited to the hallway and headed for the elevator, suddenly thinking about Mary Magdalene. He punched the down button. *What idea?* he thought. *I got shit for ideas.*

*   *   *

The Bradley Terminal at Los Angeles International Airport services airlines from more than forty countries. Fourteen million foreign travelers pass between its smoky glass walls every year. On any given day you can hear the phrase "they lost my damn luggage" in at least seventy different languages. It's a regular Tower of Babel.

Deplaning at the Bradley Terminal, the Third World Man is still wearing the clericals he stole in Addis Ababa. He likes the way people treat him when he's dressed this way. "Thank you, Father." The Customs officer waves him through with his luggage.

On the other side of Customs a man wearing casual clothes waits for his Third World friend. This man was from Africa too, originally, but lives in Los Angeles now. He says he is in the import-export business.

"Have you found the priest?" the Third World Man asks.

The import-export man shakes his head no. "But I know where to look."

"Good." The two men walk in silence to the parking structure across from the Bradley Terminal. They reach the car that belongs to the import-export man. The Third World Man gets in and looks at his friend, who points at the glove compartment. The Third World Man opens the latch and finds a .45. "Let's go see my priest," he says.

With Peg still in the hospital, Dan was in charge. Eviction was six days off and there were boxes all over the Care Center waiting to be packed. For the moment, however, Dan had stopped packing them. Instead, he was holding his mother's head steady at arm's length. "Open your mouth," he said, tilting her head back slightly. "Let me look under your tongue." Ruth tried to pull her head away, but Dan had a good grip. "I just want to make sure you swallowed your pill." He poked an index finger at her tightly pursed lips.

After a couple of pokes, Ruth shooed Dan's hand away and opened her mouth wide. She lifted her tongue and wiggled it about like a suddenly unearthed bait worm. "Being a priest wasn't enough," she said. "You have to pretend you're a doctor now."

"No, I'm pretending I care," Dan said, his voice lowered slightly.

"Don't give me that." Ruth grabbed Dan's head just like he had hers. "You care," she said, shaking his head side to side. "You've always cared."

"Mom, let go of my head." Ruth let go and sat at the kitchen table, where she was sewing Alissa's doll back together. "Thank you for taking your medicine," Dan said. He sat down at the table and screwed the top back onto the bottle of pills.

Ruth tied a tiny knot with the thread, then checked to see that the doll's head was secure. She bit through the thread, then held the doll up for inspection. "You know what I don't understand?" she asked. "I don't understand why Michael ran off to help the rest of the world instead of helping his own family."

Dan thought she sounded more puzzled about it than angry. "I guess he figured I could do it. Besides, he came back to take care of you. He didn't know he was going to die."

Ruth shrugged. "I suppose."

Dan shook the orange prescription bottle and counted the pills. Eight left. No refills. He wondered how he'd pay for the medicine after the Care Center closed and his brief career as a priest came to an end. What would happen to Alissa and Ruben and Captain Boone and Mrs. Gerbracht and Mr. Saltzman and all the others? Most of all he wondered about Peg. Since she wasn't a real nun, she wouldn't be taken care of by her order. Maybe she'd join one. It was a better option than returning to her previous line of work.

But if she entered a convent, where would that leave Dan? In love with a real nun. Great.

Maybe the answer lay in telling Peg the truth. Maybe if she knew he wasn't really a priest . . . then what? Then they'd be laypeople living on the street. Terrific. Dan pushed away from the table and looked at the partially packed boxes. Where would they take all this stuff? How the hell would they move it all? "Let me ask you," Dan said. "How is it that we have nothing to speak of yet we're going to need a large truck to move it all? How is that possible? No one here has more than a suitcase of belongings." Dan shook his head. "Unbelievable."

Ruth put her needle and thread aside. "Son, what would you say if I told you that for the past twenty years I'd been putting little bits of money in the stock market?"

Dan froze. Was this possible? Had his mother accidentally invested at the best time in the history of Wall Street? Had she used some of the money he had given her as an allowance? It was possible. He remembered hearing a story about a poor black woman in Mississippi who saved money from her job as a domestic. She invested in the market and one day, out of the blue, she donated several million dollars to a state university. Dan turned to his mother. "You own stocks?"

"Mutual funds," she said. "About a million dollars worth."

Dan nearly keeled over. "A million dollars?" He stood there, his mouth agape. As impossible as it seemed, he wanted desperately to believe it was true.

Ruth began to laugh. "Dan, I'm kidding. You think I'd be living like this if I had a million bucks? It was a joke."

Dan's jaw tightened. He was unable to locate his sense of humor. He walked over to his mother and laid his hands on her shoulders. "Don't do that," he said. "That's not funny."

"Lighten up," she said. "You'll figure something out. I got faith."

It happened every day at work. Scott would end up in a trance, mesmerized by the deluge of images coming from the wall of televisions and the forty sets of speakers that stood before him like an electronic hypnotist. Once the images of the vast wasteland had arrested Scott's eyes, his mind was free to wander, but it didn't stray far.

As he stood lost in his bewitchment, Scott weighed the pros and cons of his quest. He eventually came to the ugly realization that he was in a no-win situation. If he never found Dan, Scott was doomed. If he killed Dan and got away with it, no one would ever know that Scott had been the real genius behind the "More Is More" campaign. If he killed Dan and got caught, severe punishment loomed, but at least there was an upside. If he were put on trial for murdering Dan, Scott would at least be able to tell the world that the "More Is More" campaign was his idea. Such a revelation probably wouldn't do him any good in the prison yard, but at least his father would know that his son had accomplished something.

Ruben was looking through the want ads. There were several listings for entry-level positions as animators and graphic artists, but he wasn't sure he was qualified. He didn't really know what a graphic artist was, but it was the only job with the word *art* in it, so it was the only one that seemed to match what Ruben thought of as his only marketable skill. The jobs required several years of experience and proficiency with various computer programs, the names of which Ruben had never heard. Still, all he had to do was send a résumé. Unfortunately, Ruben didn't have a typewriter, and even if he did, Ruben didn't have the slight-

est idea how to make a résumé. He knew there were résumé services, but he figured they cost more than he had.

He reached into his back pocket and pulled out his thin
wallet. Inside were his last four bucks, not enough to do
much of anything, certainly not enough to get a résumé.
Ruben decided to do the only sensible thing. He folded the
paper and headed for the convenience store. He figured the
odds of someone like him winning the lottery were better
than the odds of winning a job. He took his time filling
out the form. He used all his best numbers—his mother's
birthday, the anniversary of his brother's death, the street
address of the Care Center—numbers that were sure to
win. He kissed the ticket and put it in his pocket. On the
way back he stopped at Holy Family Church to light a
candle and say a prayer. He promised to share the winnings.

The drawing was at seven. The jackpot was eight million dollars, enough to solve everyone's problems. Ruben
waited patiently in front of the television; he had done all
he could. Finally the machine whirred to life and the num-
bered balls began flying around the Plexiglas sphere like
tiny, round angels. Ruben knew the key was to get the first
number. If he didn't get that one, it was all over, he
couldn't win. Ruben directed his prayers at the screen as
the first ball was selected. It was one of Ruben's numbers.
At that instant, everything was still possible. For the brief
moment between the selection of the first number and the
second, the future was bright as a star in the east. Ruben
bought a big house for everyone to live in and a new Suburban and lots of food and a new television and then the
second number was selected and the dream ended. The best
that could happen was a second prize in the thousand-dollar
range and then the third number was selected and even
that hope was dashed.

*   *   *

Captain Boone smiled politely when Mrs. Gerbracht shuffled past his room, but his heart wasn't in it. In truth, he didn't feel so good. Was it melancholy or was he ill? He didn't know exactly what was wrong, but whatever it was, he didn't like it. Other than the sound of Mrs. Gerbracht shuffling sadly down the hall, the big old house was quiet. It was more despairing than peaceful. It was the quiet desperation of the disenfranchised.

Captain Boone had been sitting by the phone for three hours. He had to find a new place to live. He didn't want to burden anyone, but since he didn't have money to get his own place, he'd have to impose on someone. *I don't need much,* he'd say, if he could just think of someone to call. *Just a place to sleep and a little food—hell, I probably won't be around for much longer anyway, right?* He'd say this with a little laugh. All he wanted was a decent place to die.

He picked up his Purple Heart and looked at it. He felt an emptiness and, as he sat alone in his room, he took stock of his life. He came to grasp the significance of not having any family left, of being alone in the world, of not being able to care for himself. All his friends were either dead, in nursing homes, or dying with their own children. The VA still couldn't find his records. Captain Boone knew that lots of veterans lived on the streets. He just never thought he'd be one of them.

He looked at the medal in his hands, red and stiff with arthritis. They looked like the gnarled roots of a dying tree. He knew it was time to change his appliance, but his hands wouldn't let him. That's when he realized why he felt the way he did. It was the same way he felt as he lay in that building in France with his stomach blown open. Sitting in his quiet little room, all alone, unable to help himself, he saw what the future held for him and he was scared to death.

*   *   *

Dan was sitting on the back steps wondering how things had come to this. How was it possible, he wondered, in a nation as rich and generous as this one, that people could end up homeless and hungry? A year ago, while producing some national spots for the United Way, Dan saw all the statistics, so he knew how much money was out there. He knew that donations to the top four hundred charities in the United States were in the neighborhood of $145 *billion* annually. On top of that was all the government money. Not only did the Social Security Administration pay out $365 billion a year, but the Department of Health and Human Services, which included Food Stamps and Aid to Families with Dependent Children, spent $354 billion annually. And it wasn't as if all this charity and entitlement money had just materialized. This had been going on for decades.

Where did all that money go? Sure, the president of the United Way was convicted of embezzling funds back in '92, but not *all* the charitable money got stolen. Were things so dire that it took *half a trillion* dollars a year just to keep the number of children living in poverty down to fourteen million?

And why was it, Dan wondered, that health-related charities seemed to make progress on a regular basis—discovering successful treatments for cancer and AIDS, for example—but one never saw a headline like: *Poor Problem Solved!* or *Everybody Fed!* One would think by now the problem might be under control, but in fact, it was just getting worse. How was that possible? Was Dan missing something? Was he just stupid? Did a trillion dollars not go as far as it used to? It occurred to him that if the residents of the Care Center were in the middle of the San Diego Freeway, victims of an auto accident, in need of emergency help, they'd get it. Passersby would stop to help, ambulances would arrive. It struck Dan that the difference was that *here* there was no literal carnage, no blood, no overturned cars, nothing to entice the news cameras. It was because no one really *looked* like they needed help that no one was going to give it to them. This, it occurred to Dan, was the other side of the image-is-everything coin.

Dan considered falling to his knees to pray for divine intervention or a saint's intercession but decided that was pointless. If prayer were the answer, there wouldn't be any more questions. Dan knew it had been left to him to find the solution for the Care Center just as sure as he knew he had failed to find it. About all he could do at this point was to go back inside and start packing; however, just as he was about to stand up and go back inside, he heard a tiny voice.

"Father, where are we moving to?" It was Alissa. She had a paper bag which held her few belongings. It was the first time Dan had heard her say anything.

Dan hesitated. He didn't want to lie to her any more than he wanted to tell her the truth, but he had to tell her something. "Uh . . . it's a surprise," he said, splitting the difference.

Alissa sat down next to Dan. "Father, can we move to that place where the people are all dressed up where Sister Peg took us when I got to be like Cinderella?"

Dan put his arm around her. "Well, I don't know where that is, Alissa. But I'll ask Sister Peg when I see her."

"It was over there," Alissa said, pointing vaguely toward Los Angeles. "It was real fancy and there were people playing pretty music and there was so much food you couldn't eat it all and Sister brought her friends from TV and I even got to dance on the dance floor." She sounded amazed that something that nice had happened to her, like she didn't deserve it.

Dan was suddenly aware of the tingling. *Friends from TV?* Dan scratched his scalp and looked away as a stream of consciousness rushed into his head. *Image is everything.*

Things started to come together in Dan's mind. *Nothing to entice the news cameras.* Dan stood and started twitching like a fool. Snapsnapsnapsnapsnap. *No one really looked like they needed help* . . . Alissa looked up suspiciously as Dan snapped his fingers. "Oh. My. God," Dan said. "Right in front of me the whole time."

"Father, are you okay?"

Dan leaned down and kissed Alissa on the forehead. "I'm fine," he said. "And you, my little Cinderella, are a genius."

14

Dan decided not to tell Peg that he wasn't a priest. If he did, Peg might admit that she wasn't a nun, and Dan felt his plan would work better if she maintained her ruse for everyone.

Peg was propped up in her bed reading a magazine when Dan got to the hospital. "I'm afraid I've got bad news, Sister." Dan pulled up a chair next to her bed. "Mr. Sturholm got zoning approval for his project. But I've got some good—"

"Damn." Peg laid the magazine down on her lap. "I guess I shouldn't be surprised," she said. "Where does that leave us?"

"We've got to be out of the house in a few days."

Peg remained expressionless for a moment. "Have you told everybody?"

"They know," Dan said. "We already started packing." He wasn't sure how she would react to the news. He saw tears welling in her eyes. "You okay?"

Peg looked at the ceiling, then, after a moment, she let out a long sigh. "You know what? It's almost a relief," she said. Her lips formed a defeated smile. "Hey, at least we tried, right?" She forced a laugh. "Tell you the truth, I don't think I could have gone on much longer. It was starting to wear me out."

Dan touched her arm. "Yeah, well, I understand, but I may have—"

"Maybe it just wasn't meant to be," she interrupted. "I mean they say everything happens for a reason, right? One door closing means another one is opening, that sort of thing. Maybe this is God's way of telling me to give it up." She looked to Dan.

Dan shook his head. "I don't think so," he said. "That's not the sort of thing God tends to say."

"No? Then what do you think?"

Dan was thinking he wanted to see that snake tattoo again, but he couldn't say that. "I think it was His way of telling *me* how to solve our little problem."

"Yeah, well, maybe you're right," she said. "So, Father, how many— What?" Peg perked up and looked at Dan. "What do you mean?"

Dan swaggered a little. "It's time to kill the fatted calf."

Peg was too disillusioned to hold out much hope for Dan's idea—or anything else for that matter—but at the same time, she was encouraged by his shit-eating grin. "Father?"

Dan pushed back in his chair and made a frame of his fingers. "Okay, picture this," he said, and then he began pitching his heart out. This was the first time he had articulated the idea and it sounded even better than he thought. It was a simple plan with much to recommend it, and Dan's enthusiasm would have been hard not to catch. Five minutes later, when he finished, Dan stood at the foot of the bed, flushed and slightly out of breath. "So, whaddya think?"

Peg looked him in the eyes. "Father," she said, "you understand that's completely unethical, right?"

Dan sagged slightly. This wasn't the enthusiastic response he was looking for. "Depends on how you look at it," he said. "I think you need to consider the greater good here." He didn't think he'd have to defend his plan like this, especially to a woman who had recently helped frame a guy for assault with a deadly weapon.

Peg shook her head. "No, it doesn't matter how you look at it," she said. "It's fraudulent and dishonest and, quite frankly, the truth is I'm just pissed I didn't think of it myself." Her smile was bright as the pearly gates.

Dan smiled back. "They say the Lord helps those who help themselves."

They stayed up late working out the details. "One of the first things you have to do is meet with Monsignor Matthews," Peg said. "He's got some great contacts and leverage."

"Good," Dan said. "Put a little juice from the diocese behind this thing." Dan wasn't worried about fooling the Monsignor. The way Michael told the story, the two of them had never actually met. The thing that did worry Dan was the man's loyalties. "Sister, are you sure we can trust him with this?"

"Believe me," she said. "He's on our side."

Dan arranged the meeting and Monsignor Matthews showed up at the Care Center the next day. This was the first he'd heard about the shooting and he was keen to do anything he could.

"Hello, Monsignor," Dan said. "It's good to meet you finally. Thanks for all your help."

Matthews looked closely at Dan. "Father." His tone was cautious. Sure, he had helped Father Michael after that business in Africa, but he wasn't sure if the guy had ever returned from the deep end. His dependability was still in question. "Sister Peg tells me you have an idea that might save this place."

"Faith's a wonderful thing," Dan said. He folded his hands in front of himself, hoping he looked pious. "*Ad majorem Dei gloriam*, right?"

"Uh huh." Monsignor Matthews sensed something odd about Father Michael. He seemed to be trying awfully hard to be like a priest. *Who the hell speaks Latin anymore?* "Oh, by the way," Matthews said, "Cardinal Cooper sends his regards."

Dan responded casually, as if he weren't a bit surprised. "Well, tell him I said hello when you see him." Dan picked up a legal pad that contained some of the ideas he'd been jotting down. "Let me tell you what I—"

Monsignor Matthews stepped closer. "Does Peg know who you are?"

Oh shit, Dan thought. *That's not good.* "Uhhh, in what sense?"

"Cut the crap," Monsignor Matthews said with a scowl. "You're not Father Michael any more than I am."

Dan was busted and he knew it. He just nodded. "It was the Cardinal Cooper thing, wasn't it?"

"Let's just say Father Michael would have responded differently." Monsignor Matthews poked a finger into Dan's chest. "Let me tell you something. Sister Peg is my very dear friend," he said. "I feel very protective toward her." He poked Dan again, harder. "So just who the hell are you and what do you want?"

Dan didn't back down. "I appreciate the sentiment," he said. "I feel a little protective toward her myself." He gestured at a chair. "Sit down, I'll explain." Dan went through the whole story, from Scott Emmons to Razor Boy. After he had convinced Monsignor Matthews of who he was and what his intentions were, Dan outlined his idea.

When he finished, Dan crossed his arms and leaned against the desk. "So?"

Monsignor Matthews cleared his throat. "First of all, I'm sorry about your brother. He was a good man who deserved better than he got. Secondly, I think your idea is damn good." He snorted a chuckle. "You're my kind of priest." He extended his hand to shake. "And third," he said, "I can't believe you had something to do with those Fujioka commercials. More Is More! I love those."

Dan got on the phone and arranged a meeting with Val Logan, a segment producer at KNBC who had a good eye for this sort of thing. She welcomed Dan and Monsignor Matthews into her office that afternoon and listened to their story. "I love it," she said. "It's terrific." She flipped through her scheduling calendar. "I can give you a good ninety-second segment for tomorrow's five o'clock news, probably get a rerun at ten. How's that?" She looked quite pleased with herself.

"That's not good enough," Dan said. "We need two follow-up segments during the week, and we want live day-of-the-event coverage."

Val was shocked at the demands. "With all due respect, Father, most people are really glad to get the five- and ten-o'clock news," Val said.

Monsignor Matthews stood. "We are not most people, Ms. Logan." He leaned across her desk and tugged on the crucifix dangling from the chain around his neck. "We're with God."

Val stood up and got nose to nose with the Monsignor. "Yeah, and I'm with a network affiliate in the number two market in the country," she said. "I can't just do the same story three times." She leveled him with her steely eyes. "Are you giving me escalations?"

"Trust us," Dan said with a wink. "It's a local Emmy."

* * *

"It's so nice to meet you, Father," the woman says with a smile. "What can I do for you?"

"I am looking for my friend," the Third World Man replies. "Father Michael. We worked together briefly when he was in Africa. The refugee camps, you know."

The woman shakes her head sadly. "Ohhh, it must be so awful over there," she says. "I've heard terrible stories."

"Yes, the conditions are trying. I hope you can help me find him."

The woman is charmed by the man's accent and the way he fills out his clericals. "Always happy to help one of our own," she says as she walks over to the personnel files. "Father Michael . . ." Her voice trails off. "You know, his name sounds familiar for some reason. You say he was ordained in this diocese?"

"I believe that is right."

A moment later the woman pulls a file from the cabinet. "And here he is," she says. "Father Michael Steele." She opens the file and reads something. "Oh my." She looks up at the Third World Man, peering over the top of her glasses. "I remember now. That business with Cardinal Cooper." She closes the file. "I'm afraid Father Michael is no longer, uh, in full communion with the Church," she says gravely.

The Third World Man shakes his head. "I don't understand."

"He was excommunicated."

"I see."

The woman leans across the counter and whispers. "I don't have any of the details, but apparently Father Michael physically attacked the Cardinal without any provocation." The Third World Man watches the woman point at something in a file. "Oh, it says here that he has a brother somewhere in town." She puts the file back in the cabinet. "If you can track him down, I'm sure he'll be glad to help you."

*　　*　　*

Ruth was looking through the window at the television crew waiting in front of the Care Center. She was trying to figure out how she could get on camera. Maybe she could take the reporter hostage. He looked like a friendly guy, she thought. He'd understand it was just in fun, right? Then again, she didn't want to cause Dan any more trouble. She'd have to think of a less troublesome way to get on TV again.

The reporter's name was Jim Hamashi. He was a sharp-looking guy of Asian extraction. He was standing in front of the Care Center nonchalantly waiting for the desk anchor to throw it to him. He tucked his little earpiece in a bit tighter and suddenly the lights went on. Jim came to life like a remote-controlled action figure and addressed the lens with a practiced affability. "Thanks, Jess," he said. "Tucked away here, in a poor corner of the San Fernando Valley, is a humble place called, simply . . . the Care Center. It's a place where those who have fallen through the cracks of government programs and the safety nets of mainstream charities go for food and shelter."

Jim turned and walked up the steps into the Care Center, gesturing and narrating as he went. "As you can see, the Care Center operates on a shoestring budget, a shoestring that, unfortunately, is coming unraveled. In fact, the residents of this refuge are about to be thrown out on the street because the bank has foreclosed on their mortgage." Jim continued down the hall toward Sister Peg's office. "The person charged with trying to hold things together— the person who runs the Care Center—is a nun by the name of Sister Peg who *normally* works out of this office." Jim stepped aside so the camera could pan the cluttered but unoccupied room. "But today Sister Peg isn't here," Jim said with a hint of sadness. "For more on that, let's go to Val Logan. Val?"

"Thanks, Jim," Val said. She was framed in a close shot so that a viewer was unable to see where she was standing. "The reason you don't see Sister Peg behind that cluttered desk is that two days ago, she was gravely wounded in a drive-by shooting."

The camera pulled back to reveal that Val was standing by the automatic sliding doors of a hospital. "And if you thought things couldn't get any worse than that, think again. In another egregious example of patient dumping, the hospital where Sister Peg was treated for her wounds is kicking her out because she doesn't have the money to pay her bill."

Val turned just as the automatic doors of the hospital opened. Two orderlies emerged pushing a gurney on which Peg lay. Dan, wearing his clericals, walked alongside, apparently providing comfort. The orderlies stopped as Val approached to conduct her interview. "Sister Peg, what's your reaction to getting the bum's rush here?"

Peg slowly opened her eyes. Dan helped lift her head slightly so she could speak into the microphone. "It's not their fault," she said. "They have a business to run. I understand. I'm more concerned about the residents at the Care Center." She laid her head back on the pillow. Dan nodded to the orderlies, who rolled the gurney down the sidewalk toward the old Suburban. Dan lagged behind.

"With me now is Father Michael Steele," Val said. "Father, how is she?"

Dan played it very seriously. "Well, the doctors say she's not out of the woods by a long shot, complications are possible, but they won't let her stay here, so we're taking her back to the Care Center."

"Father, I know some of our viewers will want to help. What can they do?" In the background, viewers could see the orderlies loading Peg into the Suburban.

"Well," Dan said. "We're having a fund-raiser this Saturday. Anyone who wants to donate money or services or anything should give us a call. We'd appreciate it."

Val nodded. "For those who want to help, you can call the number on your screen and someone will gladly answer all your questions." Dan thanked Val and walked off camera. "There you have it," Val said. "A persevering Sister of Faith clinging to life in the hope that the public will pitch in and save her beloved center. Reporting from Burbank, this is Val Logan. Jess, back to you in the studio."

"Looks like a very worthy cause," Jess said with extreme unction.

"Indeed, it is," Val replied. "I encourage everyone to come out and lend a hand."

"Val, before you go, let me ask you a question," Jess said. "I know there are a lot of different orders of nuns out there. Can you explain the difference between the Maryknolls, the Ursulines, and the Carmelites?"

Val smiled innocently. "As a matter of fact, Jess, I can. Everyone knows that the Carmelites are chewier." She suppressed a big laugh. "Now, back to you in the studio."

Dan had four days to turn the residents of the Care Center into a public-relations juggernaut. *Oy*, he thought. Dan gave Ruben a list of the top ten billboard locations in Los Angeles. The idea was to co-opt the messages on these billboards, turning them into promotions for the "Save Sister Peg" campaign.

Mrs. Gerbracht, Mrs. Zamora, Mr. Avery, and Captain Boone became the direct-mail department. Peg and Ruth composed an emotionally charged letter about the poor nun struggling to help the disenfranchised, and Dan punched it up. Monsignor Matthews got a copy of the mailing list of every Catholic in Los Angeles who had ever responded to a direct-mail appeal for funding. Gerbracht, Zamora, Avery &

Boone, LLP, as they began to call themselves, addressed and stuffed the envelopes.

Mrs. Ciocchetti and Mr. Saltzman were turned into the "crackpot opposition team." Their job was to call all the local television stations and local radio talk shows and oppose—in radical terms—the notion that anyone should help this nun and her Care Center. Mrs. Ciocchetti argued loudly, frequently in Italian, and without any allegiance to logic in suggesting the whole thing smacked of socialism run amok. Mr. Saltzman played the belligerent atheist. The idea was simply to create conflict. The conflict would, at least in theory, create ratings which would result in greater awareness of the fund-raiser.

Once these parts of the machine were in motion, Dan and Monsignor Matthews hit the streets. Their first stop was the Great Western Forum in Inglewood. A call from the diocese to the Lakers' front office had arranged a face-to-face with the team. When they introduced Alissa and explained what happened to a lot of kids who got sucked into the foster care system, the players had only one question. "Can we bring some friends?"

Monsignor Matthews leaned back to look up. "You can do anything you want."

The players broke into their million-dollar endorsement smiles. They liked hearing that.

Dan and the Monsignor made similar trips to the offices of the Dodgers and the Kings and secured several more sports celebrities. Their next stop would be in Beverly Hills. They were heading for The Artist First Agency, where they hoped to sign up a few celebrities. As they struggled to get across town, slugging and cursing their way through the hordes of incompetent drivers, Dan and Monsignor Matthews talked about everything from their favorite television commercials, to the demise of the NBA after Michael Jordan, to their experiences at seminary. When Dan admitted to his agnostic leanings, Monsignor Matthews held up an index finger and said, "There lives more faith in honest doubt, believe me, than in half the creeds."

"I don't believe you'll find that in the Gospels," Dan said.

"It's Tennyson, though I forget the poem." He looked over at Dan. "But he's right."

Dan smiled. "Peg told me you didn't exactly adhere to the orthodoxy. I guess she wasn't kidding."

Matthews shrugged. "One does what one must," he said. He talked about diverting funds to Catholic-run health clinics that supplied birth control advice and materials and he took a dim view of any priest who refused to administer the sacraments to gay Catholics.

"What about, uh"—Dan snapped his fingers a few times—"that chapter and verse about they shall surely be put to death and all that?" Dan asked.

"What, Leviticus?" The Monsignor made a dismissive noise with his mouth. "Hermeneutic nonsense," he said. "Listen, I got a Jesuit friend who can cite Scripture to prove the earth is flat, but that doesn't make it so." Matthews gestured with his hands. "In my experience, when someone starts brandishing chapter and verse like a blunt object, your best strategy is to run like hell. In fact, for my money we could throw out everything except the Sermon on the Mount. You master that and everything else will follow. Sad to say, but the rest of that book is just a bad idea waiting to be interpreted."

Dan pulled into the parking garage at The Artist First Agency. "So how do you reconcile what you do when it's in opposition to Church doctrine?"

"I don't have much choice. Look, if I . . ." He stopped and thought about it. "When you consider . . ." He stopped again, still searching for the right words. "My sins are much worse if I don't follow my sense of where God is leading,"

Monsignor Matthews said. "Secondly, I have to consider
my sense of responsibility as a true disciple, and third, my
own conscience tells me what I'm doing is right. And I'm
not alone. I know a lot of priests who do the right thing,
even when it's contrary to dogma. That's what's good about
the Church. There are so many people who truly care."
Monsignor Matthews looked at The Artist First Agency's
beautiful art deco building. "So these guys represent the
stars?" He gazed at the gold-leaf sconces that dotted the
exterior of the building from top to bottom. "Looks like
they're doing pretty good business."

Dan thought about the last payday of one of the
agency's clients. "Ten percent of twenty million's nothing
to sneeze at."

Monsignor Matthews nodded. "Boy, talk about your
tithing."

The most famous billboards in Los Angeles are the ones
lining the Sunset Strip, and the granddaddy of them all is
the Marlboro ad that's been there for the past seventeen
years. The sign is a Hollywood landmark as well as a monument to the power of outdoor advertising. And lately people had been paying more attention to it, since it was
scheduled to come down on the heels of all the tobacco
legislation. That's what made it such a great target.

It was two o'clock in the morning when Ruben climbed
up the sign with a large poster board, a can of spray paint,
and some glue. Forty-five minutes later he clambered back
down and returned to the Valley. Dan called the news-
rooms of several television stations as if he were the leader
of some addlebrained terrorist group, anonymously claiming
responsibility for what had been done to the billboard. Fortunately it was a slow news day, so that was all it took to
get a reporter out at dawn's first light to see if there was
a story.

That morning both KCBS and the local Fox affiliate aired two-minute segments about the mysterious co-opting of the Marlboro sign. The billboard featured a lone malignant cowboy gazing silently out at the range, only now his silence had been broken. Ruben had attached a cartoon dialogue balloon to the crease in the cowboy's leathery mouth. "Forget the cigarettes," the Marlboro man said. "Save Sister Peg." Best of all, it looked like he meant it. The brand's famous slogan had been altered to read, "Come to where the nun is."

The KCBS reporter pointed up at the sign. "It seems to be a guerrilla PR stunt," she said. "The 'Save Sister Peg' reference is an allusion to a fund-raiser happening this weekend out at the Care Center in Sylmar." The reporter then gave all the pertinent details about the event.

The reach of the TV coverage combined with the influential demographic captured by the billboard added up to some decent gross rating points. When the print media started requesting interviews, Dan called a press conference. Two hours later the newspaper reporters and Val's TV crew were assembled in the kitchen at the Care Center. Monsignor Matthews emerged from a room at the end of the hall and walked into the kitchen. He was wearing his power cassock, black with dark red piping and buttons and a little skullcap. "Thank you for coming out on such short notice," he said gravely. "I'm afraid I have bad news this afternoon . . ." He gestured for them to follow.

"This is Val Logan with a Channel Four News exclusive," she said as she followed the Monsignor. "I'm at the Care Center, the San Fernando Valley care facility that is fast becoming a cause célèbre."

Monsignor Matthews stopped at the door from which he had come earlier. He knocked gently. A second later he opened the door and showed the reporters in. Val and her cameraman shoved their way to the front of the crowd.

The room had been transformed into a showcase of religious images. One wall was thick with representations of the Virgin Mary. Against the opposite wall was a small altar where Ruben was fervently lighting candles. Josie knelt at Peg's bedside, conspicuously working a rosary. She was wearing one of Peg's older Dominican habits, its starched cornet extending like the wingtip stabilizer on a private plane. Ruth was next to her, draped in black, veil and all. All attention was focused on Peg. She lay in the bed, motionless, her eyes closed. She appeared to be hooked up to a life-support system. Beep. Beep. Beep.

Val whispered. "Father, how is she?" She thrust the microphone toward Dan.

"Not good," Dan said as he made the sign of the cross. "Last night, around ten o'clock, Sister Peg lapsed into a coma." Dan bit his lower lip before continuing. "There's nothing we can do for her now but try to keep her dream alive . . . her dream to open a new Care Center . . . to continue her good work." Beep. Beep. Beep.

As the newspaper guys scribbled their notes, Josie noticed Peg peeking out from her coma. Josie jabbed her gently with her crucifix.

"Do the doctors give her any chance of recovering?" one of the reporters asked. He didn't have much hope in his voice.

Dan slowly shook his head. "They said it would be a miracle."

That night Dan did a short radio interview to plug the fund-raiser one last time. He left the studio at ten and headed back for the Care Center, exhausted. As he drove across the Valley, he knew his time had run out. There was nothing to do now but wait to see what tomorrow would bring.

Dan pulled off the freeway and drove along Foothill

Boulevard. Up ahead on the right was Holy Family Church. Though he hadn't planned to do so, Dan pulled into the parking lot. A minute later he was standing in the cool and quiet of the vestibule, dipping his finger into the font of holy water and crossing himself.

Holy Family wasn't exactly a cathedral. It was a simple wood-frame building that had been a VFW hall before becoming a church. Still, there was a mysterious quality about it that appealed to Dan. It was just four walls and a roof, yet it conveyed a sense of peace that Dan imagined it lacked in its VFW days. He stood still for a few moments, absorbing the serenity. It reminded him why he turned to the Church during his chaotic childhood. The calm soothed his jangled soul. Dan walked down the aisle, stopping near the front. He genuflected without thinking about it, then slid into the pew. He looked around at the stained-glass windows dimly lit by the moonlight, then closed his tired eyes and took a deep, relaxing breath.

Dan sat there a few minutes before he had the notion to ask God for help. He decided against it on the grounds that it would be bad form to ask God to get involved in a fraudulent PR campaign. For that, Dan would leave his faith in the media—a false god, perhaps, but one with whom Dan was on better terms. Still, he got down on his knees and prayed, not for the fund-raiser, but for his brother's soul.

15

Six A.M. Dan was sitting in the kitchen waiting for the coffee to brew. He wasn't feeling terribly optimistic. A few people had called asking about the fund-raiser and some ten-dollar donations had come in the mail, but there was no indication that the public had been swept away by the campaign.

Dan poured two cups of coffee and went to Peg's room. He walked in and found Peg on her knees in front of the altar Ruben had set up. "Hey, get back in bed," Dan said. "You're supposed to be in a coma."

"Just asking for a little help, Father." Peg stood up and took the coffee from Dan. "What's that?" she asked.

"Coffee, what's it look like?"

"No," Peg said. "That noise."

Dan tilted his head and listened. It was the sound of heavy equipment. *Bulldozers? Maybe Larry Sturholm had come early to raze the building.* "Get back in your coma," he said. "I'll go see." Dan was ready to tear a strip off the weaselly bastard, but then it occurred to him that, if nothing else, the bank's bulldozers destroying the Care Center would make terrific television. *One last shot of triple-strength PR wouldn't hurt*, he thought.

When he got outside Dan saw neither Larry Sturholm nor a bulldozing crew. Instead, he saw a large flatbed truck and a stout guy who Dan assumed was the driver. "Good morning, Father!" the man shouted from the road. "Could you use a small Ferris wheel?" The sign on the side of the truck read, "Southern California Carnival Rides."

Dan smiled and felt an unexpected surge of hope. "God bless you. Want some coffee?"

Seven A.M. Dan didn't know what to think when a truck pulled up loaded with lumber. "What am I supposed to do with that?" Dan asked.

"Ask those guys," the driver said. He pointed at a caravan of pickup trucks that was pulling in behind him.

It was a group of carpenters from Local 44. "Saw you on TV," one of them said. "Thought you might need a little stage and maybe some booths for games and whatnot."

Mrs. Zamora and Mrs. Ciocchetti, who were big fans of Jerry Lewis's annual telethon, imposed upon the men to build a big glittery tote board to tally the funds raised.

Eight A.M. The owner of a local doughnut shop dropped off two dozen boxes of doughnuts and muffins. Several more volunteers showed up to offer help. Captain Boone directed some of them in painting signs for the booths, and Mr. Avery got the others to spruce up the property a little. A group from a synagogue in Studio City showed up with several hundred dollars' worth of groceries and went inside to make breakfast for everyone.

Eight-thirty A.M. Val Logan and the KNBC van arrived for early coverage. "Well, Bob, the spirit of volunteerism seems to be alive and well," she reported. Val turned to stop two women who were delivering coffee and doughnuts to the other volunteers. They were both wearing tight jeans and loose sweatshirts, and they seemed to be hiding behind baseball caps and sunglasses. "Excuse me," Val said. "What brought you two out this morning?" The women seemed familiar to Val, but she couldn't place their faces.

The taller woman tossed her hair theatrically, then shrugged. "I woke up feeling charitable this morning," she said in a sort of mock-bitter tone, "which *never* happens. So I called my friend and we decided to come by and see if we could give a little back to the community, as they say."

With that, the shorter woman took off her glasses and her baseball cap and Val nearly fainted. It was Madonna. *The* Madonna. "Let's go, El Lay," she exhorted. "Save Sister Peg!"

The taller woman yelled into the camera. "Get your butts out here and bring your big fat wallets! We got a comatose nun to take care of, dammit!" They walked off cackling, leaving Val stupefied. "Uh, back to you in the studio, Bob."

Nine A.M. After the Material Girl's TV appearance, word spread like a brushfire in a Santa Ana wind. Cars full of people from all over Southern California were suddenly heading for Sylmar. Dan put Josie and Mr. Saltzman in charge of parking. "Park it over there, buster! Don't look at me that way!"

A radio van arrived, followed by a black stretch limo. Ricky D, L.A.'s most popular and outrageous radio personality, showed up to do a special Saturday broadcast. "You know what I'd like to see," Ricky said. "I'd like to see the comatose nun naked. What do you want to bet that I can get that priest to take me in there and show me some nun tit?"

"Ricky, you are awful," his sidekick said. "I shouldn't

even be sitting next to you, you're going to get struck by lightning."

"C'mon, where's the harm?" Ricky insisted. "She's in a coma, she's not gonna care."

By noon, the party had spilled onto the street and LAPD had replaced Josie and Mr. Saltzman in the parking and traffic-control department. Every television station in Los Angeles had a mobile unit on site covering the story. The amount of coverage itself had become a story within a story, with late-arriving reporters interviewing the ones who had been on the story since it broke. A quick glance at the tote board showed that they had raised $4,832.

One P.M. A half dozen middle-aged musicians showed up with roadies and equipment and asked to see Father Michael. They weren't a group per se, more of a collection of the faceless studio musicians that Los Angeles is known for. Dan recognized the keyboard player but couldn't think of his name. When the guitar player introduced the band, all he said was that they had once played backup for Jay and the Americans. They started off by playing a familiar pop song that was reminiscent of something by Horace Silver. Josie hopped onstage and sang backup.

Two P.M. Mrs. Gerbracht and Mrs. Zamora were taking in good money at their concession booth, where they were selling cheese fritters, grilled cheese sandwiches, and cheese-on-a-stick. Every now and then they would hear Alissa yell "Hello!" as she circled endlessly on the Ferris wheel.

Three P.M. The Los Angeles Lakers arrived with their crosstown rivals, the Clippers, the Laker Girls, and two portable basketball hoops which they set up on the street in front of the Care Center. They announced that they would play anybody who put up $500 for the cause. First team to ten would win. Make it, take it. They raised $10,000 in forty minutes without breaking a sweat. "Hey, big man, post one up for Sister Peg!" Two minutes later you could hear one of them yell, "Game! Next! Get off the court with that weak stuff!"

Four P.M. The streets of Sylmar were absolutely choked. The Care Center was surrounded by dozens of media vans and satellite transmission trucks. Church groups were arriving in school buses and thousands of cars were pouring off the freeways. People were parking a mile away and hiking in. It was the most amazing display of people coming together in the history of the city.

Four-thirty P.M. "This is an unprecedented event," a network news anchor said. "Police are estimating the crowd at over sixty thousand and I've just been told that they've closed the Foothill Freeway due to traffic. Let's go over to John Randall, who is somewhere near the stage. John?"

Dan ducked into Peg's room. "Hey, it's almost time."

"Ready when you are." Peg pulled back the covers, revealing a thick, full-length white cotton nightshirt. "How's it going out there?" She sat on the edge of the bed and made sure her wimple was on tight.

"It's unreal," Dan said. "We've raised close to ninety thousand dollars and people are still getting here. Oh, and Ricky D says he'll cough up ten thousand bucks if he can see you naked from the waist up."

Peg smiled and wiggled her toes. "Gosh, that's awfully tempting but . . . no."

"That's what I told him. I said, 'Ricky, for God's sake, she's a nun. She's in a coma. It's gonna cost at least fifty

K.'" Dan couldn't help staring at Peg's feet. He had worked with professional foot models in his print advertising days, but he had never seen sexier toes in his life.

Peg stood up and held her hands out to Dan. "Come here," she said. Dan walked over to her. "You saved us," she said before she kissed him on the cheek. "Thank you."

Dan held up his hands. "Enlightened self-interest," he said. "This place goes under and I'm unemployed. Plus, I think we make a pretty good team, you and me." Dan suddenly felt like a fifteen-year-old trying to sound like Bogart. "I didn't want it to end, that's all." He shrugged.

"I don't want it to end either," Peg said, gesturing for the door. "So let's make sure it doesn't."

"Well, all right then," Dan said as he opened the door. "Let's coup de grâce."

John Randall was standing halfway between the stage and the front of the Care Center. "I haven't seen this many celebrities in one place since that two-for-one special at the Betty Ford Clinic." John shaded his eyes against the bright sun as it filtered through the brown haze. "Just looking around, I can see eight or ten stars from television, film, and the recording industry." John approached an Academy Award–winning actor. "Can you believe the turnout for this thing?"

"It's unbelievable," the actor said, turning to make sure the camera was getting his best side. He looked into the lens. "Come on out here and save Sister Peg!"

In the background, a man held up a sign that read "John 3:16."

Ruben had his artwork on display in the booth nearest the stage. He had sold several of his paintings and had an offer for a gallery showing. He was just standing there, looking at the huge crowd in pure, delighted amazement, when supermodel Stacy Sanders walked by and smiled at him. He could almost hear her teeth. Unbelievable.

A moment later another beautiful woman with a winning smile walked up to the booth and started looking at Ruben's work. He didn't know it, but she was a prolific and talented film producer. She seemed to like one or two of the paintings, but something else really caught her eye. It was a multimedia sculpture composed of exactly one thousand two hundred and thirteen dollars worth of losing lottery tickets. She had to have it. "How much?" she asked.

Ruben read her lips. He smiled, then wrote a figure on a piece of paper: "$1,213."

"Sold."

Ruth was upstairs in her room. She had been sitting on the corner of her bed most of the afternoon. She felt useless, like she was doing nothing to save the Care Center, nothing to help Dan. She felt like she was just in the way. She wanted to help, so she opened the box that held her belongings and she reached in. She found the razor blade and held it between her thumb and forefinger. She had to do something, so she put it to her skin.

Oren Prescott was in his Malibu home, depressed and a little drunk. He was trying to get his mind off his inability to come up with a decent new campaign idea for Fujioka. He could feel the account slipping between his fingers. He grabbed the remote control and turned on his eighty-two-inch Fujioka big-screen, hoping for something to distract him for a little while.

What he got was a network news reporter standing in the middle of what looked like tens of thousands of people. She was interviewing a priest. "Father, in your wildest dreams did you imagine this sort of response?"

"It's fantastic," the priest said. "Unbelievable! I think

we're close to a hundred thousand dollars. I don't know what to say.''

Oren dropped his drink. He'd heard that voice a thousand times. He looked closer at the giant face spread across the screen. It was the face of Oren's savior.

The network news reporter was wrapping up her segment with Dan when suddenly there was a commotion on the front porch of the Care Center. "What's going on?" the reporter asked. The cameraman turned and zoomed in on the excitement.

Someone shouted, "It's Sister Peg!"

Peg was all but staggering across the porch with one hand on her forehead. Dan thought she was overplaying it a bit. The reporter grabbed Dan's arm. "Oh my God," she said. "It's a miracle! She's out of the coma!"

Dan pulled away from the reporter and rushed to Peg's side. He pulled her close and whispered, "Stop hamming it up, for crying out loud. You're out of a coma, not back from the dead."

A deafening chorus of cheers spread through the crowd like waves and Mrs. Ciocchetti updated the tote board to $102,900.

The Third World Man is in his room at the Sunset Palm Motor On Inn, depressed and seriously drunk. He is trying to get his mind off the fact that he can't find the damn priest. He's depressed because if he fails to collect the money or kill the priest who owes it, General Garang will kill him instead when he returns to Africa.

He decides to change clothes. He's been wearing the clericals for four days running and they're getting ripe. He puts on a white pullover shirt and some Dockers. He pours another drink and turns on the television, hoping for something to distract him from his troubles.

He surfs for a minute before he sees an attractive reporter. He likes the way she's dressed. She is interviewing a priest, and not just any priest either. The Third World Man drops his glass. He can't believe his sudden good luck. "Praise Allah," he says.

After taking Peg back to her room, Dan returned to answer a few more questions for the press. They were still talking when the front door opened again and Ruth stumbled out, blood flowing from where she had cut herself. She stood there, her arms out to her sides, as if she were nailed to an invisible cross. Her palms were bleeding.

Dan was horrified for a moment, then his mother winked at him, ever so slightly.

A devout Latina saw Ruth's bleeding wounds and collapsed in a heap.

Dan pointed at his mother and shouted, "The stigmata!"

Another woman saw it and crossed herself. "Santa Maria!" she yelled, before falling to her knees in prayer. The TV cameramen caught the whole thing. Dan rushed to the porch, where Ruth collapsed dramatically at his feet. He lifted his mother's head for the camera, then he whispered to her, "Nice one."

"Just trying to appeal to the crowd," she said. "The minorities love this stuff."

Scott Emmons was at Elite Electronics, thoroughly depressed. He'd been to confession at every Catholic church in greater Los Angeles without finding Dan. To make matters worse, and to make ends meet, he still spent his days surrounded by Fujioka products. Scott longed for something to distract him from the wall of televisions which served as a constant reminder of his father's assessment of him.

"Hey, dude," a young man said, tapping Scott. "Can

you show me how the picture-in-picture works on that Fujioka?" He pointed to a huge flat-screen television that was showing a college basketball game.

Scott handed the young man a remote control. "Okay, it's on ESPN now, right? Let's say you want to see what's on Channel Two . . ." Scott pointed at a button. "Push that."

The young man pushed the button and KCBS popped up in the corner of the screen. They were replaying the interview with Dan just before Peg emerged from her coma. Scott snatched the remote from the young man and put KCBS on full screen. He stared at it for a moment. "Jumpin' Jesus," he said.

Dan was sitting next to his mom on the edge of her bed. He was wrapping gauze around her hands. "I hate to encourage this sort of behavior," Dan said, "but that was a stroke of genius."

Ruth looked pleased. "I bet there are thousands of people out there planning a pilgrimage at this very moment," she said. "And they'll bring money."

"Yeah, well, they better hurry or they're gonna find a strip mall for a shrine." Dan finished the bandages and helped his mom into the bed. "But at least they'll be able to get a Big Gulp and some corn nuts." Dan tucked the covers under her chin. "Do me a favor, no more miracles, okay?" Dan kissed her cheek, then stood. "I'm gonna go check on Sister Peg."

Dan walked to the end of the hall and looked out the window. There were people as far as he could see. It was the most amazing thing Dan had ever experienced. *These people actually care. They want to help. They rise in times of need.* They were compassion and generosity and the best of the human spirit, and Dan felt them touch his heart.

The next thing Dan knew he was tapping his foot to

the rhythm of Los Lobos tearing through their version of "La Bamba." He looked down and saw a couple of nuns leading a conga line through the crowd. Dan felt like the benevolent patriarch of a great family. That's when it dawned on him that Michael was right. He needed this. He needed these people as much as they needed him. That's what made him get up every day and get out there. He liked that people were counting on him.

Dan backed away from the window until he could see his reflection. Technically he was a fraud, but he didn't feel like one. In fact, Dan felt like he had realized the potential of his outfit better than many. Best of all, it looked as if he could continue to do so. Dan turned and walked down the stairs, stopping near the bottom. He looked around at the old house and thought about the morning he arrived there and the strange sensation that came over him that day. He had finally come to the conclusion that the tingling was the feeling of his soul breaking free of his denial. And once again he realized his brother had been right.

He remembered the moment he first saw Peg, how he had caught himself staring at her eyes. Dan was standing on the exact step where he had been when he first saw her, and as he stood there, thinking about her eyes, Dan felt the sensation again, not the exact same tingling, but something similar, maybe better. But this time he knew what it was. He was in love, and maybe a little nervous.

Dan walked down the hall to Peg's room and knocked. She was back in bed, where Dan had taken her after her miraculous recovery. "Hi there," he said. "It's time for revelations."

Peg sat up. "Okay." She had no idea what he meant.

Dan walked to the foot of her bed and laid his hands on the footboard. He looked up at Peg and smiled. He didn't know where to start. He hadn't really thought this through, but he knew he had to do it. He smiled again, then just blurted it out. "I know you're not a real nun," he said. *Oh God*, he thought, *that sounded terrible.* Dan started waving his hands as if to erase what he'd said. "But I don't care. In fact, it's good, no, it's great because it, uh . . . oh, Jesus, what I'm trying to say is . . . let me start over."

Peg put her hand over her mouth to hide her smile. Dan's stammering display of anxiety reminded her of every infatuated boy she'd ever known. His tone and sweet expression put Peg at ease. He wasn't here to bust her. "What *are* you trying to say, Father?"

"Well, a couple of things," he said. Dan sat down on the edge of her bed. "First of all, I'm not a priest. I'm Father Michael's brother, his twin actually. My name's Dan." He told her the whole story, from Michael's hospitalization to his own epiphany the day he arrived.

Peg's expression was somewhere between a mild *you're kidding* and an extreme *I don't believe this.* "It seems like I ought to feel betrayed by this," she said.

"Do you?"

She shook her head. "How did you find out about me? Monsignor Matthews?"

Dan shook his head. "No, Josie squealed on you, but it's not her fault." He gestured at Peg's thigh. "I saw your tattoo and I made her confess." He explained how it happened. "It's a great tattoo, by the way."

Peg wasn't exactly mortified, but she wasn't bursting with pride either. She couldn't look Dan in the eyes. "So, do you think less of me?"

Dan shook his head. "Nah, I used to be a whore too."

"I was a call girl," Peg said rather indignantly.

"Excuse me, call girl," Dan said. "I was just a flat-out whore myself."

Peg was quiet for a few moments as she considered the implications of these facts.

Dan made a self-mocking face. "I was in advertising."

Peg looked at Dan. "Prove it," she said.

Dan was confused. "Prove I was in advertising?"

"Prove that you're not a priest."

Dan thought about it for a second, then he did the only thing he could think of. He leaned down and kissed Peg until her wimple fell off. To be fair, it had to be said that Peg kissed back pretty good. They both knew it didn't prove a thing about Dan's status as a priest, but they were past caring about that.

Razor Boy and Charlie Freak are swept up in the wave of charity to the extent that they are helping themselves to the contents of all the cars parked along the side streets near the Care Center. The two of them are so loaded down with stolen property that they're talking about stealing a car to get it out of there. So when a red Chrysler Le Baron pulls over, and the driver asks where the fund-raiser is being held, the two gangstas sneer at one another. "Let's jack this punk," Charlie Freak says.

Razor Boy abruptly pulls his gun and yanks the car door open. "Get outta the car, nigga!" he screams as he yanks the man out. The driver is wearing a white pullover shirt and Dockers, and he suddenly has murder in his eyes. He is annoyed that this brown idiot has jammed a gun in his face and called him a nigga.

"Cap his black ass!" Charlie Freak feels the man isn't showing proper respect.

Razor Boy thumbs back the hammer on his .38 and is about to utter a gang slogan when the Third World Man pulls his own trigger. His shot rips through Razor Boy's gut and severs the thick cord of nerve tissue that is his spine. Razor Boy dies paralyzed.

For a moment Charlie Freak is paralyzed in his own way, then he fires a shot. It knocks the Third World Man backward into his car, cracking his head. He lies there, bleeding badly. His eyes are shut. Charlie Freak walks over to finish the job, but the Third World Man suddenly opens his eyes and fires. Part of Charlie Freak's head disappears and he crumples to the ground.

Dan had never been kissed the way Peg kissed him. "Wow," he said, "you *were* a pro."

Peg shook her head. "I never kissed back then," she said. "What you got was strictly from the heart."

Dan started to imagine some of the things she might be capable of. He swallowed hard and mustered all the self-mastery he could. "I think we better go outside."

They walked out the front door and waded into the crowd, thanking everyone as they went. "Holy cow," Dan said. "Looks like the celebrities have finally opened their checkbooks." He pointed at the tote board. It showed $179,664 raised.

After grabbing some cheese-on-a-stick, Dan and Peg stopped at the dunking booth to say hello to Monsignor Matthews. He was wrinkled and wet, having spent the last two hours being dropped into the tank. "Hey, Father," he yelled. "I bet you throw like a nun!" He made some taunting gestures from his moist perch.

Peg poked Dan with her elbow. "Don't let him dis you that way."

Dan picked up a ball and tried to think of a good baptism joke for the Monsignor. As he stood there in the middle of a sea of humanity, tossing the ball from one hand to the other, surrounded by the joyous noise of the fundraiser, Dan marveled at how everything had finally come together for him. He had everything he wanted. He was truly blessed, and he knew he could drop the Monsignor with one good throw. Dan was halfway through his windup when he suddenly felt a warm breath on his ear. A familiar voice spoke to him. "Dan, can I see you for a second?"

Dan? He knew the voice just as sure as he knew there was no escape. So much for being blessed. Dan turned to face Oren. "I'm sorry," Dan said, "I'm Father Michael, but I had a twin brother named Dan." He didn't know if Prescott had come to blackmail him or what. Dan just hoped he could keep Oren from making a scene. "You must have us confused."

"Perhaps," Oren said, his throat tight. "Still, I'd like to speak to you, Father. Or should I go talk to one of those reporters?"

Peg saw Dan's face sag. "Is something wrong?" She was feeling protective of her man.

"No," Dan said. "No problem. I just need to talk to this gentleman for a minute. He wants to make a donation." He tossed Peg the ball, then pulled Oren aside. "Don't blow this for me, Oren."

"Look," Oren said, "I don't care why you faked your death and I couldn't care less why you're dressed up like a priest. I got my own fucking problems. Fujioka is going to pull their goddamn account if I don't give them a follow-up to the 'More Is More' campaign. I need your help."

"I appreciate that," Dan said, "but—"

"Holy shit!" Oren shrieked like a schoolgirl. He grabbed Dan and spun him around, using him as a human shield.

Out of the crowd the Third World Man comes staggering toward his quarry. His countenance is strained, his eyes bulging and bloodshot. He ignores the transfiguration of the faces shifting from joyous to horrified. He is the carnival's uninvited sideshow. He will provide the macabre. He clutches his bloody wound with one hand and waves his gun with the other. He is screaming, "La illah illa Allah!"

*   *   *

Dan had no idea what that meant, but it gave him the distinct impression that he was about to die for someone else's deity.

The fund-raiser came to an abrupt and complete halt. The music stopped and the Ferris wheel ground to a standstill. A hush spread through the crowd outward from the epicenter as all eyes turned to the gunman and the priest.

"General Garang wants his money," the Third World Man said. His white shirt was washed in blood. He looked thoroughly deranged. "If I must die, you must die with me," he said.

"But . . . why?" Dan asked feebly.

"It is Allah's will!" he said. *"Allah akbar!"* Before anyone could do anything, the Third World Man pressed the gun against Dan's head.

Suddenly someone in the crowd screamed, "Nooo!" A split second later, everyone heard the gunshot. The Third World Man wobbled a bit, then hit the ground like a wet puppet.

Scott Emmons emerged from the crowd with the smoking gun. He looked disappointed. He had been aiming for Dan, but he missed. A moment passed while the crowd processed the information, then they erupted with a huge cheer. They rushed Scott, hoisting him onto their shoulders, hailing him a hero. The music started back up and the Ferris wheel roared back to life.

Peg ran to Dan and wrapped her arms around him. "Are you all right?" She squeezed him tightly.

"I'm fine." He squeezed back.

Mr. Prescott pointed at the conquering hero. "Good Lord," he said, "it's that idiot Emmons! He's probably coked out of his mind."

"I hate to tell you this," Dan said, "but Scott was the

idiot behind the Fujioka campaign. I stole it, just like he said."

Oren slapped a hand against his forehead. "Fuck! Oh, pardon me, Sister." Oren waved at the guys who were parading Scott around on their shoulders. "Bring him over here!"

Scott was high above the crowd, waving his gun, yelling, "More Is More! More Is More!"

Prescott turned to Dan. "Are you sure it was his idea?" Dan nodded ruefully.

They put Scott down in front of Dan and Oren. Sister Peg snatched the gun from him, but he was too dazed to care. Scott eyed Dan suspiciously. "More Is More," he said quietly.

Oren put his hands on Scott's shoulders. "Scott, Dan tells me that was your idea."

Scott turned to Oren and blinked once. "Fujioka," he said.

"Yes, Fujioka. I need another slogan, another campaign," Oren said. "You can have Dan's old office and anything else you want. Whaddya say?"

Scott looked at Oren and smiled. "It's Miller time!" he said.

"Dan, what about you?" Oren asked. "Will you come back?" He cast a sideways glance at Emmons. "He may need some supervision."

"Sorry, no can do," Dan said. "But do me a favor, I know a guy who'd make a great addition to the production studio." He pointed at Ruben. "He's got a gift. He'll make a good art director someday."

"Fine," Oren said. "Have him at the office Monday morning."

"Thanks," Dan said, "you won't regret it. And not only is he a talented artist, he's also a handicapped minority. EEOC won't ever bother you again."

Oren put his arm over Scott's shoulder and led him away. "Did I mention the time frame we're looking at?"

Dan turned to Peg and smiled. "Well, that almost ruined a perfectly good day."

"Almost."

"Dan Steele?" The voice was serious.

Dan turned and saw two cops standing next to Butch Harnett. "Dan Steele, you're under arrest for insurance fraud, credit card fraud, obstruction of justice, and filing a false death certificate." The cops cuffed him. "You have the right to remain silent. Anything you say can and will be used against you in a court of law . . ."

Dan's trial was one-sided to the extent that the evidence was undisputed and pointed directly to Dan. Given those impediments, Dan's defense consisted primarily of heartfelt testimonials about all the good he had done, the lessons he had learned, how he was just trying to help his dying brother, and except for the credit card fraud, how he hadn't done anything for his own profit.

It took just two days to hear all the testimony. The judge then instructed the jury as to the pertinent points of law and sent them off to deliberate.

An hour later, the jury filed back into the jury box. Dan and his public defender took this as a good sign. Peg, Ruth, Ruben, Alissa, and the rest of the Care Center crowd were all in the gallery. Captain Boone gave Dan a vigorous thumbs-up in an attempt to boost his diminished spirit. Dan responded with a weak smile.

"Has the jury reached a verdict?" the judge asked.

The jury foreperson stood and smiled. "Yes, Your Honor," she said. "We have."

The truth had come out during the trial. *Fake Nun Fakes Coma!* was the headline. The newspaper articles said Sister

Peg and Father Michael were frauds, albeit well-meaning ones. The reporters explained Dan's insurance scam and pointed out that Peg had a record for prostitution. According to the papers, Dan and Peg had conned everybody who gave their time or money at the fund-raiser. But, to be balanced, they also explained why Michael had been excommunicated and didn't have any insurance. They also talked about the fact that Peg had been helping the poor for several years and, as far as they could tell, had done none of it for personal gain.

When Ruben found out the truth he was surprised. A reporter asked if he knew all along that Peg wasn't a nun. Ruben signed that he didn't have a clue. "She seemed like a nun to me." He judged her by what she did, not by whether she had taken part in a secret nun ceremony.

When the public heard the story, they reacted, almost without exception, by sending more money. They sympathized with Dan's plight and were impressed by the ingenuity of the PR campaign. In an example of the same sort of pretzel logic that led the public to give Bill Clinton positive approval ratings in the face of the facts, the popular assessment of the "Save Sister Peg" campaign was that Peg and Dan had risked their freedom in order to help those who couldn't help themselves. They became folk heros.

The bride wore off-white and said, "I do."

The chapel was small, which was all right. It was an intimate wedding. Josie was the maid of honor. Ruben was best man. Ruth was there with Alissa. Mrs. Zamora and Mrs. Gerbracht were there too, representing the rest of the Care Center crowd, all of whom were helping out at the new facility, which was located in the city of San Fernando.

Monsignor Matthews held out his hands and pronounced them husband and wife. "You may now kiss the bride," he said.

Dan lifted her veil and they kissed. The small audience cheered at the sight. None of the Care Center residents had been the least bit bothered when they found out Sister Peg and Father Michael were becoming civilians. They had promised to continue their good work and if the Church didn't see fit to let them marry as a nun and a priest, it was their loss.

The reception was modest. It was held in a small rec room. Chips and dip and soft drinks were arranged on a Ping-Pong table with the net removed. There was no champagne or alcohol of any sort. Prison rules.

Despite the general public's positive assessment of Dan's actions, the jury of his peers convicted him on all counts.

And even though there was a conjugal room available, Dan and Peg agreed to wait until he'd served his year (eight months with good behavior) before consummating their vows. "I'm saving myself for an ex-con," Peg said.

Ruth was still crying after the ceremony. She was so happy for both of them. "We're going to the cemetery tomorrow to put a proper headstone on Michael's grave," she said.

Alissa tugged on Dan's hand. When he crouched down she kissed him on the cheek. Then she giggled and put her hands over her face. "Oooh," Dan said. "Kissed by Cinderella."

Ruben presented Dan and Peg with his wedding present. Dan opened the box. It was the final drawing he had done for Scott's new Fujioka campaign, "Act Affluent!" He said early focus-group tests indicated a strong consumer response to the slogan. Dan signed "thank you" to Ruben. With all his free time, Dan had been studying ASL.

Someone put a tape in the boom box. It was time for the happy couple's first dance. Dan offered his arm to Peg and escorted her to the middle of the room. Everyone clapped. Ruth began to cry again. They danced cheek to cheek for a moment before either of them spoke. "I don't know if I mentioned this in the last five minutes," Peg said. "But I love you."

Dan pulled her closer. "I love you too."

"You know, looking back, I'm amazed at all the stuff we did to keep things going."

"Yeah," Dan agreed. "I'm amazed we got away with most of it."

Peg pulled her head back and looked at Dan. "Can I ask you a philosophical question?"

"Shoot."

"Do you think the end justifies the means?"

Dan thought about it for a moment, then shrugged. "It's not *supposed* to."

EPILOGUE

Father Michael had the strangest sensation. He heard a sound that was best described as *poof!* and he suddenly found himself standing in front of a large podium, with no clear memory of where he had come from. He smelled smoke, and when he looked down he could see that he was the source of the smell. His clothes were charred and he was smoking like Wile E. Coyote after a botched attempt on the Roadrunner. What was left of his hair was singed and standing straight up.

"Ahem!" A tall bearded man wearing wire-rim glasses suddenly appeared behind the podium clearing his throat. Father Michael looked up and saw a nameplate on the podium. It said, "St. Peter."

Gulp. Father Michael smiled weakly.

St. Peter peered sternly over the top of his glasses. "Dan Steele, I presume?"

Father Michael shook his head. "No, no, no, I'm Michael."

St. Peter held up a copy of the admission form from St. Luke's Hospital. "That's not what it says here."

Great, Father Michael thought. If he had to face the music for Dan's past, he was going to be on the next express to hell. What Dan wanted to do with that Beverly woman would be enough, by itself, to damn a guy for eternity, right? He closed his eyes and prepared for the worst.

St. Peter slammed his fist onto the podium and bellowed, "It is a fearful thing to fall into the hands of the living God!"

Father Michael cringed. *Hell yes, it's fearful,* he thought. Hebrews 10:13 didn't sound like an invitation to a picnic. He was about to face the Creator of the universe, Who would be under the impression that he was the morally challenged Dan Steele.

St. Peter suddenly started laughing. He pointed at Father Michael and slapped at the top of the podium. He stamped his foot on the ground as his laughter raced out of control. He removed his glasses and dabbed tears from his eyes using his sleeve. "I'm kidding!" he said between bursts of chuckles. "I'm just giving you a hard time," he hooted. "We know who you are, for Christ's sake. This is heaven. How disorganized do you think we are?" His face was red from laughing so hard.

Father Michael's face was—as St. Peter would later describe it—priceless. His charred clothes disappeared and he suddenly found himself wearing a beautiful white sweatshirt and matching sweatpants made of 100 percent cotton.

"God, I love my job," St. Peter said. He wrote something in his ledger, then put his pen down. "Welcome to the Kingdom and the Glory and all that other good stuff." He leaned forward and looked at Father Michael. "How's that sweatsuit fit, okay? Isn't that soft?"

Father Michael was still reeling from the weirdness of it all. "Uh, it's fine," he said.

St. Peter pointed at the radiant golden halo that was embroidered on the sweatsuit. "You like the halo? It's our trademark." He buffed his fingernails on his chest. "My design."

Father Michael looked absently at the halo, then back at St. Peter. "I don't understand. I died with sin, didn't I?"

St. Peter came out from behind the podium. "Not enough to worry about. Besides, you've been in purgatory for a while. Your brother did a good deed in your name and he said a prayer for you too, so here you are."

Father Michael looked surprised. "That really works?"

"Oh, ye of little faith," St. Peter said with a wink. He put his arm over Father Michael's shoulder. "Main reason you're here is, you were a good guy." He lowered his voice. "I especially liked it when you yanked that sanctimonious Cardinal Cooper out of the Popemobile. That was a classic!" St. Peter led Father Michael toward the gates of heaven.

The fact of the matter finally hit Father Michael. *I'm in heaven!* "Listen," he said, "let me ask you, was St. Alphonsus right about the prayers of souls in purgatory?"

St. Peter smiled. "Yep." He pulled some papers from out of nowhere. "Here's a list of answers to frequently asked questions. Read it before you start bugging the Big Guy, okay?"

Father Michael glanced at the first page and came to a sudden halt. "Darwin was right?!" He looked at St. Peter. "How is that possible?"

St. Peter smirked. "Ironic, isn't it?" They resumed walking. "I'm telling you, He works in mysterious ways."

The gates to heaven opened automatically and Father Michael looked up. It was beautiful beyond words. Rolling hills of emerald green stretched as far as he could see; brightly colored birds soared overhead. And children, all fat, happy, healthy, and laughing, played in the soft grass.

"Okay," St. Peter said, "stop me if you've heard

338 • Bill Fitzhugh

this . . . A priest, a rabbi, and a lawyer die and go to heaven—"

Father Michael held up his hand. "Got a better one. Dolly Parton and Princess Di are at the Pearly Gates—"

St. Peter cut him off. "Royal flush beats a pair every time. Listen, we've heard 'em all."